TRY

ALSO BY LILY BURANA

Strip City: A Stripper's Farewell Journey Across America

Lily Burana

TRY

St. Martin's Press

New York

This is a work of fiction. All of the characters, organizations, and events portrayed in this novel are either products of the author's imagination or are used fictitiously.

www.stmartins.com

Library of Congress Cataloging-in-Publication Data

Burana, Lily.
  Try / Lily Burana.—1st ed.
    p. cm.
  ISBN-13: 978-0-312-35505-0
  ISBN-10: 0-312-35505-X
    1. Women artists—Fiction.   2. Rodeo performers—Fiction.
  3. Wyoming—Fiction.   I. Title.
  PS3602.U69T79   2006
  813'.6—dc22   2005033027

First Edition: July 2006

10   9   8   7   6   5   4   3   2   1

To T.G.V.,
who suggested that I take a stab at fiction.
And to Chris LeDoux,
forever under Western Skies.
Rest in peace, good men.

And to the city of Cheyenne, Wyoming, with love.

Acknowledgments

Thanks to the following: Elizabeth Beier, the long, tall Texan who whipped this book into shape. My agent, Tina Bennett of Janklow and Nesbit, and J&N's Svetlana Katz and Kate Schafer for their insight. Madison Smartt Bell and Goucher College for the old-fashioned mentoring, and Ucross Foundation for the writer's residency. Slade Long and the crazy kids at ProBullStats.com for the authority and the laughs, Charidie for the Cheyenne cred-check, Al Sewell and the Sewell Ranch for the Canadian hospitality, and Dave Shelles for the sport scribe's eye view. The rodeo committees of Cheyenne Frontier Days, Greeley Stampede, Central Wyoming Fair, Sheridan, Cody Stampede, Pendleton Roundup, and Calgary Stampede. Deepest gratitude to the countless PRCA cowboys, cowgirls, and their friends, families, and fans who opened their world to me—dust, grit, gut-bombs, companion passes, one-hundred-fifteen-miles-per-hour drives and all.

On the home front, thank you to Deb DeSalvo and Jeanette

Iskat for making the best of it while weathering the worst. Thanks, most of all, to Mike, a true soldier in love and war, who has shown more *try* than I thought humanly possible.

A kiss for luck, then we'd let 'er buck—
I'd spur electric on adrenaline and lust.

—Paul Zarzyski, "The Bucking Horse Moon"

In rodeo, *try* is a noun. Try is what gets you on the back of the rankest beast and back on your feet after you bucked off into the arena dirt. Try is the part of you that just won't quit, even when every person in your life and every bone in your body begs you to. When you're broke and broken, if you've got try you count out your pennies, tape up your injuries, and get down the road anyway. Try isn't blinding yourself to consequence; it's facing risk, pressing forth, and angling for personal best. Try is your passion for rodeo and the will to persevere. Try is your mettle, your endurance, your heart.

TRY

1

BEFORE I LEFT FOR CHEYENNE, I set my ex-boyfriend on fire. I really wanted to blow his head off, but the lots are cramped in Denver's Capitol Hill neighborhood and there was no way I could shoot him unless I hung the photograph on the clothesline like a target in a carnival shooting gallery. The symbolism appealed but the possibility of taking out my neighbor's window did not. So I incinerated my ex with my glittery pink lighter while standing over the turtle-shaped wading pool that belonged to the kids next door. In the end, though, I couldn't bring myself to reduce Alex to ash. We were together for two years and I'd thought I loved him. As the little Bic inferno advanced along the edge of the picture, the paper curling and smoldering, I dropped the photo on the driveway and stomped.

"I'm sorry," I said to Alex's placid, smoke-smudged features. Then I ran over him with my truck.

At heart, Alex wasn't a bad guy; he was just the wrong guy. I didn't know it when we got together junior year at Colorado State, but he's sort of a reverse snob. He didn't seek me out because I'm model-thin or gorgeous or from some fancy bloodline. I'm none of those things. He told me he was drawn to my credibility, which I think meant he liked the idea of dating a poor chick from the middle of nowhere.

Alex had a goatee and the most inoffensive hands I've ever seen.

He didn't care much about appearances, but tried to sympathize with my frustration over my fingernails, which are always a paint-crusted mess. For my birthday last year, he gave me a fifty-dollar gift certificate to the Yes, They're Fake nail salon. I chose to ignore the significance of this.

Alex's one-room apartment in Fort Collins doubled as a vault for his sacred vinyl collection—he'd play me original recordings of jazz legends and rare AC/DC bootlegs with geeky enthusiasm that started out charming but ended up annoying the crap out of me. We both liked country music, but he had exacting alt.country standards. Alex thought Hank Williams was God and anything Top Forty was trash. George Strait and Garth Brooks he dismissed as "hat acts." Last year, we had an argument over who was the better songwriter: Steve Earle or Alan Jackson. After a point, all we shared was a love of Johnny Cash, and a nagging sense of disappointment.

But that wasn't the deal breaker. Alex was jealous, jealous of my work in the way you might get over a person. I'd come over and make him peanut butter toast when he was sweating over revisions on his collection of short stories inspired by "Kind of Blue," but if I were ever reluctant to blow off painting to hang out with him, he'd say: "An artist's work is her passion." He relied on the hipster dodge of disguising aggression as wit, and around the sour knot of irony, he spat out the words "work" and "passion" like differing strengths of the same poison.

On May Day, I informed him—calmly, I thought—that I'd rather die a workaholic loner than put up with a guy who broke out in hives whenever he heard Toby Keith. A week later, Alex got a job as a music critic for the local alternative rag, and went public with an earnest archaeology student from Nebraska named Jen who collected obscure Alison Krauss recordings and treated him like her one great discovery.

I wasn't angry immediately after our final spat but as the days ticked by, my feelings changed shape. First came a frantic arc of shortcoming—Was it me? What did I do wrong? Then, long dull spirals of doubt: Will I ever get a relationship right? Am I going to be alone forever? Finally, I augured down to flat-bottomed rage: Alex, you high-handed sack of crap. You knew what I was when you met me.

I still felt that dull burn whenever he crossed my mind. Did I miss him, miss the idea of him, or merely mourn our failure? I couldn't tell, but when my brother—freshly rehabbed on the cusp of thirty-four—summoned me north to help sell Red Hill, the family acreage on the ragged edge of Cheyenne, I knew I'd caught a break.

Only a fool gets lost driving from Denver to Cheyenne. God made it goof-proof. The plains sit directly on your right side, the Rockies, your left. Fire one hundred miles straight up 1-25, undulant grass to starboard and staunch mountain to port, and you're golden.

I rolled down the window on my brother's hand-me-down truck, a big-boned gray Chevy I christened "Count Truckula" with a Bud Light poured over the hood. At 150,000-plus miles, the only thing holding the old hoopty together is luck, but I can't turn up my nose at a free ride. The truck cab filled with hot, hay-scented air. Behind a warty growth of identical mini-mansions in a cul-de-sac that offered residents an unobstructed view of the freeway, I could see a combine working, hay rolls dotting the draught-strafed field. I tugged down the brim on my faded khaki baseball cap and rested my left arm on the driver's side door, humming along with KYGO. Sky the color of flame from an acetylene torch, zero humidity—a perfect, baggy blue jeans kind of day. I adjusted the rearview mirror, and checked the cargo out back: one grossly overweight yellow Lab named Homer, his graying muzzle high to the wind; steamer trunk; a folded-up easel; plastic-wrapped canvases; and two duct-taped supermarket boxes packed to the groaning limit with paints, brushes, pencils, and sketchpads. I'd already moved eight times in my life, so by this, my twenty-third summer, I'd learned to travel light.

Colorado melted away as I drove north. When I passed Exit 269A—Alex's exit—I tightened my grip on the wheel. *Don't turn. Don't even look.* In Weld County, the Front Range dropped to a stutter of low peaks, hazy purple and shades of deep blue in the dwindling afternoon light. Passing Owl Canyon glider port, I knew I was almost to the state line. Soon I'd see the roadside clutter of Wyoming: radio towers, steel sheds selling fireworks, billboards, futuristic turbine windmills with three-point propeller-like blades, and the dust-churning herd that meandered the rolling expanse of the Terry Bison Ranch. This riffraff was just a scare tactic. Within twenty miles, the blight of humanity—consumerism, eco-friendly folly, tourist crud—would cede to the overwhelming abundance of fuck-all. Wyoming is the country's ninth largest and least populated state, with fewer residents than the city of Denver, and more antelope than people.

Up ahead, the Devil's Tower sign marked the border. I thought the old sign was better: a blue cowboy on a bucking bronc, a background of blue mountains, and underneath, a supernatural promise. WYOMING—LIKE NO PLACE ON EARTH. Orange sunlight poured over the dun-colored hills. I followed the curve of the first exit, old yellow dog listing westward in the truck bed, clattered down the county road doing seventy-five on knobby tires, and skidded into the dusty parking lot of the Bluffs Ranch rodeo just in time.

2

"PULL 'EM UP, BOYS."

Canting to the right on his good hip, Hawley Bolinger swayed along behind the chutes, softball wad of Red Man swelling mumplike in his cheek. Creaky kneed and flat-assed spry at fifty, Hawley knew that for him, rodeoing now meant making sure the trains ran on time, that cowboys got out of the gate on the right animal at the right moment. Seven o'clock sun tinted his windburned face to shoe leather. Sweat cut rills through the dust on his neck.

"Well, if it isn't the Heartbreak Kid." My friend Kimber fluffed her tight blond curls and tossed her tinted lip balm into her purse. "I was afraid you weren't going to make it." She slid over and I creaked into the spot next to her on the rickety wooden bleachers. She offered me some of her Cracker Jack and we enjoyed the busy masculine charge in the arena as the Bluffs Ranch rodeo got under way.

The Bluffs Ranch show wasn't a megawatt production with top announcers and an electronic scoreboard and opening ceremonies full of rodeo queens riding figure-eights in spangles, but Hawley, stern and sullen in his transition from calf roper to chute boss, kept things tight. The Tuesday evening performances were staged mostly for summer vacationers who wouldn't know the Calgary Stampede from tiny old Ten Sleep, but it was good for upstarts and seasoned competitors who just want to get on some B-grade stock, exercise their horse, or throw a little rope after dinner.

A scattering of timed event hands zigzagged across the arena, warming up, the coats of their horses feathering dark with sweat. Ropes whooshed up and out, whistling as they cut the air. "Should Have Been a Cowboy" mumbled through ambient fuzz from the PA system.

My legs ached as I stood for the National Anthem. I was tired from the drive, but I came to the Bluffs Ranch anyway on account of Kimber. Kimber was on a quest, a hunt for her own cowboy king. After breaking up with her last banker by day/biker by night boyfriend, she inexplicably developed a cowboy fetish. She shipped her daughter south of Tucson to spend the summer with her ex-husband, so she was free to date whomever she pleased. Kimber doesn't mess around with this cowboy business. She'll consider how a guy wears his hat, wears his jeans, drives a truck, and a host of other points before she'll date him. She only wants the genuine article. If she could test a guy's cowboy credentials with a strip of litmus paper pressed to his forehead, she would.

We sat with Homer in the top row so Kimber could keep an eye on Danny Leigh, the calf roper she was pursuing. Kimber had a brief conversation on her cell phone as the Grand Entry wound down. She hung up smiling. "Greg says, 'I'm going to smack the brat if she doesn't start listening to me.'" She lit a Marlboro Light and shook out the flame, tucking the used match in the front pocket of her jeans.

"Do you think he would?" I thought of her girl, Aubrey, saucer-eyed at seven and constantly scowling, always in a favorite pair of hot pink sneakers.

Kimber snorted lightly and opened her purse. "Are you kidding me? She'd kick his ass." Kimber dug out a pick and set to work separating her dirty blond curls. She held the pick out to me. "Want to borrow this, or is 'Rapunzel in a wind tunnel' your look of choice?"

"That's why I've got the ball cap." I picked at one of the knots in my waist-length hair. "Ever since I used that cheapie highlighting kit, I've had this rat's nest going."

"Told you. You get what you pay for." Kimber spritzed perfume on her cleavage, covering the horsy smell around us with exotic jungle flower. She took out a leopard print pouch and started touching up her makeup.

I pulled my sketchpad from my worn leather Pony Express satchel and turned to look down at the roughstock ready area behind the stands. Bull riders looped their braided leather ropes around the center fence rail and yanked, chunks of rosin tucked in their glove palms to sticky things up. Bronc riders sat on the ground, rocking on their saddles to stretch the stirrup leathers. A clutch of bareback guys stood talking and laughing as they dusted their latigos with baby powder. A half-dozen riggings lined the top rail. I noticed a lone cowboy crouched on one knee in prayer, chin tipped down, black hat held over his face. The humility in his posture made me turn to a fresh page in my spiral-bound pad and root around my bag for an HB pencil.

I sketched as quickly as I could, hoping he wouldn't *ping*. People can sense that they're being watched, and when they feel that current they stop what they're doing and get self-conscious. I was working on the curve to his back, damn the pain in my overworked wrist, when he stood and turned his face toward the stands. Crap. Pinged, and I wasn't even halfway through an outline. He saw me, gave a half-smile, then pulled his rigging from the fence and sat in the dirt, adjusting the bolts with an open-end wrench.

Kimber zipped her makeup pouch. "My, my, looks like something tasty caught your eye. Maybe you should go down and say hello."

"Oh, please." I faced forward and twiddled my pencil in my fingers. I turned around again for a quick look. He stood and took the two leather thongs that dangled from his belt loops and wound them around his boot tops so they wouldn't fly off, then put on and tightened his riding glove, pulling the laces with his teeth. He wore brown brindle chaps with silver crosses on the leg yoke, and a starch-stiff white button-down shirt. A foam-padded brace cosseted the back of his neck, the muslin-colored straps crisscrossing his chest like bandoliers. He caught me looking and tipped his hat. I pivoted in my seat and pulled my cap down over my eyes.

Kimber bent the corner of a matchbook to nudge at a piece of caramel corn stuck in her teeth. "Why not do a little flirting at least? You could use some mindless distraction, which, I might add, would be a radical concept for you."

"Sorry. Not interested."

She-masculated. That's the best way to describe how Alex made me feel. Emasculated is the word for a man feeling less like a man. Weakened, frivolous, incapable. But there's no word for a woman feeling less womanly.

When Alex and I started going out, the attention hit me like a drug. He was an artist, too, an aspiring novelist, so I thought he'd understand—which, initially, he did. He loved the endless conversations about our art, the solidarity of being with another artist, but once we got going, he didn't much like the reality of it.

If I don't do several studio hours a day, I feel off, and that's why everything went wrong. Alex couldn't share first place with my work. He wasn't in sway of some old-school sexist mentality, like bellowing, "Get in that kitchen, missy!" or "No woman of mine is going to work outside the home!" The process of she-masculation was subtle, yet the message was loud and clear: *Oh, you don't need me. An independent woman like you doesn't need anybody.* As if a measure of self-sufficiency eliminated emotional hunger. As if the antidote for female ambition was the threat of withdrawal.

Alex slowly froze me out. The lingering hug became a perfunctory squeeze; passionate kisses turned to quick pecks. As for anything more intimate, well, we lapsed into lethargy and stayed there. Within his refusal was a tacit offer: I could have the art-girl cred, or

I could have his affection and ardor, but I couldn't have both. When I found the Lee Hazlewood mix tape in his car, *(heart), Jen* written in Sharpie on the label, I knew he was cheating. I knew it was over.

She-masculation, the dread feeling of being not enough by being too much. The thought of that happening to me ever again made my stomach hurt. No, I was not at all interested in some anonymous God-fearing cowboy, or anyone else, for that matter.

"Oh, brother. Here she comes." Kimber nudged my arm and pointed toward a girl near the timed event chutes. "Do you know her?" I guessed the girl to be about twenty, a tiny thing in Daisy Dukes, a white tank top sheer enough to broadcast her bralessness, and white Adidas, one long curl hanging loose from her platinum ponytail. She was headed right toward Kimber's conquest, Danny.

"That little skank is Crystal." Kimber fumed. "A guy could be nothing but a hat on top, boots on the bottom, and six feet of bullshit in between, and she'd throw herself at him anyway."

It occurred to me that with a population of fifty-five thousand, Cheyenne wasn't a small town, just small enough for your behavior to be assiduously policed and the gossip to cut deep.

Crystal laughed at something Danny said and touched his arm, then walked up to another guy and started petting his horse. She exuded a chemical kind of magnetism, drawing your attention to her as if she moved in a spotlight. Of course Kimber was jealous. I'd feel threatened by a female like that, too, if I considered her competition, but to me, she was in another league, maybe even another species. Women like her fascinate me.

Kimber stood. "I better get over there. You want to come? I can introduce you to some of Danny's friends."

"Hell no and thanks anyway." I pulled my sketchpad closer to me.

"Daryl Angela Heatherly, you are the most intimacy avoidant girl on God's green earth."

"Well, given your current dating habits, I know I can count on you to take up the slack."

She laughed. "You did *not* just say that to me!" She scrubbed her teeth with her finger to catch any stray lipstick and hitched up her breasts. "How do I look?"

I shielded my eyes from the setting sun and checked her out head to toe. "You look like you own this rodeo, mama."

She beamed her appreciation. "Okay, before I go, you want to tell me what I'm about to watch here?"

"Sure. The first event's always the bareback riding. When the gate opens, the cowboy's got to hold his feet above the break in the horse's shoulders until its front hooves hit the ground coming out of the chute. That's called a mark-out, and if the rider blows it, he doesn't get a score. Then the guy's gotta lean back, hold onto the rigging handle with one hand and make sure he doesn't touch anything with his other hand, turn his toes out and spur his butt off for eight seconds. The spurs are dull so the horse doesn't get injured in any way—they make sure of that. A guy can score up to a hundred points, half the points come from how the horse does, the other half from the cowboy. The better the horse bucks and the better the guy spurs, the better the score. The best ones try to look like they're right at the edge of what the horse can dish out, but they've got 'im handled. It looks kind of spazzy, but once you get an eye for it, you see there's artistry involved."

Kimber nodded as she listened. "So he wants to be in control but look like he might lose control."

"Something like that."

"Thank you. Now I'm a freaking expert."

"Yep, close to it, Calamity Jane. See ya."

I watched Kimber traipse up to Danny and sit on the bumper of a horse trailer, chatting as Danny saddled his big bay. Leaning forward with her elbows on her knees, cleavage swelling over the top of her camisole, Kimber looked severe yet somehow accommodating. She presented herself in the way of women who cultivate their beauty like a talent. A man would have to work hard to prove his worth, but she was gettable.

The bareback was about to begin. I noticed the praying cowboy setting his rigging in chute one. The announcer crackled in. "First up, we've got Alabama cowboy, J.W. Jarrett, a World Champion bareback rider who now makes his home in this great state of Wyoming. He's on a horse from the Bluffs Ranch string called Butternut Crunch. Don't let the size of this little fellow fool you—Butternut's a match for any man, even the one who won the World." So now he had a name. J.W. Jarrett. A World Champion. How could it be I'd never heard of him?

He worked his gloved fingers into the rigging and pounded his fist closed around it, thumb on top. He scrubbed under the little horse's mane with his free hand, calming the animal. When everything was in place, J.W. curled over, took his feet off the chute rails, jammed his hat down over his eyes, and tucked his chin. Everything went silent and still, the crowd a knot of anticipation. Finally, J.W. hitched his hips forward against the rigging, leaned back, raised his left arm over his head, and nodded. The puller yanked open the gate and the squat palomino made a high dive into the arena.

Bareback may not have the glamorous bloody flash of bull riding or the flowing spurs-to-cantle sophistication of saddle bronc, but there's an elemental purity to it, man versus animal stripped to wiry basics, just horse and rider and rigging. I'd read somewhere that one good jump can put several hundred pounds of pressure on a guy's arm as he grips the handhold, yet the strain only shows in the rider's particular grimace, an expression otherwise seen only on torture victims and prison brides.

After marking out, J.W. zipped his spurs straight up to the horse's withers. Butternut humped his back up like a crescent moon, front and back hooves almost touching, then launched into an erratic jump and buck. J.W.'s head snapped back, meeting the horse's rump, and his hat flew off, revealing his hair, dark sorrel red, cropped short, and sun-bleached at the temples. The horse jibbed around like a textbook dink but J.W. didn't slack. Each spur stroke had the tensile precision of a ripcord pull, mechanical, strong, and elegant. He held his free arm rigidly in place, fingers together like a presidential wave. I was impressed.

At the eight-second buzzer, my cell phone rang. "Righteous bod on that one, huh?"

"Kimber!" I swiveled around and located her standing down at the other end of the little arena.

"Just saying!" She clapped her hands together as if concluding a sales presentation. "So, what do you think?"

I ran my hand through my snarly hair. "He's good."

"Good? Daryl, are you blind?" She made a disgusted sound and hung up.

J.W. hunched over the rigging and pried his hand free. The pick-up men galloped alongside, and J.W. grabbed the nearest one around the waist and swung his feet to the ground. He mashed through the dust-choked arena, batwing chaps churning around his ankles, the silver fringe flailing like tinsel whips. A patter of applause from the stands. He raised his left arm and waved once overhead, then swooped down to pick up his hat and jogged bowlegged to the fence.

All that fine spurring only got him seventy points. I figured he'd score pretty low anyway, given that half the ride's points came from the horse, and he had drawn a certified stinker.

At the start of the calf roping, Homer picked up his leash in his mouth and rested his dusty chin on my knee. I looked down into my dog's pleading face. "All right, old boy." I snapped the leash to his collar and walked him toward the ranch house. As I rounded the porch, an Aussie shepherd/heeler mix trotted out, followed by Hawley Bolinger.

"Hey, Mr. Bolinger."

"Hello, Daryl," he said, pulling up a milk crate for me to sit. "Got to rest this withered arse and feed this miserable mutt before they start up the saddle bronc. How's your dad?"

I dropped onto the crate. "Dad's good. Doing good, thanks. Who's this?" The patchy black-and-gray dog circled with Homer, the two of them nose to tail, sniffing.

"That's Deuce." Bolinger's eyelid drooped under a glowering red cyst. His pants, a horseshoe of dirt up the thighs and across the butt, were held up with two tied-together bandanas.

When I was a kid, Dad took him on as a tile layer. Hawley always kept a bag of candy corn on the dashboard of this truck, even in summer. Every time I visited a job site, he gave me sweat-palmed handfuls that my mother never let me eat.

We talked at each other like estranged folk, harmless subjects— the weather, my art, his gout—then Hawley cracked his jaw. He looked at the canine sniff-exchange and yawned. "A dog's got a nice life, but just the same, I'm glad I don't have to greet anybody that way." He whistled and Deuce snapped to attention. "Good seeing you, Daryl. Tell your father hello." He hefted onto his cane and trundled toward the tractor shed to shake dry dog food into Deuce's dented metal bowl.

Strings of colored lights shaped like miniature covered wagons, cactus, and steer skulls swayed in the sapling branches around the perimeter of the Bluffs Ranch barbecue pit. The smoky air smelled of charcoal-grilled meat and boiled corn on the cob. A pianist with a long sandy braid started in on "Does Ft. Worth Ever Cross Your Mind?," the fiddlers folding in behind him, and a few couples got up to dance. Kimber took Danny's arm and they bumped their hips to the music, then she spun into his arms and they merged into the circular flow of two-steppers. I finished the last bite of my brisket sandwich, wiped my mouth with a paper napkin, and put my foot up on the patio fence and leaned over for a breather, Homer sniffing the air hungrily beside me.

Danny and Kimber danced past, her pelvis tilted toward his at an after-midnight angle. I first met Kimber at Grinnin' Bat Body Works, Landy Abbott's tattoo and piercing shop down on South Greeley Highway. She was leaning on the counter with her back to the door. Silver concho belt. Baby-blue Wranglers worn to onion skin. Leonine mass of curls swathing tanned shoulders. I guessed her to be your average honky-tonk goddess, but the second she turned around and I saw the determined furrow between her electric green eyes, I pegged her as an instant friend. She's as dedicated to the good times as I am to work, and though I'd never attempt half the extremes she doesn't think twice about exceeding, what can I say? She knocks me out.

The Bluffs Ranch hands rolled out a fresh keg and just as I was considering a beer, I felt a tap on my shoulder. I turned to see a fox-faced guy in a lavender neckerchief, his hat tipped to the side, à la Casey Tibbs. "Feel like dancing?"

"Oh, no thanks."

There was a sneer behind the come-on smile. "You don't know what you're missing."

I batted my lashes. "That sound you hear is the breaking of my heart." When I turned back toward the fence, Homer was gone. I scanned the crowd and saw him standing on a picnic bench amid a welter of brims and broad shoulders. A slight young guy in a black hat was feeding him a cheeseburger.

"Hey!" I called out. "Could you not do that? My dog's on a diet." He put down the remaining crescent of burger and grinned loopily. Seemed like a reasonably harmless twerp. I walked toward the table.

I think Little Black Hat tried to defend himself. Maybe he apologized. Maybe he burst into flame. I'm not sure. Once J.W. Jarrett turned around, everything else in my field of vision shut down. From under the brim of a straw Bailey with a roughstock crease, his cool gaze swung up at me and he drawled in a voice that was hard like flint rock and hickory bark. "Dog on a diet, huh?" He shook his head. I noticed the placket between the second and third button on his shirt was monogrammed in simple black letters: J.W.J.

Something about the way he looked at me made me feel like I'd been caught stealing. I hid my hands behind my back. "Yes. My dog is on a diet. Do you find that amusing?"

He picked up a stick and threw it toward the fence. Homer bolted after it. "That's what he needs. Not a diet."

"Thanks for the tip, Dog Whisperer." Kimber was crazy if she thought I could possibly be attracted to this guy.

His eyes were fixed below the aged-to-gray men's tank top I'd cropped with pinking shears. I was suddenly self-conscious about the little Buddha swell of flesh below my waistline. "What?"

He pointed. "Your belly button ring. Did it hurt to get that?"

I stiffened and wrapped my arm around my waist. "Yeah, kinda." I pointed toward his gold trophy buckle. "Did it hurt to get *that?*"

He looked down at it, looked at me, and smiled. "Yeah. Kinda."

This was the first time I'd ever seen a National Finals Rodeo buckle in real life. NFR, held every December in Las Vegas, is the cowboy World Series. Rodeo's El Dorado. I sneaked a glance at the buckle, trying to read the year on it, hoping no one would notice and think I was checking out his crotch. With a bit of discreet squinting, I found what I was looking for. I did some quick math and figured out why I'd never heard of him: He won the championship when I was eleven years old.

Homer bounded back over with the stick in his mouth and leapt up on J.W., leaving muddy paw prints all over the front of his nice white shirt.

"Down boy! Oh, I'm sorry." I grabbed a handful of napkins from the metal table dispenser. "Let me help." I started scrubbing, but that only served to grind the mud further into the fabric. "That's not helping at all now, is it? Maybe some club soda will get that out. Is there anything I can do?"

He dabbed at the shirt. When he smiled, his lower lip curled against his teeth. "You could tell me your name, for a start."

"Oh." I put down the napkins and extended my hand, marveling at his extreme Southern drawl. "I'm Daryl." He held on for an extra beat. My hand felt tiny in his.

"Daryl?" brayed the guy who had been feeding Homer. He'd sat down next to us. "Daryl's a guy's name!"

I looked at him. Dark hair curled loosely over his shirt collar, which was open to reveal a macramé choker. His eyes were black and alive like a bubbling tar pit but his smile tugged down at the corners. He obviously had more mouth than sense. I decided I disliked him, intensely.

"You'll have to pardon him. That's Beeber," J.W. said, as if making both an introduction and an apology. He blinked slowly. I thought to myself, *Man, those are some blue eyes.* Light, liquid blue— sad almost. Fragile like Monet water lilies or the first glimpse of sky after the rain—sexy, yet somehow familiar. Deep crow's feet ran in radiant lines to his cheeks. This wasn't your average bronky barstool cowboy. This was a full-grown man.

Beeber examined me from his seat on the picnic bench. He was a cute kid, discounting that tent-flap mouth of his. "You friends with that girl Kimber?" He rolled the chew around to his cheek and spit it on the ground. "I like her. She's sassy!"

Please, I thought, *Kimber wouldn't piss on you if you were on fire.* No point in being rude about it, though. "Yeah." I nodded. "She sure is."

J.W. left, then came back with a soapy sponge and two plastic cups of beer. He handed one to me, and I thanked him, then he sat down and began working at the stain on his shirt.

I figured it out, why J.W. seemed familiar. "You know who you look like?"

J.W. shrugged. "The Marlboro Man?" He smiled, one of his eye-teeth was set slightly back.

"Very funny, but no."

He put down the sponge. "Okay, I'm stumped."

"You look a little like Duff Linsey."

J.W. cleared his throat and glanced briefly at the ground, "Yeah? Imagine that." He took a shallow sip of beer, cleared his throat again, then smiled right at me.

There's not a rodeo fan anywhere who isn't familiar with Duff "The Dragon" Linsey. Even someone like me, who only follows the sport with one eye, knows the rough outline of The Linsey Legend. His rookie year in the Professional Rodeo Cowboys Association, Duff came out strong and made a hell of a first impression. But talent didn't grant him immunity from a host of hazing antics. During an unusually cold day at the Grand National in San Francisco, the temperature in the Cow Palace was so low that Duff, first man out of the chutes, blew clouds from his nostrils. Thus his buddies branded him, "Duff the Magic Dragon." As his fearlessness and his profile in the PRCA grew, he was dubbed, simply, The Dragon. Then Hollywood called.

A talent scout noticed Duff—lanky, shamble-shanked, and handsome—when he was hanging around back of the chutes during his trip to the Finals. He flew to L.A. and immediately got work as a stuntman and sometime model, then someone put a script in front of him and found he could act. Greg Van Wilder cast him as the star in a grim alternative Western called *Black Hat Blues,* about a washed-up South Texas bull rider who smuggles heroin across the Mexican border to make his entry fees. The film seemed like an excuse to make Duff into a greasy cowboy doll, with endless scenes of him wandering around shirtless and stubbled in filthy chaps and scuffed boots. The movie was only a minor success, but the role garnered Duff some fleeting visibility. The press was intrigued by this unpretentious, azure-eyed cowboy who'd had fame conferred on him yet seemed nonplussed by it. Cooler than any cowboy who had come before, he carried himself with the steel-spined resolve of a man who wouldn't be tamed, though back when they cared, the tabloids hinted he was enslaved by both bottle and pill. Jace and his friends still watch *Black Hat Blues* on DVD now and then, mumbling, "lucky sonofabitch," and "cowboy can ride, though"—a little titillated, a little awed. Duff took the Roy Rogers trip and shot it through with the glitter of nonchalance and real roughstock chops. Before devolving to D-list status, Duff Linsey was, in essence, rodeo's first rock star.

I didn't want to sound like some airhead rodeo groupie, so I let J.W. change the subject. We had an advanced conversation about boots—the virtues of pointy toes versus rounded, and both came out on the side of pointed, which made us two of a kind in a largely round-toed crowd.

"Don't see pointed toes much anymore," J.W. said.

I rotated my boot on its heel. "Yeah, you know it? But I like the pointed toes because I'm old school."

J.W. flexed his feet. "I just like 'em because I'm old."

We both laughed. J.W. adjusted his hat, looked around the patio, then leaned his elbows on his knees, focusing on me with mock seriousness. "What other kind of boots catch your fancy, ma'am?"

"I'm not particular, really. Oh, but you know what I don't like? Ostrich. Looks all pimply and weird, like the boots have a bad rash."

"I have ostrich boots!"

"I'm so sorry." I put my hand on his arm lightly. "Sorry to hear you bought such ugly boots, I mean."

We laughed again. He was all right, I guess.

He touched the toe of his boot to mine. "Yours look pretty scuffed up," he said. "Do you want me to polish them? My kit's in the truck."

What he'd said was a perfect mix of submission and aggression. I sputtered, stalled against a response. "Surely you aren't asking me to go out to your truck with you?"

"No, ma'am. I meant I'd go get my kit and bring it here." He raised a dour eyebrow and winked at me.

Those eyes. Blue. Pretty.

I was unnerved by his calm. In most attempted pick-ups, guys rush to close the deal as soon as possible. Drink? Dance? Breakfast later? But this J.W. fellow wasn't in a hurry. He wasn't even hitting on me, exactly.

"Sorry," I told him. "I've gotta go find my friend. She said she might need a ride home." I felt bad for lying but I needed an exit line before I made a complete fool of myself.

"Bye, Daryl," J.W. said, rising from his seat as I stood. "Hope we see you again sometime soon."

"Bye, Daryl!" Beeber yelled after me. "Hope you get a girl's name sometime soon!" He yelped, rubbing his arm where J.W. had socked him.

Homer lay with his head in Kimber's lap as we sat on the tailgate of my truck watching the parking lot empty out, sharing a beer. She couldn't understand why I didn't jump at J.W. Jarrett. "After you disappeared, I went over to do a little investigating, and he started asking about you. Where you were from. What you did. If you had a boyfriend."

"You don't say."

"Seriously. I don't think he filed you under 'buckle bunny.' I believe the boy has a sincere crush on you."

"Hmm," I said, in my best fake-noncommittal manner.

"I mean it. He gave me his business card to pass along."

I took it. The raised red type said he managed Dominion Lumber over on Lincolnway. "When he handed it to me, he said, 'You make sure she gets this.' Crazy accent on that guy. Wow. Anyway, he made me promise."

"I'm not ready, Kimber. And the last thing I need is to be some rodeo cowboy's latest acquisition." I folded the card and put it in my back pocket.

Kimber made a skeptical face. I could tell she thought I was being ridiculous. "Why would anyone have to know? It's nobody's business and he doesn't exactly seem like the type to talk." She folded a stick of striped spearmint gum into her mouth. "Besides, after what you've been through, you deserve to have a little fun."

"How old do you think he is?"

"Mid-thirties, maybe? An older man. Very glamorous," said the worldly wise twenty-five-year-old Kimber.

I crunched the empty beer can under my heel. "If he's so great, why don't you go for him?"

"Honey, I'm five-eleven in heels. I need to hang at the timed event end of the arena with the big boys. But a roughstock slimmy would be perfect for a half-pint like you."

I looked away. Lanterns glowed in the ranch dining room, luxury-suite diners sitting down to prime rib, boxed off in each window. Miller moths spiraled up and around the light from the street-lamps in the parking lot. The last RV turned from the drive and merged onto I-80 heading west.

"Daryl? Daryl, hey! Are you listening to me?"

3

THE PUNGENT SMELL OF FRENCH ROAST woke me up. "Good morning, Princess DeeDee," a masculine gravel voice intoned. My lids lifted to the sight of a stoneware mug full of steaming caramel-colored liquid held right under my nose.

"Good morning, Obi Jace Kenobi!" I sat up and took the coffee. My brother perched on the side of the bed, looking at me. We both have our father's eyes—wide, whiskey-ditch hazel, but Jace's have a gunfighter squint. He'd grown sideburns and a policeman moustache, his sandy brown hair cut neat. He'd also put on a lot of weight, so much he strained the seams on his brown army undershirt, but that was okay with me. Big meant healthy. Big meant clean.

Homer jumped from the bed and headed down the hallway, toenails clicking, no doubt bound for the kitchen. Jace brushed dog hair from the white matelasse coverlet. "That cuppa joe too light for you?"

"No. It's perfect." Waking up in my old bedroom was like waking up in a time warp—a *Twilight Zone* return to adolescence. The row of porcelain horse statuettes on the shelf above the mint green desk with glass pulls on the drawers, prize ribbons tacked around the perimeter of the mirror. The sun-faded Tim Cox print thumbtacked over the walnut-stained daybed. When I didn't want to take any of this stuff to college, Jace came down to our place in Colorado, packed everything up, and put it back exactly where it had been when I was a little girl.

"What time did you get in last night?" He straightened the digital alarm clock on the wobbly nightstand, shifted the lamp, and ran his finger through the dust on the mica shade.

"Not late. I think I was in bed by eleven." I yawned and stretched. "Kimber says hi, by the way."

"Ah, Kimber. Everyone's favorite bad influence."

I slapped his arm. "Shut up! You adore her."

" '*Shut up*'? Who taught you to talk that way?"

"It's like Mom always said before she'd scrub our tongues with soap when we cussed: 'The smart mouth is the Heatherly legacy.' But you love me anyway, right?"

"Yes." He put his big hand on top of my head. "In fact, I love you *so* much, you get to do morning turnout."

Four curious noses poked from the horse stalls when I walked into the barn, shouting hello. Preston and Delaney, my brother's new roping horses, were already out and tied to the porch rail for loading. The smell of cedar and yeasty grain was strong. Dust motes shimmered in soft slants of early morning light from the windows high above the breezeway. I scooped a handful of carrots from the bin by the shoeing bench, drawing the limp green stems through my fingers like doll's hair.

Tad stretched her neck out long and low over her stall door. She's my baby, a gift from my parents when I turned twelve. I kissed her by the ear and massaged her withers with the flat of my hand. "Missed you, pretty girl," I whispered into her neck. She showed me her dull yellow teeth as she carefully clamped around the carrot. Her coat was paint and dirt and hay; she'd been rolling again, the black-and-cream Holstein pattern in dire need of cleaning. I got after her with a dandy brush and ran it crackling through the black thread of her mane and tail, then went over her coat with a finishing brush until she shone like a showroom model.

When I was in high school, I cared for these horses by myself, rising early to feed, water, muck out, and if necessary, medicate, before running for the bus. But when I started looking after Dad, too, cooking and cleaning and paying bills, the horses got ridden once a week, if they were lucky. Jace intervened and brought them back to Red Hill. Now the four of them, three geldings—two bay and one roan—and my paint mare, have all the attention they need, plenty of space, and, when Jace isn't roping, the two younger horses for company.

Blob, the dyspeptic barn cat, came into Tad's stall and moiled around my ankles, his marmalade fur bristling into spikes as he arched against me. I crouched and smoothed along his spine with my index finger. "Don't worry. I know better than to pick you up." He squinted at me with his inscrutable Charlie Chan look and sauntered off to the washing stall to drink the puddled water on the floor near the drain.

When I looked into Dish's stall, his forelock was draped at a rakish angle over his left eye. With a compact muzzle like an Arabian and a cresty neck, he's got a touch of matinee idol in him. A natural performer, he earned my mother more Western equitation trophies than she could count. How she could have left him behind when she moved out is a mystery to me. That was eight years ago, and he's held his head with the tragic, wounded beauty of a jilted lover ever since.

Slade, my father's eighteen-year-old nick-eared roan, deigned to acknowledge me by stepping forward once, *tock-tock,* on his princely hooves, then turned his rump to me.

I warmed the bit in my hands and slipped it into Hodge's mouth. "It's your lucky day," I told him, walking off to fetch my saddle.

We rode up and over the rise, into the valley at the foot of Table

Mountain. Hodge is our easy chair, a gentle soul not bothered by much. He shies at snakes and unfamiliar dark spaces, but otherwise he's stout-hearted, patient with kids and dogs and tired riders. As I walked Hodge, his head bobbed up and down, *Yes. Yes, thank you*. I rode up the narrow path to the white wooden cross marking my Uncle Dee's final resting place, his ashes scattered on the mountaintop more than a dozen years ago. After my dad started construction on Red Hill, Dee bought the parcel next to ours and opened the Little Wyo Guest Ranch with Goody, his third wife. When he'd see us snaking down the road that adjoined our properties, Dee, younger than Dad by four years and my namesake, would hop up from his chair on the porch, flask of schnapps in his front shirt pocket, catch me in his arms, and scrub my head with his knuckles. "Dar-Dar, DeeDee, dip dip dot. You'd fit in a coffeepot." I extended a prayer for Dee up to the cross turning ginger beer gold in the early light. As the sun rose higher in the sky, it lit the long, flat mountain to the west. In this light, you can tell this land used to be the ocean floor, the Yorkshire pudding terrain carved by ancient sea. Looking down atop Hodge, I felt like I was sinking into familiar, if choppy, water.

Anyone who sees an open space and envisions the word "bleak" scrolling across in motion picture script won't find much to love here but Red Hill is not without charm. Tucked twenty-five miles outside Cheyenne in the sage-pocked slopes between the prairie and Medicine Bow National Forest, it's just a low-slung log home, a barn, and a shed down a winding washboard road on fifty treeless acres. Springtime drips with snowmelt and rain, leaving the grass green and supple, with broad stripes of purple columbine and blue creeping phlox sweeping across feminine curves. But the burst of flora is fleeting and by summer, the palette mutes to colors of a land uneager to impress: buff, dust, silvery sage, the alkaline soil a pinkish brown. When I rode back over the ridge, I saw the FOR SALE sign staked along Happy Jack Road, the bright yellow pressboard square like an oversize Post-It note blaring the reminder that a chapter of my life was about to slam to a close.

Jace had saddled Slade and was carefully legging him my direction up the rocky path. He brought Slade around Hodge's right side and dallied his reins on the saddlehorn. "Thought I'd give this old growler a trot before we left since I know you don't like to ride him."

We stared at the property below. *One of a Kind—4 BR/2.5BA on fifty acres near Curt Gowdy State Park. Great horse property—25×50 steel barn w/ stalls. Fenced & cross fenced. Beautiful views. Huge rooms, very private, new gourmet kit, appliances stay. Seller will not subdivide. Call for list of recent upgrades.* Red Hill sounded great on paper, at least. But from this vantage point, you could see the dark spaces where the red shingles had blown off the north side of the house in the winter winds, the weathered deck that needed to be rebuilt, a listless lean to the porch. What you couldn't see were the afternoons when my brother and I would ride bareback up and down the slopes for hours, hunting for hawk feathers, or Dee and Goody sitting on the corral fence, teaching me numbers by counting the pronghorn grazing in the brush. Or the times I'd take my sketchpad out to the big rock on the far northeast corner of the property because I couldn't take the tension in the house for one more second.

Jace waved a fly away from his face. "You gonna be sad to see this place go?"

"I don't know. Not really, I guess." I've always had ambivalent feelings about this place, love and anxiety inexorably mixed. "You?"

"Oh, you bet I'll miss it. A lot of history here. This is where our family started."

"Yeah." I clucked to give Hodge the cue to circle back toward the barn. "And where it fell apart, too."

Sun shone through the orange kitchen curtains, reflecting off the new steel appliances. From the window, I watched Kenny secure Delaney in the trailer and patiently led Preston up the ramp, while

Rosie and Josie, the red and blue heelers, rocketed in a loop around the truck, the barn, and back again. Unlike my brother, Kenny was a needle-and-spoon tragedy, and he had the jacked teeth and death-pallor complexion to show for it. Only thirty-one, the hard times had bent him into the shape of a question mark. He reminded me of a cat I saw at the pound where I found Homer. The malnourished coon wouldn't eat from its dish; he took the food a piece at a time to the corner and hunkered over it before gulping it down.

Jace inhaled, a wheeze catching at the top of the breath. He coughed and cleared his throat.

I dropped a cinnamon Pop Tart in the toaster. "I love what you did with the kitchen."

"Yeah, well, it's what every cowboy dreams of, a gold buckle and a vegetable sink." He chuckled, struggling to suppress another dry cough. "Got sick of that puny galley kitchen. A guy my size can't cook anything worth a damn in a space so small. It was like being on a submarine. Might get a buyer on the hook, too."

When his fledgling pole barn business didn't bring in enough to cover the nut on Red Hill, Jace started driving trucks, turning first to No-Doz to stay awake on the long runs, then ratcheting up to bumps of coke. When money ran thin again, he took in lodgers, most of whom paid him in party favors. By the time our mom shipped him off to the pricy Minnesota rehab, he'd snorted his way through most of a second mortgage. Now he had the property on the block, eager to make a fresh start somewhere near Centennial where the land was cheap and the neighbors sparse and indifferent. His wasn't so much a shattered life as it was a puzzle he'd let slip and drop, pieces everywhere. Far from hopeless. Just stay clean, pay down the debt, and put it all together again.

He rested his knuckles on the counter, leaned over and spat, one of those kitchen sink wads, yellowy-thick and disturbing in volume.

I wrapped the hot Pop Tart in a paper towel. "Why the coughing? Are you sick?"

"Naw, honey, I'm just tired and all the dust blowing around is gunking up my eyes and lungs. I'm all right."

I know it's silly to worry about my brother. He's built like a tanker, and my dog-eared copy of *Co-Dependent No More* says over and over that fretting is the least effective way to help a recovering addict. But the thought of him being on the road for two months, team roping on the gay rodeo circuit when he was so new to recovery and his current relationship, made me more nervous than good sense and Narc-Anon counsel allowed me to admit. The role of designated worrier is tough to shake.

Harold Gwatney, the weasel-chinned Realtor, rapped on the front door at 10 A.M. sharp to show the property to a flashy middle-aged couple from Palm Beach who, it was hinted, had pockets as deep as their tans. For the past twenty-five years, the fancypants types had been closing in all right—the neighboring land snapped up by cola heiresses, college deans, investors who wanted to sink a hook into the ever-dwindling Real West but couldn't afford the zillionaire views of the Absarokas or the Grand Tetons.

Jace insisted that I be on-premises during showings. Once he took over the mortgage for Dad and threw heft and haunch into the place, he became territorial about Red Hill, plus, the various binges of the past year had him verging on paranoid. The house looked better than I'd ever seen it. The floors, wide planks of soft pine that held dents like grudges, glowed under fresh satin varnish. While Gwatney gushed over the newly remodeled kitchen, I wandered into the living room, looking at the photos that hung on the landing of the stairway. Me, Mom, Dad, and Jace on skis at the Cowboy Downhill in 1991. Jace and Kenny standing over an enormous fallen buck, each holding an antler, the animal blank-eyed, tongue flopped out. Jace, shirtless last summer, holding me over the brimming stock tank, about to drop me in.

At the edge of the arrangement was a photo of me, nine and pigtailed, holding up Bigfoot, one of my 4-H rabbits. I wasn't particularly pretty then, and I'm not now. I started out a tomboy, later softening to what my mom calls "coltish"—which just means a tomboy who's not afraid of lipstick. Because I'd bite my lips until they swelled when I was nervous, my brother called me Monster Mouth as a child. My mother tried to console me, holding my chin in her hand. "Those are lips meant for a prince to kiss"—slim consolation to a girl who found horses better company than boys. Even now, I'm hardly the girliest girl. A denim miniskirt is formalwear to me, and while I tolerate makeup, I hate bras. Not that I need one. I'm short, sturdy, and unthreatening. Cute. A four-letter word but it fits.

In the center of the photo grouping was a large silver-framed portrait of my mother as a young woman. My mom, Raelynn, was Miss Rodeo South Dakota and an impressive trick rider. The hand-tinted photo shows her in a hippodrome stand on the back of a galloping buckskin mare: arms overhead, her body taut and curved back like the carved wooden figurehead on the prow of a ship. She's wearing a blush-rose satin jumpsuit with sequin trim. Red lipstick to match her hat, the pink fullness of her sleeves billowing out behind her like proud sails. To this day, she's a passionate horsewoman and a class act, all the way down to the underpinnings.

Next to that, in a wire frame hung from a nail, was a photo of my dad on Slade, a rope clenched between my father's teeth. The way the photos are positioned, my mom and dad look like they're running toward each other. As an adult, Dad never competed, but he was a fine roper and bulldogger, back when he was alive.

My father isn't really dead. He just acts like he is. Peter Rowan Heatherly, Jr., worked like a maniac his whole life, mowing hay, stretching fence, bolting together barns, grain bins, and sheds. He signed on at the Frontier refinery when he and Mom were first married; then an explosion of chlorine gas seared his lungs and breathing trouble came on, so he went into construction. He and a buddy revolutionized rural luxury housing, building a small development of beautifully appointed hobby ranches north of town. The two of them had a good thing going, but his partner ripped the company right out from under him. That's when the home situation erupted. My mother had accepted my dad's proposal when she was seventeen, thinking that with a hard-working, traditional husband, she'd be set for life. But when the money ran out, she conveniently had a midlife crisis and began making noises about wanting more fulfillment and "self-actualization" than life here offered. Then she left. Jace had struck out on his own years before, so it was just me and my father, and Dad's downhill roll picked up speed.

My dad loved my mother the way a tinder stick loves a match, and without her, his fire to live went away. They always fought like hell, my mom digging into my dad for never being home, him yelling back about her unreasonable demands. Her passionate rages seemed to embolden him somehow. He'd storm off and within hours complete a raft of tasks. Without that jumpstart tension, he stalled.

After the divorce, Dad and I moved down to Colorado, where he'd gotten hired as a foreman. Jace, who until then had chafed under responsibility like it was a sandpaper suit turned sandy side in, moved back to Red Hill and pressed Dad to sign over the title to him. "This is the only place you've ever had that's all your own, Dad," he reasoned, betting he'd prevail with a direct hit to the pride spot. "Either give it to me or the bank." Turned out the King of the Castle position suited Jace just fine, since he wasn't exactly hiding behind the barn door when ego was handed out, but Dad didn't handle the transition as well. He wouldn't so much as come up for a Sunday dinner. Like a typical Heatherly man, he greeted disappointment bitterly and sought its death through drowning. He drank every night, and over time he lost jobs and confidence and half his mind. As he snarled into a fraction of the man he once was, running the household fell to me, and it was hard to manage school and chores both. The grades plummeted downward and stayed there. I wrote out checks for the monthly bills and mailed them in, but they started bouncing. After several missed mortgage payments, we lost the first Colorado place and had to move every few months to a more affordable rental. In tenth grade, I moved so much I didn't bother unpacking. I knew as soon as my books and clothes came out of the boxes, they'd have to go right back in. My mother made repeated offers to let me move in with her and her new boyfriend at his huge spread in Jackson, but I was determined to prove that I didn't need her, or anybody. By seventeen I had learned that you never let a drunk sleep on his back and that you can use one credit card to pay another. While I did it all, no complaining, beneath my Supergirl stoicism, the change in my father rattled me to the core. I didn't mind the smaller and smaller houses, but the smaller and smaller Dad bothered me a lot.

The Palm Beach couple traipsed through the first floor of the house with great disinterest until the wife proclaimed, *sotto voce*, that she found Red Hill "too rustic." She clacked toward the front door on her spindle-heeled denim and leather sandals, her husband rushing forth to grab her elbow when she tripped over a chink in the foyer floor. Mr. Gwatney left Jace and me with a "better luck next time" glance and a three-page single-spaced list of suggested cosmetic improvements for the property. I ferreted through the kitchen junk drawer, found a marking pen, and offered it to my brother. First on the list: Take down the cross at the top of the rise. ("A little off-putting," Gwatney noted in shrimpy, pointed letters.) Jace took the marker, pressed the tip to Item One, and ran a thick black line right through it.

Jace folded up a map and tucked it behind the sun visor of his truck. Kenny put two bottles of pop in the cup holders. They were almost ready for the road. Homer waddled out and sniffed the dirt. Kenny called over. "Hey, Daryl, that a dog or a barrel with fur on it?"

"He's trimming down, I swear." I sat on the bottom porch step, playing cat's cradle with a length of dirty string. "Hey, Jace, you ever hear of a bareback rider named J.W. Jarrett?"

Jace picked up his war bag and stashed it behind the driver's seat. "Yep. He won the World a long time ago . . . works over at Dominion now. I see him sometimes when I'm over there. Why?"

"No reason. I just met him last night at the Bluffs Ranch is all."

He put his fists on his hips, dark oblongs of perspiration showing under his arms. "And . . . ?"

"*And* nothing. He seemed like a nice guy, so I was curious."

"Jesus, Daryl. You've had enough heartache this year. Don't you go looking for more." He came over and put his hands on my shoulders, looking into my face. "Do yourself a favor and move up into the master loft while we're gone. You can make your old room into a studio or something. Get all that good morning light." He gave me a loving squeeze. "I know I haven't exactly been Brother of the Year lately, but if you need anything at all, you call me, all right? No matter where I am, I'm here for you."

"I know that. You're my *numero uno*, Jace." I gave him a thumbs-up. "Always." I do my best to play the *golly-gee-help-me* lil' sis, but when my brother is in amends mode, I feel myself brace against it, a stiff-grinning hostage to the Fifth Step. "I'll see you in Denver in July."

Kenny slapped the front seat, and the two heelers leaped up into the truck. I went around to the passenger side and tugged the sleeve of his denim jacket. "Okay. Kenny-penny, give me a hug, you cheap son-of-a-bee."

I knew about my brother long before he told me. I never said anything, but when he had first taken over Red Hill, I came up for the weekend and one of my oil pastels rolled under the bed in the basement bedroom. I swiped my hand around under the bed, and that's when I found the box. Why did I open it? I'm not sure. But somehow when I saw that stash of bodybuilding videos from the 1980s, I knew.

Now when I meet people, I tip my head and wonder—who they really are, what they're hiding. Whether it's sex or some other secret, everyone's got a box under the bed. The only difference is that some of them will tell you about it, while with others you find out on your own.

I padded to the kitchen and broke out the pack of emergency Camel Lights I'd tossed into the freezer. I flopped onto my back on the living room couch and smoked, a striped Indian blanket rolled up under my head, looking at the water stains on the oak-paneled ceiling.

Boilerplate advice for those from dysfunctional homes is to accept your family as-is and treat them with loving detachment. I accept my brother, his addictions, his mistakes, and his ham-fisted attempts at correcting them. I accept my ever-distant dad, still drinking but at least alive and working, I think, at a sheet-metal operation. I accept my mom, remarried and refashioned as a couture cowgirl, living in a twenty-room log castle in Jackson and enjoying all the self-actualization money can buy. As for the loving detachment part, well, let's just say I'm working on it.

I ground out my cigarette in a cream-colored saucer bordered with dark red cattle brands. I said the Serenity Prayer for the heck of it and got up off the couch to make something of the day. Whatever your lot in life, it could be worse, so there's no point in feeling sorry for yourself. Or, put more bluntly, *If you want sympathy, look in the dictionary between shit and syphilis.* Something my father was fond of saying.

4

HOW COULD I MAKE A FIVE-FOOT-TWO MAN into a giant?
Resting my brush on the palette, I tilted the easel to better catch
the noon light. My T-shirt clung to my ribs in the heat. I untucked it,
twisting the fabric into a knot at my waist. Ice cubes rattled in the
glass when I took a sip of tea. My neck felt clammy.

When I got out of school and moved from Fort Collins to Denver, I got hired as an assistant to the sculptor Maxine Fish, a local
legend known for her abstract steel-and-wire renderings of the
Rocky Mountains. I had hoped the apprenticeship would instill appreciation for the artist's work ethic, but the entire time I worked
for her, I never got to see Maxine in her studio. If I so much as set a
foot across the threshold, she'd shriek like an opera diva who'd had
her cape stepped on. I was confined to her office, her supply room,
and her kitchen. The only thing the job improved was my ability to
comparison shop for solder and to visually gauge the right amount
of Amaretto to pour into someone's morning coffee. Maxine took
at least two finger's worth in her first cup, and a splash in every cup
after that.

The last time I last saw Maxine Fish, I told her I had taken up
Western landscape. She muttered, "A traditionalist," and the ser-
rated edge of that disapproval has been sawing at me ever since. "Art

doesn't document the West," she has trumpeted in the local culture pages, "art reinvents it!" But as much as Maxine relished her eye-rolling disapproval, she did do me one favor: She sent me a check for a share in a booth at the Denver Stock Show craft fair in January. Buried somewhere beneath Maxine's esoteric sensibility was a beating artist's heart. At the Stock Show, I made my first sale. It was only for a couple hundred dollars, but once you earn honest-to-God money for your honest-to-God art, you're hooked.

I tapped the butt of the paintbrush against my front teeth and wondered what was missing, why Shane McGurk read so flat on the canvas. In person, Shane had Super Ball bounce and enough psychic firepower to give a one-ton bull the what-for, though you could fit six of him in a teaspoon with room to spare. At a Ricky and the Redstreaks show during Frontier Days last year, he drank his body mass in tequila and tried to grind me on the dance floor. He reached up to drape his spindle-wristed arms over my shoulders, clamping his thighs around my leg. I winced and held my breath, certain I'd have a crushed knee by the encore of "Wild Thing." A man strong enough to hang on to a half-ton animal by just a leather rope and his legs, however short, is a dance partner to be feared.

When Shane shattered his femur in Puyallup, everyone thought he was gone for good. The damage was done by Kryptonite, a drooly white Charolais with one underdeveloped banana horn that flopped with deceptive helplessness when he bucked. Six seconds into the ride, Kryptonite swung his head up, shifted Shane forward over his neck, bonked him into the dirt like a yard dart, and spun back, bringing the rear hooves down neatly on Shane's splayed-out thigh. Shane had just turned nineteen, and X-rays showed bone chips floating like snowflakes on the screen. But he was back within a year, held together with titanium screws, though not much good for spurring with the hurt leg, and found himself in the money. He drew Kryptonite for a rematch in Guymon, and scored an arena record. Then he got mashed into the chute rails by some sorry sack of crap in the short go and broke his leg over again. Doctors say he's out for the rest of the season, but Shane was quoted as saying six months.

His mother, distraught and frantic as if absorbing through maternal osmosis the hurt Shane denied, thought a birthday portrait might cheer her son. I told Mrs. McGurk, whose husband worked with my dad, that I was only acquainted with Shane, but I'd try to get him down. The truth was, I didn't know Shane at all really, except that when he danced, he was a hazard to kneecaps everywhere. And my rodeo knowledge was limited to the basics—I scarcely followed the sport, and most of my trips to Frontier Days were when I was a girl, ceremonial outings for my mom to show me off to her former rodeo queen friends, ribbons woven into my braids, my satin shirt matching hers, our horses' hooves polished with Twinkle Toes glitter. But I couldn't turn Mrs. McGurk down in the state she was in, and I needed the money. Shane's birthday was July fifteenth. My deadline was less than six weeks away.

I lowered the shade and dropped my brush into a jelly jar on the mint green desk, swirling it in the pine-sharp-smelling thinner. Box elder bugs, their black and orange backs like tribal masks, crawled on the tarp browsing the paint tubes. I clicked the remote on the stereo and listened to George Strait tell me about the night Lefty died. I stepped back to look at the canvas and sipped my iced tea, powdered, no sugar, lemon-flavored. Strong, almost too strong—I court my muse with caffeine. Homer woke from a nap on the bed and yawned loudly. I rubbed my eyes and chewed an ice cube, then tucked the easel into the corner. Nothing was happening and nothing would. Not today.

I only work in familiar mediums—watercolor and acrylic. So it's not technical difficulty holding me up. Between Shane, who was proving himself an elusive subject, and Maxine's naysaying nattering inside my skull, it became clear that painting wasn't the problem. People, as ever, were the problem.

* * *

"Oh my God, your first tattoo," Shawna gurgled, positioning a tiny silver digital camera over her eye. "This is so exciting!" I lifted my head. The flash bounced off the mirror and the room went alien green and black. I blinked. It was almost ten o'clock, and I'd been sitting for two hours. The needle worked my skin, a screaming tingle, over and over. Peter Tosh's dusky tremolo throbbed from the boom box. I felt ill.

Grinnin' Bat Body Works had an exhausted after-hours feel. The phone kept ringing, an ancient answering machine recording a series of ranting, incoherent messages. The chair I sat in creaked and poked me in the spine, and much as I loved Shawna's boyfriend Lan, his sandalwood body oil was giving me a headache that felt like a shishkebab skewer piercing my right eye. The table fan blew clean air into my nostrils, squealing angrily as it oscillated. I kept my head tipped back so I wouldn't see the blood on my skin. *Hematophobia* is the name of my affliction—fear of blood. It isn't tough to manage; I just have to turn my head at the first sight of red and manage the guilt of never being able to let the Red Cross tap a vein. The swamp cooler clicked on and chugged miserably. I looked up. There was a psychedelic poster taped to the ceiling over the tattooing station— multicolored squares that formed a flying Pegasus if you focused your eyes a certain way. "You missed a good rodeo out at the Bluffs Ranch the other night, Shawna."

She made a fat braid over her right shoulder. "Yeah, sorry I couldn't make it. I was too busy clubbing baby harp seals." She reached behind the counter and pulled out a canvas. "Want to see the latest in the long march of the Indian maids?"

The first painting Shawna ever sold was of an Anglo-featured Indian woman in beaded buckskin, gazing into a moonlit pool. Instead of seeing her own reflection, she saw the somber face of a gray wolf. Shawna had just ripped off a particular artist who traffics in images that she considers demeaning to Indians, but our professor put the painting in a show. Not only did Shawna win first place, she got an article written about her in the *Denver Post*—"Native teen painter prodigy!"—and a rep. Now twenty-two, she sells as much as she can produce. Everyone wants a piece of Shawna Two Tribes (neé Kaplan), even though the women in the paintings represent neither her nor her vision. But it keeps the lot rent paid on the junky purple trailer home she shares with Lan south of town, and the medicine chest full of her trademark blue-black Lady Clairol. And then some.

Her most recent painting, an oil commissioned at the gob-smacking rate of $2500, was classic Two Tribes—beautiful duty, a sloe-eyed maiden leading a white horse into a night forest, feathers and fringe trailing off her sleeves and hem.

I adjusted the little pillow under my head. "They pay you for it already?"

"Yeah," she said, disdainfully. Half-Crow, half-Jew, Shawna treats her Native identity like an ambiguous shield—you're never sure if it's wielded for pride, allegiance, or defense. Once she called Kimber "pale face," and Kimber smacked her right in the mouth. Lightly, but she wasn't kidding.

Shawna stood, stretching her back. Ever since we'd declared this the year of Art First—with our debut at the Frontier Days Art Show in July as the reward for our commitment—she'd been up at all hours, painting. She pressed her hand into her lower back like an old woman, the sleeves of her long maroon crepe dress pushed up, Victorian black-and-green ivy tattoos twining up her forearms.

Lan licked the sweat from his upper lip and swiped his forehead with the back of his gloved hand. "Babe, aren't you hot in that?"

"With the thyroid condition from hell? Not really." She stroked the front of her neck. "I'm happy to report that thanks to this lag-gard little gland, I'm getting so big I only fit into dresses and leg-gings." She tapped her finger on my forehead. "And just so you know, I didn't step on the scale." Shawna and I had made a pact to never weigh ourselves. Our motto is: "Picasso didn't care if he had a fat ass."

Shawna stashed the camera between the plastic bottle of Beta-dine scrub and a half-empty box of latex gloves, size large, and sat back down, pinching my shoulder with almost maternal enthusiasm. This tattoo was her birthday gift to me. I turned twenty-three in February, and I'd been obsessed with getting a tattoo for as long as I could remember. I loved the idea of an image melding into my skin, knowing it's on me forever, secure yet dangerous in its durability. Given how much and how fast my life had shifted, I longed to claim one small thing for myself that wouldn't ever change. I wanted personal. I wanted permanent.

Lan presented a sketch for my approval, then transferred the image onto thermofax paper and rubbed Speed Stick over my ankle so the stencil adhered to my skin. The machine hummed to life in Lan's hand. He inked in the barbed-wire band and the outline of the captive heart it surrounded. "The way it is now is good, the heart and the wire. It shows your tough-but-tender dichotomy," he said, sketching crimson in the heart. He nodded, satisfied with his interpretation. "The yin and yang of Daryl."

Shawna lit a slender joint, sucked in a lungful, and waved it at me. "Smoke?" Her hair was in a twist at the base of her neck, accentuating her punky Cleopatra profile. She tweezes off her eyebrows and pencils razor-thin lines of kohl in their place, which makes her appear distant and, with the constant pursing of her generous lips, a little mean. But if you look close enough at this nimbus of hostility, you notice a spiky sweetness—hands that flutter like birds when she talks, good-apple cheeks under the pale pressed powder, a dimple on the right side of her chin.

I waved away the fingerling of pot-scented smoke that had drifted my way. "No thanks, you degenerate hippie. You know I don't indulge."

She shrugged. "Suit yourself." She rubbed her stomach lazily. "I'm so f-ing hungry, it isn't funny. Got any candy?"

Lan glanced at Shawna from behind his rig. "Emergency rations are in the drawer by the cash register." He shook a kink from his neck and frowned. Beneath his mellow-fellow facade, Lan was being driven mad by the Grinnin' Bat. As a tattoo artist, he's so gifted that people travel from as far away as Kansas to get under his gun, but for all his talent, the shop barely does enough business to stay open. He makes most of his money traveling to bike rallies. After twenty-six years in this state, he's grown tired of Wyoming and says he's dying to pack up and move to the coast. His parents, herbal tea secessionists from up near Dubois whose conversation topics were limited to genealogy, hydroponics, and *Solider of Fortune* magazine, constantly brag that Lan's great-great-great-grandfather on his mother's side was one of the state's original settlers. They named their three sons Lander, Ross, and Powell, so whether Lan stays or goes, he'll never completely leave Wyoming behind.

Shawna rummaged through the drawer, pulling out a bendable skeleton doll, a glow-in-the-dark yo-yo, a stack of crumpled tracing paper, an Iron Maiden CD, credit card slips, and a roll of postage stamps. Shawna picked up the CD. She made a gagging sound. "Iron Maiden? Heinous! Is this yours, Landybean?"

"Maybe so, Shawnabean. Maybe so." Lan swabbed excess ink off my ankle with a folded paper towel. Poochy lipped, buzz-cut, and tattooed from shoulder to wrist, Lan looks like a Gerber baby gone bad. He pinched my big toe and wiggled it. "You okay up there? Need a break? An ammonia ampule?"

"Nah, I'm good." I closed my eyes and rested my head on my arms. I didn't want to stop. The tattoo was just a lot of little pains, not one huge agony. Nowhere near as bad as the navel piercing, which felt like having a knitting needle shoved through skin thick as a rubber eraser. I could breathe through this, small sips of air through parted lips.

Lan distracted me with tattoo lore, saying how in remote island cultures, tattoos were pushed into the skin with sharpened sticks, and ink was made of ashes from the smoke of kerosene lanterns mixed with water. What he was saying magnified my pain, so I tuned out and buoyed myself on the babbling cadence of his voice.

Lan blotted my ankle again and swiped the back of his gloved hand across his forehead. "Just about done, Daryl. You did say you wanted a banner across the heart that says 'Mom' in it, right?" When I jerked my head up, he bit his lip and pressed down harder on the machine. The needle whined, red flowing. "Hee hee, I am a funny sumbuck, yes I am."

I groaned. It felt like a tiny rake was attacking my ankle. The burn was excruciating.

Lan sat back and turned off the lamp. "Okay, you're done. Be real careful when you stand up. There's a gallon of endorphins screaming through your bloodstream. You're gonna feel higher than a kite."

I sat on a bench near the door and stretched tennis socks over my feet, making sure the elastic didn't touch the bandaged tattoo. I was permanently marked, and had the sensation of floating a mile out of my skin by a silken cord. A dreamy peacefulness settled over me. I slid carefully into my boots, muscles loose and light, joints floating in their sockets. I felt cagey and catnap relaxed all at once.

Lan tossed the tattoo needles into a sterilization sack, then slid them into the autoclave. "So, you like it?"

"I beyond like it. I *love* it." I worried the tape on the bandage, trying to peak beneath. Somehow I knew in that black and red ink, my world had made a whispering shift off its rigid little axis.

Lan took his denim vest from the coat peg. "Careful there, friend. Problem with this stuff is that once you get that first taste, you immediately start thinking, *What's next?*"

"God, don't I know it?" Shawna pulled the beaded chain on the vertical blinds and twirled the sign in the window from OPEN to CLOSED. "You ready to take that brand-new beauty to the Wigwam?"

★ ★ ★

Saturday nights in Cheyenne belong to the Wigwam Wild Women. Down at the Wigwam, the rinky-dink dive bar in the Plains Hotel, the managers fixed a stern eye on their flagging business and wised up. The Wigwam used to be sad-sack central—has-beens and never-weres mooning over whiskey and vanished glory days. With Kimber now in charge, the bar was staffed with hot young women pouring kinky drinks. The tables were repurposed as go-go pedestals and a few of the old-timers stuck around, enjoying the much-improved view. Since the Wigwam "went wild" they've packed to the rafters every Saturday. Everyone under the age of forty, from Casper to Kimball, Nebraska, wanted to be near the flash and glitter of the Wild Women, as this was a region starved for youthful sexual electricity, a little edgy glamour. The Wigwam Wild Women Revue rolled out the rocking country songs and liquor, and the cash rolled in.

We found Kimber by the beer cooler in the stock room, sitting on a stepladder putting double-sided tape on the soles of her brown boots. "I spend so much time standing on the bar, this keeps me from slipping," she said, tearing a piece from the roll with her teeth. She stood and straightened the legs of her tight, chocolate-colored fake leather pants. She arranged the stack over her boots, then adjusted her tan suede vest and matter-of-factly fluffed out her long blond curls. "C'mon, kids, it's feeding time at the zoo!"

Four of the Wild Women were busy setting up shooters and drawing beers for the thirsty crowd. Alizé, atop the bar in shiny red patent pants, matching halter, and vintage stack-heeled boots with gold-tone spurs, sucked in a mouthful of 151 rum, brandished a lighter, and blew out a flailing cone-shaped plume of orange fire. A delighted, drunken roar rocked the room.

Shawna can't drink for crap, never could. During her second beer, she clutched my leg and yelled in Kimber's face. "Hey, you wanna see Daryl's new tattoo?"

Kimber leaned over the bar. "Of course I do!"

I took off my boot, poking people on either side with my elbows, and swung my leg up. My ankle was warm to the touch when I pulled the tape and peeled back the gauze. The tattoo gleamed under the thick coat of antibacterial ointment, the scabs forming over the ink fine and barely visible.

I turned my foot so Kimber could see the entire design, the salve shining pink and orange in the bar neons. She let out a low whistle. "That's a beauty!"

"Much obliged." Lan preened. "Now cover up. Your tat's a germ vector while the skin is still open."

While I struggled to reattach the gauze bandage, some yahoo ran over and swiped my boot.

"You'll have to give me a kiss if you want this back," he snickered over my shoulder and bolted across the room with my boot tucked under his arm. His rancid beer and cigarette breath made my stomach lurch. He'd have better luck if he'd offered to trade my boot for a Certs.

"Hey, Gomer!" I yelled, "Give me my boot!" I hopped off the barstool and took off after the guy, walking on my heel and limping like a peg-leg pirate.

Lan wove ahead of me and yanked my boot from the guy. He gave Lan a brawler's once-over, but decided not to press the issue after registering the shaved head and wrist-to-shoulder tattoos.

The red siren spun and wailed and at the plucking electric guitar intro, Kimber came out on a little hobbyhorse and "galloped" across the barroom floor in nothing but her hat, boots, bun-hugging faded denim cutoffs, and a skintight leather vest. Men swiveled on their barstools to look at her, eyes bright with eighty-proof and hope. Her bare midriff ranged tawny and taut between where the vest ended and the shorts began. In front of every dollar-bearing hand, she did a dip and curtsy on her stick horse, plucked bills, then shinnied up a stool onto the bar for the song's climax.

Her body articulated sex, but her expression was all business. She ripped open her vest, revealing a red sequined push-up bra. Fists thrust into the air and everyone hollered along with the song: *We're from the country!*

In her red spangled bikini, she twirled the shucked-off shorts over her head like a lasso. Everyone in the bar shouted, making the walls shake: *We're from the country and we like it that way!*

At half past one, Shawna, Lan, and I decided to hit the Village Inn down the street to sober up for the ride home. We forged a path through the Wigwam crowd, which had grown thick and stubborn as gumbo mud. People were grabbing, grinding against each other, huddling in packs near the jukebox and pool table. A bouncer wrestled darts from the grip of a drunk in a plaid shirt and Coors cap. I led the way through the crush of asses and elbows, making a slow, steady beeline for the exit, distracted by the chaos around me. As I reached out to push open the door, it swung forward and hit me square in the face.

Tiny glimmering pink comets blitzed back and forth in front of my eyes, hundreds of them. I put my hands to my forehead, palming my eye sockets and wobbling on my boot heels. Stunned tears ran down my cheeks. My pulse pounded and a soprano chorus of adrenaline shrieked in as the music from the jukebox faded out. I heard a man's voice wavering in on a distant galactic frequency, "Oh my God! I'm so sorry!"

Once the light show behind my eyelids stopped, I dropped my hands and looked up. There, clutching me with both hands, was J.W. Jarrett. His gaze was concerned, amused. My mouth dropped open, and he started laughing. Tightening his grip, he pulled me in close, then wrapped his arms around me so my cheek pressed against his shoulder. I could feel the whiskey-buzz on him.

His lips were right by my ear. "I'm so sorry, precious. I didn't hurt that pretty face, did I?"

I shook my head no.

"Do you need some ice?"

I shook my head again.

"Not too bad then, huh? Just a little bump?"

I nodded and sniffled.

He pulled back, took my head between his hands, and kissed the tender spot on my forehead where no doubt a big ugly bruise was egging up. Then he folded me back into his embrace. I came just up to his chin, my head resting perfectly on his shoulder. His neck smelled like spices and shaving cream. "Hey, Daryl," he whispered into my ear, that honey drawl vibrating against my skin, plinking down my backbone one vertebra at a time. "I wanted you to call me."

My pulse still hammered in my head, a band of pain spanning temple to temple. My tongue felt loose in the back of my throat. We fell silent, pressed together from shoulder to knee, and kept hugging. Beneath the spicy scent on his skin, I caught a note of clean male sweat. I breathed deeply. The pain in my head dulled to a heavy, wonderful wooziness.

I broke the embrace and held out my hand. "Give me your cell."

He pulled the phone from his belt.

"I'm not going to call you," I said, flipping through the phone's menu to the directory. I punched my cellular number into the keypad. "But you can call me." I handed the phone back to him with a smile and a curt nod, then strolled through the barroom door, letting it swing wide behind me.

Lan and Shawna followed me out to the marble-floored brightness.

Shawna caught my arm. "Who was that?"

"I have no idea!" I said with a shrug. I stepped into the wedge-shaped glass chamber of the revolving door and twirled from the lobby, presenting my freshly bruised face to the cool night air.

5

I STOOD IN THE FUSTY OFFICE of the Twin Pines motel with a folded-over copy of the *Tribune-Eagle* want ads stuffed in my satchel. I hadn't planned on working this summer, but Count Truckula had started making threatening noises and my piggy bank had cobwebs in it. By noon, I'd been turned down at six restaurants in town, two stores in the Frontier Mall, the Western-wear store on Lincolnway, and I'd even left an application at Target. The last thing I wanted to do was to clean up after other people, but with no promising leads and truck Armageddon on the horizon, here I was.

The office smelled like moldy carpet, antiseptic, and jasmine incense. An older Vietnamese woman in a lime sherbet muumuu and pink crystal chandelier earrings stepped out from behind the desk and said, with a voice that managed to be both quiet and mean, "Can I help you?" She patted her cascading black pompadour with the bored hand of a lady-in-waiting who'd been waiting too long.

"I'm here about the housekeeping position." I slid the newspaper across the counter, and the muumuu woman snatched it up and looked it over, her glasses slid to the tip of her beige-powdered nose. She wore cocktail rings on every finger, clustered with diamonds the color of cloudy beer.

"Full-time or part-time?"

"Part-time."

"I'll take this, Grandma." A teenage girl came in, a Vuitton purse tucked under her arm, and introduced herself as Giselle. She walked me through the process of filling out an application, then took me down the hall and showed me the laundry room and the supply closet. She opened a metal locker and pulled out an ugly mustard-yellow smock that tied on the sides. "You'll have to wear this."

I put it on over my shirt.

Giselle pressed her glossed lips together archly. "That looks great." She smoothed the front of her white slacks and we walked into the hall. "Here's the deal. If you want a day off, you have to call one of the other housekeepers to cover for you. We don't care who it is, but getting a replacement is your responsibility." She handed me a list of phone numbers.

"So, does that mean I have the job, or . . . ?"

Grandma stuck her tall-hairdo'd head out the office door and yelled down the hall at Giselle. "Nguyen, go to Wal-Mart. Get more cleanser."

"Oh my gawd," Giselle moaned, hugging her Vuitton purse close to her little body. "Anyway, yes. You've got the job. Stick around and I'll train you myself."

I watched the bobbing platinum-blond ponytail bounce down the sidewalk by the pool. The sass of it suggested a high-stepping palomino, the hair almost angelic golden-white in the morning sun.

Giselle helped me load a cart with clean linens, and we pushed it toward Room One, where the girl stood facing into the stand of pines, cigarette in hand. Under a purple miniskirt, her tan legs shimmered, light catching the outer rim of the calf muscles in golden arcs that curved into a pair of white cowboy boots. A car stopped at the light on Lincolnway honked, and she squinted at the passenger and waved. I knew I'd seen her before, somewhere. She was wearing a mustard-yellow Twin Pines cleaning smock. Giselle rolled the cart up to Room One and rapped on the door with her key. "Housekeeping."

The girl turned around. "Hi," she said to me, crushing her cigarette under the toe of her boot. "I'm Crystal. Welcome to the party."

I stood in the barn, sweating like a steelworker. Slade was doing his best to give me a hard time, twisting his head to the right and blowing whenever I tried to put the bit in his mouth. I'd spent the entire morning at the Twin Pines motel, stripping and making beds, emptying trash, vacuuming, dusting, and scrubbing bathrooms. I guess the Dam family was striving for some kind of thematic unity, because the industrial cleanser they used was pine scented, which gave me a pain like pinecones had been shoved up my nose and taken root in my sinuses.

"Come on, mule. Work with me." Tempting Slade with a bucket of oats didn't help any, and neither did opening his stall window to sunlight and birdsong, though he usually found the breeze delicious and would spend hours warming his nostrils while taking in the view. I had just stepped away from his kicking back leg when my cell rang.

"Daryl, it's J.W. Jarrett. How's your head?"

My mouth went dry. "Only slightly dented, don't worry."

"Well, I feel terrible about what happened. I'd like to make it up to you if I could."

"You don't have to do that," I said, pressing the phone to my ear with my shoulder so I could tempt Slade with half a Macintosh apple. He took it and nipped my fingers in the process. "I know you didn't hurt me on purpose."

"Of course not," J.W. said, waspishly. He took a deep breath and his tone changed. "But I'd like to take you out for supper sometime anyway." A tense pause. "If you'd want to, I mean." He paused again. "If there's someplace around here that you like to go. Heck, we could go to Fort Collins or maybe Loveland even."

J.W.'s hesitance was touching—it had been some time since I'd heard a man say *heck*. "That's very nice of you," I said. "But I'm really busy, I've got work and chores, and I won't be free for a while."

"Oh. Now that's too bad. I'm fixing to rodeo for a couple days, and I was hoping I could maybe see you before I left."

"Where you off to?"

"Well, there's Ute Mountain in Cortez Saturday, then I'm going down to Grover. I'll be back late Sunday night."

Slade finally accepted his bit and I led him into the round pen. A flock of starlings littered the sky, pointed wings, black bodies swooping down, then banking west in tandem. Sun baked the sage, furling its peppery scent into the stagnant air. I considered my schedule. J.W. sounded sincere. "You could come here if you're free now," I suggested. "I'm out on Happy Jack, turn right off Lincolnway onto Missile Drive, then we're twenty-five miles out, right-hand side. The log house with the red roof. I'm in the barn doing chores but I'll be done soon."

"Well, don't do any more. I'll help."

The second we hung up I raced to the house. I figured he'd take half an hour to drive out. I needed to change out of my sweaty clothes, but I didn't have anything clean in the bedroom. I ran to the basement laundry room in just my underpants and sprinted back upstairs clutching my Wranglers and a ribbed khaki tank top. Hopping inelegantly on one foot, I tried to work the jeans up to my hips. I lay down on the bed and zipped them, then sneered at my reflection. The party-girl pants were overly snug for the occasion, and who does chores in clean clothes? I got back into my old grungy men's Levi's. In the mirror, I caught sight of the green-brown bruise on my forehead and panicked. Makeup wouldn't cover it. My hat was nowhere to be found. No bandanas in the drawer, either. I unearthed a pair of scissors from the nightstand, finger-combed the front section of my hair over my face, and cut myself some shaggy bangs, then braided the rest into history's hastiest pigtails.

Why I spazzed so much over J.W.'s imminent arrival was beyond me. I wasn't like Kimber. Cowboys were never my thing, especially the rodeo kind. I remember countless weekend afternoons when I was small, tucked behind my dad's knee as he leaned his elbow on the fireplace mantel, lording over the living room while he and his buddies held forth, trying to outdo each other with good-old-bad-old-days stories of the wildest buckers, the most unruly steers. My knees quaked at their booming voices coaxing me out, teasing and rattling the ice cubes in their glasses, asking me to freshen their drinks when I wasn't even strong enough to hoist a lemonade pitcher or crack open a beer. My mom would laugh along with them and send me out from the kitchen with one full highball at a time, condensation chilling my fingers as I gripped the heavy glass for dear life. For my efforts, they'd pat my head and tug at my braids. One time, someone slipped a dollar in my pocket, and that was all right until my mom made me give it back. My dad and Uncle Dee would hoist their glasses to those assembled and recite a Curly Fletcher poem:

> You've been tramped full of shit about cowboys.
> They're known as a romantic band.
> Bold knights of the saddle who round up wild cattle
> And roll cigarettes with one hand.

> According to movie and story
> He's a sheik in a ten-gallon hat.
> All he knows of romance is the crotch of his pants.
> What the hell do you think about that?

> It's high time somebody debunked him.
> He's so plumb full of crap and besides
> A bull-shittin' bastard who's always half-plastered
> Is no hero just 'cause he rides.

The women would blush and giggle. Every one of these women was as tough as her man, so the pink cheeks mystified me. I didn't figure out until I was much older that they were seduced by the spark of romantic badness that flew up around the fire of rodeo. The hook was macho spectacle—flashy chaps and blood and bruises and the glint of spurs—and didn't the women just love it? Rodeo cowboys have been getting away with their own special brand of murder forever, and I heed that fact. Paint one? Sure. Date one? Never.

I heard the throaty hum of a diesel engine and stuck my head out the stall window just as J.W.'s pickup bounced over the cattle guard. I watched from the window as he hopped from the pearl green dually and shut the gate, his walk one part stiffness, two parts swagger. There was an alert set to his shoulders and neck as if there were something tightly wound inside of him. I stepped away from the window and propped my foot on an overturned washtub next to Dish.

"Hello?" His voice echoed down the alley between the stalls. Tad shifted in her straw and nickered.

"Hi, J.W., second stall on the right." I was inspecting the frogs on Dish's front hooves with as much busyness as I could front.

J.W. leaned on the stall door and crossed his arms. He wore a dark blue Cabela's cap and wire-framed glasses. "What do you know, she's a true cowgirl!"

I lifted my head and smiled, welcoming but a little aloof. "She was raised a cowgirl, anyway. I identify more as an artist now." The sentence sank under the weight of its pretension. J.W. smiled gamely and pushed his glasses up the bridge of his nose with one finger. My cheeks reddened. "Hand me that hoof pick, will you?"

The horses loitered in the round pen, walking lazy circles. Black-flies launched their kamikaze drills, whizzing around our ears. The horses swatted testily with their tails. J.W. motioned me to him. "Let me see." He brushed my bangs off of my forehead and took my chin in his hand.

I watched his face while he examined my bruise. Behind his glasses, his eyes were eerie pale like beach glass and webbed at the side in deep, sweet lines. The sun caught the blond tips of his chestnut lashes. They made him look boyish, though he was far from a boy. The hair on his temples, which looked sun-bleached when I saw him at the Bluffs Ranch, was tinged with gray.

He sighed. "I can't believe I did that. I hope you forgive me."

I was aware of the gentle weight of his fingers gripping my jaw and how close his face was to mine. I shook my head free. "Oh, it's nothing." I clapped my hands together. "Let's get to work!"

If cowboys are expected to be stoical and quiet, J.W. missed the memo. While we attacked the chores, he talked and talked some more, drawling companionably as we raked and piled the straw in the stalls, pitched apples into the cart, and refilled hay nets and water buckets. He told me that he'd quit competing nationally, and for the last five years he'd stuck to the Mountain Circuit, moving between rodeos in Colorado and Wyoming. He said, pride close to the vest, that he'd qualified for the Circuit Finals in Pocatello eight times, and until a second shoulder reconstruction surgery last winter, he'd planned to keep doing it until they got tired of seeing him, or until he won it—whichever came first. Now he was just hoping for a second chance. "I spent three months in rehab," he said. "Hate to say it, but if this shoulder don't hold up, it may be the end of the line for me."

As he steered the cart into Dish's stall, J.W. paused. He took his glasses off and scrubbed barn dust from the lenses. "I like you in those pigtails."

I kept my expression neutral. "We thank you for your vote."

"I mean it. They're adorable."

"Adorable, huh?" I rolled my eyes. "Here, grab this." I tossed him a shovel. "It's getting pretty deep in here."

★ ★ ★

We had the stalls cleaned in record time. J.W. leaned out the window and took in the view of Table Mountain. "Sure is a pretty place. Why're you selling?"

I believe you owe a stranger courtesy, but you don't necessarily owe him the truth. "Oh, my brother just decided it was getting a little crowded up here. That's Wyoming claustrophobia for you—any neighbor within two miles is too close." I walked beside him down the breezeway, steering the conversation elsewhere. "Do you miss competing full-time?"

"Not really. The travel wore me down. That whole 'If the rodeoin' don't kill you, the commute will' deal is no lie. A hundred-plus rodeos in a year gets to you, multiply that by nine or ten years and you're toast. Besides, I pretty much met my goals, winning the World and all. I would've liked to win it again, but one's better than none. Excuse me a sec . . ." He leaned off the concrete pad and spit tobacco juice into the dirt. "Sorry. The only big ones left I want to win are Calgary and Cheyenne. We'll see if I get 'er done before I retire."

"Retire?" I walked a little slower. "How old are you, anyway?" I saw the look on his face and regretted asking.

"Forty-one. Almost forty-two now, sad to say." We walked out of the barn and rounded the corner.

"You don't look it," I said. Which wasn't exactly what I meant. I meant that I recognized there was a breadth of years between us and didn't mind.

"Well, thank you, but that doesn't change the facts." The shadow from the barn cut a diagonal across his face. He shifted the cart forward and dumped the manure onto the pile. "I'm a fossil."

I led J.W. to the tack room and took my saddle down from its peg. "Feel like a morning ride?"

"Absolutely." He reached to take the saddle from me.

A sudden spike of anger sent me whirling from his grasp. I jerked the saddle close to my hip. "I'm used to doing for myself. Thanks, though."

He took a step back. "Oh. All right."

J.W. took Hodge and I took Dish. He sat a horse well, as I knew he would, swinging up into the saddle with acrobatic ease. He tilted his face to the sun. "I never get to do this. Long time since I been on a horse that wasn't trying to get me off its back as fast as it could."

"You don't have your own horse?"

"Nah, no room. I live in an apartment downtown. No time, either, even if I boarded. Sometimes I ride with Beeber out where he starts colts, but that's about it."

"What kind of name's Beeber anyhow?"

"His real name's Chester, but don't tell him I told you that. He's real sensitive to it. Anyway, Beeber's like my baby brother. I kind of adopted him, I guess. Got him a job working for a doctor out north of town. He bunks up there in her spare bedroom, runs her stable, and seems to be glad for the company. He don't have any people."

I turned the horse around, leaning with my outside leg. I wiped sweat from my nose. "Hey, watch this." I pulled on Dish's reins just so, calling "up, up!" and he stood on his back legs in a perfect Lavade. He stretched his front hooves and pawed the sky.

"*Hi-ho Silver!*" J.W. called out. "Just like the movies."

"Actually, it's an old battle move." I turned Dish around Hodge's flank in a tight circle, drew up along J.W., and spoke out the side of my mouth in a stage whisper. "We don't have the heart to tell him the war's over." J.W. laughed like I was light as air.

I guided Dish to face downhill, the breeze tossing his forelock into a bad-boy tangle. "Race you back to the barn?"

J.W. pulled Hodge alongside me. The horses were nose to nose. "You're on."

I leaned forward in the saddle. "Just so you know, I'm not going to let you win to flatter your male ego."

"That's just fine, because I'm not going to let you win, period."

He whooped and took off though the fringe sage. I wasn't about to eat his dust. I nudged Dish in the ribs and bolted down the hill after him. Being jockey-size carried certain advantages, as did riding a horse I knew better than I knew myself. Dish threw down the throttle and I blew by J.W. with a victorious yelp. I drew up short at the barn door, trying to restrain my grin. When he stopped Hodge at my side, I was still panting. "About time you showed up!"

J.W. accepted my offer of a cold drink. We paused to take off our shoes at the door. The house was quiet and cool. Miller moths stuck to the screen on the kitchen window. While I mixed iced tea, J.W. wandered the living room. I heard his voice, low and awed. "Oh my."

I carried two glasses into the living room. "What?"

J.W. stood with his nose pressed against the leaded window of Jace's gun case, his face filled with longing. He cocked his head. "Is that Winchester a pre-'sixty-four?"

"Sure is. You hunt?"

"You bet."

"Would you like to see?" I took the case key from the kitchen drawer.

"Could I?"

"The old Model Seventy." He handled the gun like he was about to propose to it. "This is dang beautiful. All these your brother's, huh? I like him already."

"They're Jace's, but I've been known to get around with that Browning a little bit, if you can believe that."

J.W. looked at me. "Why wouldn't I believe it?"

"Most guys I know wouldn't."

J.W. pressed the butt of the Winchester to his shoulder and sighted down the barrel. "Sounds like a city boy problem."

I walked him to his truck. When he opened the driver's side door, J.W. cleared his throat. "Well, I had a wonderful time out here, but this wasn't hardly what I had in mind for making it up to you."

I put my hands in my pockets and swayed from side to side as I deliberated. Maybe Kimber was right. Maybe a harmless rebound romp with a cowboy would be just the thing. I felt wicked for even considering it. "How about you take me to dinner? I'm free Wednesday, if that works."

"Day after tomorrow?" He reached into the glove box and pulled out a leather datebook stuffed with notes, receipts, and a folded-up PRCA Business Journal. He flipped through the June pages and nodded. "I've got to work 'til six, but after that I'm wide open." He wrote it down, then snapped the book shut. "It's a date." He moved toward me. I resisted the urge to step back. He took my face in his hands, like he did at the Wigwam. I closed my eyes and waited for the press of his lips on mine.

I felt a touch on the tip of my nose like a fly had landed on it. "Bye, cowgirl," he said, then climbed behind the wheel of his truck and swung the door shut.

6

WEDNESDAY AFTERNOON, THE TEMPERATURE in the pro-
duce section at the Safeway on Pershing Boulevard was sub-polar,
damp air tainted with the bosky smell of vegetal rot. I had just left
work, reeking once again of industrial pine, wearing my cleaning
outfit of shorts and a tank top with my beat-up sneakers. My teeth
chattered as I navigated the gummy linoleum-tiled aisle, dropping
fruit into a basket. I admired the orderly piles of apples and oranges, grapes in plastic mesh bags, bananas cradled on tiers of As-
troturf. I sorted through a bin of nectarines, rolling their cool flesh
in my hand as I picked out a half-dozen and dropped them into a
plastic bag.

Jace had left grocery money and it was a pleasure to shop without wondering "how much does that cost?" with every single item I
picked up. When I bought food in Denver—tins of store-brand vegetables, brittle bricks of six-for-a-dollar ramen—the question played
in my head as a constant refrain.

In the frozen foods aisle, I tossed a bag of chicken fingers into the
cart and reached for a box of pizza rolls. I leaned over an open case
and decided on a small carton of strawberry ice cream.

"Daryl? Daryl Heatherly!" The voice carried on the blast of frost
from the freezer. I'd recognize that chirpy inflection anywhere.

Jordan Rivers.

I straightened up and there she was, dimples and giggles on cue. Just my luck. Jordan looks sweet as a cupcake from the church bake sale, but she's a nightmare. She and I were best friends in grade school until I realized she was only friends with me for my horse. When she got her own, I was squat to her.

Jordan, who didn't know a horse from a hamster in grammar school, got her dad to lay out a king's ransom for a specially trained barrel racing horse from a well-known Sheridan string for her thirteenth birthday. She raced a little and was actually pretty good. Her real mission was to collect tiaras, however. She took up horses and 4-H just so she could win rodeo-queen pageants. She also got private riding instruction, and piano, ballet, and tap lessons. I only knew this because she made a point of mentioning every accomplishment or acquisition to anyone who would listen. I didn't think her bragging indicated an inflated sense of self. It was more of a verbal tic, like the way some people end every sentence with, "you know?"

I wasn't surprised when Jordan married the insufferable Darcey Rivers right out of high school. Darcey and Jordan were cut from the same cloth—town kids who play rodeo games. Jordan's parents own the tack store and a few construction companies, and they spent as much money as needed to get Darcey launched as a steer wrestler. Now he competes full-time, the pride of Cheyenne.

I stood behind my cart, smiling at Jordan, and she smiled back, checking me out. She blinked and waved her hand. "Oh, where are my manners?" She hitched her boy on her hip. "This is Dustin, and you know Naomi." She rubbed the head of the little girl at her side. She patted her tummy. "And number three is on the way." She widened her stance and put Dustin down with an exhausted *whoof.* He started wailing and Naomi offered him the cookie she was holding.

"Heard your family's place is up for sale. Moving on to bigger and better things?"

"Yeah, pretty much."

"Well, we might just come out to take a look. We're practically busting out of the house we built over in Mustang Ridge. Have to make room for the new addition." She patted her stomach again. "How's your dad?"

Jordan loved to bring up my family. Thanks to her, everyone we went to high school with knew my parents divorced and my father cracked up.

"He's fine."

"Well, we sure would like to see that old place of yours. Maybe you can show us around."

"That's great, Jordan. Harold Gwatney Real Estate, just give him a call." I pushed a paint-speckled shank of hair behind my shoulders.

"Heard your artistic career is doing just great," Jordan chirped, oblivious. For someone with two kids on the ground and one on the way, she sure had a lot of time to talk. Her daughter hid behind the leg of Jordan's fashionable loose-cut maternity pants, drooling over half a butter cookie. I smiled at her.

"How's that cookie, sweetie? Good?"

Dustin wandered off and started pulling cereal boxes from an end display. Jordan smoothed her daughter's hair. "I'd love to see what you're doing now."

"Well, I'll have stuff at the art show at Frontier Days. Opens July seventeenth, if you want to check it out."

"Oh, I will. I will. I'm sure it's wonderful."

"Thanks, Jordan. Nice seeing you," I said, wiggling my fingers at her and her daughter.

"God bless," she sang at me, then darted to shoo her son away from the cereal display. I pushed my basket toward the dairy section. I think on some level Jordan tried to be nice. She just didn't try real hard or real often.

★ ★ ★

"Jarrett, party of two, eight o'clock reservation. Right this way." The hostess scratched our name off the list, jammed two gilt-scripted menus under her arm, and sped us through the restaurant.

The Little Bear Inn is north of town on I-25, blue swells of the Front Range in the distance and grassland all around. Pebbles wedged under my toes as I skidded across the parking lot in my too-big sandals. I paused to clear my shoes, holding onto J.W.'s arm to stay balanced. He made a small ceremony of holding the door open and let me pass through.

Our table was in the back dining room overlooking the patio, which was populated with bears of all sizes. Concrete grizzlies pawing the clouds. Stone honeybears huddled around pots, teddy bear planters with ferns springing from their bellies. We ordered cocktails—red wine for me, Jack and Coke for him, and scrutinized the menu in silence. The strap of my dress slipped down. The dress, on loan from Kimber, was brilliant—white cotton patterned with red cherries, a red ribbon gathering the sweetheart neckline. The waist was tight, the skirt full, and the hem had a slight but devastating flare. On Kimber, it would be almost a mini-dress, but it skimmed my knees. When I pulled the dress from the bag, a note fluttered to the floor. *I call this dress "cowboy bait." Works like magic! Have fun and don't do anything I wouldn't do. Ha ha. Love, K.*

Confidence—feminine confidence—does not come naturally to me, but as I readied myself at Shawna and Lan's to spare J.W. the haul out to Red Hill, I told myself I could at least try to fake it convincingly. Under Kimber's dress, I was wearing bikini underwear, white with small baby blue satin bows at each hip, and a coordinating push-up bra, size 34A—dainty things with a painful history.

It so happened that the very day I received word that my work had been accepted at the Frontier Days art show, Alex got a form rejection letter in the mail from *Tin House*. He tried to be happy for me, but it was clear he didn't like that I had succeeded when he had not. Things were awkward between us for days. I bought the lingerie in an attempt to restore the peace. When I came out of his bathroom wearing it, he looked up from his computer. "You don't have to be a seductress." Like many things he said, it was nicely phrased but had a nasty resound. That I didn't have to be a seductress was beside the point. I'd *wanted* to be one.

There was an element of revenge in accepting a date with J.W. Alex might have his opinion but tonight I'd prove that not only could I be seductive, I would. I pushed up the dress strap demurely and sent a darting glance at J.W. from behind my menu. The beauty of this first date that was also the last date was that I could really pour it on. Pacing wasn't an issue. Was I boring? Didn't matter. Too talkative? Too bad. I'd just have to dust myself off and step prettily away from the wreckage. Any way was a win.

Our steaks arrived, tender and running with juice. The waitress lingered over J.W.'s shoulder. He smiled up at her. "Miss, she needs another glass of wine when you've got a sec." A little of that humid Southern charm goes a long way in this arid environment. I thought she'd melt right into the floor.

"I'm curious," I said, splitting my baked potato and salting it. "What's J.W. stand for? John Wayne?"

He smiled, dabbing a pat of butter into a multi-grain roll. "No. James Willis. Jamie when I was a boy."

"So, Jamie-when-you-were-a-boy, what brought you to Cheyenne from Alabama?"

"Well, I'm divorced," he said carefully. "And I have a son. Troy. He's eleven. His mama is from Cheyenne, which is why I'm here. Her dad passed on from cancer about six years ago, so we came up from Alabama to take care of her mom. Her mom took ill and left us, but my wife wanted to stay here. I only lived in Alabama for a couple years, right across the Georgia line. I'm from Georgia, originally."

"Oh, that's interesting." *Oh, that's interesting! Nice response, social genius.* I lunged for recovery. "What do you do when you're not rodeoing?"

His expression shifted, like at some point he'd been surprised to have adulthood thrust upon him. "I work at Dominion over there on Lincolnway. They don't give me a hard time about taking weekends off, so I'm on call for them a lot. Means a lot of late nights on short notice, but it's a good deal. Circuit guys do all kinds of stuff. Other guys I know work construction, drive trucks. Whatever's flexible. Friend of mine carves headstones up there in Dillon, Montana."

"That's pretty grim." I took a sip of wine. "Your steak okay?"

"Excellent, thanks. You want to try it?"

I said sure and he held out a bite on his fork. I wrapped my fingers around his wrist and drew his hand toward my mouth, slowly closed my teeth around the tines, and drew back to take the meat like a cowgirl straight out of *Cosmo.*

He stared at me, his mouth set in that enigmatic half-smile. I had him fully entranced. I blinked once and leaned forward, my chin in my hand. "What?"

He reached over and wiped my chin with his middle finger. "You got a spot of A-1 sauce on your face." He cleaned his finger on his napkin and winked at me. My face got hot.

I excused myself and went to the ladies' room. While I stood at the mirror refreshing my makeup, our waitress came in. She washed her hands at the next sink. I looked at her in our shared reflection. Her brows were tweezed into surprised arches, olive green eyeliner mudding the corners of her eyes. "You two are a cute couple," she told me as I sifted through my purse for lipstick. Her affable tone veiled her intentions.

"Oh, we're not a couple," I said airily, filling in my lips with a fresh coat of my new shade, a red called Vice is Nice. I was alarmed at how false my voice sounded. *I'm just planning to ravish this man and send him on his way,* I thought to myself. But I wouldn't have admitted that to her; I could barely admit it to myself. Something inside me caught, a whisper of "shouldn't be doing this." My good-girl reflexes were intact and I was rather disgusted with the fact.

I eased back into my chair and rested my elbows on the table. In the other room, the band started up. A stand-up bass *thump thumpa thumped* the intro to "Walking After Midnight." J.W. hitched his chair closer to mine. Sometime during the *crème brulée*, I realized Alex hadn't crossed my mind in hours. He flashed into view when J.W. opened his mouth to take a bite of sugar-slivered custard from the tiny spoon I held to his lips. *I'm hand-feeding dessert to a world champion rodeo cowboy. Take that, Evil Ex.* Then, just as quickly as he came, Alex vanished.

By the time we left the restaurant night had settled in, drawing a chilly light blue rim around the half moon. Dew drifted onto my neck and the skin on my shoulders and arms puckered, the tiny hairs saluting the dark. J.W. helped me up into the truck. "You are just covered in chill bumps. Here, take this." He pulled a black-and-white checked blanket from behind the seat and wrapped it around me. "Come prepared. Right, cowgirl?"

J.W. had an internally imposed sense of order that gave him a surprisingly cerebral air. He would make sure things were squared away—a blanket around the shoulders, a drink order, a detail in a story—then joke, as if he lived by a long to-do list with "lighten up" penciled in as the last item. He wasn't what I'd have thought. He was serious.

I twisted to look at the rear window. "No guns in your gun rack?"

"Not today. Why? Do I need one?" When I turned around, I caught him looking at my legs, then quickly redirecting his focus to the dashboard.

I tipped my head back and laughed, resting my hand on his knee, fully inhabiting Kimber's dress. "Maybe."

"Check the glove box."

I flipped down the door and saw a Ruger Blackhawk .44 in a

canvas holster, underneath the registration and insurance forms and a pair of oil-stained leather work gloves.

"You see I'm suitably equipped." He was looking my way, his thin lips fixed in a shy smile. We both knew this was the point in the movie where we were supposed to kiss. Tiny cupids were flying around with their bows drawn, chanting, "Do it! Do it!" but we just sat there.

I pulled the blanket tight around me and tucked it between my thighs. "I call them goose bumps."

He did a little dip with his head. "Oh . . . goose bumps."

I was feeling all those drinks. I flapped my arms inside the blanket and yelled, "Honk!"

We both laughed, embarrassed. His eyes were fiery, as if he was gleefully relieved by my lameness. He put the key in the ignition and started up the truck. He jammed the gas pedal. The engine roared, a beastly aggressive noise. "Feel like hitting the Cowboy?"

I sat back and looked ahead. "Sure."

We picked our way carefully across the Cowboy's potholed parking lot. I tried not to twist my ankle. The black-vested doorman, posted atop a stack of milk crates, tapped me on the shoulder as we passed and asked for my ID. A blast of neon and bar music rushed forward, almost mowing us down. The din-and-light blast made me feel curiously exposed. I grabbed J.W.'s hand, and we wove through the crowd: denim, work shirts, big sprayed hair, "Hey, buddy!" and Saturday-night hats. All the tables were full, so we leaned on the wooden rail by the dance floor. The waitress brought us beers. I leaned back against the rail, which gave me an air of nonchalance but made my boobs look great. I was having fun with the push-up bra, pointing my small swell of cleavage this way and that. Dancers moved in synchronized rows to a song called "Strokin'." Their dancing was giddily idiotic and stiff in a sort of sexual way. J.W. flipped the lid off his Copenhagen can. I poked him in the ribs. "Hey, why aren't you out there line dancing?"

He adjusted his hat and talked over his shoulder. "Because I'm sane." He brushed his fingers on his pant leg and packed chew down below his gumline with his tongue. "But I can go out there and shake it around a little bit if it would make you happy, do a little Boot Scootin' Boogie, maybe an Electric Slide." He tucked the can back in his jeans pocket, and bit back a smirk.

"Actually, I'll thank you in advance for *not* doing that."

Doug Cathcart came shrugging through the door, in his trademark gray duster and black felt hat with the eagle feather tucked under the hatband. I turned my back to him. Everybody knew Doug Cathcart was rabid-dog crazy. Jace thought they napalmed his brain in Vietnam or something. He used to be quite a hand, on friendly terms at ranches all around the state, but what civility he had was hammered flat by years of basement speed or booze or both. Last year, my brother hired him to help set trusses, even put him up in the guest room after long workdays, but turned him loose after six months when some expensive tools went missing.

"Hello, J.W.," he said, stopping next to us at the rail. The duster coat molded to his wiry body like a carapace. He looked down at me. His eyes were dark green silted with gold flecks, pinched to comma shape at the outer corner. His pupils did a vertical jiggle as he grinned as us; his teeth the color of dirty grout. The scarred cheekbones were high and wide, probably Indian blood in there somewhere. Under the scrunge, it was easy to see he was once a beautiful man. Rumor was he bit a guy's ear off in a fight some years ago. He'd been off the rails for so long nobody in town would hire him. Now he just collected disability checks and enemies by the score. He slapped J.W. on the back and yanked his thumb my direction. "That ain't the one I seen you with just a while ago, is it?"

J.W. examined his knuckles and put his arm around my shoulders for punctuation. He did not think much of Doug Cathcart. The band started a waltz and J.W. hustled me off for a turn around the dance floor. We fit together well; J.W. steering us more than serviceably through the movements, holding our hands high and out like an eighteenth-century courtier. Whatever antipathy I felt toward my mom, I was in this moment grateful for the dance lessons. I could hear her voice as she forced Jace and me to practice in the living room: *On your toes, DeeDee. On your toes!* When the song ended, I excused myself and headed to the second-floor ladies' room.

As I approached the top of the stairs, Doug Cathcart rounded the closest pool table, trailing his fingers across the watermarked felt. Half his pinkie was missing. He stopped in front of me, blocking my path. "Out with J.W. Jarrett, huh?"

"Yeah," I said toward his shoulder, silently willing him to get out of my way. I didn't want to make eye contact with him, set him off, God knows what.

He leaned in too close and leered. "J.W. Jarrett ain't a real cowboy. None of them rodeo guys are."

I steeled myself and squeezed my lips into a cold smile. "Close enough for me," I said, then stepped around him like he wasn't even there.

I leaned on the railing to keep my sandals from falling off. J.W. was waiting for me at the bottom of the staircase. The band started in on Chris LeDoux's "Look at You, Girl."

J.W. held out his hand. "Well, come on, we got to dance to this."

The song floated down and sealed us off from the crowd. J.W. folded me into his arms. I pressed my face against his neck and inhaled. Someone should bottle the scent of fresh-scrubbed cowboy. They'd make a mint. I lifted my head from J.W.'s shoulder and looked at him. We danced a little slower, swaying in one spot, grinning at each other.

"That's better," J.W. said, tipping his chin down.

"What's better?"

"That's the first time you looked me in the eye all night."

Cosmo composure be damned, I stood on my tiptoes and kissed his lower lip, right on the spot where the tobacco mounded up. He pressed his cheek against my temple and whispered in my ear, "You want to get out of here?"

We wrestled each other across the parking lot, elbowing and leaping over the pits and ditches. When we got to his truck, I sat on the back bumper. J.W. stood in front of me with his thumbs hooked in his belt loops, his knees locked. He was making that awkward face again. Fortified by beer and mindful of my mission, I leaned against the tailgate and crossed my ankles. "You want to kiss me, don't you?"

J.W. adjusted his hat and scratched the back of his neck. "Maybe I wouldn't mind it. But you're just a kid."

"I'm not a kid. I'm twenty-three."

"That's a kid to me."

"What if I kissed you first?" I tilted my head.

"That'd be against cowboy law, I think."

I stood and put my hands on his shoulders. "You wouldn't press charges against a minor," I said as I leaned in. "I can tell."

A great kiss is a hosanna in your bloodstream, chords of exultant heat singing through your entire body. I was fully and blissfully engaged in our kissing, not distracted by anything—not people, not traffic, not the music that barged into the parking lot each time the door opened—until our legs touched. The brush of denim on my bare skin made me go rubbery. I grabbed his belt loops to regain my bearings, which he took as a signal to kiss me more deeply. I stepped back from him and turned toward the truck door. "It's getting late. We should go."

J.W. draped his arm over the steering wheel and faced me. "Should I take you back to Lan's?"

Here was my turning point. Was I going to follow through or fold? I clasped my hands over my knee and looked at my skirt. "No."

The ride to his place was tense and almost unbearably quiet. His apartment was right across the street from the railroad tracks, in a row of two- and three-story redbrick buildings that lapsed together and spaced apart like old teeth. He came around the front of the truck and opened my door. The moon hung tiny in the sky, shrouded still in pale blue mist. Our footfalls echoed along the sidewalk in incriminating staccato bursts as we made our way to his front door. We creaked up a flight of splinter-ridden stairs to his flat above King's Metal Shop. He turned the key in the top lock and we stepped inside. I could tell from his hesitation before crossing the threshold that he hated the way he lived.

J.W.'s living room was long and narrow and religiously organized, decorated in late twentieth-century bachelor—a leather couch that had seen better days, a recliner, and a television a good bit larger than it had to be. The walls were tenant white. On the far wall leaned a grandfather clock and a mahogany-stained pie safe with hammered tin doors. The distinguishing element was a corner dedicated to every type of rodeo trophy and citation a person could get—saddles, spurs, buckles, bits, framed photographs and newspaper clippings.

Instinctively, I walked toward the display—it threw off its own energy like a force field. Pride of place in the arrangement belonged to his World Champion saddle, magnificent as any sculpture, covered in elaborate hand-tooled scrollwork with the event and year on the stirrup straps. In the faint light of the desk lamp, the brown leather glowed.

I ran my hand along the smooth curve of the cantle. "Beautiful. It looks like a Severe."

J.W. drew alongside me and joined his hands behind his back. "The girl knows her saddle makers, but no. They were from Oklahoma City Saddlery that year."

I looked around the room. "I like that you've got all your trophies out where you can see them. I think that's important."

"Twenty-five years of rodeoing and that's what I've got to show for it. A bunch of buckles, a little leather, and a mess of scars." He removed his hat and placed it brim-up on the end table. The big old clock ticked murderously. I crossed my legs at the knee and dangled my sandal off my left foot, waiting for J.W. to make the next move.

He offered me a drink but I declined. He rubbed his hands to-gether. They made a dry, papery sound. His shyness was surprising. He cleared his throat. "Why don't I give you the grand tour?"

It didn't take long—the pale yellow kitchenette with a table and three chairs that I recognized as being from Sam's Club, his son's small bedroom with a knotty pine bunk bed and toy chest, bath-room with old blue fixtures and a hexagonal tile floor. Then he opened a door at the end of the long living room and we walked in-side. A white iron bed was angled in the corner, positioned so it looked like a crouched animal in the dark. A desk and ladderback chair stood next to a tall oak wardrobe. I was in his bedroom. This was what I came for, wasn't it? I hovered near the door, hesitating. J.W. lowered the wooden blinds and looked my way, his expression small and serious.

"Show me." My voice was louder than I wanted. I covered up my wince with a smile.

"I'm sorry?"

"Show me your scars."

J.W. folded his shirt lengthwise and laid it on the bed. He turned on the small green bedside lamp. His torso was lashed with faint pink lines like patching seams on a cloth doll. He named them all for me with the vocabulary of a Latin scholar—shoulder reconstruc-tion, broken pelvis, wrist and ankle held together with plates and pins. "My legs are the real show. My knees, especially," he said, try-ing to slide up his pant leg to show me the repair of his "anterior cruciate ligament."

He explained the how and when of each scar, not with porno-graphic pride in the injury process, but a cataloger's laconic attach-ment to the remains—*been there, got that*—his body a traveler's trunk plastered with souvenirs from South Dakota and Texas, Idaho and Oregon. Arizona, Alberta, Nevada, too. "Compared to some guys, I got off pretty easy. I never been badly injured. I got a lot more adhesions than scars," he said. "Most of the damage is on the inside." I suspected he was telling me more than he realized.

When he turned away, I let my eyes roam all over him. I never imagined what a forty-one-year-old man would look like half-naked, but if I had, I wouldn't have pictured anything like this, sculpted through the lats and chest, hips and waist whittled flat, solid neck like a draft horse. Forearms veined and thick under a light dusting of red-blond hair. Every part of him was forcefully compact and exceptional, but what impressed me most were his hands. I'd been looking at them all night—stout-wristed, knot-knuckled, show no mercy hands. They weren't big or scary looking, just seasoned enough to stop my heart.

I took his left thumb, rotating it until his palm faced up, and began rubbing the innocent spaces between his fingers and the tendons ridging the back. "That's amazing," J.W. whispered. He leaned back against the headboard, closed his eyes, and swallowed hard. As I massaged him, my eyes kept coming back to the angry pink scar on his shoulder. Less than six months old, it was neat and precise, almost ornamental. I wanted to touch it, follow the slender vertical curve with a fingertip, but it seemed too personal.

After several minutes J.W.'s lids fluttered open. "Would you excuse me?" He got up and backed out of the room.

I managed to get out of my dress and into bed before J.W. came back. I lay besieged with doubt, staring at the distressed flower-and-vine molding that ran the perimeter of the ceiling. Should I have worn black underwear instead? Was this too forward? I might have had an easier go of it if I'd drunk more beer after dinner. I would have been eager to proceed with the hit and run, but the conversation and his hands and that beautiful shoulder scar changed my view on things, and my attraction seemed bigger, scarier somehow. My seduction plan was shredding like rain-soaked paper.

J.W. came into the bedroom, still in his jeans but barefoot. He lifted the comforter, politely avoiding looking underneath, and edged over alongside me. His breath was cold peppermint; he'd brushed his teeth. He came in for a full-frontal hug.

I shrieked.

He jerked back as if snakebit. "Jesus! What?"

"Your belt buckle . . . it's freezing!"

"Right! Sorry." He scurried up and stripped to blue plaid boxers, laying his jeans over the back of a chair with his belt draped on top. His leg muscles banded and flexed. *Percheron thighs,* I thought abstractly as he padded back to the bed.

"Better?"

I nodded.

J.W. reached over and snapped off the lamp. Orange streetlight glowed at the edge of the window blinds. We pressed together, kissing. My pulse thrummed in my temples. J.W. wasn't a card-trick kisser—no nibbling or tongue sucking; he didn't trace the outline of my lips with his tongue. He kissed like a man should, pure and straightforward. Every time we separated, the air in the room cooled my lips and I'd roll back toward him, seeking his mouth. My resistance was weakening. I had to throw the brakes on and soon. I forced myself to pull fully away and sat up.

His eyes opened, liquidy and loving. The look of a man happy to be received. He stroked my upper arm. "Everything okay?"

I pulled the quilt up under my arms and tucked a lock of fallen hair behind my ear. "I hope you don't mind but I'm really not ready to—"

He smiled and lazily dragged two fingers down my back. "It's okay."

"You sure? I'm sorry, I—"

"Shhh, it's all right." He pulled me close so my head rested on his chest. I could hear his heart thudding, loud. Strong.

He kissed me deeply, our legs entwined, rubbing. He laced his fingers in mine and slid my hand to the fly of his shorts. When I didn't pull back, he placed his hand over mine, guiding me. We kissed again, still touching. His grip was faster now, a little harder. After several minutes, his breath became labored, teeth clenched. He tipped his head back, grabbed at the sheets, and twisted.

J.W.'s neck and chest were gleaming, his eyes closed, peaceful. I wasn't sure what to do. After handing him the tissue box from the nightstand I rolled onto my side and presented my back to him for spooning.

J.W. kissed my shoulder and fiddled absently with my bra strap. He rested his chin against my shoulder blade. "I'm sorry, were we done?"

I turned halfway over. "Aren't you?"

"That wasn't my question."

I shrugged.

He slid out from between the covers and walked around to my side of the bed. As he drew close, light through the wooden blinds threw blurred slats of shadow across his chest. He patted the sheet, urging me to move over and lie flat on my back. He sat down and began rubbing the toes on my right foot.

"Cute foot you got here." He smiled, running his thumbnail along the arch, making my toes curl.

I bit my lip to keep from laughing.

"Sweet little tattoo." He cupped my heel in his palm and kissed the inside of my ankle.

Then he kissed the inside of my knee. Then my inner thigh.

He reached up, hooked his fingers in the sides of my panties, and in one smooth motion, pulled them down and off.

There's a joke in Wyoming: Why do cowgirls walk bow-legged? Because cowboys eat with their hats on.

It's not true.

7

I'M IN TROUBLE NOW. My first thought when I woke up. Not good.

A patch of sunlight warmed the bottom of the bed. My feet felt hot and I could smell my own boozy sweat and traces of dirty hair. The trains had started up across the street, wheels clacking as they lumbered past and screeching when they braked. I wriggled in the sheets and rubbed my eyes, salted with regret. I had more or less successfully completed a one-night stand. Instead of feeling sexy and triumphant, I was embarrassed and deeply confused. On the desk near the window, an old walnut clock said five-twenty. Obviously stopped. It had to be at least seven. My head buzzed dully from wine chased with beer, and I felt sleazy having slept in just my push-up bra. I looked around the room. The sheets and the checks in the comforter were a perfect match of ivory. They had the stiffness of new poly-cotton blend. I felt the prickly sensation of being watched. I turned my head. J.W. was lying on his side, head resting on his arm, looking at me.

I scratched the corners of my mouth, hoping there wasn't any crusted lipstick. "Can you see me without your glasses?"

He reached over and began groping blindly, feeling my face. "Hello? Hello? Is somebody there?"

I batted his hands away and sat up, hugging the sheet to my

chest. "Is there a parallel universe out there where you're actually considered funny?"

J.W. rolled over on his stomach, the back of his hair mashed flat to his head. He still had his shorts on. "Come on, I am funny. Admit it."

"Funny looking, maybe."

"That does it." He pounced to kneeling and began tickling my sides.

"No tickling." I kicked at him, flailing in the sheets. "No tickling! Ever." One of my breasts popped out of my bra.

He rolled me onto my back and pinned me with his legs, which were inhumanly strong. "Make me stop. If you can." He dove for my armpits.

"Quit it, you psycho!"

That just made him laugh: Yeah, I *am* psycho. You got one *vaquero loco* here, ma'am.

I jammed my arms down at my sides, trapping his hands. "If you keep tickling me, I'm going to pee on you. I mean it."

His eyes flashed. "Yeah? I might like that."

"Gross! Get off of me!"

We lay side by side panting and giggling. Sun flooded the room, heating it so we were both dewed with perspiration. J.W. lifted his arms over his head and stretched. His shoulder popped. I smelled the scent rising from his skin, male like musky fern and faded cologne. I gathered the sheet around me and chewed the inside of my lower lip to slow my breathing.

He looked at me again. His gaze was unnerving, like he was appraising me. With tenderness, but still.

I looked back at him. "Tin Man," I said.

He blinked. "Mmm?"

"You have eyes like the Tin Man. You've seen *The Wizard of Oz*, right?"

"Sure." He rolled over and gingerly pushed himself up to sitting. He groaned.

"You okay?"

"Yep, this just takes a while. Some men get up in the morning, I unfold." He leaned forward, freckled shoulders aslope in frustration. At the top of his crown was a whorl of thinning hair, the pink of his scalp showing through. He took a bottle of ibuprofen from the nightstand drawer and tapped three into his palm, swallowing them dry.

I felt a sympathetic pang and ran my hand across his back, my arm dark olive against his milk-toned skin. "Your back is so smooth. You're a regular Georgia peach."

"That ain't Georgia. It's Lubriderm. If I don't use it every day, I look like a piece of jerky." J.W. rooted around in the bottom drawer of the dresser. He slipped into a pair of baggy maroon sweatpants and took his glasses from the nightstand. He picked up my hand and kissed my knuckles. "Take your time. I'll get coffee started." His scars shone in shades of white and pink as he moved.

For fifteen minutes, I lay staring around the room, eyes wide like a nervous cat. I was mortified that I hadn't thought to bring a change of clothes. I'd have to Walk of Shame it in last night's dress. I could hear J.W. bustling around the living room.

The bedroom door creaked when I opened it. I tripped over an electrical cord, bringing down an iron and ironing board with a loud crash. I stubbed my toe on the doorsill.

"Good morning to you, too, Daryl."

Shirts hung from the closet doorknob on wire hangers. I noticed he even ironed his T-shirts. A can of spray starch stood atop the pie safe. I picked up the ironing board and turned around, expecting to see J.W.'s face. Instead I saw his feet. His scary, scary feet. He was in a headstand against the wall.

"I thought you were sore."

"Shoot, if I let being sore keep me from getting after it every day, I'd be hitting the snooze button for the rest of my life." He wiggled and pointed his toes, then flexed his feet. He had gnarled toenails like an alligator, some of them yellowed, others half-gone. "Pretty, ain't they? Every time I got my foot stomped, the toenail never did grow back right. The boots I wear probably don't help." He swung down to the floor and stood upright. "Let me get you coffee."

"No, no. It's fine. Don't let me interrupt." This was fascinating, watching him in action. I sat on the couch and watched as he did five, ten, fifteen, twenty, one-handed push-ups. He lay on his stomach and chucked his chin up at me. "What do you say, cowgirl, feel like gettin' on one?"

"Bad for your shoulder, don't you think?"

"Little bit like you? Not a chance."

I folded my legs under me on the couch. "Thanks anyway."

"Come on, I dare you." He wasn't about to give up on this idea, I could tell.

"Fine. If you're daring me, that's different." I walked over and awkwardly arranged myself along his prone body, holding him by the shoulders like I was body surfing on his back.

"How many would you like, ma'am?"

"Ten, please."

Up and down we went to the count of ten. He inhaled, lowering himself with a grimacing hiss and exhaling with a resolute puff when he pushed up. Strangely, this prank felt more intimate than last night when I lay against the pillows spent and shocked—in twenty-three years, I had only ever had an orgasm by my own hand—J.W.'s sweaty cheek pressed to my belly.

He sank to his stomach with me on top of him. "How do you take your coffee?"

I rolled off and sat cross-legged on the floor, pulling the dress down over my knees. "Just milk."

"No milk. I'll run out and get some."

"Don't bother. It's okay."

He adjusted the waistband on his sweats. "Won't take a minute."

He jammed his feet into tennis shoes and pulled on one of his freshly ironed T-shirts. On the way to the door, he leaned over and kissed the top of my head. "Help yourself to anything you want in the kitchen."

I used his Listerine, then washed my face and scrubbed my neck with a stiff blue washcloth. I wondered if he lived here when he was married, if his then-wife had chosen the towels, the washcloth I'd used. Was she the one to angle the bed in the corner? No guy would think to do that. Did she walk in here one day, dropping off their son maybe, look at his stripped-down digs and move it in a disgusted attempt to make the place more "livable"? I felt like her shadow was everywhere—not so much in what was in the apartment, but what wasn't. J.W. had so little for a man his age. I put on lipstick and knotted my dirty hair at the nape of my neck. The last squeeze from my tube of concealer went over the dark half-moons under my eyes.

I browsed around the apartment, waiting for J.W.'s return. In a silver 8 × 10 frame on the television was a photo of J.W. on the ground, pulling his son by the leg, laughing. Troy was just a small boy; the picture must have been taken five or six years ago. The edge was folded down. Curiosity seized me. I wondered if his ex-wife was on the folded part. I flipped the frame over and started to slide off the felt backing. I heard J.W. coming up the stairs. I placed the frame next to the others and went to the kitchen.

I watched as J.W. poured condensed milk into his mug along with a teaspoon of sugar. "A little coffee with your milk and sugar?"

J.W. took a sip and smiled rapturously. "If the spoon's not standing straight up in the mug, it ain't coffee. I confess to a bit of a sweet tooth." He topped off my mug.

This isn't so bad, I thought. The sleaziness had burned off with the morning haze. *I'm still the same person. Same feet, same knees, same Daryl.* I felt grand and worldly. I stirred more milk into my coffee and tinked the spoon on the rim. "Are you working today?"

"No. I'm going down to Cortez tonight, so I'm free until about noon," he said cheerily. The clock on the stove said 8:15. "Sorry I didn't have much in the kitchen. To be honest, I wasn't expecting company."

I dropped my spoon into the mug. I'm sure he didn't mean it the way it sounded, but I felt like such a whore. "So it's not a problem to drive me back to Lan's then?" I patted my lips with a napkin. "After your coffee, I mean."

Playfulness drained from J.W.'s face. He knew he blew it. "Oh. I was going to take you to breakfast."

I pictured myself cowering behind a big plastic menu with lurid color pictures of sausages and syrup-drizzled french toast, praying no one noticed me in this cherry-print hooker dress. "That's sweet, J.W., but totally unnecessary." I put my mug in the sink.

We left J.W.'s apartment in silence. His manner had turned stiff and formal; Fancy Dan was back. The sky was headache blue, the sun unrelenting. I got in his truck and leaned against the passenger side door, shielding my eyes. J.W. gave me a pair of his sunglasses from the glove box, sparing my retinas. They were too big but I kept them on anyway. I could see my black, bug-eyed reflection in the windshield glass. I rolled down the window. I was desperate to get home and shower, but I had to be at work by nine.

J.W. turned on the country oldies show and tapped his fingertips on the gear shift. "You like rock music or are you pretty much a country person?"

"I like it all, I guess." I sunk my head into my hand and looked out the window, dry prairie grass speeding by in a biscuit-colored blur. The thrill of last night was hardly worth the anguish of this morning.

Homer was staked outside Lan's trailer on a length of logging chain. He stood up and grinned when we pulled into the driveway, tail tickling the air like a whip antenna. I thanked J.W. for a nice time and he thanked me back. I knew Lan and Shawna would still be asleep. I took my keys from my purse and let Homer into the truck. Grandma Dam would surely yell at me for bringing my dog to the job. I motioned and J.W. rolled down his window.

"Yeah?"

"You know how you said you've never been badly injured? May I ask what you consider bad?"

"That's a different deal for everybody, I guess. But the way I see it, if it doesn't lead to organ damage, diminished mental capacity, a wheelchair, blindness, or adult diapers, I'm all right. If I can still get on, it's not serious." He straightened behind the wheel with the smile you'd see on a boy wading from a pond with a box full of just-caught frogs. Next to his Mr. Smooth date-night pose, impetuous kid seemed to be his preferred role.

"Ah. Well, I just wondered."

Still in performance mode, he shifted his truck into gear, waved casually, and said, "I'll call you."

"Don't bother," I said to his tailgate as he drove away.

8

SHOWING THE HOUSE CHAPPED MY HIDE.

At the outset, I'd thought it would be easy—people breezing in and out, admiring, asking questions, tottering after the Realtor with heads full of interest rates and ideas about where they might put the couch. And I anticipated swells of warmth between me and my brother, him grateful for my help, me deeply touched that he thought I was responsible enough to bear the load. But I hated everything about it. Even the simplest conversation Jace and I had about the house turned terse and nervy, and the violation of having people tromp right through what remained of our family history, surmising and deciding, wrecked me.

The problem with showing a house is that your lifestyle becomes a tourist attraction. Strangers drifting around judging the creaky stairs or trying to guess the soundness of the barn roof in winter wind, even disliking the color of the kitchen linoleum, felt like a personal affront. It wasn't until someone commented on it that I realized it was a pretty odd place—no privacy in the master suite loft, two bedrooms on the first floor, one more in the basement, as if specifically designed for a fractured family. Westward-facing floor-to-ceiling windows in the living room afforded a stirring view of the valley below Table Mountain, but let in so much sun you'd bake like a human casserole from noon until sundown.

The heat wave didn't help. Once the average daily temperature hit ninety, Gwatney tried to bring clients out in the morning, so we wouldn't have to hear another mom and pop groan, "What? No central air?" as they fanned themselves with the real-estate brochure.

After every showing, I'd feel soiled, as if I'd discovered someone rooting through my underwear drawer. Hated it.

The showings taxed me so much I actually looked forward to my shifts at the Twin Pines motel. I'd gotten my chops as a maid, figuring out how to get a whole room done in fifteen flat. Strip the bed, hit the rug with the carpet sweeper, dust the furniture, 409 the tub, sink, toilet. Fresh linens, stack two crinkle-wrapped plastic cups on the vanity, sliver-sized bars of Cashmere Bouquet in the soap dishes, then spray the bathroom floor with disinfectant and switch on the heat lamp to dry it. Over and done and out.

When it was slow, Crystal would hang out with me. Kimber found her loathsome, and Giselle and her grandmother were offended by her tube tops and short skirts, but I didn't mind her. She worked hard, and she had a coarse naivete that I liked. She had grown up in a geodesic dome two miles off the nearest paved road in the blush-topped clinker buttes of Johnson County, where her dad and brothers worked drilling coalbed methane wells. She left school when she was twelve and Cheyenne meant the big-time. She lived with her four-year-old daughter, Keely, in one of the motel's kitchenette units and did massage for guests when she wasn't cleaning rooms. She told me this stuff while I worked, leaning against the cigarette-burned dresser, smelling like coconut massage lotion. I watched as she pulled her cell phone from her cleaning smock and checked her messages, her nails so long she had to push the buttons with a knuckle.

Being a maid at the Twin Pines was a low-stress gig. Grandma

Dam dispatched Giselle to fetch any supplies we needed, while she sequestered herself in the office, snacking and watching talk shows, her black bangs rolled into foam rollers, the front of her chenille housecoat covered in peanut hulls the translucent copper of beetle wings. Sometimes she'd make us lunch, a delicious tamarind shrimp soup that she brought to us steaming in square porcelain bowls.

After work, I decided to tackle one of the points on Gwatney's home improvement list: replace the missing trim on the baseboards in the renovated kitchen. I could charge the supplies to Jace's corporate account. Adamant about supporting local businesses, Jace deals exclusively with Dominion Lumber. What a coincidence that I had energy to go there on a Sunday, when I could safely assume J.W. would be out of town at a rodeo.

Or so I thought. When I went into the trim section at the very back of the store, I saw him there. He had his glasses on and was frowning at sheets on a clipboard, pencil in his hand. Of course, the thing I needed was in the aisle closest to him.

I stole into the aisle and hurriedly surveyed the baseboard trim. A couple twelve-foot lengths of quarter round would do. I could see J.W. right across from me. He scratched his temple with the pencil eraser and punched a couple keys on a calculator.

"Can I help you?"

I jumped about a foot in the air. A salesman with a slick gray pompadour was at my side, his expression the studied patience of those paid to feign interest in helping people. His nose was broad and flat, a burst of purple veins on either large-pored cheek.

"No, I'm good."

J.W.'s head snapped up and he peered through the shelves. "Daryl?"

I didn't move.

He came around the end display of rope-trim molding and into my aisle. "I thought that was you."

"Oh, hi, J.W. What are you doing here?"

"I work here. Remember?"

"Of course." *Floor, open and swallow me up now. Please.* "I meant, I thought you were out of town."

"I didn't draw anything good down in Grover so I turned out. Me and Beeber took my son fishing instead." J.W. was dressed for work—jeans, dress boots, a white button-down with the green Dominion logo embroidered on the collar. Pens and a small ruler filled a plastic sheath in his pocket. I nodded at it. "Nice pocket protector you've got there."

"Yes, ma'am, that's me, the original cowboy nerd. All's I need is a slide rule and I'm plum irresistible. Hey, I left a message for you. Did you get it?"

"Yeah, I've been kind of swamped."

"Well, how about it, Daryl? Can I take you to another dinner or a movie sometime?"

"Oh, I don't think that's a good idea, J.W. I mean, you know, I'm just, well, I'm busy."

"Was it something I said?" Kidding/not kidding. Maybe he remembered the "I wasn't expecting company" comment.

"No. And I mean that. I guess I hadn't planned on dating while I was up here. I kind of wanted the summer to work and unwind." I took out my wallet. "And I shouldn't be accepting dates from a cowboy anyway."

He rested his clipboard on a shelf and folded his arms. "Really now. Why?"

I scrambled, shoring up with the first stanza of the Curly Fletcher poem. *"You've been tramped full of shit . . ."*

J.W. tipped his head to the side and listened, less than enchanted. "Shoot, if that's what you think about cowboys, it's a wonder I got you to go out even once."

"I'm sorry. It's not that you're not a great guy." I regressed to seventh-grade soothing. "We could be friends."

Merciful fellow, he saw I was trying to let him down easy. "All right. Friends it is. Hello, friend." He bowed.

"Hello," I said, curtseying back.

He picked up the three lengths of trim I needed and carried them to the checkout. "I bet you got a saw out there to cut this down, but do you have a miter box to get it angled right?"

"Sure."

"Know how to use it?"

"Yes, I know how to use a miter box, thank you. I worked my way through school in a frame shop."

"How about nails? You're gonna use a nail gun for this, right?"

"I hadn't thought to."

"You might want to reconsider. A nail gun'll save you a lot of time. We rent them here, but I have a feeling I can get you one for free." He cupped his hand to his mouth. "I have an in with the manager."

Being a belt-and-suspenders type, J.W. showed up at Red Hill with the right tool for the task and two kinds of backup. The inventory's remaining nail gun had a tendency to short out, so he hauled in his nail bags and a couple hammers, just in case. Technology was on his side, however, so he shot down the quarter round, and in no time we were drinking tea at the kitchen counter.

I helped him gather up the tools, enjoying his aftershave. Was there any situation in which this guy didn't smell great? He bent to pick up the nail bags and the belt slipped from his hand. The bags opened, sending thousands of nails to the floor in a musical shower of steel.

"Oh shit." He grimaced. "I mean, shoot."

After fifteen frantic minutes on our hands and knees, we'd chased down most of the nails. They had rolled under furniture, counters, into corners. J.W. scouted around under the kitchen table. "One more," he said, emerging.

We crawled toward each other, knees squeaking on the linoleum, and met in the middle of the room. When he dropped the nail into my outstretched hand, his fingers met my palm in a little circle of heat. This was the first time we'd touched since I spent the night at his apartment.

His fingers lingered on my palm. I took the nail and quickly looked away. "Thank you." The nail was warm from his hand. We stood and I dusted off my hands. "Now I guess I owe *you* a dinner." I tucked the nail into my sweatshirt pocket.

He looked happy. "I might just take you up on that. Dyewwy-delk?"

His accent. For the first time, I couldn't understand it. "Pardon?"

"I said, Do you eat elk?"

"Oh! I do. I can cook it, even." After every hunt, Jace would come down to see Dad and me, and stock the freezer. During the Super-girl phase I'd taught myself to season and braise the back strap. My dad fell asleep before it came out of the oven, so I ate it by myself.

"By no means necessary to cook. I'll do it. How about before I leave for Evergreen this weekend, we grill some elk steaks?"

When I came down for breakfast in the morning, the nail bags were still on the kitchen floor, forgotten in the clumsy steps of lurching toward the platonic.

After work, I went to Country General to pick up some grain for the horses and special diet dog food for Homer. Instead of heading straight home, I drove east to the end of Lincolnway and made the long loop around Cheyenne on College Road, touching the nail that was still in my pocket. Though we'd agreed to friendship, J.W.'s departure from Red Hill had the medicinal aftertaste of virtue.

The plains sulked under cloud shadow. A herd of black baldies speckled the slopes across the road from High Plains Tack, mixed in with some fine young Corientes. In the distance, I could see the pipe organ gutworks of the Frontier Refinery, orange flame from the cat cracker lapping the lavender afternoon sky. I sped along listening to the radio, wondering what having J.W. over to dinner might be like.

I meant to hold to my decision to not see him again but something made me invite him to the house. When I pictured him, I felt a welling tenderness, not because of anything he said to me or anything we did, but because of what I'd seen that morning in his apartment when he left to get milk, telling me to help myself in the kitchen.

I'd opened the freezer. It was stuffed with microwave entrees, unidentifiable items wrapped in foil, minute steaks. Aside from a stack of Cold Paks and a box of orange Popsicles, it was nothing but ice and fixings for can't-be-bothered dinners—sandwiches eaten over the sink, pot pies in front of the ten o'clock news.

The fridge was equally spare—a half-full pitcher of tea, three kids' juice boxes, plastic bags of sliced lunchmeat and cheese in a casual pile. A loaf of Wonder bread, a couple heels of whole wheat. An open can of condensed milk. The middle shelf held a jar of mayonnaise, a withered old wedge of onion, and a squeeze bottle of spicy mustard. The racks on the door teemed with supplement bottles—glucosamine, ginko biloba, something called Muscle Repair Complex, and an alphabet's worth of vitamins. The eggcups were vacant and gritty.

I shifted where I stood and a sharp sadness cut through me. I closed the door. It was the loneliest refrigerator I'd ever seen.

9

FRIDAY NIGHT WAS THE BIKINI BULL RIDE competition at the Cowboy, and Kimber strolled toward the club's front door with her sights set on winning. Shawna and I panted behind, her bag-toting minions. We grabbed three longnecks from the girl selling them out of an ice-filled tub in the parking lot and headed straight for the ladies' room. Kimber dropped her purse in the middle of the floor and started stripping off her clothes. I gave apologetic glances to the women she'd displaced as they stood in line for the toilets and clustered at the mirror, combing and making up. Kimber peeled down to a gold metallic bikini and pulled a pair of three-buckle chaps from her gym bag. She stood in her stocking feet and fastened the chaps, black with gold stars down the legs and trimmed with black-and-gold party streamer fringe.

Shawna perched on the edge of a sink, clearly agitated. "So this client calls about the commission I'm working on for her, and she says, 'Can you make it a mother-daughter painting, with the mama Indian—I quote verbatim, 'mama Indian'—carrying the baby in a papoose?' And I was like, lady, we carry our babies in Bjorns these days like everybody else, and my mom wasn't into the papoose action when I was born, either, and she was living with my dad up in Crow Agency at the time." Her father, Bobby Black Foot, is a schemer who seduced her mom, a self-described "hippie exile from Rhode Island's middle-class Jewsoisie." He ekes out a living selling dream catchers and painted steer skulls, and holding fake sweat lodge ceremonies in a steer-hide-covered Coleman camping tent he hauls from town to town. Shawna has half-siblings from New Mexico to northern Montana, and of all of them, Shawna fared the best. When Shawna was ten, her mother settled in Colorado, took healing arts classes, and became successful enough to send Shawna to a private liberal arts high school in Boulder, where her talent was immediately recognized. By the time I met her at college, she was already a prolific painter. Buyers fall in love with the Indian Maiden in the Moonlight tableaux that have become her trademark. Since she started selling her work, her sole departure from type was a darkly distorted portrait she did of her father, whom she calls "Chief Black Book." She titled the painting *You Can't Spell 'Shaman' Without 'Sham,'* and it was the only thing she ever touched a brush to that didn't sell.

Kimber dug in her bag for her makeup case. "What did you tell her?"

Shawna bit her thumbnail, chipping off the silver glitter polish. "I said I'd do it, but instead of charging her the usual twenty-five hundred, I told her it would be three thousand."

My eyes bugged. "Holy shit." Three-thousand bucks. I love this girl with every fiber of my being, but that love's got little gnaw-marks of envy all over it.

"Jesus, Spooky, at that price, *I'd* paint the damn thing." Kimber strapped on a pair of gold platform sandals with six-inch spike heels. Pick in hand, she bent at the waist and worked on separating her curls. She stood straight, rearranged her man-made breasts in her shiny top, and fluffed her torso with sparkly dusting powder.

Shawna scowled and spat a polish chip to the concrete floor. "Just another profitable day in the life of a boutique minority." Since I've known her, Shawna has always been just a few yoga postures away from atomic rage.

Kimber balanced a can of vanilla SlimFast and a package of beef jerky on the edge of the sink. She tore open the jerky with her teeth. "Dinner. Stopped at Conoco on the way over."

"Ew!" Shawna clapped her hand over her mouth. "I am going to vomit if you eat that, Kimber. I really am. I was nauseous to begin with, and that is the most disgusting thing ever." Shawna has been a vegetarian since sixth grade, and an agent for the cause just as long.

I picked up the plastic tab from the jerky and tossed it in the trash. "Even as a sworn carnivore, I have to agree with her, Kimber. It's a sickness you've got."

"Tell it to me when I'm not trying to lose five pounds for Frontier Days. I need the protein, ladies, so suck it up." Kimber popped a sliver of jerky into her mouth.

Shawna cupped her hands and called out, "Murderer!"

"Oh, come on now, Shawnzy." Kimber's jaws labored. That jerky looked tough enough to sole a boot. "You know I love animals. They're delicious."

I leaned back against the stall door, watching Kimber in the full-length mirror on the far wall. "You're looking particularly bodacious tonight."

"Yeah, this bra's got so much padding in it, in the event of a water landing I can be used as a floatation device." Kimber adjusted her thong so it best flattered her figure. She slapped her butt. "Not bad for a white girl," she said to her reflection. The women in the bathroom stared, the full range from curiosity to disgust.

Kimber pulled her black Stetson with the rhinestone band low over her eyes. "Okay. Let's roll."

The bikini bull ride contestants had to sell strands of Mardi Gras beads for a dollar, and the girl who got the most beads tossed to her during her ride was the winner. The three of us grabbed an armful apiece and started working every corner of the room. The place was a throbbing mess of dancers, every secretary and loan officer in town done up in whatever was hot off the racks at Corral West. They swung around the wood dance floor in liquored abandon, and the corner tables were filled with guys from the Air Force base, smoking cigars and skidding on new boots. One of them did a double take when he saw Shawna approach in her black Torrid bondage skirt and vintage pearl-snap shirt with red fringe and piping. "Hey, Halloween's not 'til October!"

"So why are you dressed like a jackass?" Kimber stared down her nose at him. The guy shut his piehole and bought five strings of beads, but Kimber made him bark like a dog before she'd hand them over.

"Yee-ha," Shawna said sardonically as we advanced to the next table.

Kimber tapped a guy on the shoulder, and when he turned around, we were face-to-face with Cheyenne's own hotshot bull-dogger, Darcey Rivers. I was watching him take in the sight of Kimber, full eyeball suction from head to toe, when I heard that sugary-sweet voice.

"Oh, Daryl! Hi!" Jordan waved from behind Darcey's broad back. Her ivory sequined off-the-shoulder top looked expensive. "We're here for date night. My sister's got the kids."

Kimber twirled a string of beads on her finger and spoke over Darcey's head. "Well, nothing says romance like taking your pregnant wife to a smoky bar where any old mess could happen." She wasn't fooling. I had my first legal drink here, and that night I saw a guy get into a fight with a trucker, pick up a pool cue, swing it around, and accidentally smash his wife right across the bridge of her nose.

Shawna stuck out her arm. "In the name of supporting hard-working women everywhere, would you be interested in buying some beads?"

"Okay. Sure." Jordan squinched her button nose. "I like your braids. Are you an Indian?"

"Yep, honest Injun," Shawna said. "Just like this guy here." She pointed to the Indianhead logo on her American Spirit cigarettes.

I spotted Crystal a few tables over in her white boots and a bikini the shade of Barbie-flesh peach, which clashed horribly with her tan. She was plying her wares to a couple of the old guys who ran Linda Kenny's stables north of town. "Boys, you need to buy some beads!" Crystal dropped into one guy's lap, touched her nose to his, and drew the beads down over both their heads. She was playing the *come and get it* card, hardly a rarity in places like this where the redneck girls come to turn it on. That spotlight-grabbing quality I caught the first time I saw her out at the Bluffs Ranch wasn't some God-given magnetism. Her aggression was well practiced. I'd seen her pull guys out of their lounge chairs by the Twin Pines pool and haul them into her room for a massage, saying, "You look tense." Once she even corralled a married couple using that same tactic.

When Cystal came over to us, Kimber crossed her arms like a bored queen. "Entering the contest, Crystal?"

"You bet."

"Best of luck to you then." She twirled her beads again and slid smoothly away.

"Haven't seen you in a while." Crystal leaned down and put her hand on Darcey's knee. "What's up? Don't you miss my magic hands?"

"Busy. You know. Rodeo." He nodded his head toward Jordan, made a tortured, ball-and-chain face. "Family." His wife tapped her toes to the music and played with the stem on the maraschino cherry in the cup of seltzer she'd balanced on her pumpkin-proud belly. The atmosphere's pretty dense on Planet Jordan.

The band started "The Devil Went Down to Georgia." When Crystal walked away, ten strands of beads lighter, Jordan reached for her husband. "Honey, if you're sore, *I* can give you a massage." She started kneading Darcey's shoulders.

"Quit, Jordan." He slapped her hand away. She cast her eyes down and forced her home-hearth-happy smile.

Outsiders who view this sparsely populated state through sage-colored glasses can think what they want about our simple way of life. But life isn't simpler here; the drama's just done to scale.

The bucking machine was pushed out into a caged-off corner of the parking lot. When we walked outside, the crowd cleared the way for us as if Kimber were a prizefighter doing a perp-walk toward the boxing ring. Her casual strut emphasized her coolness, and she left a trailing aroma of jungle flower in her wake. Shawna and I pushed our way to the front where people clustered on the hay bales around the machine.

The first contestant was strictly Amateur Hour, wearing a faded American flag bikini, work boots, and a ratty old hat. She hopped up on the bull and kind of ground around a lot and posed, like Sissy in *Urban Cowboy*. Worth a whistle or two and a few strings of beads but wouldn't really cut it in cowboy country.

Crystal was next. She was even cheesier than the girl before, which was too bad, because I'd secretly hoped for her to win at least a little money. I mean, Kimber's my good friend, but I knew for a fact she made a nice wage and hundreds in tips at the Wigwam. Plus, Greg may have been a jerk to her when they were married, but he kept up with Aubrey's child support. Crystal was on her own with her kid, scrubbing toilets at the Twin Pines and giving the occasional massage. I don't know what Crystal was doing on that bull exactly, but I'm pretty sure it was illegal in twenty-three states. I actually felt bad for her. Kimber's lip curled in disgust. Turns out she's disliked Crystal ever since the night she'd seen her take off her thong during a chaps-and-cheeks contest at Goofy's Tavern. If there's one thing Kimber hates more than a gal who doesn't play fair, it's a gal who gives away more than she needs to.

Kimber stood with her hands on her hips. Under a neutral gaze, she scoped out the rest of her competition. Two girls in matching baby blue chaps stood next to her, slouching their pelvises forward, giving her dirty looks. The crease in her brow deepened, though she kept a hail-fellow-well-met smile plastered on her face. One whispered something to the other, and they both laughed pointedly—a little honky-tonk chin music this fine Friday night. Kimber hitched up the sides of her thong, and her hands went back to her hips. The smile stayed put. An attempted psyche-out only fortifies her. That's just the kind of girl she is.

Modesty won't get you anywhere in this type of situation, least of all to first place. You don't need to wear a thong to curry favor with the judges, Kimber explained: It was a matter of logistics—your butt cheeks provide traction. It was worth stripping down. First place paid a thousand bucks. I could have used a thousand bucks myself, but no way. I looked around at the half-blotto crowd. I went to grammar school with some of these people.

When it was her turn, a bouncer helped Kimber squash across the foot-thick padding to the mechanical bull, painted with spots and flaking from age, a pair of plastic red horns strapped to the front. She swung one star-spangled leg up and over and set her right hand in the grip. She raised her left arm, stuck out her chest, and nodded.

The machine humped once and began a leisurely spin with Kimber on top. It was quite a sight, her up there, the machine rocking back and forth and up and down in MTV-style suggestiveness. Around and around she went, like a glittering rotisserie cowgirl. Kimber kept her arm in the air and her hips forward like a real bull rider up on the rope. People began tossing beads to the mat like roses before a matador. The consummate performer, she was smiling, but I could tell she wasn't happy. The machine was only being pushed to 30 percent strength, and her talent was being underutilized. After another pathetic Sunday drive of a spin, Kimber blasted the guy at the controls with a disgusted look. "Stop!"

He slowed the machine. Everyone leaned in, wondering what was going on. Kimber put her hands on her hips, chest expanding as she yelled. "Listen, buddy, I don't know what kind of rhinestone cowgirl you usually get on this thing, but I came here to get on something that bucks!"

The crowd roared. The guy's head bobbled in assent, and he leaned on the lever. The machine leaped and whirled as the cowbell clanged with each jerking movement. Kimber had the crowd right where she wanted it, eyes front-and-center on her. She bucked around and around, sexual energy flying off of her like shrapnel. The guy kept the bull going hard to the left, but the girl was sticky. The lights glittered on her sweaty, sparkle-dusted chest as she rode away from her hand.

The crowd really started yelling when Kimber opened up with her outside leg and began spurring the bucking machine with her stiletto heel. Finally, atop a huge undulating swell, she flipped off the bull and flew through the air, a meteor of fringe and cleavage, landing on the bead-covered mat right at the feet of Beeber, who watched slack-jawed next to a doughy kid with a SPURRIN' WITH JESUS patch on his shirt pocket. Kimber stood, dusted off her hands, and swatted Beeber's hat brim down over his eyes. "Hello, Junior!"

Beeber turned gradient shades of red, and Kimber put her index finger under his hung-open mouth and popped her thumb like she was pulling a trigger. "You gonna stand there catching flies or give me a hand with these beads?" Beeber scurried around the mat, and soon Kimber had so many strands of beads around her neck she looked like Mr. T. *Ladies and gentleman, we had a winner.* She sauntered off to change, the scent of victory and jungle flower following like a cloud.

Back in her jeans and T-shirt, Kimber collected her money and treated Shawna and me to watermelon Pucker shots and beers. We stood alongside the dance floor railing, and she pressed a cold bottled water to her neck. An Air Force guy sidled up to her. His hair was cut high and tight. Close-set brown eyes and hawklike eyebrows made him look dreamy. He smiled at her. "That was a heck of a bull ride there. Can I buy you a drink?"

Kimber just looked at him blankly, like, *I'm sorry. I don't recognize you as a carbon-based life-form.* F. E. Warren Air Force Base might as well have been on the moon, for all she knew.

"I'm sorry." He blushed profusely, reddening up to his scalp. "I should have introduced myself first. My name is Jeff." Poor guy had no idea he'd queered the deal already. Kimber may go through the full Discovery Channel spectrum of mating strategies, but one thing remains constant: Kimber picks.

She blinked and smiled wanly. A flyboy is no cowboy. Flanny Rupert walked past in his tightest jeans and Frontier Days buckle. Kimber watched his ass as he went by.

Flyboy Jeff's face fell. "Oh, I get it. You're one of those cowboy-chaser types."

Kimber brightened. "Yeah, maybe. Sorry, honey."

"Let me tell you something. Rodeo isn't a legitimate profession or a testament to manhood. It's a hobby." He pivoted and walked away.

Shawna rolled her eyes. "Got some issues there." She sipped her beer and made a face. "Does this taste funny to you?" It tasted fine when I took a sip. I returned the bottle to her, and Shawna started peeling the label.

Kimber scanned the crowd and spotted a gorgeous black-haired guy pushing himself along in a wheelchair. "Oh, hey, that guy comes into the Wigwam all the time."

It was Tazer Mendez. No one knew what to do about Tazer. He'd been paralyzed from the waist down since a bull riding accident the summer before his sophomore year of high school. He wasn't tearing around in a golf cart, working a ranch, and staging his own rodeos like Jerome Davis, the World Champion who was similarly paralyzed a couple years back. Tazer was confined to his wheelchair. People were polite in his presence but definitely freaked out. I'd even seen a few guys avoid him because they thought he was bad luck.

Not Kimber. She sauntered Tazer's way and dropped into his lap. "Excuse me, is this seat taken?"

Tazer narrowed his long, slanted eyes. He was scanning for pity or ridicule.

Kimber looked impatient and luscious. She folded her hands. "You offer to buy a lady bull rider a drink, if you're a gentleman."

Tazer smirked. "That right? I've been called a lot things, sweetheart, but never a gentleman."

Kimber leaned into him and put her arm around his shoulder. "So they tell me. To the bar . . ." They rolled forward, crowd parting like the Red Sea at Kimber's command.

Beeber stopped next to Shawna and me, shaking his head, entranced. "She's something else."

"Yep." I killed my beer. "You got that right."

I lay on the couch watching a Patty Duke rerun, a bag of ice resting on my sore wrist when J.W. called me from the truck. He was on his way back from a night show in Durango. "Hey, Daryl. I thought maybe if you weren't busy I could come get those nail bags now."

"Oh God, I meant to drop them off for you at Dominion. Sure, come on over. I just got home from the Cowboy, and I'll be in my studio, so if I don't hear you, go on and let yourself in. I'll be up way late. Whenever you get here is fine."

He hesitated for a minute. "I've got my boy with me, if that's all right."

An hour later, I heard the front door open. The wood floor echoed as J.W. slipped off his boots.

I shouted from my studio. "Be out in a second."

Father and son sat at the kitchen counter, bottle of iodine and cotton balls between them, cleaning Troy's thumb. They were both in riding clothes—long sleeved button-downs and loose 20X jeans. Troy even had a monogram on his shirt placket. J.W.'s Mini-Me.

Troy fidgeted while J.W. swabbed his bloody thumb. I averted my eyes. Troy's voice was plaintive. "Can I do it, Dad?"

"Not if you're going to sit like that, you can't."

The boy's back went ramrod straight, narrow shoulders squared. J.W. slid the iodine bottle over to him. Troy soaked a cotton ball and scrubbed at the cut.

J.W. was a strict guide, but he'd let the kid walk himself to manhood. I liked this.

J.W. looked up at me. "Daryl, this is Troy."

Troy stood and nodded formally. "Nice to meet you, ma'am."

"Nice to meet you, too. But I'd rather be Daryl than 'ma'am', if you don't mind." I gestured at his thumb. "What happened here?"

"Caught it dallying my rope. Never done it this bad before."

"Hey, your first battle scar! This calls for ice cream."

Troy looked hopeful.

J.W. took off his glasses and cleaned the lenses with a paper towel. "No. It's too close to bedtime for sweets. Besides, he already got a treat today. I let him eat fried dough for lunch." When he put his glasses back on, he saw his son's crestfallen face. "Sorry, buddy."

When J.W. went to the truck to stow the nail bags, I took out the strawberry ice cream and zapped it for fifteen seconds in the microwave so it was soft. I held the container out to Troy. "Sure you don't want any?"

"I'll get in trouble."

"Not if your dad doesn't know, you won't."

Troy showed a crafty smile. He could be tempted. His father's boy, for sure. I gave him a soup spoon and whispered, "One, two, three . . . go!"

We shoveled ice cream into our mouths as fast as we could until we heard the slam of the front screen. I grabbed the container and lobbed it into the freezer, then leaned nonchalantly against the door. Troy wiped his mouth on his sleeve and ducked his head like he was inspecting his socks for holes.

J.W. put his hands on Troy's shoulders and gave him a little shake. "We'd better get going. It's late."

"It's a long way back to town. Why don't you two just stay over? You look exhausted, and I've got plenty of room."

"Oh, well . . ."

"Oh, well, nothing. The couch is a sleeper, and there's a daybed in the bedroom down the hall, if that's okay. There's video games on the TV in the basement guest room."

"Troy's not allowed to play video games when I've got him. If he wants something to occupy his mind, he can practice his roping."

"That's a yes then?"

J.W. looked at Troy, who nodded. "Yes," J.W. said. "We 'preciate the offer."

They went outside to get their bags, and I brought them linens and pillows. I said goodnight to J.W., pointed to the cereal and coffee, and he went off to make sure Troy was tucked in down the hall.

I turned on the ceiling fan and crawled between the covers. I'd thought I was tired, but I couldn't sleep. My brain was a clutter of woes: money, the Shane portrait, Red Hill, which, despite all Gwatney's boosterism, showed no sign of selling. But most of all, I was kept awake by my awareness of J.W. just below me, stretched out on the couch. I sighed.

J.W. called up, quietly. "You okay up there?"

"Can't sleep."

"Me, neither. Feel like talking?"

"Sure. Come on up."

He took the steps two at a time. I could smell him the second he came into the loft, strong with horse and sweat and dirt. He looked pleasantly rumpled in his untucked shirt and jeans. He sat on the side of the bed. I plumped a pillow and motioned for him to join me.

He put his glasses on the nightstand and leaned against the headboard, knees drawn up. "Why can't you sleep? Something on your mind?"

"I don't know. Lots of stuff, I guess. How was your horse?"

"How was my horse," J.W. repeated. He stifled a laugh. "My horse was pretty, uh, pretty windy." He went on to tell me about drawing Colorado's champion farting bronc, replete with sound effects. "He almost blew me into the next chute. I think he did it just to spite me."

"Ah, the romance of cowboy life. How'd you do?"

"I won second. I've got a little jingle."

"That's awesome." I reached up and ruffled his hair. "Hair's getting long. I can see your cowlicks."

"Yeah, I got a couple bad ones. Troy's got a mess of them, too."

"Troy looks just like you. He's cool."

"He thinks you're cool, too." J.W. eyed me. "He really liked the ice cream."

I pulled the sheet over my head.

He gave me a light shove. "I'm just teasing."

I peered over the edge of the sheet, afraid to say anything.

J.W. leaned over. "Hey, I'm not mad. I was only fooling with you."

Safe to emerge, I tucked the sheet under my chin and felt my eyelids start to droop. "How'd you find out?"

"He didn't tattle. He's not that kind of kid. I smelled strawberries on his breath when I went in to check on him."

"I apologize for corrupting your child."

"Not a problem."

I yawned.

"Sleepy?" He reached over and smoothed my bangs away from my forehead. I closed my eyes. I heard him whisper, "Yeah, she's sleepy." He turned off the lamp and stretched out next to me on top of the covers. I felt him extend, reaching, and the second he put his arm around me, I fell dead asleep.

Goody called first thing in the morning, hysterical because the scatty Basque cook at the Little Wyo had gotten into the cooking sherry again and sidelined the trail guides with some bad huevos rancheros, so there was no one to take the dudes out for their ride along Brush Creek. Since I had the day off, I promised to come over on Tad.

I'd felt J.W. get up from the bed last night and head downstairs to the couch. Now he stood at the sink, filling the coffeemaker. Troy was next to him, washing his cereal bowl.

J.W. wiped the counter with a green-and-white plaid dishtowel. "I don't have to go to work until noon. Want a couple extra hands?"

"I'd never say no to that. And if you want to do my poor aunt a favor by making a half-dozen dudes into repeat customers, maybe you could wear your chaps when we go?"

The three of us saddled up and pounded along the dirt road, over the hill, and down again. When we rounded the bend on the Little Wyo road, Troy stopped Hodge. "Whoa!" The reservoir sparkled in the light and the foothills rolled off in subtle shades of sere and green. Cotton-roll clouds bunched up in the west, the rest of the sky a flat sheet of deep Wyoming blue.

I reset my hat. "Awesome, isn't it?"

He nodded sagely. I liked this kid, trying so hard to be the stalwart little man. I recognize the attitude—perfection will yield peace, the psychology of someone who's seen trouble at home. His disposition reflected well on J.W., and Troy's mom, too, surely, though I still couldn't picture her and what she might be like.

"There are people waiting. Let's go, boy." J.W. sunk his heels into Slade's sides, and we were off. Everything he said to his son, however loving, had the subtext of *I could fold you like origami, kid.* Maybe he leaned so hard because he had to do his fathering in compressed noncustodial bursts.

At the ranch house, we found the six dudes mounted in a semi-circle, expectant and saddle sore, a family of four from Minneapolis and two honeymooning playwrights from Vermont. J.W. shot the cuffs on his shirt, tipped his hat, and transformed suddenly into Hopalong Jarrett. "Well, howdy, folks!"

Goody rushed out onto the porch, her red calico apron dusted with tortilla flour. "Oh, my gosh!" Her Swedish accent lilted each vowel. She tossed her silvery blond plait over her shoulder. Even at sixty, she was the hugest flirt. "J.W. Jarrett! It's such an honor to have you here."

"Thank you, ma'am." J.W. tipped his hat again. "It's an honor to be of service." J.W.'s molasses drawl had turned to a phony buckaroo twang. Troy and I kept our eyes on our saddle horns, not sure where this Sunday matinee act was off to next. J.W. turned Slade in a showy spin. "How's about y'all come along on a little late-morning trail ride with my ranch friends, Troy and Daryl here. We've got some real pretty country we'd just love to show you." Troy did his best to not bust out laughing, hiding his mouth behind his shirt collar.

The dudes moaned and creaked in their saddles as we led them along the trail that wound through limber pine and Engleman spruce and fans of aqua sage. The teenage boy rode behind J.W. "Where'd you get those cool chaps?"

J.W. shifted in the saddle to face him, his hands gentle on Slade's reins. "They're rodeo chaps." With that, everyone knew they were in the presence of a real-deal rodeo cowboy, and the questions started to fly. J.W. handled himself graciously.

"The chaps I wear are different from yours," he said, leading us up a rocky path that bisected a shale-covered slope. "Fancier and cut different. The batwings flap when we ride to show off our spurring action. We flip the legs of the chaps up to show the judges that our feet are in the proper place when we leave the chute."

The pines saluted, bent, and waved, their resinous scent taking the air. J.W. raised his voice over the scratch of branches as he led us single-file down the slope along the creek. "I've been a professional rodeo cowboy for over twenty years. Rodeo is the only American sport that has roots in an occupation. It began on ranches as a pastime for the hands who would compete against each other in a show of skill. There's debate about where it started. Some say Chile, some Mexico, others, the United States. I say it doesn't matter, just be glad we've got it."

Maybe another guy would've laid off the history lesson in favor of flaunting his own résumé, but J.W. was humble enough to keep his ego out of the recitation. "There are Indian rodeos, black rodeos, women's rodeos, military rodeos, and rodeos just for kids. There are PRCA rodeos in forty states and rodeos every month of the year. Cowboys don't just come from the West. There are cowboys in Connecticut, cowboys in Hawaii, even cowboys from the Deep South. I'm from New York City, though I guess you couldn't tell by my accent."

The dudes laughed. The father of the foursome tipped his ears with sunscreen and rubbed some vigorously on his perspiring nose. "How exactly do you hang onto the animals?"

"I ride bareback, so I only have to hang onto one kind of animal. A horse that was bred to buck. We have a rigging and pad that basically strap around the horse's girth, and we wear a heavy leather glove on our riding hand. Before we work into the rigging, we coat the glove with rosin, which helps our grip."

I raised my hand.

J.W. pointed at me. "A question. Yes, miss?"

I leaned forward and spoke loudly so everyone could hear. "Can you explain how you got that gold buckle you're wearing?"

Troy tipped his hat back slyly. "Tell 'em, Dad."

He confessed his World Championship, and the men sat taller on their mounts while the women twittered. The honeymooning bride pulled up next to him on her little grullo, hat bumping between her

shoulder blades on stampede strings. Her short hair was the color of
winter wheat. "When did you win that?"

He didn't much like being advanced upon by someone's brand-
new wife. He smiled curtly. "Back when dinosaurs roamed the
earth, ma'am."

He clucked to urge Slade on. "Most cowboys and cowgirls have
farm and ranch backgrounds like me and Daryl." To a tourist, I
could pass, but I wasn't any more a ranch kid than the teenager in
the Tupac T-shirt hanging on J.W.'s every word. Summer sightseers
driving down Happy Jack would stop when they saw my dad mend-
ing fence along the road and say, "Whadda ya ranch?" He'd lift his
head. "Hot air and plenty of it!" Dad's parents, though, were
second-generation cattle ranchers of the blood-and-blister variety.
Salt of the earth at core and granite on the surface, they weren't exactly the doting kind. My father and Dee, brought up seething under their father's leaden hand, rebelled by failing to follow suit, and I
was glad. Except for my grandmother's amazing blackberry pies,
every visit to their outfit near Torrington was an exercise in dread.
We'd go up to help with calvings and brandings, and the ooze of fe-
cundity and stench of burning cattle hair made me green at the
gills.

The dudes kept tight hold on their reins, enraptured by J.W.'s lecture. "I've met cowboys who learned to bulldog off of videotapes,
and bull riders from the South Bronx and South Central Los Ange-
les. Charlie Sampson was the first black World Champion bull rider,
and he's from Watts. We respect Charlie—well, Charles now—
because he sure paid his dues. A bull stepped on his ear one time and
tore it clean off. If you ever see a black cowboy wandering out there
with one fake ear, please tell Charles I said hello."

"Rodeo can be a family affair. Ford, Marvel, Etbauer, these are
families now on their second and third and fourth generation of
competitors. My uncle, who was like a daddy to me, well, he rode
broncs and bulls a little, in his day. He hasn't been on any bucking

stock since Nixon was president, but he still critiques every ride of mine he sees. And I do appreciate it."

They laughed again. Sarcasm didn't fit their presumed cowboy model, which allowed him to act as his own straight man.

J.W. led the group to the water's edge and around the perimeter of the reservoir. "Some people view rodeo as pure entertainment, like back in the day of Buffalo Bill Cody's Wild West Show, but to-day's rodeo cowboys are professional athletes. If you don't win, you don't get paid, your career is pretty short, and you've got to do a lot of driving."

Minneapolis Mom, hair a mass of wind-tangled, frosted ringlets, spoke huskily through pink lips that glimmered like fish scales. "So why would you do it then, cowboy?"

Gross. I didn't know I was squeezing my heels in until Tad stamped a protest. I rubbed her neck.

"Question isn't why I would do it, ma'am." J.W. looked at her with a face that was equal parts sincerity and mischief—straight out of every cornball Western and, probably, this gal's friskiest dreams. "Question is why *wouldn't* I?"

When we were done, J.W., Troy, and I walked the horses back to-ward Red Hill, the clop of hooves a homey sound on the dusty road. Toadflax and purple lupine bloomed on the hillside. I rode up along-side J.W. "Nice speechifying you did there, J-dub. Above and beyond the call of duty, really."

"Yeah, well, figured it's the least I could do what with you puttin' us up last night." He squinted at the sun. "I pretty much bullshitted my way through the whole thing anyway."

Troy laughed to hear his father cuss.

10

WEDNESDAY AFTERNOON, I CAME HOME from work and grabbed the mail. I stood at the top of the dirt drive, truck idling, sun scorching the back of my neck as I sorted through bills and fly-ers. Heat phantoms rose from the pavement. I remembered Jace and Dad and Uncle Dee coming up the road on horseback on the way back from The Bunkhouse Bar ten miles down Happy Jack, roping every street sign and mile marker along the way. I tossed the mail in the front seat. When I looked up, I saw Doug Cathcart driving by in a white truck with BROTHER'S ABATEMENT COMPANY stenciled on the doors. I'd never seen him in daylight before and was shocked, like he existed as a bar specter that only drifted up in the presence of neon and beer. He slowed and leaned over to yell out the window. "Selling the ol' homestead?"

"Looks that way."

"Where's your brother at?"

"Not here right now." I slammed the mailbox door shut.

"You out here all alone, little flower?"

"No." I contemplated saying something about having the com-pany of my friends Smith and Wesson, but then Gwatney pulled up with his Range Rover full of kids and a harried-looking mom. He'd said they were from Wisconsin. I waved, then headed to the barn and saddled Tad. I rode her to the top of the rise and didn't come down until they'd left.

I went downstairs to Jace's computer in the basement bedroom and got online. Experience had taught me to steer clear of Jace's bookmarks—dozens of sites that indicated an interest in rough trade and high volume. I once opened a folder marked Bears, thinking it would be about hunting, and found out more about my brother's erotic proclivities than any sister would ever want to know.

I called up a big search engine and typed in "J.W. Jarrett." It yielded four hundred entries. Most were links to a hyperactive blogger in Ohio with the same name. I narrowed it down to "J.W. Jarrett" and "rodeo" which brought up about a hundred entries. I clicked through the first fifty, mostly scores from local rodeos. I kept clicking.

I knew I was cyber-stalking but I didn't care. Unlike real-life stalking, there was no possibility of witnesses and it didn't involve any particular strategy. It was something I could do in my spare time.

"J.W. Jarrett" and "rodeo" and "bareback" didn't yield anything productive, just more old scores. My adrenaline ramped each time I followed a new link. It was weird to see someone's existence itemized and indexed by category. I typed "J.W. Jarrett" and "rodeo" and "family." Thirty entries. I tried them all.

The first twenty-nine were links to rodeo sites and old articles, none of which focused on J.W. beyond a passing mention. There were rodeo history sites that mentioned his World Championship, though far fewer than I would have thought, mere blips on the data radar. But then, he won it a long time ago, in the barely fathomable days before the Web. Entry thirty was a homemade fan site for Duff Linsey. There was an extensive photo gallery featuring various promotional and paparazzi shots. It listed his movie credits, the highlights of his rodeo career, and his biographical information: "Cowboy-turned-actor Duff Linsey, 38, born in Commerce, Georgia, has rodeo in his blood. He's not the only bronc-stompin' champion in the family . . ." So there was a reason I noticed a resemblance between him and J.W.

They were brothers.

J.W. showed up for dinner at eight, Italian seasoned elk steaks in one hand and a box of rigatoni in the other. He shrugged off his Carhartt and left his boots by the door. When I saw his beautiful starched blue dress shirt and creased jeans, I felt underdressed in my old denim mini, tank top, and flip-flops. He inhaled. "Smells like heaven in here."

For dessert, I'd cruised cooking sites online. In a section of Southern foods, I found a recipe for red velvet cake. The layers cooled on a wire rack, filling the entire house with the aroma of chocolate.

The phone rang. I leaned over and saw the Jackson exchange on digital readout and decided to let the machine get it. Necessity is the mother of invention, and mothers necessitated the invention of caller ID. "DeeDee, I want you to call soon if you need Larry to fly down to get you for the Fifth of July party. The chairman of the elk preserve is going to be there and he's *very* interested in meeting you. They've got a calendar they need illustrated. And where's our invitation to the Frontier Days art show gala? I'm getting impatient. Kisses, sweetheart."

"DeeDee, huh?" J.W. laid the steaks on a plate, a smile threatening to break out. "Say, DeeDee, how would *this* elk look on that calendar?"

I swatted him with a dish towel. "Not one more word about it."

J.W. looked lordly and content as he stood over the grill, long two-tined fork in his hand. I put on a Frank Sinatra CD, and J.W. left the steaks grilling and came into the kitchen to start the salad. The frosting for the cake was supposed to have turned red in the freezer overnight, but when I took it out, it was a feeble carnation pink. I squeezed in more food coloring, drop by drop until the frosting was red like the perfect valentine heart. I scooped up the frosting and scalloped the sides of the stacked cake layers with a plastic paddle. "Got a question for you, my friend."

"Shoot."

"I saw you praying behind the chutes at the Bluffs Ranch. Do you pray to win or something?"

"No. Nothing like that. That's asking to get jinxed, if you ask me. I keep it simple, same thing every time: 'Keep me healthy, Lord. And thank you.'" He looked embarrassed. "Corny, I guess."

I put down the plastic paddle. "If there's a world where prayer is corny, I hope to never live in it."

I rooted through the utensil drawer for a corkscrew. When I'd gone to the Town and Country liquor store to find a wine for dinner, the clerk followed me down the reds aisle, reciting every option: Zins, Merlots, Cabernets. Sweating in his Fleetwood Mac T-shirt, he radiated the obsessive eagerness to connect that I recognized in people being driven mad from boredom in this small-town city. He bounced on his toes as he presented the Rocca de la Macie. "The Cowboy Chianti. The guy who owns the vineyard used to star in spaghetti Westerns!" He raised his fingers to his lips and kissed, "RO-kah DAY-la MA-chee-uh—perfect for Italian!" Twenty bucks a bottle. I went next door to the Safeway and bought fresh basil, vine-ripened tomatoes, and a Napa Valley mozzarella for a salad. I put everything on a charge card.

J.W. prepared the salad. I looked over at the hands that I had such a crush on. Even slicing tomatoes took on militaristic formality, as if making a salad deserved singular focus. I fussed over the sauce. We were fully in concert regarding seasoning. More oregano. More garlic. More everything.

When "They Can't Take That Away from Me" came on, I flicked J.W.s hat brim when Sinatra sang "the way you wear your hat," and he flinched.

"Calm down now, cowboy. It's just a hat."

"It is not just a hat." J.W. slid his eyes at me while he snapped the stems off the basil. "You don't like cowboys much, do you?"

"I never said that."

"Not in so many words, you didn't." He unwrapped the mozzarella and set it on a plate, ringing it with tomato slices interspersed with basil leaves. "On canvas, we're okay. But in person, not so much, huh? A real man too much for you to handle there, Daryl?"

"Not even." I picked up the bottle of wine. "Could you open this for me?"

"Happy to."

"You sure, cowboy?" I pointed to the cork. "'Cuz it's special fancy, see? It doesn't have a pop-top like you're used to."

"Oh, you are hilarious." The cork made a satisfying pop as it came out and J.W. set the bottle on the counter to breathe. "A hat is more than just protection for a cowboy's head. It's his allegiance to a dying breed. Looking the part is as much a part of the code as his honesty or his word."

I poured two glasses and handed one to him. "You forget that there's cowboying in the Heatherly blood. I've heard this code stuff before."

"Then you ought to know there's something to it. Don't you think qualities like honesty are important?"

"Of course." I sipped my wine. It was excellent. "And I *honestly* believe that you cowboys just use that 'last of a dying breed' business to impress chicks."

He choked and spat, pitching forward to keep the wine from staining his shirt. "I do not!" He put his wineglass on the counter. "I swear. I don't." He wiped his mouth and laughed into the napkin. "Anymore."

"A-ha! I knew it." I put my hands on my hips. "Come clean. How long has it been?"

"I don't know. A long time. Twenty years, maybe?"

"Well, I wouldn't have been able to call you on it then, since I was in nursery school at the time." I could see my reflection grinning in his glasses.

He leaned forward, putting a hand on either side of me so I was pinned with my back against the counter. "So what's your point?"

"My point is simply that you're a man of experience." I heard my mother's voice in my head: *It's not nice to tease boys.* But if a boy was teasing you first, I figured all bets were off.

"That a plus or a minus?" His eyes narrowed.

"Well, they say there's no substitute for experience."

He leaned in closer. "That's a plus then, I guess."

"I guess."

He was right in my face then, our noses almost touching.

By the time he might have leaned in for a kiss, I was already headed toward the deck. Gray smoke boiled out from under the grill hood. J.W. raced outside ahead of me, but it was too late. The steaks were reduced to charred, inedible elk pucks. He picked up one with the tongs, and it promptly disintegrated into black flakes. "Look out, Julia Child."

We piled the plates high with salad and pasta and carried them outside. We ate with our feet dangling over the edge of the deck as the sun set. I passed J.W. a napkin. "How's your boy?"

His face darkened. "He's fine."

"Do you not like to talk about him?"

"No, nothing like that." He wiped his mouth. "It's just that some people don't like hearing about a kid that's not theirs."

"Why would I care, though?"

"I'm sorry. I probably shouldn't have mentioned it. I had a less than ideal date in Cortez last weekend."

Jealousy plugged me between the ribs. "Oh?"

"She said her friend told her she should pass on a divorced guy with a kid. I believe the term that came up was 'damaged goods.'"

"That's bullshit." I said "bullshit" much too loud. I dropped my voice. "That's bullshit. No woman in her right mind could judge someone for that. Who hasn't had a busted-up relationship? God knows I have."

"Yeah, I never did get the background there. Didn't want to ask."

"Long story."

"Aren't they all?"

As I tried to explain what happened with Alex as discreetly as possible, I skewered rigatoni with my fork. One noodle. Two noodles. Three. "The simplest way to put it is that he never failed to tell me he respected my ambition."

He swirled the last sip of wine around in his glass and swallowed it. "Big of him." As far as putdowns went, it had the lethal economy of a heart-lung shot.

I served the cake. He didn't care that the red food coloring turned his teeth pink. "It'll balance out the yellow from the chew."

"Sorry about that," I said, pouring him a cup of coffee. "I guess neither of us is a domesticated animal."

We talked about his own failed relationship. How they'd come to town when Troy was six, moved into a split-level in Buffalo Ridge, tried half-heartedly to have another child. They fought, separated, and bang, thirteen years to the week after saying "I do" under a bower of pink roses in an Alabama botanical garden, he moved into the apartment on Fifteenth Street. I watched him while he spoke. He attempted a poker face, but I saw a definite shadow of culpability. He sipped his coffee. "Not that fun to talk about, I know."

"Well," I said, holding up my mug, "here's to getting it out of your system." We toasted our friendship and toasted our respective recovery, agreeing that the loneliness you feel when you're lying next to someone who's supposed to love you is the most pitiful kind of lonely there is.

When our mugs met, that brassy cold bolt of pain shot up my arm again. I rotated my wrists. "That copper bracelet you wear really work?"

"My riding arm hurt all the time 'til I got it. That's all I know."

He cracked his neck. Without thinking, I reached out and gave him a quick scrub under the collar, then just as quickly stopped. There was a reflexive answering in his shoulders, though our eyes never met.

He asked to see my art, and I felt comfortable enough to indulge him. I pulled out a laser print of the painting that would hang in the Frontier Days art show, a watercolor of a pickup pulling a two-horse trailer down an empty highway. "When you paint in shades of gray like this, the technique is called *grisaille.*"

"*Grisaille.*" J.W. sampled the word. From his Southern tongue, it came out "griz-AH." He looked mighty pleased. "You're the first real artist I've ever met. I'm impressed." I still hadn't told him I was a maid. No one had ever been impressed by me before. He held the picture. "What do you call it?"

" 'Passion Is a Lonely Road.' " I felt suddenly stupid. "I was in a dark mood that day."

He focused on the truck driving off into the sunset alone. "Where you suppose he's headed?"

"It's a she."

We'd reached the bottom of the wine bottle. "The Chair" came on the stereo. J.W. pulled me up to standing and put his arms around me. "You already got my hat off of me. The least you can do is give me one dance."

We made an ideal match, height-wise. While not a tall man, J.W. was still a head taller than me. We maintained self-conscious distance, like fifth-graders practicing a box step. I matched his neat turns. "I have to admit you're a pretty good dancer."

He pulled me closer. "I'm just rising to your standard." Was there some charm requisite that Southern boys took to make them this slick? J.W. danced me around the kitchen island. "Ready for the dip?"

"Dip away." When he leaned me back, I fumbled a little on the way up. "Whoops."

J.W. steadied me with a hand to my lower back. "My fault, precious."

I broke away from him. "What's with this 'precious' business?"

"What do you mean?"

"That's the second time you've called me that. You did it that night you hit me in the head at the Wigwam, too. Is that how you say you're sorry?"

"I guess I didn't even think about it. Does it bother you or do you like it?"

"If you want to know you the truth, I do." I could feel the tips of my ears glowing. "Bother me, I mean. It does bother me."

He saw the snag in my composure and moved in closer to tug the thread. "What if you are precious? Shouldn't somebody tell you so?"

"Stop it."

He put his arm around me and squeezed. "Stop what, precious? Mmm?"

"Cut it *out*." I punched him in the chest. "It's not funny, J.W." I stepped away from him. "So, Ace Comedian, were you ever planning to tell me Duff Linsey is your brother?"

He stopped smiling and the temperature in the room dropped about ten degrees. "I didn't see the point. We're not close. He's got his life, I've got mine." He took his arm from around my shoulders. "Listen, let me help you with these dishes, then I'll take you to town so we can do some real dancing."

The night was hot, a little stick to it, but not actually humid. I lowered the passenger's side window and took in a faceful of soft rushing air, which chased away the last effects of the red wine. J.W. put Roy Acuff on the CD player and gently drummed the steering wheel with his thumbs. We sang along with "Tennessee Waltz," in a dead heat for first place as Wyoming's Worst Vocalist. When we were almost to town, I had a change of heart. "Let's not go dancing."

The ground lights vanished as we turned onto County Road 225.

Out of the dark, the Coastal Chem plant rose up, lit like a NASA launch facility. Thick, white steam clouds spumed from the tall concrete stacks. A few miles farther and there weren't even ranch lights, just occasional pairs of shining eyes headlight-caught on the gravel road that ran alongside the railroad tracks. I told J.W. to pull up next to an old snow fence and park. We climbed into the truck bed and lay flat, cooling our backs against the dusty steel, smelling creosote. We tipped our chins to the sky, which was mad with stars and planets.

"You know," J.W. said, folding his arms behind his head. "I never done this."

"Really? In all the years you've been here?" I kicked off my flip-flops. "It's neat. You just look up, and voilà, the best show in town."

I'd been to this spot a million times when I lived here, with friends and sometimes boyfriends. When we couldn't barricade ourselves in a den or a living room, we camped here. This was where I learned to kiss in eighth grade, where I had my first taste of beer and discovered that I hated smoking pot. Freshman and sophomore year provided me with a string of inconsequential boys who would take me out, and we'd occasionally wind up this way. They'd try their lines and their luck, and wearily, I'd put them off. Every so often, we'd ease our boredom by making big romantic declarations to each other that we didn't mean but recited anyway, practicing them for future occasions when we would.

When I was in ninth grade, I let Jim Ringold take me out here one night over Thanksgiving break. A long-limbed, tetchy junior, Jim bounced his knee all the time and picked his cuticles, but he was sweet enough, and he drove. We parked here after he'd come over for dinner. I hunkered down into my navy blue parka and he killed the lights. Through the windshield, the stars glared frigid and bright. We spent a few stilted hours sipping beer that he sneaked into the trunk from his father's refrigerator in the garage. Freezing beer in early winter didn't richen the atmosphere or ease Jim's fidgeting. I don't remember much about the night except for his hard, nervous fingers on my cold breasts. Jim and I were a typical hook-up—together more to keep the teenage lonelies at bay than for any real reason. I never got in over my head with guys like him because it was all so incredibly dull.

But tonight was different because J.W. was different, and so, almost a decade hence, was I. The heavens were doing their best to entertain us. The Milky Way arced overhead, filmy white and silver. Stars shimmered through the night heat and far to the west, pink forks of lightning flashed and exploded behind a scrim of light blue clouds.

A small gold dot cruised through the sky just south of Jupiter, too steady to be a shooting star, too far away to be a plane. I pointed up. "Know what that is? It's a satellite."

Some people hate the sky being orbited by junk, but I like that there are so many things being shot into space, each with its own purpose. Every time I see one, I think, *that's someone's big idea up there.* We counted satellites, found at least a dozen before tiring of the game. The Big Dipper was still low to the horizon, spanning the width between five telephone poles.

I stretched out on my side and tucked my elbow under my head. "Think you'll ever make the NFR again?"

He shook his head. "No way. I'd have to win three times the money I do just to get to the bottom hole. There's about twenty guys between me and the top fifteen. Fourth of July run's coming up. That's when it gets really hectic, but it's not near as bad as the years I tried to make Finals. I'd be gone the whole month. I added it up once. I've traveled more than a million miles in my career."

"You've done so much cool stuff, J.W. You're lucky. I haven't done squat."

"You went to college. I didn't. I'd say college counts for something, wouldn't you?

"I guess." I stretched out again, looking at the sky. We lay side by side in silence. I could almost hear the legs of grasshoppers rasping together in the brush. A small brown spider ran along the edge of the toolbox lid. I hugged my knees to my chest and stretched my back. The lightning moved off in the distance and the sky was perfectly clear. Something brilliant zipped across the sky over the train tracks. "Hey, shooting star. You've got to make a wish." I looked at him. "Did you see?"

"Sure did." He leaned against the toolbox and closed his eyes.

I blotted my forehead with my cuff. "Jesus, this weather is making me nuts. Let me get this off. You must like this heat, huh?"

"Love it. Closest thing to home I felt since I got here." J.W. helped me wriggle out of the sweatshirt. When I tugged my arms from the sleeves, they turned inside out and something fell from the pocket, clattering to the truck bed.

I reached out but it was too late.

The last nail. J.W. picked it up. "What's this here?"

My face burned. I couldn't speak.

He held it in front of his face, between his thumb and forefinger. "It's a nail." His expression was solemn. "The kind from your house. From the other night."

I could feel the red creeping up my neck.

"Did you hold onto it for a reason?"

I knew if I spoke above a whisper, my voice would crack. "Yes."

In that instant he tore through the flimsy fiction of Just Friends. Through the hot, still night, I could hear the eighteen-wheelers throttling along Route 80, engines singing, far away. Neither of us moved.

The metal of the truck bed started vibrating, like it was coming to life. I put my hand on top of his. "Train's coming. Feel it?"

He pulled back, watching my face. "Yeah." His look was intense and direct, telling me that this whole time, he'd been waiting and wanting me, too.

I knew that once I did what I was about to do, Just Friends would become null and void. I leaned in and kissed him.

J.W. relaxed into the kiss for a second, then raised his hand to his lips. "I've got a chew in."

I didn't care. The sharp spark of tobacco only made me want him more. I brushed my lips along his and eased my tongue into his warm, yielding mouth. He took my face in his hands, the heels of his palms resting under my cheekbones, his calluses cupping my temples. He paused to spit, took off his glasses, and pulled me into his lap.

A train roared up, a big long hauler with car after car of coal. The cloverleaf of white lights on the engine exposed us in a blinding blast but we kept on kissing. We were still kissing long after the train passed and the rumbling in its wake faded. The thinnest sliver of moon rose above us and looked on, mute and impartial.

J.W. spread the blanket out on the metal truck bed and we lay down. Both of us moved stiffly, every touch preceded by hesitation. We were facing the next level scared and completely sober.

We'd been kissing for a long time when his hand found the hem of my skirt and disappeared underneath. As his fingers traveled below the waistband of my panties, his hand slowed. He stroked once between my legs and inhaled with what I thought was appreciation when he felt that I was shaved, then sat up and tucked his hands between his thighs.

When I'd showered after work, I perched on the side of the tub examining the dense triangle of hair between my legs. I usually trim it short with manicure scissors and shape it around the edges with a razor. I squirted a dollop of raspberry-scented shave cream into my palm and edged in tighter this time, shaving the hair down to the narrowest strip. I looked at it for a minute, then took up the razor again and made the impulsive decision to take everything off. When I saw the results, pink and sleek and sweet, I felt a sinister thrill in my belly. My step felt light as I walked into the empty bedroom to get dressed. I couldn't believe how free I felt. It was dizzyingly erotic, like I was smooth even on the inside of my body.

I came up onto my elbows on the blanket. "I'm sorry. Do you not like it?"

"No. Oh, God no. It's not that." He glanced at the hard-on straining his zipper and laughed a miserable laugh.

Even with his face turned away, I could read his expression: Dirty. Wrong. Musn't touch. The weight of self-recrimination deepened the lines around his eyes and mouth. I finally grasped that what I'd taken for shyness—in the barn doing chores, at his apartment after dinner at the Little Bear—was guilt. I'd expected assurance, confidence being the purported mark of the older man, and came upon this in its place. The phrase "age appropriate" probably taunted him, as I suppose it should have taunted me. But it didn't. When confronted squarely with the notion, I resented it.

Seeing someone so strong bent at the mercy of desire moved me in a way I'd never known before. I sat back and let one knee drop to the side, revealing myself to him. He lifted his head and faced me. My heartbeat surged. I let the other knee fall.

I regretted it instantly. When he put his hand on me, I squirmed. The few guys that I'd let touch me down there seemed to have a Mount Everest mentality, jabbing inside just to prove they'd conquered the area. Either that or they'd find a good spot and rub so hard you'd think they were trying to erase it.

I focused on the stars above, trying to relax, but my body made up my mind for me. Clamped shut. J.W. backed off. "You all right?"

"Could we slow down?"

Between kisses, J.W. breathed in the scent of my hair, my neck, the valley of my throat. He spent a long time stroking the side of my ribs, and tracing just inside the ridge of my hip bone, then behind my knee. The soft touches had a hypnotic effect. When I was relaxed and pliant, he slid his fingers back into place, his thumb light on my clit. I worried that I might take too long to come, or not come at all—I had nothing in common with those effortlessly, endlessly orgasmic Harlequin Romance damsels. But J.W. didn't appear to be in any hurry. He put his lips to my ear, telling me in a low, adoring voice that I was beautiful, precious, and a host of other things that I would never have expected to come from the mouth of a God-fearing Southern boy. Then he did a quarter-turn with his fingers and curled them slightly toward my navel, brushing back and forth over a spot deep inside, like he was beckoning me. When the sensation grew from a single trilling point of heat to a burn that flanged through my entire body, I squeezed my eyes shut, turned my head away, and let it happen.

When I turned my face back toward him, J.W. was watching me with those wide, sad eyes. I reached over and touched his cheek as gently as I could. "How'd you get so talented?"

Even in the dark, I could see his face turn red. "That's a heck of a question."

"Too nosy?"

His eyebrows vaulted in disbelief. "No. But do you really want to know?"

I adjusted my skirt, clambered to my knees, and knelt next to him. "Sure, why not?"

He fixed on a passing cloud. "The time I broke my pelvis was just after I got married. I couldn't move for months, let alone have much by way of sex. *Sex* sex, you know? I had to develop other ways of keeping my wife interested."

"So rodeo enhances your life on a lot of levels, huh?"

J.W. smoothed the hair on the back of his head. "Yep. It's quite an education."

I lay beside him on the blanket, watching his profile. "I didn't meet you that long ago but it'll be weird to not see you. When you leave for the Fourth of July, I mean."

He propped himself on his side. "You oughta come with me."

I laughed. "Are you kidding?"

J.W. sat straight up. "No, I'm not kidding. I'm completely serious. You should come."

I thought about it, trying to puzzle out if it could possibly happen. There was so much to do. "But my work . . ."

"Can't it wait for a couple days?"

"And the horses . . ."

"Have Beeber take care of them. He's not coming with me; he'll do it. He's a hand."

"But I've got my mom's Fifth of July party in Jackson."

"So I'll take you there. We're gonna wind up in Cody on the Fourth." He tugged the sleeve of my robe. "We'll have a big time, I promise. Say yes, Daryl, come on."

"I can't." I crossed my arms.

"Then say maybe."

"Okay, okay. Maybe."

He leaned over me, cupping my cheek in his hand, and brushed his thumb across my lips. He tasted like salt and skin, tasted like me. Our gaze caught and held, his eyes shining platinum pale in the starlight. I took the tip of his thumb into my mouth, suckling it. A shiver ran up his leg, so strong I could feel it in the column of my neck. "Come with me," he whispered. "Please say you will."

"I'll think about it."

We were closer to town than to Red Hill, so we drove to his apartment. When we were curled up in a tight ball on the bed, J.W. ran the tip of his nose up the back of my neck, then kissed the hollow at the base of my skull. "You're a pretty tough customer, I can tell. But sometimes you're just like a little girl."

He dropped off to sleep, his mouth open slightly. I stared out the window, the night contained in a pitch black rectangle, and wondered what he meant by that.

The next morning, I sat at the kitchen table, wearing J.W.'s blue button-down shirt, drinking coffee from a green chipped-rim mug stamped BURLINGTON NORTHERN in white letters. The warm morning tangled the hair on my neck into a wet lace.

He came smiling into the kitchen dressed for work. His eyes were still lazy from sleep. Caffeinated into high gear, I bounced onto his knee and slung my arm around his neck. Three small blood dots from shaving rode above his collar. I nuzzled him. "Sleep well?"

"Well enough," he said, holding me about the waist. "And you?"

"Like a rock."

"Did you have a good time last night?"

"Amazing." I handed him an ultra-light coffee and topped off my mug.

"I'm glad. Me, too." He hugged me to him and we sat quietly that way for a long while, his chin resting atop my shoulder.

He placed his empty cup on the edge of the table and gave me a light squeeze. I settled back in his arms and sipped my coffee. "Underneath all that cowboy stuff you're just a sweet old daddy, aren't you, J-dub?"

J.W. lifted the hair up off my neck and ran his fingers from root to tip, carefully brushing it out. He let the damp strands underneath fall. My scalp prickled as things took a decidedly less innocent turn. I rocked back on him so my shoulders pressed against his chest, and he slid his hand into the shirt. His callused palm grazed my nipple, radiating warmth. He kissed me behind the ear and spoke with his lips against my neck. "What if you had a daddy who took care of you like that all the time?"

His voice held two distinct strains of teasing, one coaxing me toward him, the other bracing me at arm's length, cautious.

My eyes dropped to the mug in my hand. A tingling wave of heat fanned upward from the soles of my feet and wrapped its way up my belly and neck, spreading to my face. I flushed deeply. I turned, intending to meet his gaze, but found I could look no higher than his chin.

I whispered, "If you're offering, then yes." My lips were dry. I licked them and the spreading heat turned to ice in my stomach.

What had he just asked me? What had I just said?

He was silent for several moments and still, as if considering the direction the exchange was taking. His breathing deepened and slowed. I looked at his face. His eyes were glassed with a sheen of need and fear. He pulled me tight to him and ran his hand hungrily along my hip. I felt him harden against my thigh. In one swift motion he stood, hefting me up from where I was sitting in his lap, and carried me toward the bedroom. The coffee cup smashed to the kitchen floor, splintering in a dozen ceramic pieces.

II

THE NICE WISCONSIN FAMILY came for a second showing later that morning, the father helming the expedition. He followed me and the agent around, big hands in and out of his twill pockets, asking questions about the septic system, how many wells there were. I was so distracted it was as if he were speaking to me from the bottom of an aquarium, his words a stream of shiny bubbles from his mouth. The wife and kids ping-ponged between the house, the barn, and the shed. I drifted behind to make sure they didn't disturb the horses, oblivious to the meddling din, Gwatney singing praises and low taxes at my side.

After the Range Rover scooted out the driveway, spumes of grit curling from the tires, I stood at the easel feeling almost hungover. Though I longed for him, I was glad J.W. was gone. I didn't want him anywhere near me. I was too blown out from what happened between us earlier.

I didn't know what to make of what we'd started in the kitchen. On the face of it, *daddy* was a damn stupid term of endearment. We've all heard it: "Who's your daddy?" It was pimp talk. Crude talk. Joke talk. But there was no denying how my body reacted, how we tore at each other when he carried me to his room and laid me down on the bed, his touch paternalistic care coupled with a lover's ache.

Daddy had nothing to do with kin. It had nothing to do with anyone or anything I knew beyond the recognition of a gentle authority that sent a scald through me like biting down on an exposed wire.

At first, he wasn't sure where to touch me, or how. I wrapped myself around him, his blue dress shirt sliding down my shoulders as my breasts disappeared under his hands. The sex flush came up on his chest and neck, pink like nothing I'd ever seen. He unzipped and half-in, half-out of his pants, began rubbing against me. I could feel how hot he was through my cotton bikini underwear. It was agonizingly hard to resist shifting the fabric aside and taking him inside me. A guilty sweat broke out on my upper lip. I toyed with his earlobe. "Sweet thing," I whispered. Yes. We kissed; he tasted like coffee and cream. I kept my lips right against his as the friction increased. When I whispered "daddy," a huge shudder passed through him, heavy warm spurts hitting the tails of his shirt while it was still on me.

He was mortified to have fired off like an overheated teenager, but his loss of control aroused a sympathetic throb between my legs. I kept my knees splayed, not caring how it looked, waiting. J.W.'s fingers crept under my waistband, and he repeated what he had done to me the night before. I was used to coming only after endless cajoling and repositioning, and strictly solo at that, but my response to his deft hand was sharp and sudden, like it was ripped from me. I shouldn't have liked it as much as I did. I stared at him wild-eyed, then stripped off the messed shirt and pushed him onto his back so I could relieve him of his jeans.

His touch was seductive, but reciprocating brought unexpected pleasure, scent of the dark red hair down there innocent and fresh like laundry soap when he slipped off his navy briefs. I knelt, coaxing him back to hardness and bowed my head. When I had him in my mouth, he looked down at me and said, "You feel so good," with such gratitude I thought I might cry. His fingers twined in my hair, I stroked and sucked him until I felt his entire body tighten, thighs trembling as he pulsed into my mouth.

All morning, I'd be standing at the easel or sketching a line on a page and find myself thinking of him, the Tin Man eyes, the daddy voice, and the coffee-flavored kisses. And I'd picture us together, images settling one over the other like sketches on tracing paper. I was startled by the realization, but we came into the most intense focus with me on my knees, his loving hands cradling the base of my neck.

Kimber's eyes glittered with sympathy as she set the egg-shaped timer to seven minutes. She reached across the wet bar top and squeezed Shawna's arm. "What do you think you're going to do if it's positive, kiddo?"

Shawna leaned her elbows on the bar, chin sunk in her hands, as she stared at the pages of an old *Love and Rockets* comic. "I don't know." Possible pregnancy wasn't typical lunchtime conversation at the Wigwam, but Thursdays from 11 until 2 was the Wild Women's rehearsal and it was Ladies Only.

I shook some black pepper into my Bloody Mary. "Did you tell Lan yet?"

"No, and I don't know if I'm going to." Shawna crumpled the paper Hoy's Pharmacy sack into a ball, aware of every second ticking by.

Kimber set up the Wigwam's CD player. Three of the girls ducked behind the storeroom doors to change into leotards and shorts, but there was no need. Teal, the only boy dog on the premises, didn't have much interest in women or any other form of companionship; he just set up refills, read *Newsweek*, and polished the tap spigots with a stringy old rag.

I'd picked up the latest issue of *ProRodeo Sports News* at The Wrangler on the way over. I paged through the magazine while Shawna read her comic. Duff Linsey and his travel partners were on the cover under the headline, "Bull Riding Buddies: Rodeo's Three Amigos," decked out in their gear—chaps, protective vests, and deerskin gloves. Clint Weeks stood on the left, arms crossed, cheeks chubby as dumplings; Kenton Whitley glowered on the right, most of his face shadowed under his crow's wing mustache and dark brows. Duff stood in the middle, hip cocked, hat pushed down low over his aquamarine eyes and a tight, practiced *aw, shucks* smile hiding his million-dollar teeth. His return to pro-bull riding was big news.

Hollywood didn't care, my Web surfing revealed. He was yesterday's bad boy to them, but the rodeo press was going batshit, tracking his every move, stoking the resurgent Dragon-mania. It said something about his unique appeal that even his traveling partners luxuriated in runoff glamour.

The feature story praised Duff for not being a cartoon cowpoke, but the real deal, down to the root. "I'm just the cowboy next door" was how he described himself, which explained why he couldn't be coerced to trade in his pickup for a Porsche, why he wore pressed Wranglers rather than more fashionable torn-up, faded Levi's, and why he insisted on doing his own stunts. He said all his best friends had four legs and a warm beer was a crime, which only charmed the media more. *People* magazine had even put him on their Fifty Most Beautiful People list one year.

If the mainstream profile weren't unusual enough, the article gushed, when the Hollywood ops slowed to a trickle, Duff went on to be a rodeo commentator on TV. Becoming a commentator is the rodeo equivalent of being kicked upstairs—definite silverback territory, which made sense for him since he was into his thirties by then. But Duff was always known as a wild card, a reputation reinforced three years ago when he quit the microphone jockeying, undertook a rigorous physical fitness regimen he designed himself, and went back on the circuit riding bulls, a move virtually unheard of in pro rodeo. He told everyone he was determined to make the Finals by forty—a bold claim for a guy in roughstock, where men feel their mortality at twenty-five and all but the very best start ticking down around thirty. A torn rotator cuff in his riding arm sidelined him halfway through his comeback summer last year. So far this season he'd barely cracked the Top Fifty.

"Duff Linsey," Kimber read over my shoulder. "What I wouldn't do to get a piece of that. Mmm hmm."

I closed the *Sports News*. "Bet you didn't know J.W. and Duff Linsey are brothers."

"Was that in the article?" Shawna glanced up from her comic.

"The article doesn't even mention it in passing. I found out on the Internet, and when I asked J.W. about it, he changed the subject. I don't know why."

Kimber flipped the cover open. "I guess I can see a little resemblance. Around the eyes. Yeah." She slid the magazine back to me across the bar. "He probably doesn't want to sound like he's bragging," she said. "Seems like something J.W. might do."

"Sounds a little shifty if you ask me." Shawna raised an expertly penciled brow. "I don't know about this J.W. guy. When he came over to get you for that date, he seemed a little, I don't know, bubba. Is he a Republican?"

"He's not so bubba that he wouldn't help with the dishes after dinner last night. And he grilled his own elk steaks, too. Or at least he tried to."

"Great. So he rides in the rodeo *and* hunts. Not to mention, he's a little on the *mature* side." Shawna licked a finger and turned the page of her comic.

"Who cares about his politics?" Kimber was incredulous. "Or his age, for that matter? You think she'd be better off with some kid who can't even pay for dinner?" She stretched from side to side, limbering up her waist.

"You mean you have no reservations about J.W. whatsoever?" Shawna craned her neck to check the timer. Still ticking. Two minutes to go.

Kimber shrugged. "He could be taller, I guess."

"Yeah, and I could be fifteen pounds lighter but I'm not." I crunched the celery from my bloody Mary.

Shawna lit a cigarette and the smoke curled up over her lip in a French inhale. "You're not weighing yourself, are you?"

"I was making a point. Nobody's perfect." I could hear an embarrassing edge of defensiveness creeping into my voice. "Besides, J.W.'s more than tall enough for me."

"Oh my, sounds like somebody might get an upgrade on his Just Friends status," Kimber teased.

"Maybe somebody already did." They looked at me covetously but I wasn't going to give them any more than that. "Speaking of status, how's it going with Danny Leigh?"

Kimber threw her hands in the air. "It's gone. He picked me up the other night and he had one of those gross window decals, you know, of a kid peeing on a truck logo? At dinner all he talked about was his new horse trailer. Then, oh God, you're gonna love this. When he took me home, we sat in the truck and he started whining about how he hadn't gotten any in so long, he was worried it wouldn't work anymore." She did a pitiful Droopy Dog voice. "Pwease, Kimber, I need a widdle wuvvin."

Even Teal snickered behind his crossword puzzle.

"I swear, I took him inside just to shut him up. I figured I could waste half an hour trying to get rid of him, or get it over with and send him home after." She patted her hair. "Did you ever do that? Just give in to get rid of someone?"

I raised my hand. "That pretty much covers eleventh grade for me, sad to say."

Kimber poured herself a glass of seltzer from the soda gun. "What about you and J.W.?"

"I don't know, we haven't gotten that far."

Shawna and Kimber looked surprised.

"I'm not saying we sit around holding hands, but no, we haven't officially had sex. But he asked me to rodeo with him during Cowboy Christmas—the whole Fourth of July weekend."

Kimber choked on her seltzer. "Oh my God. That's huge."

"Why didn't you tell me?" Shawna snapped her comic book shut.

"Because I knew what you'd say."

Kimber grabbed my arm. "You're going to go, aren't you?"

Shawna grabbed my other arm. "You're *not* going to go, are you?"

"I don't know." It was the right answer for either question.

Kimber squatted on the bar. "What do you mean you don't know? Daryl, J.W. is a cowboy. A real cowboy who would rope the moon for you. This is every woman's fantasy come true! If you don't go, you're crazy."

"I don't know," I said. "It might not look so good if I'm out at rodeos traipsing behind J.W. like some scuzzy . . ."

Kimber glared. "Don't even say it."

"Like what?" Shawna's eyes flicked from me to Kimber. "Hello?" Shawna waved her comic book in my face. "Like some scuzzy *what?*"

I watched Shawna's face twist into a knot of P.C. indignation as Kimber explained. Every sport has its groupie: baseball has the baseball Annie; NASCAR has the pit lizard. Rodeo has the buckle bunny.

When I was younger and I first heard the term "buckle bunny," I was intrigued. Bunnies were cute, soft. Feminine. In my tomboy view, that meant glamour. When I learned that buckle bunnies followed rodeo hoping to bed cowboys, I imagined them as a sexy roving tribe. I thought maybe you had to audition to be one, like a Laker Girl or a Dallas Cowboys Cheerleader. But eventually I realized that being a buckle bunny wasn't something one aspired to. A buckle bunny was somewhere between a throwaway fuck and a punchline.

Kimber laughed at me. "Who cares what anyone thinks? If you don't go, you are insane."

The five other Wild Women assembled on the barstools, in tights and sports bras and high heels, waiting for Kimber to lead them through their new routine.

"Looks like it's time for me to get to work." Kimber stood on the bar and addressed them with the command of a junior high drama club president. "I know it's hot in here but we've got a lot of work to do. Listen, about last Saturday. You know that this is a classy show. I don't care what kind of tip a customer offers you; you are not allowed to show your boobs or your butt." Kimber came down rather hard on the five Wild Women, but she'd busted her tail to recruit the perfect testosterone-boiling ensemble—a range of big and little, curvy and sporty, two blondes, two brunettes, and a redhead, lured to the Wigwam from as far away as Billings, and nicknamed after the sexiest drinks—Alizé, Brandy, Sherry, Bubbles, and Tequila Rose. Plus, with no kid to boss around this summer, she was at a loss as to where to direct her commanding energy, and I knew she missed Aubrey something fierce. Whenever she'd talk to her on the phone, she'd hang up wet-eyed. Kimber paced the bartop and clasped her breasts. "I love my girls as much as you love yours, but if you don't keep 'em covered, Teal could lose his liquor license, and you could lose your job. Teal just had the overhead glass rack reinforced, so we're going practice our back flips. Everybody on the bar."

The timer dinged and Shawna raced toward the ladies' room. I watched the louvered wood doors swing shut behind her. The desperate wail made everyone in the bar turn around. By some mysterious pharmaceutical alchemy, her fate had been determined in two purple stripes. Shawna was pregnant.

J.W. met me for dinner at Lexie's on Seventeenth Street. I ordered chicken marsala and a glass of white wine. J.W. was in his work clothes. He kept rearranging his silverware, straightening his plate, a nervous strain to his lips. Conversation was spotty and awkward, niceties choked out between sips of water.

We were halfway through our meal when Jordan Rivers and her

two sisters came in, trailing a gaggle of kids. They sat at the only table big enough to accommodate them. Right next to us. Once Jordan hoisted her little boy into his booster seat, she noticed J.W. and said hello, told him the deck they'd built from the lumber he delivered last summer was holding up great. Then she saw me sitting across the table. I could read her face: *How interesting.*

I panicked, wondering if we should leave but we had just ordered dessert.

The waiter put down our coffee and apple crumb cake. Jordan was busy tying a bib around Dustin's neck. J.W. touched my arm, anxious, like he was desperate to say something. *Hey, I'm not that slob from this morning who came with his boots still on.* He looked at me. "How do you feel?" He was casting for assurance I wasn't sure I could muster. Jordan was watching us. I pulled back. He excused himself and got up to use the restroom.

Jordan whispered over her menu, eyes round and hard like shooter marbles under the blond Kewpie doll curls. "Are you two an item?"

I shook my head behind my coffee cup. No, no. Of course not.

J.W. returned, pulling his chair in close to the table. He winced as the metal legs screamed along the saltillo tiles. "Listen. About Fourth of July. You don't have to come if you don't want."

I glanced over at Jordan. She was struggling to hear every word.

Everyone has a defining internal image, a mental picture that illuminates their sense of self. Standing on a mountaintop, holding a child, sweating at a podium, driving through a storm. My image is of me at age four, gripping the cement ledge of a swimming pool, my mom and brother in the water five feet away with their arms open, trying to get me to paddle over. No matter what Mom or Jace said to me, no matter how buoyant the little flowered water wings, I was frozen with fear and would not let go.

Nice as he seemed, J.W. was a mystery to me. He was something I'd been cautioned against my whole life. And he'd admitted to dating around, at least a little. That gal in Cortez and who else? Plus, he'd never mentioned that Duff Linsey was his brother, and didn't like me bringing it up, either, which made me wonder what else he might be hiding. Legitimate concerns all, but my chief reservation about J.W. was that he moved me in ways I didn't quite trust.

But something about Jordan staring at me kicked over that girl in the pool image. I lifted one finger from the ledge, preparing to push off.

I reached out and picked up J.W.'s hand, feeling Jordan's eyes burning into me. "Oh no," I said quite loudly. "I'm coming with you."

It wasn't until we got to our trucks that I realized I had lost an earring. I wore three—a pair of small silver hoops, and on the left lobe, a smaller hoop with a silver four-leaf clover on it. We checked and no one had turned it in at the restaurant. J.W. and I searched the sidewalk, to no avail. I finally found it wedged under the floormat of my truck. The catch on the earring was broken. I tossed it in the ashtray.

J.W. was headed down to Steamboat, and we wouldn't see each other for a couple days. The parking lot was empty. Before he got in his truck, we stood shielded by the driver-side door, hugging long and hard to the serenade of the door-open chime. When I let go, he held both my hands and focused on my face. "So, you're okay?"

"I'm more than okay." I reached up and smoothed his collar. I wanted to tell him, *I started it, remember?* Instead, I looked him in the eye. "And how's Daddy doing?"

He looked at the ground, flushed positively scarlet, then flashed a relieved smile. "He's just fine."

We hugged again. We drew apart slowly and I dropped the clover charm in his shirt pocket. "There."

"What's this for?"

"Luck."

He patted his pocket. "Well, I can always use more of that."

12

IF YOU ASK ME, EQUINE THERAPY is the ultimate form of stress relief. On a quest for a little artist's retreat, the painter and her paint horse took off from Red Hill in the hazy afternoon, saddlebags loaded with a pencil box, a watercolor board, photos of Shane McGurk—the subject in question, and plenty of water for me and my dog to drink. The sky was tinged smoky gray from wildfires raging down in Larimer County. They'd brought in volunteer firemen from as far away as Idaho and as the blaze edged toward a fancy mountaintop development, there was talk of evacuation.

But here it was just another hot, dry day. We were a half-mile away from Vedauwoo, my favorite part of Medicine Bow National Forest. I looked up the road. Often trunk-to-tail with RVs this time of year, the two-lane was almost empty. Much in the way that you'd crave to open up a Ferrari on the Autobahn, the siren's call of curving asphalt proved too much to resist. I gave Tad a loose rein and we galloped right down the middle of Happy Jack Road, Homer bounding behind. Soothed by the rhythm of the ride, I savored the gift of this day, the chance to work in solitude, the basic animal truth of loyalty. The important things in life. Values you don't learn through formal education.

Even though my marks were poor due to the Dad situation, I did enjoy school and admired the smart kids. Shawna had skipped a grade, but by the time we met at CSU, we both pretty much regarded all non-art classes as time-killers between trips to the Visual Arts Building. We did try to broaden our minds, though. In our American Poetry class, the professor started the semester with a Louise Bogan quote: "Women have no wilderness in them." When he read that, Shawna kicked the back of my molded plastic chair.

Is it true women contain no wilderness, or do they just have singular means of expressing it? Even my mother, in her sophisticated way, cultivated a wild streak. She took tremendous pleasure in teaching me how to jump horses—our best times were spent working Dish and Tad inside the ring. She was a patient and keenly sensitive instructor. Easter Sunday when I was thirteen, she set up some low PVC jumps and we went through the basics, even though a spring squall had blown through the night before. My dad showed up on the deck covered in April snow, waving his arms. "Hey, missus, I think the ham is done!" Fifteen minutes later, there he was again. "Rae, I smell something burning!"

When my mother was satisfied with my progress, we gave the horses heaping scoops of sweet feed for a job well done, stamped the mucky slush from our boots, and went inside. She turned off the oven and set the perfect clove-studded ham on the counter trivet, the meat gleaming under brown sugar glaze. Uncle Dee, Aunt Goody, me, and my dad were gathered around the table in the dining nook, napkins on our laps, waiting. Jace had been excused from the festivities. He'd packed up his recurve bow and Mossy Oak camo, and disappeared into the Sierra Madres to catch the close of black bear season. Mom brought out the roasted new potatoes and green beans with slivered almonds first, then the rolls and a pitcher of ice water. After a brief but poignant absence, she emerged from the kitchen bearing the Easter ham ringed with her first-place equitation ribbons instead of pineapple slices. When my mother set down the china platter with that big ol' ham wreathed in royal blue right in front of my dad, he put down his carving set and said, "I see your point, Raelynn."

Just inside the dirt road turnoff for Vedauwoo was a short span of split rail fence, maybe eighteen inches high. I adjusted my seat and said to Tad. "What do you say, sweet girl? How's about you and me kick up some trouble?" She'd seen the fence before I had and fairly danced with anticipation. She picked up the pace at my subtle cue and I felt her front hooves lift off. No wilderness in women? *Dubious,* I thought as Tad sailed cleanly over that silly little fence.

"Earthborn spirits." That's what Vedauwoo means in Arapahoe, and I loved it here, for it was impossible to be in a bad mood in such a silly and majestic place. Ten square miles of weathered Sherman granite, the Vedauwoo formation is an array of slabs, pedestal rocks, and honey-colored loaf-like formations. Native Americans thought playful spirits piled up the all the rocks, and you could believe it, because they made a random and comical setting, like any minute, the Road Runner might come whipping by, followed by Wile E. Coyote and his latest Acme gadget. I tied off Tad high on the trunk of a young aspen and sat cross-legged on a flat rock.

A good painting starts with a good sketch, and a satisfactory sketch can take fifteen minutes or three weeks. But more often than not, it's the fast ones that contain the crucial spark that says "keeper." Once I have a sketch I like, the painting part is like dessert, plunging into the decadent world of cadmium yellow, sleeping beauty turquoise, quinacridone violet, rose madder, and lunar earth. On paper or canvas, watercolor or acrylic, imposto or wash, it doesn't matter. Color is the reward. Forget rubies, hashish, trips to Paris, designer purses. The ultimate indulgence for me would be unlimited tubes of Daniel Smith paint. I clipped a profile shot of Shane McGurk to the upper right corner of the watercolor board, slid a piece of paper under my hand, and started in with my graphite pencil.

After weeks of artist's block, my hand felt steady and sure. Maybe I'd never make the big bucks like Shawna but this was *it* for me. No mind for the percolating summer heat, just the cool paste of creation. When it flows, it's like there's a hint of the divine in what I do, as if God's got my output on the agenda.

I paused and scratched my ankle. There was a mosquito bite right in the middle of my tattoo, which had healed beautifully. I was more in love every time I looked at it, the dense red of the heart, the spiked perfection of the barbed wire. Shawna was right that I'd get the itch for another body mod. I could feel the urge gaining strength in the back of my mind.

Homer parked himself at my feet, barking at prairie dogs and snapping at flies. He was a good boy; even the workers at the pound were crazy about him. They'd had him for a long time before I took him home. *A little gray in the muzzle and*, pfft, *they trade 'em in for a pup.* My horse and my dog. Them, plus my pain-in-the-butt brother were all the family I needed. *Need* seemed like a lot of pressure to put on any other kind of relationship, too knotty a connection to another person, and an unnecessary complication at this stage of my life. Best to count on keeping associations light for now. Detach. Detach.

Seriously, Daryl, you're too good for this buckeye crap. There he was, Tiny Alex sitting on my shoulder, judging me when I was halfway through my sketch. His negative influence would have been easier to refute if he were some blundering hack, but Alex was an excellent writer. An essay he'd published in *A*, the school literary journal, about the effects of suburban living on the artist's soul, drew me to him in the first place. We went out for greasy pad Thai, split a big bottle of Singha, and talked for hours about politics and art, the intellectual bond florid and fast, which was why, when it came, the loss of his respect had such a lasting sting.

I moved down to Denver after graduation because I needed to

lose myself in the chaos and the press of bodies. But this part of Wyoming showed up more and more in my painting. I tried other things—still lifes of fruit, urban street scenes, but I could no sooner change the hold that this land had on me than I could change my own fingerprint. It was where I was from, and it would become the key subject in my work. My "personal idiom," to coin the B.F.A. lingo.

When I asked Alex why he thought landscape seemed like a waste of my talent, he said, "It's so *sentimental*." Sentimental. The ultimate dirty bomb. Even a simple country girl could recognize the affront, even if I couldn't rebut it.

I hated the approval-seeking part of me that rose up whenever Alex was in one of his critic's moods, the girl at the front of the class, hand raised, *pick me*. Alex and I were too alike, a couple of junior talents hooked to the towrope of artistic aspiration. If I pulled ahead, he'd resent being left behind. He was a serious writer after all, and what were horses and grasses and mountains compared to weighty matters like suburban ennui?

One work of mine that Alex truly appreciated was a series of ink drawings of a galloping horse that I did on brown grocery sacks because I didn't have the funds for my beloved Arches paper. I bound the dozen bags together with white twine, making an oversized flip book motion study that I called, *Eadweard Muybridge Goes to Safeway—or—Locomotion in Fifteen Items or Less*. It was the ironic title that got him. He liked my art in air quotes.

I mentally pictured dangling Tiny Alex out the window of a speeding train, his little legs slicing the air in terror, and started sketching the outline of a roughstock silhouette, ignoring the chilling pain in my forearm. Where was the real Alex now, I wondered. Deeply immersed in archaeological study, no doubt.

Alex had Jen, but now, I had J.W. The whole thing seemed sort of ridiculous at first, but most of the time I found the differences between us relaxing. We weren't jostling for space on the same rung of life's ladder, and J.W. didn't know enough about art to fashion any kind of estimation of merit, only that he was—and he really said this—"plum tickled" by what I did. I still hadn't told him about my day job at the Twin Pines, but why should I? A touch of mystery is a compliment to a relationship, really. Especially a relationship like ours that was built so much on the huggy-kissy. That was what it was, just the chemical surge of infatuation. A summer fling. Though I was glad no one was around in the big park to see it, I hugged myself a little at the thought.

There were so many attractive things about J.W., I could make a list: Smart. Polite. Hard working. Thoughtful. Devastating eyes and brilliant hands. Plus, he was so clean—meticulous to a fault, really. Why does every starry-eyed hack describe cowboys as "rugged?" J.W. wasn't rugged. Something about him was smooth as bone, almost elegant. He was Christian, too, but not straight-laced. Like me, he dithered with religious practice but was smart enough to keep an eye toward shore. And like me, he was not inured to fleshly temptation.

I recalled him turning over in the sheets that first night at his apartment, reaching for me in the dark. He was hungry, but there was gentleness to him, too. I couldn't remember a second when he wasn't smiling his shy little smile. And those thin lips gave some thick, syrupy kisses. Once the reserved shell of him fell away, he became like another person. In his clothes, he smelled like aftershave and starch, but up close and naked, his scent was more primitive. Private, like hot fern and skin. The monitored speech gave way and his voice dropped to a knowing whisper, his drawl slow and loose and pure redneck. He wasn't so refined underneath it all.

He clearly cared whether he satisfied me or not and enjoyed the hell out of it when he did. A stark contrast to Alex who, despite his best efforts, made going down on me feel like a pity fuck delivered by mouth. There's not a woman on earth who wants oral sex to be a mission of mercy, and you can always tell.

I closed my eyes at the memory of J.W. shouldering in, his soft lips blooming open, tongue a swipe of warm velvet as he tried a slow, exploratory lick. "Sweet," he'd whispered to himself, then melded his mouth to me like, *Damn, I need this*. It was something he craved, not the due diligence of an all right guy.

I could itemize what was wrong with J.W., too: So much older than me. Divorced. A dad. Nothing I'd judge him for, but nothing I was set up to handle, either.

A crush is great when there's nothing better to do, but when the clock is ticking it's a deadly distraction. I looked down at the sketch in my lap. Homer swiveled his head when I groaned. It wasn't Shane's form taking shape on the page, but J.W.'s. Maybe God didn't have an agenda, but he had a sense of humor, sure enough.

I came back to the house to find my aunt Goody on the porch with her Irish wolfhound, Shooter, curled at her feet. When I stepped down from the truck, she raised her arms, the tanned flesh loose on her lean biceps. "You can't visit your crazy aunt the whole summer?" Homer did an ecstatic jig as she dug her short nails into his fur and scrubbed. She stood and breathed deeply. "I love that sweet timothy your mother planted there in the shade. The smell is like new hay."

When Goody came to Cheyenne thirty years ago to work as a nanny for the governor's family, she found the high plains vistas comforting and decided to stay. She developed a foreigner's fanaticism for rodeo, and never missed a perf when Frontier Days rolled around. Uncle Dee was mugging in the wild horse race one year and saw her at a picnic table eating a coconut-topped candy apple in her hot pants and cork-heeled sandals. From that moment on, they were inseparable. No shining example of Scandinavian reserve, she matched Dee drink for drink, flirt for flirt, and slap for slap. They lived like a pair of hell-raising turtledoves until the January night when Dee, coming home in a closing-time blizzard, tried to sneak his Suburban around the roadblock and spun into a ditch. When the phone rang and Goody said that Dee hadn't come home, my dad and Jace went exploring in the frigid pre-dawn and found him ten miles down Happy Jack, frozen to death in the front seat, clutching a schnapps bottle as if drawing warmth from it.

"Sorry, G. I'm a bad niece, I know." I hugged her, her graying blond hair blowing around me in a tickling aureole perfumed with rosemary and lavender. She held me at arm's length. "Something's going on with you. Something big. Tell me!"

Unlike my mother, who observed me to see how closely I matched her reflection, Goody viewed me as a friend. I'd already convinced her that J.W. and I were just buddies, but her mischievous smile could unlock me in an instant so I leaned down and started pulling weeds from between the porch steps. "Same old. Except that I have my very first commissioned portrait due in exactly two weeks and I've made *exactly* no progress on it."

"Someone's buying a portrait from you! It's fabulous! Why don't you tell me these things?" She pushed her hair off her face. "Well, let me feed my not-so-starving artist. Half the dudes I've got this week are vegetarian and I made too many meatballs. You'll come over for supper."

I was grateful for the invitation. Even lone wolves hate dinner alone. The dudes were out on the sunset trail ride, so I helped Goody set the table, then we had strawberry lemonade in the great-room by the enormous stone hearth. I examined the library she stocked with Western books and periodicals for the guests. She had an extensive collection of *ProRodeo Sports News*.

I knelt in front of the low shelf. "Goody, you got any older issues of *Sports News*? Like from ten-fifteen years ago?"

"Sure." She pushed up from the wing chair. "In storage. Let me get them for you."

I waited on the lodgepole couch topped with leather cushions. The room was furnished with so many sticks and twigs it felt like being in a bird's nest. The mantel was a shrine to my uncle Dee—his antique silver revolver, a photo of him with one of Goody's laying hens tucked under his arm like a football, his spinning rope with the brass honda, their wedding portrait, the newlyweds kissing with cake-smeared faces. I asked Goody once if she ever thought of dating any of the men who called to see if she needed help with the guest ranch, anything at all. She said, "If one of those gigolos shows up on my porch, I will chase him off with a broom." No, in her heart it was settled—Dee or going solo. Sometimes when I'm out with the horses, I see her up on the rise tying fresh flowers to his cross.

Goody pulled the magazines from the storage closet and handed the cedar-scented stack to me. *"Var sa gout."*

I dug through the pile until I found the issue when J.W. won the Finals. There he was on the cover. "Not Just Whistlin' Dixie: J.W. Jarrett Bucks His Way to Bareback Crown." He appeared walled-off, almost arrogant, his bulked-up build suggesting a bull elk with a swollen neck, ready to lock antlers. He was sexier now, more approachable-looking. The difference, I supposed, was that back then he looked like a man with something to prove, and now, twelve years later, he'd proven it.

I opened to the center spread. On the left side, a full-page photo of his title-clinching ride, free arm stiff in his signature style, floated under a pull quote in red: "I knew that as long as I had the good Lord on my side, I could do whatever it took to win." The right side was a column of text and a portrait of the God-fearing champion, eyes bright as his brand-new gold buckle and the brand-new pair of brass *cojones* that rounded out the ensemble.

I turned the page and there she was. Melissa. Mrs. Gold Buckle, right by her husband's side, hands clasped proprietarily on his shoulder. My heart raced as I inspected the photo. She was lovely—I knew she would be—with dark hair and long, slender fingers, one graced with a decent-sized rock, thank you very much. Though the picture was small, I could see her eyes were a startling "gotcha" blue. I was sort of grossed out by their matching button-down shirts, but visually, as a couple they made sense.

Goody came up behind me. "What'd you find?"

I shut the magazine. "Nothing." There, next in the pile, was an issue with J.W. and Duff Linsey on the cover. "Blood Brothers: Roughstock's Friendly Family Feud."

I tore through the pages and skimmed quickly when I found the article. J.W. had come into the Finals that year fourth place in the bareback, Duff in second, and eleventh in bull riding, hoping for a shot at the all-around. The brothers were separated by just a couple thousand dollars in the ninth round of bareback, then during the final go, Duff missed his mark-out and J.W. got the title. A quote from gracious loser Duff: "J.W. is one of the most consistent bareback riders going. My older brother isn't my competition; he's my inspiration." There was a montage of the two of them together at junior rodeos, and a photo of them wearing buckles that they'd swapped when they won their respective rounds at the Finals on the same night.

I showed Goody the article. "Do you remember when this happened?"

"Oh, J.W. Jarrett and Duff Linsey. That was a big deal. Duff didn't think the missed mark-out was fair so he quit rodeo after that and moved out to Hollywood. He even stopped speaking to J.W., saying he might have bribed the judges."

I started sifting through the magazines. "Is that in any of these?"

"No," she laughed. "This is rodeo, not like the big-time sports. They don't print scandals. Only the good stuff. But at the time, it was all anybody talked about."

"First I've heard of it."

Goody gathered up the magazines and fixed them in a pile. "It goes fast, Daryl, and people forget. Faster than you can imagine."

13

ON JULY FIRST, COWBOY CHRISTMAS EVE, I sat on J.W.'s couch, watching him siphon health supplements into glassine envelopes. He'd already starched his shirts and ironed the creases into his jeans. He had the exacting routine of someone leading a monastic life. The apartment had a still feeling, like the air was rarely stirred by visitors. I wondered if I didn't represent a break in a celibate stretch.

Spread out on the living room table were five days' worth of multivitamins, minerals, and gel capsules of fish oil. He put one of each into an envelope, sealed it, and put it into his toiletry kit. A small assortment of prescription bottles was clustered on the table.

I leaned back and rested my elbow on a pillow. "Now that we're here, I guess we should discuss the weekend ahead. I don't want to get in your way. In fact, I've got plenty to keep me occupied, so I'll cut you a deal. We'll each make work our priority. Art first for me. Rodeo for you." Pleased with my pronouncement, I felt like a pulp fiction heroine, the sophisticated lady artist steering toward a throwaway affair with a hot cowboy.

"Sounds good, Daryl. It's a deal."

J.W. clicked off the television and we sat side by side looking at his photo albums. There were dozens of photos of Troy. J.W.

pointed to one when he was just minutes old, his confused, mushed-up face, head lumpy like a soft orange in a blue knit cap. "When he was born, his whole arm was as long as my hand."

As we flipped through, I noticed there were no wedding pictures. No ex, period.

We came to a snapshot of a dark-haired wild child on a pony, grinning like a devil. I pointed. "Who's this gorgeous little squirt?"

"Beeber."

"Wow. You've known him that long?"

"You bet."

When he tried to bypass a page with a teenage J.W. in a black tuxedo and cowboy hat, I slapped the album open. "Prom! Oh my God, you look so cute!" He stood proud as a young lord next to his date seated in a large wicker peacock chair. The girl had her hair on top of her head in a bouffant bun, her red dress so ruffled she looked like a lasagna. Her corsage went halfway to her elbow. "Who was your date?"

"Tracy Mulvaney. My first love."

I liked that his first love was a Tracy. Good name. No fuss. I could tell by looking at this Tracy girl that she knew horses.

"Boy, I tell you what, I went all out—took her to dinner, got a limo, bought her a gold necklace. Prom was a huge deal back in Georgia."

"I can see that. Love the red tie and matching hatband."

J.W. nudged my ribs. "Your prom pictures are probably just as embarrassing. I bet you still looked pretty, though."

"I didn't go to the prom." I turned to the next page.

"Why not? Don't tell me nobody asked you."

"Somebody asked me. I didn't go to the prom because I couldn't afford a dress."

"Damn, Daryl. I didn't know." He was making this soft face at me that I just hated.

"J.W., that was years ago. Who cares?"

* * *

The next afternoon, I sat on the curb in front of J.W.'s, hands folded and knees together like I was in a reception area, waiting to interview for an important job. I'd act right and clean up nice, just like my mother raised me to. The stand-up-straight-and-smile ritual of our family trips to the rodeo is so deeply ingrained in me that to this day when I hear the "Star Spangled Banner," I tuck in my shirt.

Even though I could chalk this trip up to research, I felt guilty for going. I'd left my cell phone number for Gwatney and a detailed list of chores for the hands at the Little Wyo, so nothing would slip through the cracks. I calculated the exact number of days until Shane's birthday—only thirteen to go. Not nearly time enough to waste this way. But, I rationalized, if I took a few days off I could rest my hand. And no rodeo research opportunity should go wasted, right?

That last person I'd discussed it with was Jace. "And who will you be traveling with? That Grits and Gravy fella?"

"Yeah, and a bunch of his buddies will be there, too."

"Will any of their girlfriends be going?"

"I don't think so, no."

"Are you sure you wanna do that?" His disapproval was palpable.

A black-and-silver Dodge dually, half the length of a downtown block and fitted with a Capri camper top, rounded the corner and purred to a stop. From the passenger side stepped Brandon Drew, tugging the cuffs of his Wranglers over the tops of his Lucchese boots. Brandon, famous as a state politician's kid who could take on any bronc, wore his clothes and burgeoning celebrity with equal finesse. He snapped his heels together and saluted J.W. "Hey, Jarhead."

"Hey, Boo Boo. I'd like you to meet Daryl."

Brandon looked at me from under his 20X beaver hat. Slender, with dark hair and palm-green eyes with long black lashes, he had the hygienic, oddly sexless sex appeal of a singer in a boy band. On his nose was a small scar shaped like a lucky seven from a fight after dancing with the wrong girl at Crabby's Bar in Pendleton. Always quoted in the press as stressing that rodeo cowboys are genuine athletes, he had a reputation so clean you could serve Sunday dinner on it. Totaling a rented Corvette at the Finals last year was the only ding in his reputation, but he blew clean, so the incident was chalked up to youthful exuberance. He helped load our bags into the truck with the cheerful ease of a kid who never had to make his own bed.

The driver's side door slammed, heralding the arrival of Clete "Mad Man" Maddex, a cowboy notoriously short in stature and long on opinion. Clete had a huge black mustache pointed with wax, thick eyebrows, and a mouth like a split knuckle. Hard to believe that before scaling back to the Mountain Circuit, this five-foot-mumble ball of aggression had won the World three times.

He gawped at J.W. and slapped the heel of his palm to his forehead. "Christ on a pogo stick, Jarhead, you get uglier every time I see you."

J.W. sucked his teeth and snorted affectionately. "You're one to talk, Clete. Everyone knows you only wear that hat to cover your horns."

Clete pulled in his stomach and held in his waist with his hands. "I like to think I possess a certain inner beauty." He actually sounded a little wounded. He pivoted and jabbed his blocky hand at me. "I'm Clete." He squeezed pretty hard.

I squeezed back harder. "Clete, sure. Ninety points at Deadwood last year, right?" Eager to make a favorable first impression, I'd pored over the boys' stats online.

"None other." He straightened, obviously flattered. He sniffed the air deeply. "So, you're the *artiste*. Well, welcome to the exciting world of rodeo. It's a thrill a minute, if you couldn't already tell. Not sure why you want to do this, but welcome aboard."

"I'm ready to get rugged."

"Hey, you're not in for rugged with this crew. There are eight trips to the Finals between the three of us. We're pros. We travel different."

"Like how?"

Clete hitched his foot up on the bumper. "Well, every night about sundown, we set up camp under the stars. Tell stories, take out a guitar, maybe sing a little. Then one of us rolls out of his rack at the crack of dawn, gets a fire going, and whips up a big breakfast on our old camp stove. Flapjacks and buttermilk biscuits from scratch, scrambled eggs, potatoes, mess of sausages. It's a gourmet deal."

J.W. came around the side of the truck with his stuffed-full rigging bag. "Don't forget the fresh-squeezed orange juice and cappuccino."

I looked at them. "Are you serious?"

That's when they started laughing. Brandon had to press his lower lip in with his fingers to keep his tobacco from falling out. "She don't have no idea."

J.W. wiped his eyes. "What did we have for breakfast last day we were out together? When we were hell bent to get to Steamboat in time? I think a couple of us fought over the day-old hot dogs at the Seven-eleven."

Clete said, "I had a bear claw and coffee that purt near took the shine off my beautiful teeth."

Brandon chuckled. "I finished off a cup of Wendy's chili that was on the backseat. Remember?"

Clete snorted. "Shit yes, we remember. We had to ride home with the windows down because you were farting like a sick wizard."

J.W. held up his hand. "Fellas, please, there's a lady present."

Clete raised his satanic eyebrows at me. "Well, Miss Girly Girl, I hope you brought some smelling salts, because the road's no place for ladies."

The Greeley arena was big and bulky, like a concrete tub. I couldn't get to the back of the chutes with the guys, so I took a companion pass and found an empty seat up near the top of the stands. I could see the carnival rides blinking as the sun set, the mingled odor of popcorn and horse manure thick around me. I rolled the day sheet in my hands. Through the grand entry and anthem, there was a mounting tension, something pulling at my insides.

When it was J.W.'s turn, he got down in the chute carefully, like he was lowering himself into a hot bath. A couple guys helped him get ready. The stock contractor came along to check the setup. It seemed to be taking forever. I was nervous, my toes tapping, my lips dry, everything in me *en point* and on guard. *Please*, I prayed, *let this go well*.

Finally, the grate cracked wide and he came flying into the arena on a haunchy gray named Unforgiven. The horse circled back to the left and sunfished in front of the chutes. The crowd was a distant roar, the announcer a nattering hum. All I could hear was my heart rattling, strained to breaking against its cage. J.W. made the whistle and got an eighty-one. It was like no other ride I'd ever watched. I was shocked that I took it so personally.

J.W. climbed up and sat on the fence, watching the other riders with acute concentration as he rolled up his sleeves and pulled the tape from his left arm. His chest heaved and sweat streaked his cheeks. He licked his lips and spit vigorously. There wasn't a trace of his usual cool in evidence. Maybe, I thought, his placidity was site-specific, or maybe it was just a lie he was particularly good at telling.

Amped on adrenaline, I raced down the steps and left the arena to meet J.W. before the round even finished. I bought a bag of cookies and found a seat near the concrete mouth of the contestant's entrance. When J.W. came strolling around the corner of the medical trailer, I leapt up. "Hey, pretty spurs, you want an elephant ear?"

"Too shaky just yet. Thanks, though." He put his arm around my shoulders. The tips of his fingers trembled hot against my skin. "Let me get the buzz out of my arm, then we'll go eat cotton candy and ride the Ferris wheel until we puke."

When we were up in the air looking down on the whirl and flash of the midway, I congratulated J.W. on his good score.

"Why, thank you. Looks like I won the round."

"Awesome! I didn't know."

"Yep. Means we'll have to come back down here on the fourth for the short go, then get a little plane up to Cody, but heck, that's all right. First time in a while my feet have felt that good." He sniffed the night air, sweet with diesel fumes and burnt sugar. "I've got reason to believe my luck's changing for the better."

"What makes you think that?"

He tipped his head and looked at me, the orange and yellow Ferris wheel lights blinking against his skin.

I held out the bag of elephant ears. He took one.

We left Greeley early, the sun dithering behind morning haze, aiming to make Red Lodge, Montana, by three. We passed fields of wild daisies and fluffy hay rolls patchworked around glimmering office parks that rose from wide aprons of asphalt. A five-hundred-mile trek ahead of us, Clete jostled the radar detector to life and set cruise control at ninety-five miles per hour.

North of Cheyenne, the landscape smoothed to yellow grass and dry creek beds, yielding shortly to a hundred-plus miles of sun-scalded oblivion, hawks circling on updrafts overhead. Countless bugs met their juicy demise against the windshield, protein-rich chunks that stuck to the glass no matter how hard Clete leaned on the wiper-fluid button. After breakfast, I insisted on driving, the guys laughing when they saw how far up I had to pull the seat to reach the pedals. I punched the radio buttons and found a station playing "Funkytown." I looked at Brandon, my co-pilot. He gestured his approval.

Twenty seconds later the back curtain parted and Clete's head poked out from the camper, like Jack Nicholson axing his way through the door in *The Shining*. "What are you doing?"

I called over my shoulder. "I believe we're getting funky, Clete."

"Not in my truck, you're not."

I turned down the radio. "I thought if I was driving, I got to play whatever I wanted."

"No. This truck is not a democracy." His disappeared behind the curtain.

From the backseat, J.W. glanced apologetically at me in the rearview mirror, shook his head, and went back to his *Sports Illustrated*.

They say that rodeo is like one big family. It is. And just like your real family, when you spend too much time with them, you become homicidal. I wasn't about to say anything, but I was rapidly growing weary of Clete. He was so damn bossy.

At Red Lodge, we shopped for a late lunch at the Beartooth IGA. While we waited for sandwiches at the deli counter, J.W. pulled an iced tea out of the cooler and pressed speed dial on his cell phone. "Hey, Troy! Happy birthday, buddy." . . . "We're gonna fish when I get home, right?" . . . "Well, yeah, we'll sleep in the truck like we always do, *dos caballeros*."

I opened a *Rolling Stone* while Brandon flipped through *Maxim*. "Does his son ever travel with you?"

"Oh, yeah. We've got T-bone with us most of the time, but his mom wouldn't let him come at all this month. She was mad that the last time J.W. had him he kept Troy a night more than he was scheduled for."

I put the magazine back on the rack. That was the night J.W. and Troy were at my house.

The phone chirped and J.W. exchanged brief unpleasantries with the female caller while looking over the August page in his date book. He hung up and joined us, neck stiff and shoulders pinched as if he swung from a hanger, full of starch.

I inspected the selection of tortilla chips, and Brandon reached toward an end display. "Oh, hey, Little Debbie snack cakes. Ain't seen them in a while." Clete pulled the paper tab on a twelve pack of cream-filled oatmeal cookies. He handed one to J.W., then dropped the open box next to the bubble gum, sandwiches, Rolaids, and a stack of Cope tins waiting at the register. J.W. bit through the cookie like he was chewing glass.

Red Lodge was a funky, down-home rodeo with a wooden arena on a flat overlooking the picturesque town, a welcome contrast to the Greeley behemoth. The white afternoon sun dappled the jagged peaks of the Beartooth Mountains.

After the boys checked in at the office to pay their entry fees and get their back numbers, the veil of focus began its descent. J.W., Clete, and Brandon grabbed their rigging bags and started getting into knee braces and Lycra compression shorts, each taping his riding arm to hold the slight bend in the elbow. They were attentive as lace tatters, lost in the minutia of the riders' rituals. J.W. was especially methodical. The nickname "Jarhead" wasn't hard to understand. Clete, not exactly a man of order, grumbled, "He's only late when he takes extra time getting that stick up his ass." J.W. tucked his shirt into his shorts and zipped the fly on his Wranglers. In a sport where guys thought it bad juju to wear yellow in the arena, throw out or even wash a lucky shirt, or eat chicken lest *you are what you eat* make them ride chicken, J.W. hewed to no superstition beyond reaching under the camper bed for his hatbox and changing into his cheap black felt hat.

When they finished their preparations, we started our walk toward the chutes. Around us, kids were practicing, spurring hay bales and roping Coleman coolers. We passed the farrier's trailer, noses twitching at the sweaty metal smell of welding flux and hoof cuttings. In their chaps and immaculate pressed shirts with back numbers pinned on, the men looked imposing. I watched everybody watching us, the *tink* of spurs calling cadence as we passed. I looked at J.W., the thin blade of his nose in profile, the blue of his eyes seeming to deepen in concentration. Shoulders erect and that proud chin. I knew I was supposed to be observing for research purposes but when I saw him like this, I had to admit my interest was more than academic.

After seeing J.W. ride—eighty points, second place after Clete's eighty-two, Brandon bucked off at three seconds—there wasn't much for me to do except wait for the guys and sketch. I noticed they had milkshakes and floats at the refreshment stand, so I bought J.W. a vanilla shake.

I couldn't find J.W. but Brandon was leaning on the fence, talking to Trav Carlsson. "You should've seen this lady who came around looking for J-dub. She had on this itty-bitty red top and the biggest, bounciest—"

Trav coughed and made a *hey-now* with his eyes. Brandon turned around. "Oh, hello, Daryl."

"You seen J.W.?"

Brandon veered into my path. "Um, no." He was steering me away from the catch pen. J.W. was there, talking to a woman with tousled blond hair down to her waist. She was built like a Coke bottle—long neck, long torso, and big breasts. Their interaction had an air of unease mixed with familiarity.

When I walked over, J.W. stiffened. He forced a genial sweep of his arm. "Taffy, this is Daryl. Daryl, this here's Taffy. She's an old friend."

I knew in that instant that they'd Done It. I didn't know which bothered me more, that J.W. had been intimate with this woman, or that he'd been intimate with a woman whose name was, of all things, Taffy.

Taffy had freckles under peach cover-up and friendly crinkles at the corner of her eyes. I imagined cookies sent on J.W.'s birthday and "Thinking of You" cards throughout the year. She seemed perfectly pleasant and otherwise worthy of a swift kick in the shins.

My stomach clenched to a tight fist. "Well, I'll leave you two to catch up."

J.W. moved in, panicked. "That's not necessary. Taffy here was just leaving." Taffy didn't budge, just smiled bemusedly, squared her shoulders so her breasts jiggled, and blinked her glued-on lashes. She gave off a distinct city vibe. Probably had a great job managing a bank or a real estate office in Billings or Missoula, spent weekdays in suits with tastefully low-cut blouses that showed off her long neck, and only ran with the bunnies a couple weekends a year.

"I hate to break up a happy reunion," I said, backing away. I raised the milkshake. "Catch you later."

Taffy waved with a phony fizz of a laugh. "Nice to meet you, *Darren*."

Given the circumstances, I said the only thing I could say. "And it was nice meeting you, *Tammy*." I walked away palming the waxed paper cup, my hand covered in a cold sweat of condensation. I sucked down the top layer of melted vanilla. Naïve. Damn, I'm naïve. He hadn't been celibate; he gets it to go. What did I expect? The guy knew what he was doing; skill isn't a product of luck. So he got around a little. It was interesting. Well, it was something.

Bucking horses and bulls were eating hay in the maze of stock pens. I sat on a rust-freckled step and watched them nose around. Maybe Taffy-types were like roaches—for every one you saw, tight pants, false eyelashes and all—there were dozens scurrying just out of view. That J.W. had hooked up with such a class act made me feel both better and worse about him. I wished suddenly for some lipstick, a troweling of foundation, but nothing would bring me to a Taffy level of sophistication. Paint or no paint, I was destined to suffer the needling tyranny of cute. What was he doing with me anyway? Was I a new flavor in his assortment of females, some ragamuffin speedbump with kitchen-sink highlights he brought along to break up the long hours on the road?

I had no right to judge, really, given that I was essentially rebounding my way across three states in his company, but I couldn't help myself. I wondered if he said the same things to her as he did to me. I wondered how creative she got with those monstrous boobs. I wondered if she swallowed.

I threw out the milkshake.

Kimber was in the tanning bed when I called. Against the hum of UV lights, she sounded irritated. "What, you meet a girl he dated and now you're convinced he lays more pipe than a union plumber?" She sighed. "He's been single a long time. It's reasonable that there'd be women around him."

"I'm a long way from reasonable right now, Kimber."

"I know, baby. I know. But remember, you're a bona fide cute young thing. I'm sure the shiny bright veterans aren't happy to see you, either. It'd be different if you were some worn-out bar skank."

Kimber does love the word "skank." I hate the very shape of it, harpooning from someone's mouth. See a woman you want to take down, open up, and *skank!,* there's blood in the water.

"Tell you what," she said. "If you want to test him, stay away for a while. Watch the bull riding or sit and draw or whatever. You'll know you've got him if he comes looking for you. If he didn't care, he'd make you come to him."

"How'd you get so smart about men?"

"I'm a bartender. I'm a walking index on human nature. Oh, listen, speaking of . . . If you go to the bars with J.W. at any point during the weekend, make sure of one thing—"

"What's that?"

"Whenever you two arrive someplace, you go in the door first." I heard the creak of the tanning bed as she shifted. "So, you'll never guess who I took out for a spin last night."

"Shock me."

"That kid Beeber."

"You're shitting me."

"Shit you not. He came into the Wigwam when I was shooting pool and I said if he won two out of three, he could take me to Sanfords, and one thing led to another. For a youngster, he's quite a talent. Maybe it's all that time he spends taming animals." Kimber chuckled devilishly.

A Kimber-Beeber alliance. When I hung up, I had an awful feeling about it.

Half an hour later, J.W. found me stepping from the ladies' room. "I was about to send out a search party." He draped his arm around my shoulder, hand dangling from the thick wrist, relaxed. The sun struck his copper bracelet and a dull rose-colored reflection the size of a dime winked on my breastbone. He handed over his beer so I could take a sip, then led me to a group of friends and introduced me. A new-dad saddle bronc rider was passing out cigars and a photo of an infant bundled in pink and bows. J.W. tilted the picture my way. "She's a real pretty baby, don't you think?"

The father beamed. I stood assured.

After the rodeo, we left to bunk with Clete's cousin, Big Sue. We eased to the outskirts of town and pulled up to a redbrick Victorian with a wide front porch and a terraced cupola. In a dilapidated corral out back, two lumpish sorrels and a swayback blue roan were slurping at a metal trough. Big Sue stood on the porch, watering big hanging baskets of geraniums, the collar of her oversize striped workshirt fluttering in the hot breeze.

Clete stuck his head out the window. "Hey, dog breath!"

Big Sue, broad through both shoulder and hip, thudded the green plastic watering can on the porch railing. "Hey, asshole!"

When we were introduced, she looked me up and down. "Good grief, you're just pocket-sized, aren't you? Well, how do, Little Peanut."

I went ahead to take my bags into the house. Sue smacked J.W.'s arm. "You remember to bring her baby blanket?"

Sue had prepared an Italian feast, breaded cutlets and pasta, which we ate in the company of her silent husband, Tim. She forked extra salad around the two stuffed shells arranged primly on her plate.

J.W. sawed into his cutlet and wound cheese around his fork. "Sue, I can help Tim with that boiler problem if you want."

Sue put a pitcher of tea on the table. "That's why I like you guys staying here. Two days ago, Wendell Pagan came through here with a bunch of his boys and left it looking like a tornado hit. Which leads me to say that if you bastards clog my toilet, fix it yourself. Plunger's by the can. And if you bring a girl over, tell her to stay the hell out of my collectible perfumes."

I could see why the guys loved Big Sue. What made her appealing was the obvious fact that she didn't give a red-hot damn. She'd seen it all and done it twice.

The guys cleared the table and I helped Sue with the dishes. She handed me a khaki dish towel. "You sure put a kick in J.W.'s step. What've you been mixing into his feed?"

"What do you mean?" I ran the towel around a plate rim.

"Shoot, I haven't seen him this happy in years. He got so serious after a while." She drizzled soap in the marinara-crusted baking dish. "He used to be buck wild, hell, we all were. If Tim knew half my stories, I'd still be single. J.W. and Clete, my God, they could shut down a bar at night and finish first and second the next day. J.W. was cocky, but in a way that made you think it was because he couldn't believe all that good luck was his, so he had to parade it around like a kid trying on his dad's shoes."

The hot, soapy water felt good on my wrist. "What changed?"

Sue shook her head and smiled. "We got old, I guess! As for J.W. personally, I don't know—Troy, getting divorced, all that tedious grown-up stuff. Women seem to weather those things better than men. We're wired for upheaval, I suppose." Long past the town-to town rodeo hijinx, Sue's wild ways had burned off and left her a knowing, welcoming woman. But just how wild was Sue back then, I wondered.

As if reading my mind, Sue said, "Oh, don't worry. J.W. and I never . . ." She cracked up at the thought. "He liked 'em slim and glammed up and prettified," (Taffy fit the profile, I noted) "and at the time, I liked 'em stocky and raw and mouthy." She smiled at the thought of silent Tim. "So there was not one smidge of attraction. He's as much a relative to me as Clete. Anyway, I'm glad to see him with someone down to earth. It's what he needs, not some fancy little miss who can't open her own pudding cup."

J.W. was in the basement with Tim. Clete and Brandon tossed a football in the yard with a half-dozen other cowboys who had just pulled up. Sue walked around the yard, passing the hat. Board and laundry were free, but she appreciated money for her grocery bill, which swelled considerably during rodeo week. She approached a thick-thighed roper named Beef. "Feel like making a contribution to the cause?"

He was tossing rope around a metal roping calf and didn't want to interrupt his practicing. "Get my wallet out of my room and I'll square you away." It was more an order than a suggestion.

Sue was astounded that someone would boss her in her own home. "Okay. Where is it?"

"In the end pocket of the black-and-green bag on the bed."

Sue called to where I was sitting on the porch swing. "C'mon, Little Peanut. You can help."

Beef had turned his corner of the room into a mess of mahogany leather rope cans, a pouch of Beech Nut, a green bottle of Excedrin on the nightstand. On the bed were two tan canvas bags, one large, like you'd use to carry your gear, the other an overnight-sized duffel. Big Sue grabbed the duffel bag. "You think he means this one?"

"Probably."

She unzipped the end pocket. "There's a mess of stuff in here. I'll bet this is it. Just a sec." She turned the bag on its back and wiggled her fingers down into the pocket. With some effort, she pulled her hand out, dislodging the contents. A surge of porn magazines came flooding forth, not just a couple, a landslide of porn, a river.

Big Sue and I stared disbelieving at the fleshy spectacle that slid onto the polyester bedspread. The glossy covers reflected the lamplight, shining like grease. The magazine on top was called *Fuck My Ass*.

We laughed until pain knifed us in the ribs. "We better put them back," I said, "Beef'll crap himself."

Big Sue crouched next to the bed, flipping through a well-thumbed copy of *Comely Coeds*. She eyeballed a layout with a tan girl holding an erect penis as if pondering it, then two pages later, the same girl smiling with clots of semen pearling on her baked-to-orange stomach. Big Sue snorted and grabbed another magazine, then another.

I sat down, picked up a *Hustler* and opened to the centerfold. The woman was lying on her back, spread so far you could see her esophagus. Her full, brown-nippled breasts jutted severely from her rib cage. "Do you think these are real?"

Big Sue inspected the photo. "Hell no, Peanut. God-given big ones don't stand that high on their own."

"There's like a dozen magazines here," I said, sifting through them. "Why would anyone need so many?"

"Maybe it's like day-of-the-week underwear, you know, oral on Monday, up the butt Tuesday."

Beef called up from the driveway. "Hey, what the hell's taking you so long?" Classic irritated male.

Big Sue poked her head out the window.

He yelled. "Did you find my wallet?"

"Nope," Big Sue yelled back. She wasn't going to let this clown off easy. "We found your porn, though!"

A hoot from Clete and Brandon cut the night air.

Big Sue looked at me and we doubled over.

"You did what?" Beef sounded like he was strangling. "You come out of there!"

"No!" Big Sue slammed the door. Fingers racing, she secured the chain. She was pink from laughing.

Seconds later, Beef tried to get into the room, cussing blue fire at the chain bolt. We could see his bulging, angry eye in the gap between the door and sill. "Let me in there, you bitch. I'll put a hurt on you. I mean it!"

Big Sue braced her back against the door, straining to get it shut, but Beef jammed his shoulder into the space behind the chain and kept yelling. Big Sue motioned for me to bring the magazines over. She tucked a bunch under her arm. Her eyes glittered. "Beef," she said calmly, "if you stop pushing on the door, I can close it enough to undo the chain."

He eased off. Big Sue shut the door, slid the chain, and stepped aside. Beef barreled into the room and grabbed at Big Sue, but she squirted past him and ran out the door. She ran down the hall to the balcony and hopped up on tiptoe at the edge, the copy of *Fuck My Ass* dangling over the railing. "You come near me, Beefy Boy, and this one's a goner."

He started toward her, pushing up his shirtsleeves. "Aw, fuck you, you stupid—"

Big Sue clucked her tongue. "Such language!" Her hands went to her hips. "That does it, Beefaroni." She whistled, two fingers in her mouth, and shouted, "Hey, everybody! Free porn!" She wound up her pitch and hurled *Fuck My Ass* as hard as she could. The magazine sailed over the balcony and landed with a papery splat on the hood of a maroon Monte Carlo. "It's raining!" she warbled not unlike an Appalachian yodeler. "It's raining porn!"

Big Sue tossed *Comely Coeds* up over the wood railing. "Wear your rubbers everybody," she sang out. "It's raining porn." Eight different magazines hit the ground, one by one, Big Sue calling out each title, from *Bad Little Babysitter* to *Kissin' Cousins*, which attracted quite a few guys from neighboring rooms. Downstairs, a dozen of them stumbled off the porch, squinting up at the balcony. Beef paced, frothing for vengeance, but he was compelled to back down. He knew he'd get no reinforcement. The cowboys on the lawn were laughing too hard.

J.W. and Tim were busy wrestling the boiler pipes so J.W. sent me off to the Bull and Bear Saloon with Clete and Brandon. I bought a rum and Coke with the twenty J.W. gave me and watched as the guy next to me groped a girl's butt so thoroughly he could count the change in her pockets.

A pert-nosed blonde at my back shook her head, her laugh like a chickadee peep. "Typical."

"You really think?"

She squeezed in beside me at the bar. "Yeah. Oh, yeah. My name's Cassie." She held out her hand, short nails painted flamingo pink. Her shirt was a cropped sports jersey, number 77. The faded cutoffs were baggy but short. She wore low-top sneakers, no socks. "Here for the rodeo?"

"Sort of. I'm traveling with someone."

"That's cool. My brother's a bull rider." She pointed to a knot-headed kid on the dance floor with two girls pressed up against him. "Your boyfriend rodeo?"

"He's not my boyfriend, but yeah."

"Husband?" She took a gulp of her draft.

"No." I had to laugh at that. "No. Just, you know . . ."

"Totally." She licked the beer foam from her upper lip. "It's better that way. You don't want to be married to one of these guys."

"Why not?"

"Because they cheat! Not on their girlfriends, but they all cheat on their wives." Cassie treated me solicitously, as one who *must be told*.

"How do you know?"

"Oh, I know." With her hand on my arm like my most staunch conspirator, she launched into a riff about which guys cheated, which girls gossiped, which wives should know better but didn't—I think there was even a saxophone solo in there—I mean, the girl went on and on.

She pointed to two sizable girls in tight pants, standing in the corner. "See them over there? The big gals?" One of them shimmered in a lavender lace top. "Those are bottom-feeders. If a guy's not hooked up by closing time, he'll glom onto a fat chick, get laid, a place to sleep, and some breakfast." She bit her stubby nails as she talked. "I'm sure the guy you're with is nice, but most of them, you can't trust for shit."

The song ended, creating an awkward pause. People tittered nervously in the silence, and somewhere close, a glass smashed against the dance floor parquet. I sipped the dregs of my watery rum and Coke though the red straw. "Hey, Cassie, you know about Cassandra's curse? From Greek myth?" I leaned meaningfully into her puzzled face. "She spoke the truth and people thought she was crazy."

The music cranked on again. She perked up and yelled over the onslaught of Hank Williams, Jr. "Cool! I like that."

"Cassie! Where you been?" The cowboy lisped through train-wreck teeth. He had a bull riding buckle and a dimpled sweet potato chin. There was a devilish tilt to his posture as he leaned back on his heels.

Cassie grabbed both his hands. "Carlos Lacerda! The Brazilian Bomber. You did *great* today!" Leading with his hips, Carlos squired her to the dance floor. She turned over her shoulder and waved frantically. "Gotta go, Daryl. Bye!"

I wandered through the crowd with a grody alkaline buzz in my head, the way I felt whenever I pigged out and ate a whole bag of Doritos for dinner. Was Cassie a truth-teller or just some random psycho-bunny? Were the things she told me what a girl could bank on—hooking up, then hoping against hope your man won't disappear down a rabbit hole?

I found Clete holding up the end of the bar. You could get Crown for a dollar until midnight. Clete had one in his hand and another at his elbow. Now and then, a girl drifted up and asked him to dance. He turned them all down.

"Clete, we're going to have to set up a triage center if you keep breaking hearts like you do."

"Possibly."

"Why isn't a guy like you married?"

"Who's to say I'm not?" He leaned his crossed arms on the bar.

"Oh."

"I'm on my way out of that one. Didn't work out so good."

"I'm sorry".

Clete sipped his drink and grimaced. "Nah, don't worry about it." He folded his napkin. His squared hands were smooth, almost pretty. "So, Daryl, you like our boy J.W., do ya?"

"Sure. He's pretty great."

"First cowboy you been with? Dating, I mean."

"Yeah, why?" I wasn't sure I liked him prying but I wanted to see where this was headed.

He nodded. "Like it?"

"So far."

"This is the fun part, isn't it?"

I looked at him.

"Most girls don't have what it takes to be with a rodeo cowboy. Sure, for a night or two, maybe a couple months. Looks real glamorous at first—you get to sit in the stands knowing you got something a lot of other girls want real bad, watch him win, maybe even travel a little bit if you want to.

"It's a choice for you, but rodeo isn't really a choice for us. Once it hits your system, it camps out. Like a disease, a virus maybe. For the woman at home, that means a lot of alone time. That guy with the pictures today? His baby girl is two weeks old and he's down the road already. Shoot, when Troy was born, they'd tried so hard for a baby that J.W. drove nineteen hours from St. George, Utah, to catch him, then drove seventeen hours to get on in Prescott the next day. You don't just stop when you become a dad. Sometimes you go harder because you got a little one depending on you.

"Now I saw your face back there by the catch pen with J.W. earlier. Don't worry about ol' Taffy. She's just his Montana sure thing for a few years now."

I winced. *Sure thing.* Clete talked to me like I was one of the guys. He was democratic in that regard, at least.

"It's nothing serious," he said. "I guarantee. J.W. seems to like you fine. A couple weeks ago he made me stop on the way back from Pueblo to pick you flowers by the highway," he said in a tone of admiration and disgust. "Spent the rest of the ride home picking bugs out of his clothes."

J.W. had never brought me flowers but I didn't mention it.

"He went a little wild after he split up with Melissa, made a bunch of new friends, one of whom you had the pleasure to meet, but he keeps that business pretty well sewn up. He's not after permanent with any of them, and whether they like it or not, they know it. We never had no ride-along before, that's for sure. You might want to know that." He picked up his drink and faced me.

"You know J.W. and his brother don't get along so good, right? And you know why, too, huh?" Thinking he meant the Finals, I nodded.

"I've known J.W. for a lot of years, back when he and Melissa were just dating, and I was with him after it fell apart. Seen it coming, in fact." He smoothed his moustache and looked up at the old neon clock over the bar.

"Tell you what, Daryl, I like you. You exhibit a quality I appreciate—you know how to keep your dee mouth shut. So I'm go-

ing to let you in on something and trust you to keep it to yourself."
He leaned in. "I seen it, Melissa and Duff in the bar together. I knew
something unsavory was going on. She denied it, but I know what
I saw."

So there was more to their sibling rivalry than rodeo.

"J.W. figured it out when he called home one night and she
wasn't there. He tracked her down the next day and she finally
owned up. We found him curled up under a table in the beer tent
and hauled him out of there. She's one of those females who sets
the bar high, and he never did feel like he could do enough to make
her happy. We ended up at an Applebee's outside of Del Rio,
thought maybe I'd get him something to eat so he could think better. Here's what I remember about that day—this old boy sitting in
front of a plate of ribs that was getting cold, the barbecue sauce
turning to glue. He just sat there staring into space like he'd been
gut-punched. He was on fire up until then but once that happened,
he never got back on track. Cost him his shot at the Finals that year,
I'm sure of that.

"Let me tell you another thing, Daryl. Near as I can tell, J.W.
didn't mess up once. Not one time. That gold buckle attracts a lot of
opportunities, even for an ugly old cuss like me. A lot of guys let it
go to their head, think the extra girls are gravy on the side. Theory
is what happens on the road stays on the road, so why not, right?

"Only thing I didn't know at that time is whether I should have
said something. I still don't. Maybe I could've spared his pride a little. Maybe it would have ended up the exact same way."

"I think you did the right thing, Clete."

"Daryl, I'm only going to ask you one thing."

"What's that?"

"Once J.W. gets hold of an idea, he follows it through to the very
end, so I request that you not lead him anyplace you're not willing
to go yourself."

I excused myself and went to the ladies' room. There was only a faint trickle from the faucet, but I filled my cupped hands and splashed cold water on my face. The water went in my ears and rolled down my neck. I cranked the dispenser handle and dried myself with a length of pulpy brown towel that smelled like old wet wood.

When I came back out to the bar, Clete stood wary, watching a couple next to him fight. The man raised his long arm and smacked his palm flat on the bar, then stormed away. The woman, short and substantial with a sad mouth under wings of frizzed ash-blond hair, frowned into her hands.

Clete nodded at her. "You live in town, hon?"

"I came up from Douglas," she said to her fingers.

Clete nudged his untouched Crown and water under her nose. "Need that?"

The woman looked up at him, eyes brimming, and shook her head. "Oh, no thanks." She tried to smile.

He shifted his toothpick and leaned back against the bar. "How about steak and eggs? You need that?"

She brightened at his audacity and laughed, showing a crooked front tooth. "Sure."

Clete took her arm and called to me over the bossy cha-cha that had started up. "When J.W. comes in, let him know I took off, would you?"

"Where should I tell him you went?"

"He'll know." Clete put his arm around the woman's rounded shoulders, ruffling the sleeve of her white cotton blouse. She leaned into his side, the conchos on their belts kissing. Clete tipped his hat to me. "See you, Miss Daryl."

I angled toward the bar, nursing my drink and checking my watch, wondering how much longer J.W. would be. I felt a hand around my waist.

"You need a small."

I turned and saw that the hand belonged to a very uncowboy guy in a cowboy hat. He had a long, greasy blond ponytail and a Dale, Jr. T-shirt. Must've taken a wrong turn at the stock car track.

I cocked my head. "What did you say?"

He raised his shot glass and yelled, "I said, you look depressed. You need a small."

I realized he was saying, "You need to smile," at the same time I realized his hand was traveling toward my ass. Out the corner of my eye, I caught sight of J.W. coming into the bar. He saw what was going on and started bulldozing through the crowd.

A redheaded buckle bunny undulated up to him and slid her hand inside his shirt buttons. I'd seen her palling around with Taffy earlier. "Heard you fuck like a bastard," she hollered over the music. I immediately understood Kimber's *you-go-in-the-door-first* instruction but I was helpless to defend my stake, pinned as I was at the bar.

"Really? Imagine that." J.W. eased her off and she slunk away, cursing. Her friends started laughing and clanked their beer bottles together in salute to her failure. The redhead yelled, "I heard your brother was better anyway!" then slammed back a tequila shot so hard she coughed. A lot was happening.

When J.W. got to us, he came full-on redneck. He threw his arm around the guy's shoulders and shook him to his side. He tilted up his chin and that flintrock voice boomed out. "Make a habit of touching women you don't know?"

Happy Hands sized up J.W. "Maybe. Don't see it's much business of yours, though." He turned back toward me.

J.W. grabbed Happy Hands by both shoulders and spun him around, pushing him so the hard lip of the bar slammed into his lower back. He yanked the guy up by his T-shirt. "Point of fact it is my business."

Happy Hands's friend put down his drink and took a step in. Rodeo brings the drama to a sleepy town, and the local boys were all overstimulated and itchy, their territorial sap flowing. They might have been up for a fight, but I wasn't. "Let's go dance," I said, dragging J.W. toward the dance floor.

J.W. kept his head turned, staring down the guy and his friend. A ballad started. We rocked stiffly back and forth, tension knotting the muscles in his shoulders. I leaned into his neck. "It's not worth it." He glared over my shoulder, the spangled light from the mirror ball overhead dancing across his face. When Birch Witting waltzed by with the redheaded buckle bunny, J.W. shouted something in his ear and jabbed his finger at the two guys, making sure they saw. Birch and the redhead left the dance floor.

The two men stood by the dance floor, waiting for the song to end. Birch was mobilized. He told Brandon, who told Morris Washington, a huge, black bulldogger, who went over and tapped another guy on the shoulder.

Morris and Brandon stepped on either side of the two knuckleheads. Morris popped a fresh chew in his mouth and Brandon stared straight ahead, sipping his Coors Light. Neither said anything. Every rodeo guy in the bar was on alert, forming an invisible net. Cowboy law was in effect and would be enforced.

The two men surveyed the situation and left. Within minutes, everything returned to normal, whatever normal meant in a full bar on rodeo night.

14

I WOKE TO THE SOUND OF TWO MEN talking on Sue's landing, their voices muffled by the bedroom door. "Where's the Jar?" The guy had a chips-and-Foster's Australian accent.

"Probably tanglin' blankets with his cuddling partner," said Brandon.

The Australian voice came back. "Tastes like chicken." Both men laughed, the buffered thud of boots receding down the carpeted stairs.

I rolled over. The other bed was empty, yellow flowered sheets rumpled, pillows mounded up. I nudged J.W.'s side. "Hey, cowboy, guess what?"

He lifted his head.

"We're alone. I mean *alone* alone."

"Then get over here. Daddy needs a snuggle." He pulled me to him playfully, but he meant it. It was splendid to feel his skin on mine. He had that warm sleep smell on him. We kissed. Hands began wandering, things started to stir.

Someone knocked on the door and we broke apart. Brandon crept in on tiptoe. "Sorry, forgot my phone." He grabbed it from the nightstand and left.

J.W. sat up and checked his watch. "Might as well get after it."

I sat on the bed, brushing my hair. J.W. came behind me and took the brush. I watched him in the mirror, those seasoned hands moving gently, then watched us together. No wonder people were scandalized. With no makeup, swimming in my oversized T-shirt, I looked half his age.

I was at the bathroom sink when Clete banged on the bedroom door, hollering that breakfast was on. J.W. pulled on his jeans and excused himself.

I leaned against the door, toothbrush tucked in my cheek. I could hear J.W.'s voice low and furious. "Before I tear your head off and shit down your neck, I want to tell you something. If you ever leave her alone when I ask you not to . . ." The anger poured from him, hot and pure like steam through a kettle spout. Remarkably, I heard nothing from Clete.

The bathroom was a tiny pass-through with an entrance on either side. Everyone was down at breakfast, rattling dishes and cutlery, so I locked both doors, pinned up my hair, and got in the clawfoot soaking tub. I was lathering my neck when J.W. called into the guest room.

"Where's my lucky charm at?"

"Bathtub." I reached over and unlocked the door.

J.W. leaned against the sink and stared down at me. He looked impossibly huge. We had done so well keeping a congenial distance that an observer might have thought we were approaching this trip as friends. But as J.W. stood above me, a keening need announced itself in my bones. I wanted him to reach under the water and do to me what he'd done that night when we were lying in the truck bed under the stars. I tried to reason back the intense longing—*This is crazy. There are other people around*—but I couldn't. What I felt for him wasn't right, but it was real.

He knelt at the side of the tub, took up the washcloth, and wordlessly began washing me. I closed my eyes and wrapped my fingers around the porcelain lip of the tub. He rubbed my hands between his, the soapy cloth bristling on my skin. "Wrist still hurting?" I shook my head no.

He kissed the inside of my wrist. I watched the blue pulse under his lips. I wanted to kiss him but I couldn't because I knew once I started, I'd never stop. My entire body ached with the memory of him loving on me, how tender he was, and how strong.

We'd had a dozen opportunities to get something going if we didn't mind it crude and fast—in the little camper, or heaven forbid, on the bed in a room we were sharing with other people. But J.W. didn't want to offend me. He was cautious—no swearing, ever, and whenever we stopped to eat, he wouldn't let me walk from counter to restroom without a visual patrol and I couldn't so much as touch a check. I suddenly remembered when he came to Red Hill with Troy, that moment before I dropped off to sleep with his arm around me. His hand atop my wrist. He was praying on it.

I put my wet hand to his cheek. "I miss you, Daddy."

His face became almost sorrowful. "I miss you, too, baby girl." With the washcloth, he made long strokes up my arms, then curved down my shoulders, advancing toward my breasts.

Brandon yelled up the stairs. "J-dub. Sue made these poached eggs special for you. You better get down here before I feed them to the dog."

I nodded for J.W. to get out. He nodded back, a silent contract.

Alone again, I pulled my knees up under my chin and hugged my legs to my chest. No man had ever had this effect on me before, made me want him so bad I could feel him from the inside out. But where my body goes, my heart follows, and I was losing my grip on the throwaway affair idea.

Sue and Tim had already left for work, but the kitchen was full of people. A long row of shoes lined the wall near the back door, mud-stiffened sneakers, boots with buckaroo straps and heels that knew more dirt than concrete, ropers in varying states of disrepair. Clete's girl from last night, who poured me a cup of coffee and introduced herself as Margie, was making waffles in an electric iron. J.W. dropped his poached eggs into a Green Bay Packers mug, warmed them in the microwave, and ate them with a teaspoon. He pulled up a chair next to a long-headed guy with a big nose and a grid of sun lines on the back of his Spam-colored neck. "What do you know, Preacher? Haven't seen you in a coon's age."

"Immigration. Gone four months," he said around a mouthful of dry wheat toast. I recognized the accent. He was the guy on the stairs.

"Four months gone, huh?" Clete put his hand on the guy's gut. "When's it due?"

"Get stuffed, old man."

Clete grabbed my shoulder so my coffee spilled. "Daryl, the schnoz from Oz over here is Wick Scuno. Don't mind him—he's harmless."

Wick sipped his grapefruit juice. There was a Bible next to his plate and a gold cross dangling from a chain at his throat, but I felt like I needed a penicillin shot just looking at him.

A young kid came in and put an empty porridge bowl in the sink, his upper lip covered in cobbler-crust scabs. I felt just the slightest mosquito whine of anxiety when he showed Margie the two teeth he'd been carrying wrapped in a wet paper towel in his shirt pocket. "Gettin' them put back in later today," he lisped. "If I have time. I'm up in Livingston."

This trip was doing quite a bit for my squeamishness. I was getting used to seeing men stitched up like Frankenstein, biceps balled up and torn from the bone, fingernails ripped off, Technicolor bruises, and bodies all but mummified in white medical tape. And those were just the injuries you could see on the surface. J.W. had steel in his wrist and ankle; Clete, his jaw; and Brandon, over an eye, a hard pea-sized knot you could feel when he put your finger to it. If I pulled every plate and screw and bit and bolt from the competitors I had met, I'd have enough metal to build my own cowboy robot.

J.W. and I gathered our things and met the guys at the truck, blinking tiredly in the sun, as we'd been up until four, assaulted by whiffs of ditchweed, shrieking giggles, and the jounce of bedsprings through the thin walls. "Has a sense of humor, doesn't she?" I'd whispered to J.W. He moaned back. "I hate to break it to you, but that's Clete." Then he told me something about a rumored fondness for tickling that I wished I hadn't heard.

J.W. held out the truck keys with an obvious yawn. "Since we didn't sleep last night, neither one of us is driving." Clete took the keys and climbed into the driver's seat. Beneath the dirty sheet grin, he was reasonably subdued.

I watched the guys closely, made notes or quick sketches whenever I could. But more than anything, I listened. They talked shortcuts and stock contractors, and, carefully in my company, girls. And always there was talk of horses. They shared information as readily as they shared equipment. Guys calling each other: *Four Bars, what's she like? How'd you do on Weaselhead?* In the scheme of their performance, their cell phones were as important as their spurs. They'd discuss which broncs you spur, which ones buck better if you just set your feet and hold on, all in the unique rural-rodeo argot—*waspy, salty, rank, squatty, strong,* with an occasional *beauty* thrown in, Canadian-style, as an affirmative. Talking distracted them, stimulated them, united them. They all talked at once. Two talked while one slept. They talked through the requisite road piss.

When I had to go, they'd wait politely in the truck while I relieved myself in the weeds and hastily zipped up praying against ticks, sunlight catching bumper chrome. Through peeing I realized how apart I was. I didn't count on fitting in, and I was happy that I didn't. It made me feel spy-like, stealthy. I liked being the shotgun chick. The girl alone at the rodeo.

When I got back in the truck after a pit stop outside Roscoe, Brandon was mulling a potential sponsorship. He already had so many stickers and patches and logos on his gear, he looked like a Monopoly board. The company was looking for "the new breed of old-fashioned hero" to promote their line of Western jeans. Who could blame a guy for seeking extra income? After travel expenses and entry fees, even the most successful bareback rider earned less per year than the average NFL player spent on lap dances.

"Oh, shit on that. Heroes." Clete veered around a bloated porcupine in the road, lip of red flesh showing under the leg quills. "Heeee-roes. All that's left of the Old West! Tell you what, cowboys weren't heroes back then neither. If they came after me with that garbage, I'd turn 'em down flat. I'll leave that Saint Cowboy crap to the Mr. Cleans like you, Brandon, or my good buddy, Studly Do-Right over there. I am nobody's hero. I am selfish as shit. Day job? No thank you. Suit and tie? Don't think so. Bust hump at the ranch? Yeah, I'll get around to that. But not right now, not anytime soon. I ain't gonna change who I am for free pants. Watch my temper, what I say. Free pants." He raised a finger for emphasis. "A true cowboy wears no man's brand." Jealousy was plain in that WANTED poster face.

When I was heading to the companion seating in Livingston, a seraphic blonde yelled down from the stands, "Hey! Didn't I see you down in Greeley?" I mounted the stairs. She held out her hand. "Tara Dunny. My husband Cord used to travel with J.W." She introduced me to the pageant party. This was the foxiest assemblage of wives I'd ever seen. I felt a little out of my league, what with all the babies being passed around and the pretty hair. I took a seat off to the side, feeling insufficiently blond.

It was just like when I started at a new high school, merging into the edge of whatever shitkicker clique I could find. I listened to Stephonie Carlsson tell Tara about how she gave up her career as a professional volleyball player to support Trav while he rode bulls. "I used to make good money at it, too, but you know, Trav's only got one shot at this, I figure. I like working at the bank anyway. Short hours and most weekends off."

The spotlights turned on, and the beams tracked the barrelman as he stood in the center of the arena, pulling a length of multicolored scarves from the pocket of his baggy shorts. I sipped a bottled water, my gut clenching. Stephonie looked closely at me. "You okay, Daryl?"

"Oh, me? Yeah."

"You sure? You look a little pale there."

"It's just the heat." Stephonie's baby boy dropped his sippy cup, the lid exploding off, grape juice flying onto everyone's legs. I took off my hat to cool my head. These women, so nice and quiescent in the scheme of their husbands' plans—I wasn't sure I could ever adopt their power behind the saddle position.

"You from around here?" Tara asked, mopping up her baby's purple-splattered legs with her sweatshirt.

"No, I live in Cheyenne."

"Well, great then. We'll see you at Frontier Days!"

Hours later, J.W. and Clete were still behind the chutes, helping Clete's ex-brother-in-law, a novice bull rider, set his rope. I sat by myself at a table near the beer tent, passing the time. It was almost eleven o'clock.

"Little Daryl. You should paint me sometime. Do you do nudes?" I looked up from my sketchpad. Wick Scuno stood in the shadow of the tent with his thumb crooked in his waistband. Wick was an import, but not one of the great talents who flew in from overseas and stormed to the top of the standings. I wondered if he had a box checked "wannabe" on his work visa.

Wick held a white plastic cup of beer in his hand. He looked down his long nose, grinning in the dark. "You're a tiny one, aren't you?"

The announcer boomed out a reverberating thank you to the sponsors. A stiff rubber band sensation started in my shoulders as my neck stretched back. I didn't like the girl-alone-at-the-rodeo feeling any longer.

Wick squatted so he was right by my ear. "J.W. says you've got the prettiest little pussy he's ever seen."

Part of me broke when he said that. I heard a hot buzzing in my ears as rage and sorrow spiked through me. J.W. How could he?

Wick leaned in. "I'd like to see for myself. In fact, I'd like to lick you until you cream all over my face." He stayed put, watching my face for a reaction.

Shock rooted me to my seat. My lips felt numb, my tongue a fat worm in my mouth. Around us, streams of families were going by, kids running after their parents, parents running after their kids. A black-haired girl held a shiny, horse-shaped balloon. It wove in the air and spun on a pink string. I stopped breathing. The trip had been going so great. Everyone had been nice and welcoming and decent. Had I said something to bring this on, I wondered. What did I do?

I'd heard things like this before, high school boys hissing nasty words over the girls' shoulders as they passed in the hall, then running away. But Wick wasn't leaving. He touched his curled fingers to the side of my neck and blew a beery stream of air in my ear. "I'd lay you down, push your knees up to your earlobes and run my tongue from your asshole to the tip of your clit. I bet you taste clean as a virgin."

The line between tamed and untamed in rodeo is slight, and that line is exploited baldly: *Ho ho, better keep an eye on those cowboys!* But it's all nudge-wink innuendo. The suggestion of badness fills the seats. Would specifics like this, I wondered, empty them for good?

Wick cracked his jaw and his lips spread in a reptilian smile. "Just so you know, J.W. is telling every guy he knows that you're the best fuck he's ever had."

I knew then that Wick was full of shit. I looked ahead, refusing to acknowledge him. Where was J.W.? Why was I sitting here alone?

Wick stood and clasped my shoulder, like, "Okay, we're friends now." I thought of rapists who embraced their victims for hours afterward and how the women said it was worse than the actual rape.

Wick walked away, sipping his beer. He stopped to autograph a young boy's hat. There was a burst of laughter from the grandstand as the clown started his trained chicken act. J.W. would snap Wick's neck if he knew he'd talked to me this way. But I couldn't tell and I knew I never would. Wick was his friend.

I walked, legs pumping, toward the darkened parking lot. I found myself wishing a horse would ram Wick into a fence, smash his face to pulp, cripple him to a crab-walking wreck. Recrimination clanged in my ears, a chorus of accusing voices. *How dare you sully our nice clean sport! This is a family entertainment! You're out here on your own, young lady, what did you expect would happen?* The blame was on Wick, but somehow, the shame was all mine.

I heard J.W.'s voice behind me. "Daryl, where you going?" I kept walking.

He came after me and caught my arm. "Hey, why didn't you stop? I was calling you."

I jerked away. "Let go of me! I'm not your stupid rodeo whore."

He dropped my arm. "Where did that come from?"

"You think you can leave me alone the whole night and I'll come running whenever you call me? Forget it."

"You know I can't be with you every second. It's not possible." He mistook my anger for a prima donna tantrum, that I was pissed because he wasn't tacked to my side. "If you don't want to be here, I will pack you home right now."

I pressed my fingers to my temples and squeezed my eyes shut. "No, I'm sorry." I shook my head clear. "I don't want to go home. I'm just tired. I think I'll lie down in the camper for a while, if you don't mind."

"Are you sure?" He started to look concerned.

"Yeah. I didn't mean to yell. I'm really sorry, I mean it."

I kicked through the dirt and crushed cans toward the truck, counting every step. I was in the cowboy's world now, so I'd make like the cowboys do and walk it off.

15

AT MIDNIGHT, J.W. AND I STOPPED outside Thermopolis and bought two jumbo coffees and microwave gutbomb burritos at a fuel plaza with a food mart big as an Albertson's. With so little sleep, the fluorescent world of the market took on a psychedelic sheen. We tripped out into the concrete parking lot giggling thievishly, jostling each other, coffee sloshing under plastic lids.

By now I had accepted that even witnessing rodeo required its own unique courage, that when the chute gate opened, my heart was joined up to J.W.'s, as if I were the one in front of the roaring crowd, hand vised in the rigging. I was getting used to my blood pressure ballooning in my head, breath leaving me, adrenaline coursing, the contact high in full effect. I was glad for the downtime of the road when we could drive the anxiety away.

It seemed the ideal pursuit, this rodeo. I loved the single-minded focus and the gypsy lifestyle, the dazzle of city neon one night and empty two-lane under black sky the next. I figured trouble and hurt couldn't stick to you if you just kept moving. Your duty was as uncomplicated as putting together a fast run or a good ride. It was as simple as winning.

Clete lent his truck to J.W. so we could drive the six hundred miles to Greeley for the final round. A saddle bronc rider named

Hale, who also made the short go, packed in with his saddle. Hale took the first driving shift, so I crawled in back to watch a movie with J.W. I was dozing lightly when my cell phone vibrated against my hip. I looked at the screen. It was 2 A.M. Shawna sounded wide-awake, a butterfly tremble to her voice. "Well, I finally told Lan. I waited until he was in Hollister tattooing at the rally."

"And . . . ?"

"He was so excited, he packed up and flew home last night. Then this morning, he ran outside the trailer and did a backflip off the porch, landed on the garden gnome, and broke it clean in two."

Shawna had once described the abortion she had when she was fifteen. Trays of stainless steel instruments, days of cramping and bleeding into sanitary pads, the guilt and confused relief. To a res-olute, if hodgepodge, spiritualist, the "clump of cells" argument was fairly thin. I couldn't bear her going through that again. "I am so happy for you! So this means you're going to give it a go?"

"Guess so. I had to tell him. I kept having dreams where I was getting pecked by storks. It hurt!" She coughed. "But you know what this means—I can't keep doing my own stuff. I'll need all the money I can get now. Art First is going on hold for a while."

J.W. roused from his sleep. "Everything okay?"

I settled back against the pillow. "Yeah." My best friend was going to have a baby. I was so pleased.

At three-thirty, Hale pulled over so we could switch. J.W. held open the passenger side door for me and came around front to get behind the wheel. I watched the flash of him in the headlights. I'd had so much time to observe J.W. these past few days. He'd swap seats and drive at a mere suggestion of fatigue, give a broke guy twenty bucks, even lend out his equipment. *Unspoiled,* I thought approvingly.

He pawed through the CDs tucked in the sun visor. "The Eagles. Christ. 'Best of Cowboy Poetry.' How about that?"

"Please, no. Bunch of old buckaroos struggling to come up with rhymes for 'branding iron' and 'dutch oven'? Can't do it. I'll find something." I flipped around, searching late-night radio. The only station that came in played the same ten songs as every other country station. In a genre that exalts tradition, they sure don't waste any time chasing the oldies off the air. I found a retro show at the very end of the dial and soon the cab filled with "You're the Reason God Made Oklahoma."

We were quiet for a while. He looked up through the windshield. "Rodeo moon tonight."

"Rodeo moon?"

"When it's bright enough to drive by. Watch." He killed the headlights and the moon was so bright you could still see perfectly.

J.W. turned the high beams back on. It was almost 4 A.M. Looking at him by dashboard's early light, you couldn't see the lines on his face or the flesh just a little loose under the chin. He looked like the punkin roller kid who slept eight to a motel room and lived on bologna sandwiches. The one who, when he won his first check, kept taking it from his pocket to see if it was real, smoothing the paper flat and folding it again. He was as far as you could get from the old, broken-down cowboy of Western lore. Was J.W. old? For a roughstock rider, unquestionably, yes. But he was hardly broken down. Maybe that sad character was stalled at the side of the road somewhere. Not J.W. He had plenty of fuel left to burn.

I leaned my head against the glass and watched the sky going by, Mars a red dot skimming the black strip of horizon. J.W. took a sip of coffee and rubbed my knee. "How's our moon doing out there?"

One could rope the moon, hang it, or pine beneath it, but only J.W. had the brass to all-out claim it. I curled up as best I could around the seat belt. My head got heavy, my eyes filled with sand, and I drifted off.

When I woke, I sat straight and yawned. Strings of lights waved in the heat, sieving through the darkness. "What's that up ahead?"

"That's home, baby. Old Cheyenne."

Something about the way he said it struck a deep chord, like we'd been together forever, like he'd talked to me that way a million times and always would. When we drove past the Frontier Days sign, white lights flashed that there were only fifteen days to go.

"Going to win it this year, cowboy?"

"Depends. Am I going to have my lucky charm with me?"

I put my hand on top of his and he curled his fingers around mine. Together we palmed the gearshift to put it in fourth and didn't let go until we pulled up in Greeley.

J.W.'s friends had a full house so we parked in the driveway to crash for a few hours in the camper. Hale tossed his saddle into the back of his ex-girlfriend's old beater Sunbird and sped off.

Fresh from the shower, J.W. came across the dew-spangled lawn in his sweatpants, wet towel around his neck. I watched as he perched on the edge of the camper bed, struggling to slap lotion on his back. I found it impossible to separate him from his physicality; his body and body of work were one. He was a head-to-toe contradiction—youthful in shape, but punctuated by scars, bruises, and breaks. He was solid, as if assembled from packed earth, yet nimble. Indifferent to pain yet responsive to my touch in a way that was both heady and alarming.

His cell phone rang. He turned from me, wet hair combed into points that curled behind his earlobes. I looked over his shoulder at the caller ID. Taffy. He didn't answer it.

I'd decided that I didn't really care that J.W. had had a relationship with Taffy. What bothered me was that she had intelligence on him that I didn't. I picked up the tube of lotion. "Here, let me."

He stripped and lay on his stomach and I rubbed lotion on him, circling his shoulder blades, pressing my thumbs into his spine while he moaned gratefully. The phone started up again and I knew who it was. So did he. It stopped halfway through the third ring. I squeezed a dollop onto the small of his back and smoothed it into his butt. He tensed and hugged the pillow.

This is what girls check out on a rodeo guy: buckle, eyes, smile. Then the appraisal goes around back. Cowboy butt is the stuff of legend. J.W. did indeed have one of those Eighth Wonder asses, hard and muscled to almost equine perfection. He gulped wetly as I massaged deeper, his eyes closed, mouth open. He was shocked but he liked it, too. There are, it appears, firsts even at forty-one.

I felt a malevolent slant to the air, crackling with new energy. Taffy had never done this. I stroked over and over like an old hand working saddle leather until he unhitched the muscles, then ran the side of my hand along the gully in between. He shifted, thighs spreading a little as if offering.

I had a sincere desire to make him feel good, but there was anger there, too. I had a grandiose thought about how I might invade him as men have invaded women's bodies for centuries. Work a greasy finger inside. Feel the exquisite pleasure of being in there, flesh yielding around me, warm and tight.

Though the virgin territory tempted like wet cement, I held back. J.W.'s body wasn't grounds for a gender battle. This conflict was more personal. Wick and his ever-ready tongue had made me curious about this spot, but it was Taffy who led me to it.

"On your back now, okay?"

He flipped over. He came up on his elbows, ready as I'd ever seen him, erection curved against his flat stomach. Our gazes locked. I lowered my head and he held his breath in anticipation. I bit the soft flesh of his inner thigh. He nodded down at me: *As much as you like.* His largesse was supremely annoying.

I bit down harder. *How's this for a pain game?*

His gasp was high, almost girlish. I heard him groan, could smell him sweating. I kept my eyes fixed on his. *How dare you let her cross my path?*

He couldn't play stoic now. He was starving hard, straining toward the wetness of my mouth. I gloated over his erection, dusky
and weeping clear fluid at the tip. *Cowboy up.*

He put his hand on my shoulder. The sheet rustled under his
thighs as he rolled his hips forward. "Please."

"Please what?" After the Wick incident, this surge of aggression
felt almost necessary.

"Your mouth. Please."

I could plunge down and finish him off in less than a minute, or
say something mean and deflate him, but I had already done what I
wanted to do. This trip was leaving its mark on me; I thought it only
fair to leave my mark on him, too.

Like a car that's dropped a rusty old muffler, I was ready to roar
on down the road. Part of growing up is assuming your own rendi-
tion of the world that was painted for you as a child and I was raised
in the light of rodeo's chiaroscuro—Yes, ma'am, Praise Jesus, and
God Bless America. Rodeo had community spirit and godliness and
patriotism, it was true, but it also had shadows where a girl could
find as much trouble as she could handle. Maybe more. I gathered
my toiletry bag and change of clothes, and left him panting on the
camper bed.

I showered and got into the one sort-of sexy outfit I'd brought—
a little red plaid skirt, a white tank top, and boots. I tugged up my
knee-high, red-striped tube socks, snapped elastics around my pigtails, then painted my lips glossy vermilion and pulled down my hat.

I swung open the camper door, looking like a schoolgirl but feeling like a gangster. J.W. sat on the bed, buttoning up his shirt. He
took in what I was wearing. "Are you trying to kill me?"

"No. But we're running late."

He laughed uncomfortably. "You can put that on and make yourself cozy in my lap any old time, but I don't think I much like you
wearing that out in public."

"Too late to change and I doubt I'd do it if you asked me to."

He shook out his jeans and stood to put them on, the imprint of my teeth purple in his skin like a crescent of pomegranate seeds. "I'll tell you what, little girl. You got a hell of a bite on you."

Let the Taffys of the world take note and take heed.

The ready area at Cody was fenced off and guarded by a rent-a-cop so I was on my own. I climbed the metal steps to the companion seating. I hadn't killed J.W. I didn't even put in a crimp in him. He blasted into the final round at Greeley in seventh place, put on a great show atop Jaxon and Sunny's Whiskey Walk for eighty-two points and finished second. We didn't have time to collect the check; we raced to the airstrip with the satisfaction that he was six-thousand-dollars richer.

On the step ahead of me, a gorgeous white-haired Indian in a pricey silver belly dropped his cane. When it clattered down the metal step, I stooped forward and picked it up. He clasped my hand gratefully when I gave it back.

"Old war wound there?"

"Pretty much so," he said, speech slow and nicotine-frail.

I climbed after him. "Got a favorite ride?" It probably was a nosy question, but I wasn't going to sit on the sidelines anymore. I'd ask what I wanted, go where I pleased.

He stopped and turned, a happy flush dawning on his face. "Reno, forty years ago. I still got those silver spurs. I gave away almost all my stuff, to my grandbabies, mostly. They live in Pasadena and like to hear about their Paw-paw the cowboy."

"So what was it about Reno?"

"Well, every cowboy wants a pair of those Reno spurs, for one thing. I wasn't any different. The bull was named Dragonfly. It was a clutch situation . . ." He recounted the ride as if it had happened yesterday. The hum. The horns hooking roan dirt. He returned to the well, eager to reminisce, the story cast-in-amber intact.

I took his arm and we eased carefully up the stairs. He coughed and we stopped to rest. He fumbled a pack of Winstons, his nail beds flat and stained yellow. "You ever hear of a guy named Sleepy Levon?" He tapped a cigarette from the pack.

"No, who's he?"

"He's an old bull rider; he was old even when I was riding and that was back a ways. Anyhow, Sleepy lost his leg in Vietnam and he had a prosthetic that came just above the knee. Didn't stop him from getting on bulls, but because of his one bad leg, he had a real hard time holding on for eight seconds. He usually bucked off but everybody was real proud of him for trying. This one time he finally made the whistle, he had kind of a messy get-off and the bull turned around when Sleep was still on the ground and hooked him right in his false leg. Well, you should've seen the bullfighters' faces when they saw that leg flying through the air! Long as I live I'll never forget it."

"Was that the end of Sleepy's career?"

"No, ma'am. No. We took up a collection, got him a new leg and he kept riding for years after that."

"That's amazing."

"No, that's rodeo." A perfect gold bicuspid glimmered from his smile. "Once it gets in your blood, it stays there." He gripped his cane with raptor-claw fingers and rattled off to watch from the top row.

J.W. had drawn a black-socked buckskin named Lucky Strike. Parrot-nosed, tall, and skinny, she was ugly as sin. The men in the chutes helped steady the horse so J.W. could prepare his mount. He'd already spun the latigo through the D rings, laid the free end across the handhold, and tied off. He tightened up his cinches.

"Now we're on to one of our old guard cowboys, J.W. Jarrett . . ."

J.W. pulled his hat down tight, worked his riding hand into the rigging, and cracked back. With his other hand, he slapped his face, both cheeks, hard. He nodded his head quick and short, *yesyesyes*, and the gate snapped open. He marked out, toes pointed east and west, then Lucky Strike rocketed forth and blew up right out of the chute.

Oh, she was glorious, sunlight glinting off her wheat-colored coat, her black mane thrashing and whipping at first jump. J.W. made his mark-out, then brought his spurs up in a seamless zip across her shoulders. Over and over she bucked, not covering any ground, just staying right there by the chutes, back hooves up and planing the air sixty degrees from the ground. Through each jump and buck, J.W. gapped open and slammed his spurs into the pocket, raking them across the horse's withers, finding a groove. It was just the prettiest ride.

At the whistle, J.W. hunched over the rigging, business as usual, but as he tried to break the bind, he struggled. One of the pick-up men galloped up and tried to jerk him free, but J.W. flipped over Lucky Strike's side, hung up in the rigging. He bounced jerkily against her flank as he dangled away from his hand. I rose from my seat.

Clete stood up on the chute rails, hollering, "Keep on your feet, J.W.!"

I could see the pick-up men shouting, their mouths working furiously as they tried to subdue the horse long enough to wrest J.W. from his rigging. Then the rigging slipped to the side, J.W.s arm locked in, and he lost his footing. I watched in horror as Lucky Strike dragged him along the arena on his face. He was struggling to stay face up, the pick-up men yelling down at him and him yelling back.

Next thing I knew, Lucky Strike sped up, running so fast I saw six inches of daylight between J.W. and the dirt. She'd lifted him clear off the ground.

The stock contractor came in from the side waving a white plastic garbage bag billowed out to try to stop Lucky Strike, but she turned and took off running like a buckskin demoness, churning the dirt with hooves the size of dinner plates. J.W. caught a hoof to the temple that knocked him clean out. The horse dragged him around the arena, limp as an empty puppet. Someone put a bracing arm around my shoulder. It was Tara Dunny.

The three men surrounded Lucky Strike so she had no place to go. One leapt from his horse and pried up the fingers on J.W.'s riding glove. He lay motionless in the dirt. After a moment he stirred and waved off the paramedics with the backboard. When they pulled him to his feet, I saw his eye, a big purple-red mass like a stewed plum, the lid a distended black slit.

J.W. lurched and bent forward, struggling to get by the pain and shock, but he couldn't. He knelt and put his head in his hands, three fingers of blood snaking down from his forehead.

Wick Scuno, Brandon, and Clete had already jumped the arena fence and bolted across the dirt. Brandon and Clete helped the EMTs hold J.W. still while Wick dropped to his knees and quickly undid the four buckles on his chaps. They flanked him on either side and helped him stagger from the arena, Wick with J.W.'s chaps over his arm like a soldier shouldering a fallen comrade's rifle.

The clown tried for some comic relief. He ponied over, mugging with his tape-wrapped microphone. "Gave us quite a scare there, J.W. What do you have to say to these worried fans of yours?"

J.W.'s head lolled toward the mike. "That hurt."

He limped off with an escort of pick-up men on their mounts. For all that, his reward was seventy-four measly points and an arena-full of pity applause.

Over the manic clatter of my heart, I heard Tara say, "Come on, let's get you down there." I clutched her as she led me down the metal bleacher steps by my elbow and through the chain-link fence behind the chutes. I squeezed into the medical room, screen door slamming behind me. J.W. was stretched out on an exam table. The doctor walked his fingers around J.W.'s eye socket. A disembodied voice said, "girlfriend," and the crowd parted to let me in.

I stood next to the gurney opposite him, my feet fading. "Why isn't the cut on his eye bleeding?" My voice echoed off the cinder block walls. I noticed a poster of acupressure points.

"Got to that already," the doctor said over his shoulder. "He's lucky he didn't lose the eye altogether."

I fainted on the spot.

When I came around, there was a blanket draped over me, a sour metal taste in my mouth, and a nurse in a squash-blossom necklace pressing a Cold Pak to the inside of my wrists. I lay on the gurney, my feet up on a hard wedge of orange foam. I heard J.W.'s miserable-sounding voice. "Is she all right?"

My eyeballs reeled up under my lids. I tried to move.

"Take it easy, honey, he's fine and you're fine," the nurse said, patting my arm. She had a thin, sympathetic face that was deeply tanned, and bright coral lipstick. She held out her hand and I took it so I could roll onto my side. I curled my knees under my chin.

"Can I see her? Where is she?" Behind the doctor's hovering form, I could see the top of J.W.'s head covered in white paper. "Just hold on, J.W. One more stitch and you're good." The doctor balled up the paper and threw it into the medical waste bin, then he and the nurse took J.W. under the arms and carefully helped him sit up.

He looked awful. The whole of his right side was streaked in dirt, his sleeve torn at the shoulder. From forehead to chin, it looked like someone had sloughed the skin from the edge of his face with 30-grit sandpaper. The wound was bulbous and purple, with a fresh line of cobalt-blue suture running through. His good eye was glassy and flat. He sank back against the wall and smiled sheepishly. "Got kinda Western out there, didn't it, baby girl?"

Brandon and Wick took J.W. under the armpits and hoisted him up. Clete and the nurse eased me over to a chair. I sipped from a bottle of water. Ten minutes later, they were loading us out with a plastic baggie full of ice cubes pressed to J.W.'s face, a bolus of crushed ice Saran Wrapped around his elbow, and some packets of Tylenol.

"Tonight he'll need codeine," the nurse said, pressing an envelope in my hand. "If anybody asks, you didn't get it from me. Try to persuade him to take it."

While J.W. scrawled his signature on a waiver to decline further treatment, I looked at the implements on the counter. "Why would you need a defibrillator kit? Do cowboys really have heart attacks at the rodeo?"

The nurse smiled coolly. "Oh, cowboys aren't at much risk for heart attack, honey. We keep that on hand for their girlfriends."

After the rodeo, our room was busy with people stopping by. I helped J.W. undress while Brandon and Clete rounded up some Ziploc bags and filled the wastebasket with ice cubes. We laid him down under the sheet and packed his right side up and down with ice. Birch Wittig poked his head into the room. "Hey, bud. Ya doin' okay? I could've sewed you up, you know. Not any different than a calving cow with uterine prolapse. A couple stitches and I'd pop the eyeball right back into yer head."

A pizza materialized and J.W. carefully ate two slices that Brandon cut into bite-size pieces with his pocketknife. Every guy had to tell his version of what he saw. They'd make fun of J.W.—*Got your bell rung, did ya*—and he'd try to laugh, but he was too sore. Just like in the bar, they formed a protective net around him, not with the pledge of their fists but with their stories. That they were blasé about injury was unremarkable to me—*No Pain, No Gain* found its start point in rodeo. What surprised me was that they healed through talking. The stories salved the wound.

J.W. didn't want to take any codeine but he was so sore and miserable he couldn't sleep. He lay on his back, too cricked up to sit propped against pillows to watch television. I chased everyone from the room. "Let's get you under the covers, Daddy Rabbit." Once he was tucked in, I was able to convince him to take a single pill. Within a half-hour, the ice in the baggies had melted down but J.W.

didn't mind. He was riding a slow wave of druggy euphoria. He yawned and settled into the blankets.

I sat on the side of his bed. J.W. half-opened his eyes. "Go on out, Daryl. No point missing the show. There's nothing anyone can do for me right now anyway." He lifted his head a little. "But when you come back maybe you can give me my medicine."

"What medicine?"

A sly smile from the patient. "You know what I mean. You owe me after this morning."

"I think that wreck knocked you dingy, cowboy." I turned out the light. "Get some rest and I'll check on you in a bit."

I went out to the pool. Everyone had changed into swimsuits and cutoffs and splashed around waiting for the fireworks to begin. The manager floated on a raft, listening to Verdi on a yellow waterproof transistor radio. I sat on the edge, dangling my legs in the water. Brandon sloshed over. "You okay there, Daryl? J-dub's gonna be just fine." When I turned down a beer, he offered to get me a soda from the vending machine.

Clete sat down and put his arm around me. "You did great today, kid."

I looked at the upturned faces of the cowboys and cowgirls, watching as fireworks exploded overhead and shimmied down against the black sky backdrop like tossed confetti. None of them wasted a second deliberating whether or not to come to J.W.'s aid, and it was what I'd seen so much of this weekend—people not hesitating to help, as if helping were as important as winning. Rodeo derives from a Spanish word, *rodear*, meaning "to surround or encircle." As we sat there, it occurred to me that the encircling doesn't so much happen in the ring as just outside of it.

I walked barefoot across the dirt parking lot and poked my head into the room. "We're missing you out there, cowboy. Ready for fireworks?"

J.W. didn't answer. I stood still until my eyes adjusted to the darkness, his shape emerging as I gained focus. He was lying on the bed, flat on his back asleep, fingers steepled over his chest, his chin tucked down. Half his face was rough and crazy looking, swollen and gruesome from injury. The other was chiseled calm, passive and strong as ever. His lips curled in a peaceful smile.

I wanted to gather him up in my arms, but I wouldn't dream of interrupting his sleep. As I looked at him, it dawned on me, why I'd been so self-conscious around his friends, why I was so jealous of Taffy, why I'd been completely unnerved by his wreck. I couldn't understand why my reactions were so strong, but I finally caught the thread that held those feelings together. A rush of blood flooded from my chest to my face, a surge of ecstasy laced with dread. *Oh my God,* I thought. *I love him.*

I woke early. Brandon was out swimming laps, everyone else off to breakfast. I squeezed some skin cream into my palm and rubbed it into my cracked knuckles. The dry Western summer was annihilating my skin. A hand reached across my pillow. J.W. wiggled his fingers, signaling for lotion. "I'll do it," I said, crawling under the sheets. I rubbed him with the cream, massaging it briskly into his feet and legs. I didn't have any anger toward him this morning, only the urgent need to nurture. J.W.'s insensitivity around the Taffy issue had been a product of my imagination. His vulnerability, however, was entirely real. I could lose him at any time.

The room was dark like a secret cell. J.W. emerged from the sheets and allowed me access to his entire body without restraint, which made me feel guilty for the camper stunt. I smoothed lotion carefully over the bruises up and down his side, and the bite mark on his inner thigh already fading. As the sun climbed higher in the sky, light poured through a split in the flimsy blinds, a broad beam shining on the cheap comforter. He lolled in the strip of sunlight like a golden cub. "You take good care of me."

"I like taking care of you." When I said it, I realized it was true. I kept massaging him, moving down his abdomen, my touch firm and slow. When he got hard, I wrapped my fingers around him, returned my other hand to the scene of my transgression, and took care of him as sweetly and lovingly as I could.

His face was no longer puffy, but his eye was blacker than before, the prune-dark bruise ringed by dots of gray-green and blue. The scabs made him look like he'd slid down a cheese grater cheek first. I straddled him carefully, avoiding his sore side, and lay with my ear against his chest. "Guess I'm not so lucky for you after all, huh?"

He rubbed my temples. "Don't say that. Think how much worse that wreck could have been. I got off easy because you were there. I'm certain of that."

I called Jace from the bathroom, the sink faucet on full blast to give us some privacy.

"How's Dangerboy?" Jace was fueling the truck. I could hear cars zooming by in the background.

"Fine. We're having a nice, relaxing trip." An awkward thing to say, with J.W. in the other room zipping up like a sailor on leave. He was so mindful of time I expected to look in his eyes and find a second hand sweeping across the pale blue iris.

"You run across his glamourpuss brother out there on the road?"

I kept my voice low. "No. I overheard someone in the stands saying Duff's out with a concussion and may be cutting back for the rest of the summer. J.W. doesn't talk about him at all, though. People won't even mention Duff's name when he's around. Some bad blood there."

Jace harrumphed. "A guy who can't let bygones be bygones isn't a good sign." But Jace didn't know what really blew the brothers apart, so I let him nurse his disapproval.

I turned off the faucet. "So, guess who's having a baby?"

Jace sucked in his breath. "Oh Jesus, do I want to hear this?"

"Not me! Shawna."

J.W. had our bags packed, waiting on a chair by the door. "Checking in with CIA headquarters?"

"Almost. My brother. If I don't call every couple days, he freaks."

He hugged me. "Your big brother's worried about you. That's a good man."

At the gate inside Cody's toy airport, our tight band of four split up. Clete was headed to Belle Fourche, Brandon to Saint Paul, and J.W. and I would loop through Jackson and take the truck back to Cheyenne for Clete to gather later. I watched as Brandon put a dip in. This morning, I'd seen him emerge from the pool in his swim goggles, smooth body a perfect V in snug trunks. Brandon was my age, a good guy with talent and funds; he was what I was supposed to want, but compared to J.W., he just didn't scan. When I looked at him, I saw a flawless surface that everything slid right off. He caught me looking, misunderstood, and held out the Copenhagen tin. "Want to bum a dip, Miss Daryl?"

"Maybe."

"Oh, you do not." He looked at J.W., green eyes wide as an ingenue's. "She does not."

J.W. shrugged. "I dunno, bud. She's got her own mind."

"Seriously, Brandon. Give me some."

I put a big pinch in my cheek and spit it out onto the pavement when my entire mouth starting stinging, tobacco juice welling under my tongue. I wiped my mouth with the back of my hand. "I don't know how you guys do it. That stuff tastes like straight-up ass!"

Clete laughed and hugged me to his side with one arm. "Aw, I'm gonna miss you, Little Peanut. You're like the baby sister I never had."

All things considered, Clete and I had been through quite a lot these past few days. Underneath the guff and bluster, he had a heart the size of a pot roast. I put my arm around his waist and squeezed back. "I'm gonna miss you, too, Clete. You're like the annoying big brother I never wanted."

While I drove along the Buffalo Bill Highway on the way to Jackson, J.W. told me about Clete's wife, Ronnie, how she left him last year. Together, they'd had seventeen years, four kids, and even (don't you dare bring it up before Clete does) two grandkids.

I sipped from my cardboard pint of orange juice. "She take everything?"

"Worse. He had given her his first Finals buckle and she sold it on eBay. Heard she got thousands for it, too. Clete's a pain in the you-know-what a lot of the time but that was a dirty move he didn't deserve." J.W. adjusted the rearview mirror. "For the longest time, he practically lived in that camper of his. In his own driveway, in front of a house he paid cash for." The broad history of rodeo includes several stripes of insult and injury, but never the pain of lump-sum alimony or relationships where you both get too tired and just let go of the rope.

It was late afternoon when we turned onto the swank macadam that led to my mother's house. The drive was lined with Range Rovers, Subaru wagons, and sedate late-model trucks. We rounded the aspen stand in the center island and pulled up to her front door. J.W. pressed his forehead to the window, taking in the tall columns of river rock and the vaulted blue spruce atrium ceiling you could see through the glass walls around the front door. "Wow. I'm out of my depth."

My mother left the kitchen staff chopping vegetables and rushed into the foyer. Hanging from the ceiling was one of those ridiculous antler chandeliers that looked like a fatal collision between all of Santa's reindeer. I told her I was bringing a friend, but I could read the shock in her raised brow when she saw J.W. She greeted him graciously, then gave me a hug and a look that said, *Interesting choice in chauffeur, hmm?*

J.W. pulled his hat down a little. "I'm sure sorry about the state of my face, ma'am. This wasn't the impression I was wanting to make."

"Hey, is that our resident artistic genius?" My mother's husband came in, doffing his grilling mitts. His apron said WORLD'S BEST BARSTOOL COWBOY. He put his hand on my head. "My, how you've grown!" He laughed at his comic ingenuity.

"Hi, Larry." I liked Larry fine, even though he was nervous and so oddly shaped, he would need a pillow to fill out the butt of his Wranglers. He pumped J.W.'s hand. "You look like a man who knows his way around a grill. Why don't you come out on the palazzo and help me stir the mesquite chips in the smoker and we'll get some steaks over the gas flames?"

My mom put her arm around my shoulder and led me through the living room and into the yard, introducing me to every single guest. After sixty handshakes, "you bet I'm excited to be in the Frontier Days art show this year" and "yes, that's right, her hair's darker but we do look just alike," I was thirsty.

My mom had the bartender ladle me a glass of sangria and took me into the bedroom. "I got you a new hat. I had the manager of the Jackson Hole Hat Company custom-make it for you." We were alone but she offered no comment about J.W., just hummed around me as she fetched the shiny hatbox and set it on the bed. I almost wanted her to say something, but I knew she wouldn't. She'd long ago segued from rodeo royalty to the reigning queen of Everything's Fine. I lifted the hat from the gold lasso-print tissue paper. It was a beautiful chocolate-brown beaver-and-rabbit blend, nicer than anything I could ever afford on my own. I wasn't sure how I felt about that.

When I wore the new hat out onto the palazzo and showed it to J.W., he approved. "We've got to turn you into a roughie girl." My mom watched in amusement as J.W. strolled into the kitchen, shooed cook Rosa from the stove, and shaped my hat brim over the steam from the tea kettle.

J.W. and my mom sat down together and she seized the opportunity to tell J.W. about the one and only time she tried to curl my hair like hers. "You should've seen her, this tiny five-year-old girl running down the hall in her My Little Pony nightgown, trying to tear the pink rollers out of her hair. I'd never seen anything so funny. The way she was acting, you'd have thought her hair was on fire!"

I was afraid of what she might tell him next, so I excused myself to "mingle." Since taking up with Larry, my mother had done a fabulous job of merging into the gourmet West. Her guests were local politicians, business owners, several guys on the board of the elk preserve, and their various wives and kids.

Some of the women were getting ready for a barrel race in the huge, larch-bordered arena out back. The Cathedral Peaks loomed behind, prettier than any postcard. I stood at the fence while they rolled out the cans, my tongue weighted down by rage. No one copped an attitude when they saw my holey jeans and worn boots. No one had been even remotely rude to me. But I hated them all anyway. They looked so comfortable. So moisturized.

The women entered in the race trotted around, with their sun-affirmed salon highlights and religiously maintained thighs. A restaurateur named Elayna picked up her horse's front legs and stretched them. The horse was a flax mane sorrel with a gorgeously dished head. He must have cost a fortune. Elayna swung up into the saddle and tapped him in the ribs. They entered the ring. Gold-flecked dust stirred under the horse's hooves as they cantered in circles, warming up.

No, I thought as I watched, *you can't have this. You can't put this on and show it off like some high-dollar accessory.* I marched back to the patio where J.W. sat on a carved stone bench telling my mom and Larry about the time a bronc bit him on the nipple.

"Mom, I need to borrow your ropers."

She flipped up her Chanel sunglasses. "Why?"

"I'm racing."

My heartbeats turned to hammer strikes as I took the last spot in the line of racers. It had been years since I'd done this. *They're amateurs,* I reminded myself. *No fear.* I was on Circe, my mom's best barrel horse. Circe threw her head back; she really wanted to go. When the last woman in front of me took off, Circe went hot-footed, dancing behind the chalk line. I guided her to starting position and when Larry signaled, I jabbed into her sides and she took off, a precision missile. Within a second, I had the old familiar feeling of my heart being pulled out through my eyes.

I headed straight for the money can and circled it tight and true. God, this was a great horse. Riding her was like playing a perfectly tuned instrument. No, it was better, like being instrument and player both. I could hear the wind singing in my ears and cheering from the fence. I came around the second can too wide, but no matter. I kicked ahead. The last can. I put my hand out. It bobbled but didn't fall. Now for the straightaway. I shifted forward in the saddle. Circe was coming full on and I whipped her, whipped her, whipped her with the reins.

Larry looked up from his stopwatch and waved his arms over his head. "Sixteen fifty-three." Everyone applauded and whistled. I nodded my head, my chest heaving. I won. Circe was a mama's girl, so I pulled her reins and up she went on her back hooves just like I knew she would. *Hi-ho Circe, and screw you, Jackson.*

My mom loped up on her black Arabian with the white blaze, a tall filigreed rhinestone tiara in her hands. I leaned down and let her fasten the tiara around my hat. We smiled as Larry circled us with his video camera. I waved to everyone at the fence and said through my teeth, "You've been waiting twenty-three years to get one of these on my head, haven't you, Mom?"

"Damn right," she said and kept right on smiling and waving.

A tall woman, about forty, I guessed, came up to the fence. "Quite a ride. Your mom tells me you're a painter like me." Her hair was curly black with plenty of gray mixed in. She looked neither comfortable nor moisturized. I smiled at her. "I am. Give me a sec to put her pony away and we'll have a drink."

Mom rode Circe into the stable and I met the woman at the bar. She handed me a glass of sangria. She told me her name was Bettina and she painted Western equine scenes.

"I'd love to see your stuff sometime."

"My book's in the truck. Let's go." When I looked surprised, she laughed. "I always have it with me. Every waking moment is a networking opportunity."

I flipped through her print portfolio. Her work was colorful abstract expressionism, suggesting Walter Piehl. "Wow, your stuff is great! Did you study out here?"

Bettina topped off my sangria and offered me a taquito from her plate. "No, I'm from Connecticut. I went to school back East. Yale."

"No kidding. How in God's name did you end up in Jackson? Does your family have a house here?"

"Hardly. My dad was an accountant. He wasn't exactly making Jackson money. I got every grant, loan, and scholarship I could scrounge. By the time I got my MFA, I had student loans out my ass. I went back to New Haven and taught for a while, but I got sick of it and came out here fifteen years ago."

"And all you do is paint? That's awesome."

Bettina nodded. "Get in the right galleries and you can do really well. First, you've got the hidebound plutocrats that live here. Then you've got the tourists whose idea of going country is eating at Cracker Barrel. They're sitting ducks, every last one. You could make some spurs out of tin foil, say they're from Billy the Kid, and they'd whip out their checkbooks faster than you can say *yippee-ki-ay*. The other day I was in my friend's shop down by the Betty Rock Café and he was selling an old secondhand cowboy boot with a lamp inside it for five hundred bucks! Five hundred bucks for a two-dollar boot, a three-dollar fixture, and a Kmart shade that he stitched up with rawhide string around the edges. Suckers."

I looked around. "To tell you the truth, I don't know if I'd even want these people to buy my work."

She looked at me, nostalgic and bemused like I was reflecting her old silly self back to her. She tipped her goblet my way. "But my darling, that's the first lesson one learns as a professional artist—if you don't like your buyers, you deal with the displeasure by depositing their checks."

I saw someone familiar at the buffet table. "Huh. That guy over there eating all the Buffalo wings looks like Dan Rather."

Bettina leaned over. "Um, I think that is Dan Rather." She squinted. "No, wait, maybe it's Tom Brokaw." We couldn't figure out which newscaster it was, but we were pretty sure it wasn't Ted Koppel. This really was just too much.

J.W. found me sitting on the porch fifteen minutes later. "What are you doin' out here?"

"I was just trying to figure how many paintings I'd have to sell to afford a place like this."

"How many?"

"More than I could ever paint."

"So?" He set his beer on the porch railing and leaned against the post. "Let me ask you something. Do you pay your taxes?"

"Yeah."

"Self-employed?"

"Right." I picked up an aspen leaf and shredded it.

"What do you put on your Schedule C form where they ask for your occupation?"

"Artist."

"Right. And I get a W-2 from Dominion Lumber, but I also fill out a Schedule C where I get to write 'rodeo cowboy' in that little box. What do you think these people put?"

"I don't know, but I bet they're deducting all these second homes that they live in two weeks out of the year."

He sat on the step above me and wrapped his arms around my waist. "Yeah, probably." A voluptuous chuckle. "But you know what, Daryl? In a million years, they'll never be like us. You can always make more money, if that's what you want. Can't buy what we've got."

"You think so?"

"I know so." His arms nestled under my breasts. "Money can't buy respect," he whispered. "And it won't get you much by way of talent, neither." His breath was hot and fierce on my neck.

Underneath his humility and sure 'nuff simple stuff was bedrock pride, pride that had nothing to do with wealth or status, just the satisfaction of being skilled, of living an independent life, and being smarter—much smarter—than people think. When he said it that way, I was part of it, too—me and him versus everybody else. I settled into his arms. I was less afraid of how I felt. In that moment, I embraced it with certainty: I love this cowboy, and I love his cowboy heart.

16

J.W. LAY ON TOP OF THE QUILT in the master loft, keeping cool. We'd pulled into the drive at Red Hill at 4 A.M. and fell asleep without even getting under the covers. On three hours' sleep, he'd already done two loads of laundry, made a pot of coffee, and was packed up and set to go again, due to leave at noon for the thousand-mile drive to Calgary. There was something to be said for keeping company with an in-and-out guy—just enough time together, and plenty of time to myself. I was looking forward to some quality time at the easel where I could pour everything I'd learned over Cowboy Christmas onto untrammeled canvas.

I folded edges of the quilt over him, one atop the other.

He opened his eyes. "What are you doing?"

"Making a cowboy burrito."

He lifted his head and wiggled his feet. "Cowboy burrito?"

"Yeah, you wrap one edge over the other, then stuff the ends underneath." I did it. "Now you're a cowboy burrito. Good enough to eat."

"I can't move, though." He wiggled his legs. He looked at me and smiled crookedly. "Ah, but you don't *want* me to move. You don't want me to leave, do you?"

"I never said that. You're free to go now, in fact. Cowboy up, bud! Gas it. Let's go. Come on." I slapped his sides.

"What if I don't want to leave? What if I like being a burrito? What if my true destiny is to lie here being a burrito?"

I climbed on top of him and hugged him to me. "Whether you like it or not isn't the point. You *have* to leave. We made a deal, didn't we? Art first for me, rodeo first for you."

He raised his eyebrows. "Any other guys you're making into burritos?" I opened my mouth to say something fresh, then stopped. "No."

Jace had called earlier. When he found out J.W. was over, he was irate. "Jesus, Daryl. Haven't you gotten that old cowboy out of your system yet?" When I tried to defend myself, Jace cut me off. "Just so you know, J.W. is forty-one. I checked."

"I know. I'm sure you're wondering what a guy his age is doing with me."

Jace sounded mad enough to spit shoeing nails. "No, I don't wonder at all. I know *exactly* what he's doing with you."

J.W. nudged me from under his mummy wrap. "Something wrong?"

I rested my chin on his chest. "You ever get the sense that people think you're dating me for the wrong reasons?"

"Any particular people?"

"Not really," I lied.

"I can't guess what people think, and I don't know that I care. But it's different for girls, I reckon." He was the first male I'd ever heard acknowledge this and it raised him in my esteem. "I know when we were out on the road together, a lot more guys were slapping me on the back, that's for sure." He got up and took his laundered shirts off the bedpost. "Iron's in here, right?" He swung open the closet door.

"J.W., *don't.*"

He saw the back numbers before I could stop him. A blind man could see them. Jace had tacked every back number from every gay rodeo he'd ever been to up and down the inside of the closet door.

"What the heck is all this?"

I knew we would have to have this conversation, but I hadn't wanted to have it this soon, this way. I could have lectured, I could have held forth about rainbow rodeo and stumped for tolerance and diversity, but I didn't. For the past five years I'd been testing my ability to make people understand, massaging, spinning, half-truthing. But I wasn't the one who needed testing. I'd been anxious for weeks anticipating this moment, but now that it was here, I didn't feel one twitch of retreat. I just said it. This brother of mine, my hunting, cowboying, truck-driving brother was Like That.

I waited for the reaction. *Be a man,* I dared J.W. silently. *Go on, be a man about it.*

He pursed his lips and set his neck. "Oh."

We had toast on the deck, then I walked him to his truck. "J.W., about what happened upstairs . . ."

He rapped a fresh can of chew on the steering wheel, pinched up a big loamy dip, and packed it down beneath his gumline. His face was unreadable. "Don't worry about it, Daryl. I don't." He flicked a grasshopper off his shirt.

The "queering of America" hadn't hit the back forty. It was just a fact. There may be pockets of liberalism in the NPR heartland, but you weren't safe making any assumptions. The truck engine hummed. J.W. put on his sunglasses and tugged his cap down. "And as far as my intentions where you're concerned? You'll see. And so will everyone else." He leaned out the window and gave me a quick kiss. "I'll call you when I get up to Marv Stewart's place in Calgary. Be good."

After my shift at the Twin Pines, I got back to Red Hill at the tail end of the open house. The horses in the round pen made a picturesque "country living" scene. Newly purchased flowerboxes lined the porch railing and tubs of red geraniums sat on either side of the front door. Old Hawaiian pedal steel wafted from the stereo speakers, further fleshing out the image of Red Hill as the ultimate rural idyll. Trays of stale Danish ranged across the kitchen counter. A chrome coffee urn stood on the table, surrounded by Styrofoam cups. Gwatney, sleeves of his olive-green jacket pushed up to his knobby elbows, looked over the sign-in sheet. "Twenty-four people," he said, satisfied.

Jordan Rivers held tightly to the brass banister on the stairway as her two children slid down the carpeted stairs on their behinds. She looked huge in a pink-and-white awning-striped sundress with floppy sleeves. Her daughter Naomi picked up a cup of juice and ran over to her mother.

"Careful, sweetie, careful. We can't get punch on our clothes. We're having our picture taken later." She flushed a little. In her hand, I saw a list of action items: grade driveway. Pave front walk. Paint barn. Take down cross on hill, "Darcey's going to be the cover story in the next *Sports News*."

Standing next to Jordan, powdered and pink, I felt grimy in my work clothes. "That's something, Jordan. Congratulations. You must be very proud." I started upstairs so I could change.

"Oh, I am. I am. This season has been such a blessing. We'll just have time for the photo shoot before Darcey leaves for Calgary. I'm joining him at the Stampede for a few days, then I'll be vacationing in Banff with the family. Doesn't that sound fun?"

I didn't answer. I looked at the dust-haloed spot on the wall of the stairway. The photo of me and Jace was missing.

Jordan Rivers called the next night, sounding breathless. I thought maybe she had a question about the property that couldn't wait for a call to the Realtor, but she didn't. "I don't want to have to tell you this . . ." I could tell by her tone that whatever it was, she not only wanted to tell me, she was *dying* to tell me. "Darcey called me and said that Steve Lukkins told him something about J.W. and all the guys staying at Marv Stewart's place that I think you might like to know." She took a deep breath. "I heard they headed out to Ranchman's and after Ranchman's they went to a rub-and-tug."

I sat on the kitchen floor, wondering what in God's name she was talking about.

"Do you know what a rub-and-tug is?" There was a concerned smirk to that *la-di-da* voice.

I thought about Pak'nSave supermarkets and Kum & Go convenience stores. "I imagine it's a store of some sort."

"Well, kind of. It's . . . it's a massage parlor."

"So?"

Her voice dropped to a satisfied whisper. "I mean, *a massage parlor.*"

I was stunned. I thought J.W. wasn't like that, but maybe I was wrong.

My dander was up when J.W. called me at midnight.

"How's it going?"

"Good as planned, I guess." I mixed paint while we talked. "How'd you fare today?"

"Eighty-eight points. I won the round, if you can believe. Had to work my tail off, but I did it. One win away from getting to the fifty-thousand-dollar round."

"Well, I'm glad to hear it. You managing to have some fun, too?"

"Yeah."

"I'll bet." Acid floated on the surface of my voice.

"What's that supposed to mean?"

"Nothing." I swirled my brush in a cup full of gouache. "It's just that Jordan Rivers took it upon herself to tell me about your little trip to the rub-and-tug."

"The *what*?" He was incredulous. "How the heck would some timey's bossyboots wife know my business when the only guys who stay at Stewart's are bronc and bareback riders? I went to Ranch-man's for a couple hours last night, then I came back to the ranch and went to sleep on the living room couch. Go ahead, ask anyone." He paused. "You trust me, don't you?"

I waited too long to answer him. "Yeah."

"Just so you know, when I'm out, I make it real clear I'm seeing someone. Which brings me to something I been wanting to talk about with you. I seen your truck outside the Twin Pines motel a couple times."

"When?"

"I seen it when I was on my way to work. In the morning. I didn't want to mention it but now seems like a good time to bring it up."

For a second, I thought someone had told him I worked there and he was confronting me about keeping it from him. Then it dawned on me that he was accusing me of something far worse. "What exactly are you implying, J.W.?"

His snort was bullish.

"How dare you police my behavior," I hissed into the receiver. "Let me remind you that you don't have any claim on me."

"Yeah, I guessed as much. So what do we have here, Daryl? Anything?"

"You tell me. We agreed it was work first, so I don't bother you. But I can start calling you to ask where you're at, what you're doing, who you're with. I can keep you on the phone all the damn time if you want."

He was spoiling to fight. "Yeah? Well, do me a favor, don't bother."

"No problem. Starting now." I slammed down the phone.

He called me back right away. "I don't want to do it like this, Daryl."

"Me, neither." I struggled to gain control. This guy riled me up in every possible way. "About the Twin Pines. If you must know . . ."

"Don't. You're right, it's none of my business. I wasn't meaning to pry. What I'm saying is, I'm not out there with anyone else, and I'm not much inclined to share you, either. If that means making a formal bid, then I will."

17

"YOU'RE COMING WITH US." Shawna and Kimber grabbed my elbows and hustled me out of Room Twelve and into the Twin Pines parking lot. I blinked against the blinding afternoon sunlight, catching the briefest glimpse of Lan's orange Rally Sport parked diagonally across the handicapped spot before a dark cloth covered my eyes and blotted out the day.

I stumbled as they pulled me along. "What the hell's going on, you guys?" They didn't answer me, just shoved me down and into the car. I heard the doors slam, felt the muscular pressure of their legs on either side of mine in the backseat.

I heard Lan's voice. "No talking. This is a kidnapping," then, the firing of the engine.

"What about my dog? And did you forget I have four horses to feed?"

I felt Kimber's hand pat my thigh. "Got it covered."

"Would you mind filling me in here?"

The three voices in unison. "Soon enough."

"Soon enough" turned out to be almost three hours, if four play-throughs of Metallica's *Ride the Lightning* were any kind of time-keeping. When the blindfold came off, I found myself surrounded by toilet stalls and a row of sinks. Stray bits of straw littered the concrete floor. I had no idea where I was but I heard carnival music and the livestock odor was unmistakable.

"We don't have much time," Shawna said, pulling a pouf of crimson fabric from a shopping bag. "Hurry and try this on." She stepped back. "I hope you don't mind Salvation Army. We got our fairy godmother orders at the last minute." She zipped me into a strapless 1950's cocktail dress with a full crinoline skirt. The fabric smelled sweet, like old perfume. Shawna inhaled deeply. "I think that's Ivoire de Balmain. My grandmother wears it." With tortoiseshell combs and clips between her teeth, Kimber rolled my hair up on the sides, with loose tendrils hanging down around my face and long waves flowing down my back. Shawna dropped to her knees and tacked up the hem of the dress with safety pins so it skimmed the tops of my worn oxblood boots.

"If you won't tell me where I am, can you at least tell me what I'm getting dolled up for?" I really don't like surprises, especially the kind that involve scratchy dresses.

Kimber winked. "Like we said: soon enough. Wait here."

They disappeared into toilet stalls and when they emerged, Kimber was in a magenta sequined mini-dress and Shawna wore a black lace sheath, a mantilla comb stuck in her center-parted hair. They grabbed my hands and pulled me out of the bathroom and into the dusk.

Lan leaned against the cinder block wall, holding a giant stuffed yellow brontosaurus in a Central Wyoming State Fair and Rodeo T-shirt. He'd changed into a black rockabilly tux with silver skull cuff links. "Geez, ladies. In the time it took you, I could've won six more dinos." He took Shawna's arm. "But it was worth the wait to see my girl like this. Now come on, the show's almost half over."

I knew J.W. was entered here tonight, so I wondered if Lan and Shawna hadn't thought it would be a lark to see him ride dressed in formal attire, a novel way to celebrate his second awesome score in Calgary, which made him a serious contender for the short go and the coveted $50,000 bonus round coming the next weekend. If so, whoopee. We stepped carefully through the rocky grounds to the contestant area, Kimber dodging fresh piles of horse manure in her strappy gold stilettos. Shawna gathered the hem of my dress in her hand and I climbed the diamond steel stairs to the arena seating.

I felt my breath catch when I spotted J.W. pacing back and forth on the riser behind the chutes. If I ever had a dream man, he looked like this: boots, skintight Wranglers, a tuxedo jacket, and the lingering traces of a black eye. I went to the railing and called his name. When he saw me in my party dress, he took off his hat and clutched it to his chest like he was having a heart attack, his knees buckling. I'd never had a man look at me that way in my life, like I was the only girl on earth. I felt beautiful. Worship-worthy. The very opposite of she-masculated.

He climbed up the stairs holding a clear plastic box containing a red rose corsage. He sat on the metal rail and motioned me to him. When he tried to fasten the corsage to my dress, he fumbled and the pearl-topped pin fell between the slats in the stands. "Well, there goes that idea." He thought a minute and snapped his fingers. "I got it." He unwrapped his leather boot tie and lashed the corsage to my wrist. "Just right!"

I looked at the roses. "What's this for, anyway?"

"Remember that night when we were looking at the stars? You took me someplace I'd never been before. Now I'm returning the favor."

The five of us squeezed into the hot rod, me sandwiched between J.W. and Kimber. Lan blew through a yellow light on the main drag and stayed in the passing lane. I felt like a cowgirl Cinderella en route to the ball, screaming up Wyoming Boulevard in my orange metal-flake Camaro pumpkin coach. We screeched to a halt in front of the Beacon Club. Strings of white lights bobbed in the wind and in a chain-link cage off the back door, the bucking machine flung a rider to the mat.

All eyes were on us as we walked into the main room. Just off the dance floor was a long table. Around it, in formal attire, sat Beeber, Big Sue, Tim, Brandon and his model girlfriend, Clete, and Margie from Douglas. Clete wore his best shirt, a loud paisley of purples and blues that matched Margie's azure cocktail dress, which dragged a little at the décolleté. Shawna bussed J.W. on the cheek and Lan slapped his back. Kimber raised her shot glass my way and everyone at the table yelled, "HAPPY PROM!"

J.W. held out his arms, circus master-style. "Better late than never." It was just crazy enough to thrill me to the core. I hopped up and kissed him.

We drank and talked and ate barbecue, Beeber beaming to have Kimber eat cornbread from his plate, hovering over her like her own Secret Service detail. Then we got up and stormed the dance floor. J.W. took great pleasure in spinning me out, the skirt flying up around my thighs. Whenever I crashed into another couple, we'd laugh, apologize, and keep right on dancing.

Everyone cheered when "Cotton-Eyed Joe" came on. As silly dances go, Cotton-Eyed Joe takes the cake. You don't want to do it, but you can't resist. Every barn dance or Saddle Tramps memory rages back and goes straight to your feet. Lan and J.W. yanked me in between the two of them. Tim hooked arms with Shawna and a wallflower hanging on the side and dragged them onto the floor in front of us, and Clete, Sue, and Margie joined up behind us. Three by three, dancers moved around the floor in a circle.

At the end of the song, we collapsed into our seats. I fanned myself with a napkin. "Thanks, guys. I know that took some guts."

"You've gotta do Cotton-Eyed Joe!" Lan pounded his chest, then shook his fist. "It's roots, man. It's core!"

J.W. looked toward the DJ and made a motion with his hand. "Look at You, Girl" came on. He held out his hand to me. "Remember this?"

I rose. "Who could forget?"

J.W. led me to the very center of the dance floor. He put his arms around me and we danced. Then we weren't dancing anymore. We were standing in the middle of the dance floor holding each other. He whispered in my ear. "You enjoying your prom, sweetheart?"

I knew that if I looked at him, I would cry. It was the nicest thing anyone had ever done for me. I hugged him closer and nodded into his lapels.

We went outside to the bullpen. "Can't have a prom without a portrait. You ready?" J.W. hopped up behind me on the bucking machine and we got a five-dollar Polaroid of us together, him in his tux, me in my secondhand gown. We both had an arm up like we were ready to nod, the corsage around my wrist raised with the celebratory thrust of a tossed bouquet. When J.W. jumped down and the machine started up, I lasted two seconds. After a tremendous heave and surge, I was flung to the mat.

"My turn," Shawna said. Lan gently boosted Shawna onto the bucking machine. As it slowly rocked to life, Lan whistled to the guy at the controls. "Hold on a sec there, chief."

Shawna put her hands on her hips as the mechanical bull came to a stop. "What's going on? I was doing pretty good up here."

"I need to ask you something." Lan dropped to one knee on the padded mat and opened a small black box, the excited angle of his arms threatening the seams on his sharkskin jacket.

Shawna clapped her hands over her mouth.

Lan held up the box with trembling hands. "Shawna Shalom Two Tribes, will you marry me?"

At closing time, my personal prom wound down. Everyone hugged Shawna and pumped Lan's hand. J.W. led me to his truck. "You've made it past midnight, Cinderella. Night's just beginning." We took a winding road and drove into the hills above town.

We parked at a remote turnoff and started making out like

teenagers. I did everything he liked, kissing on his neck and calling him Daddy. We steamed up the windows in the cab. I unbuttoned his shirt and slid it off of him, and J.W. sat back, a blissed-out look on his face, lips slightly swollen and pink at the rim.

He reached into the backseat and brandished a champagne bottle icing in a feed bucket. We grabbed the black-and-white checkered blanket and spread it on the ground outside. We sat in the dark, the lights of Casper down below like handfuls of scattered citrines, the hard rise of the Bighorns looming black behind. I put my arms around him. "That whole prom thing was just a scheme to get me out here, wasn't it?"

"Possibly."

"Don't get your hopes up, Romeo. I'm a good girl. I only go to second base. On the outside of the clothes."

"Oh, don't worry. I'm a gentleman. I'll stick by the rules."

We kissed, his hands tracing the contours of my body through my dress. "How about one more base?" It was like he was reading my mind. When J.W. was good, he was very good, and when he was bad, it was just the kind of bad I needed.

If you looked at us, you wouldn't be able to tell what we were doing. Don't I look like I'm relaxing in his lap? Don't we look like innocent stargazers? You couldn't see his hand under my dress, petting me through the thin fabric of my panties.

History is filled with millions of furtive post-prom explorations like this, so what we were doing was nothing new, but it was new to me. I felt guilty when I touched myself; to have another person do it was almost too much.

"You said to stay outside the clothes, right?" His hand cupped my sex. "Like this?"

I moved up a fraction. I needed him to do it softer.

"Is this it right here?"

I was too self-conscious to tell him what I wanted. I wished he'd just figure it out on his own, but he wasn't a mind reader. "Slow," I whispered, so soft I could barely hear myself. I didn't know why, but it was probably the most difficult thing I'd ever said.

He eased up and everything receded but the stiff tulle scratching my legs, the sound of my breathing, and his fingers rubbing pink satin. He'd touched me there before, but his way. Now he was touching me exactly the way I touch myself, something intensely private and almost shameful. "It's okay, sweetheart," he whispered when I tried to move his hand. "It's okay." He kept touching me and right about the time he began whispering everything he wanted to do to me that he hadn't yet, I squeezed my thighs together tight and orgasmed against his hand.

While I caught my breath, J.W. picked a wild daisy. "She loves me. She loves me not." One by one, petals floated to the ground. "She loves me. She loves me not." Soon there was a drift of yellow petals at J.W.'s feet and only a few on the stem. "She loves me . . ."

I grabbed his wrist. "Stop."

He stood up and held out his hands to me. "Come on. Let's get you to the hotel."

"You're not going to put on a shirt?"

"I'm not standing on ceremony, Daryl. Not tonight."

When we got to the hotel, J.W. carried me down the hall. I cradled a bottle of champagne in one hand and my boots in the other. We passed an older man and woman coming out of the elevator. She had on a ruffle-necked peasant dress, he a tan reproduction Nudie suit and a Boss of the Plains Stetson. J.W. turned sideways to squeeze by and nodded at the couple. He dialed up the cowboy corn with a dip of his chin. "Evenin', sir. Ma'am."

Before the elevator door shut, the lady slapped her companion's arm. "How come we never do that, Roy?"

My feet throbbed when J.W. set me down inside our room. My scalp itched from the hairpins. "I feel scrungy."

"How about a bath?" He opened the bathroom door. The tub

was ringed in candles. He lit them and turned on the faucets full-blast. There were black-eyed Susans and daisies in a plastic vase. He unzipped my dress so I could step out of it, then he skinned off my underwear. I hid behind my hand. "I need to shave."

He leaned forward. "Let me do it."

"It'll be cold."

"I shave with hot water just like anybody else."

J.W. filled the sink basin while the bath was running. I perched on the edge of the tub, and he knelt between my legs and started working. He finger-painted me with shaving cream and it tingled. I bounced my knee anxiously. J.W. trapped my leg under his elbow. "I've been skilled with a razor for as long as you've been alive. Now quit fussing."

The task intensified as he shaved lower. Him doing this was the most excruciating, exhilarating intimacy I could imagine. He had me splayed on the bathmat, my foot on his shoulder. It was making him crazy, having me this vulnerable, this helpless in his hands. He wiped the excess cream away with his thumbs and spread the fragile lips apart. "That's beautiful."

He finished up and rinsed me with a warm washcloth. "Okay, you can stop holding your breath now. I'm done."

We got in the tub, me sitting between his legs like a nesting doll. I could only feel him behind me, soaping my shoulders and back. I ran more hot water and we passed the champagne back and forth. I took a pull off the bottle. The bubbles nipped my gums. "When did you know?"

J.W. squeezed the washcloth so hot water ran down my back. "Know what?"

"That you wanted to be with me."

"From the second I saw you in the stands at the Bluffs Ranch."

"That soon?"

"Well, that was when you first caught my attention, and it only got better from there. You're the most fearless girl I've ever met."

"Fearless how? I pass out at the sight of blood."

"That's just a phobia. I mean grand-scheme fearless. You're not living small. You went after what you wanted with the painting. Cowboy Christmas, you hopped right in with us. You drove. When I got hurt at Cody you were amazing. But you know what I like most?"

"What?"

"You never ask me to be any different than what I am. Shoot, you'll even kiss me when I got a chew in. That alone about breaks my heart."

Rosy from the bath, J.W. dried me off, even hooking the towel over his fingertip to get between each individual toe. He tapped powder on me and smoothed it in. He carried me to the bed like I was weightless and switched the lamp to low. The nightstand drawer slid open on plastic rollers. At the sight of the yellow foil strip of condoms, I seized up. I counted the freckles on his back as he sat on the side of the bed and rolled on a rubber.

He took me in his arms, but the more he kissed me, the farther away I pulled. He shifted his hips over mine, poised for entry, and it turned out the girl he saw as fearless wasn't so fearless after all. "I can't," I whispered, turning my head away. "I'm sorry."

I awoke to a rush of cold air. J.W. whipped the blanket to his side. "It's eight-forty-five, sleepyface. We've got fifteen minutes to get on the road. I told Lan and Shawna I'd drop you off at nine."

I opened one eye to a champagne headache. "Why is it so late? Did you just get up?"

"Are you kidding? I been up for hours now." He opened the blinds.

"Nooo," I groaned, diving under the pillow to escape the light. I looked out from under the pillow at the flowers in the vases. "You know, Clete said you'd picked me flowers in Colorado once."

"I did. I drove out to your house, but I turned around and came home. I figured you didn't need me pestering you like that."

He sat on the end of the bed, waiting for me. He picked up my foot. Holding my ankle, he traced the barbed wire over the heart with the edge of his nail. "This is a good tattoo for you."

I lifted the pillow from my head. "Because it perfectly captures the dichotomy of my personality?"

His lips quirked into a smile. "Yeah, something like that."

"Oh my God. That almost makes me cry." Shawna touched her hand to her cheek when I told her about J.W. and the flowers. She pushed away her tofu scrambles. The tofu tasted rotten, she said. The waitress returned the plate to the kitchen, came back, and reported, aggrieved, that the cook had tasted it and couldn't tell the difference.

When Lan slid away to the men's room, I turned toward Shawna. "I don't know what's going on with me. Why can't I just get down to it with this guy?" I was on such good terms with my internal jury. As much as I wanted J.W., there was an equally strong opposing force inside of me telling me no. I picked at my fruit and yogurt parfait. "I tell you, I wish I were more like Kimber sometimes."

"Look, we totally love Kimber, okay? But she mounts these elaborate campaigns to distract herself from the fact that she has no life right now." However brief, the analysis was apt. "It's different if you care. I think you're smart to be cautious." She popped an echinacea capsule in her mouth and washed it down with orange juice. "In the beginning I had my doubts, but he seems good for you." The ring on her finger caught the hard light, a dark oval ruby set in a Celtic braid of white gold. Only a man who knew and loved her well could make such a perfect choice.

"I gave him an invitation to the Frontier Days art show before he left. I asked him to be my date."

"That's pretty big. He's gotta know that at least." She put her arm around me. "Right?"

"I guess. But I'm sure it wasn't what he was hoping for. I keep looking for some sign, like, okay, it's safe now."

She twisted the ring on her finger like she wasn't quite used to it being there. Around and around. "Well, when you know, you know."

18

I TUMBLED OUT OF THE RALLY SPORT into the Twin Pines parking lot wearing yesterday's clothes. A family was making lunch at the warped redwood picnic table between the eponymous pines in the driveway. The father tinkered with a small hibachi, laying a pink coil of frankfurters over the coals. Amid the swooping branches, the mother snapped a towel to shoo bees away from glasses of toxic green Hawaiian Punch.

Giselle pulled the drapes in Room Three and came out when she saw me loading change into the Coke machine. "Crystal's on her fourth massage this morning and you're three hours later than you said you'd be. We're way behind." She rushed on, stubbing her toe on the uneven pavement as she tried to push the cleaning cart down the sidewalk in her high-heeled mules.

The walls of the Twin Pines held no secrets. I heard it all—squalling babies, shower singing, coughing fits, loud television shows, louder fights. The dull choir of life's proceedings, with occasional weirdness mixed in. One guy checked in with his clarinet and played "Ave Maria" over and over for an hour, then left. A woman who left her husband when he wouldn't give up the dog she was allergic to cried in her room for two days. I listened to her story after she'd called the desk to have her Kleenex-stuffed trash baskets emptied. She left me a fifty-dollar tip.

When I finished everything else, I went into Room Eleven, which shared a wall with Crystal's. I hovered at the open bathroom window. She had a client in her room. A chime rang and I heard her say, "Ten minutes left in the hour."

The man's voice was a relaxed drone. "Is this the end of the story?"

"Do you want it to be?"

"I like my stories to have a happy ending."

"Thirty extra," she said.

"Watch the nails, Crystal!" he said. Two minutes later, I heard his heaving groan.

I put away my cart, went around back, and sat on the curb next to the laundry room. Bleach- and detergent-scented steam poured from the vent. The heat of the sun drilled down on my back and shoulders. I watched hundreds of tiny red ants descend single-file from the chipped masonry and swarm around a melting chocolate kiss mashed flat in the foil shell.

I wasn't blind to the extracurricular potential of this job. More than one male guest had made it known that he'd tip generously if I'd rub tanning oil on him while his wife was off shopping, or let him take me for a drink at the Redwood Tavern when my shift was over. Did I care what Crystal was doing? I didn't know. But it wasn't my damn business, and if I didn't want someone minding mine, I'd best not mind hers.

I felt differently when I saw the next client emerge from Crystal's room. I recognized his beefy back in the black-and-yellow plaid short-sleeved shirt. Darcey Rivers. He looked both ways, making sure the coast was clear, before he stepped out the door. I watched him put on his wedding ring, start up his Bronco, and nose out the back alley entrance. Wife out of town, husband on the loose.

I felt a numb shock, like I'd just witnessed a gruesome accident or someone held up at gunpoint. I was filled with an awful feeling of doom, so heavy I drove home half-expecting to find Happy Jack Road surrounded in flames or that the horses had gotten loose and run away. But when I got to the house, all was well. Homer slept soundly in his run, the horses were calm and in place. The morning mail even contained a small check from a freelance assignment. The only thing wrong was that I was running out of time on the portrait of Shane McGurk. And Jace. He was pissed that I had been gone overnight.

"This isn't like you, Daryl," he hollered on the answering machine. "What the hell is going on?"

J.W. came over for an early dinner. He was up at Jubilee Days in Laramie at eight. A chicken was roasting in the oven and baby red potatoes were set to boil in the pot. I sat on the deck, the hot vinyl cushion sticking to the back of my legs, and fondled a 12-gauge shotgun shell while J.W. set up the thrower. The shell looked like it slipped from a woman's makeup case, the cylindrical plastic hull canary yellow with a six-point crimp at the top like a daisy. I shook it by my ear; the lead shot dancing inside sounded like a baby's rattle. The heft felt good in my hand.

A cardboard case of clay pigeons was out next to the pedal-operated launcher. J.W. loaded clays in the arm of the thrower at the other end of the deck. He stood and checked the sight on his gun. "What've you got on your mind, precious?"

I was tempted to tell him about seeing Darcey at the Twin Pines, but then I'd have to explain why I was there in the first place. And maybe Darcey just saw Crystal for a regular old massage. I appeased myself with this possibility.

"This portrait I've got due next week is important to the client and I'm totally choking. If I didn't care so much and she didn't expect so much, I'd blaze right through it. But I try to focus and my mind skates off in the opposite direction."

We each put on a pair of safety glasses. J.W. set his foot on the launcher. "Well, run the metal to that muse of yours. She'll give you want you want."

I shouldered my shotgun and nodded. "Pull!" J.W. stepped on the launcher and two clays arced into the sky. I followed them with the shotgun barrel and fired. Missed them both. "Damn, I can't believe that shot."

"It's been a while. Try 'er again." He loaded another couple pigeons.

"Okay, pull!" I missed again, clipping a chunk off of one. I lowered the gun. "Let's switch." I watched as J.W. fired, pegging both clays on the first try. "How do you maintain your focus every time you ride?"

"I don't think about it." He shrugged. "Athlete's no different from an artist in that respect."

"I don't understand."

"I'll give you an example." He put the shotgun down at his side and turned to me. "You don't think about your reaction when I do this"—J.W. jabbed his finger toward my eye and I flinched behind the safety glasses—"See? It's like that. It's an instinct." He sat. "Somewhere in there, you know exactly what you've got to do. You clear your mind to react. That's all focus is. Rodeo is ninety percent mental."

"You're never afraid?"

"I'm never *not* afraid. It's like Donny Gay said about bull riding, 'If a guy tells you he ain't scared, either he's lying or he ain't draggin' a full string of fish.' Same goes for bareback."

J.W. flipped up his glasses, rubbed his dominant eye. "The thing to do is to make your try bigger than your fear. When I'm under a lot of pressure, I visualize it. I break it down into letters: T. R. Y., over and over until it's the only thing in my head. I use T. R. Y. as shorthand for the whole deal—not over-thinking, not over-riding, just keeping with it. Trust yourself. Stay true. Try."

"Is that what you're thinking about when you look so preoccupied before you get on?"

"Well, it's what's on my mind, though I don't guess you'd call it thinking."

I sat down next to him. "So it's kind of like meditation, a mantra or something."

"Maybe. Every guy's got his own way of focusing, because when you lose focus, you get hurt. Or worse. For me, it all comes down to T-R-Y."

I wrapped my hand around the barrel of the shotgun. The gunmetal was warm in my fingers. "I don't see how you can stand the risks. No matter how good you are, you still get bucked off, and you can always get injured. It seems kind of nuts, when you consider the odds."

"Risk is just one of those deals you get comfortable with over time. People might think we're nuts, but then again, we're what they come to see." He flipped his safety glasses back down and squinted into the sun. "Besides, look at what you do."

"What about it?"

"Everyone knows artists are insane, right? Drugs. Alcohol. All kinds of screwed-up relationships. Suicide. Those are some serious risks right there. Why would anyone want that life?"

I closed my hand around his and he helped me stand. "What other life is there?" I said. "If I couldn't paint or draw, I'd die. I'm serious. It's a struggle to produce a lot of the time, but sometimes it just flows right out of you. When you're in that space, it's like you're touched by the hand of God." I put the shotgun down. It was something I'd never said aloud. "Okay, now I do sound like a nut job."

"Not to me, you don't. Cowboys get in that space, too, where it's like God's cracking out right along with you. Getting tapped off— when you're perfectly in sync. No feeling like it in the world."

I braced the gun butt to the cradle of my shoulder. "How's that for the lives we lead—we're either going to end up crazy or dead."

"We're all going to die, Daryl. If living crazy means dying happy, then I'm okay with that."

I yelled, "Pull!" J.W. brought his foot down hard, launching two clays. I fired once, twice, and they both exploded into clean bits.

J.W. slapped his leg. "Beauty!"

"Thank you." I took a little bow.

"God, you make a picture with that shotgun." He sat down and shook his head. "Girls and ammo. It's a beautiful thing."

We went inside the house. I took the chicken from the oven and set it to cool on the counter. J.W. opened the refrigerator. "Fresh out of tea." He picked up the glass pitcher from the sink and rinsed it. "This would be a good opportunity for you to learn how to make real iced tea."

I poured milk into the potatoes and started mashing. "I drink real tea; it's just from a mix is all."

"That powdered stuff you drink is not tea. I don't know what it is, exactly, but tea it ain't. It doesn't even have any sugar in it, which as you know disqualifies it as a real drink far as I'm concerned." He pulled a stockpot from the cabinet and turned on the faucet.

"Okay, I'm game." I set aside the potato masher and dried my hands. "Teach me."

"First thing, you put about a quarter pitcher of water on to boil, like I've got going here. Then you pour the sugar in." He stirred sugar from a five-pound bag into the pot with a wooden spoon.

Waxy yellow sun slanted knowingly through the dust-flecked kitchen window. Sweat ran in a slow trickle between my breasts and down my stomach. J.W. came up behind me. He picked up two lemons from the fruit bowl and took up a paring knife. "Then, while that's heating up, you slice the lemons so they're ready when the tea is boiled." Still behind me, he slid his arms under mine. His chest was pressing against my shoulder blades. I could feel his body heat coming through my worn cotton shirt.

Pressing the lemon down firmly under his palm on the cutting board, he said, "First, you roll the lemon like this to wring juice out of the pulp." He ran the fruit back and forth a dozen times. I picked up the other lemon and did the same.

J.W. put his chin on my shoulder. "You know something?"

"What's that?"

"Watching you with that shotgun was killing me."

I wasn't going to give the smooth mouth any play. "Is this how every Southerner makes tea?"

"This is how *I* make tea. Everyone's got his own idea about it back home. Sweet tea is a source of passionate debate." He chose a heavy, wood-handled knife, the blade ringing out of the holder with the *tang* of a sword being drawn from the scabbard. "You got to cut the lemons thin as you can." He slid the knife though the lemon, a slice folding slowly away from the body of the fruit as if languishing in the heat. He held it up and turned toward the window. "You want the sun to shine through them. See? Just like that. You try."

I took the knife from him and began making careful slices. While I worked, J.W. kissed my neck.

"Dammit!" In the split-second of distraction, I ran the knife neatly through the flesh on my left index finger. The lemon juice in the cut stung mightily. I dropped the knife on the counter.

J.W. spun me around to face him. "Baby, I'm sorry. Here, let me."

I felt swoony and weird.

"You okay?"

I shook my head no and grabbed the edge of the counter.

"Come on. Take a deep breath. You feel your feet? You won't fall if you think of your legs and feet being solid. Wiggle your toes. You feel that?" He shifted me away from the counter and pressed up against me so I was braced against the refrigerator. A weird electricity buzzed around my molars and forked down the underside of my tongue. I fought to stay vertical.

J.W. brought my finger to his lips and kissed the cut. A smear of blood shone on his lower lip, fresh, translucent red. A burst of nerves seized my stomach. "J.W., your lip . . ."

Before I could finish, he ran his tongue over the spot and it disappeared. An acquisitive smile flickered on his face when he tasted the salted tin flavor of my blood. I heard myself gasp.

The edges of the room went black and began to curl in on themselves. White spots raced up the walls and back down again. J.W. pressed me harder against the refrigerator, his full weight against me, and pulled my arms around his waist. "Come on, Daryl, breathe. You can do this. Remember, ninety percent mental."

I grabbed onto him and ground my cheek against his shoulder as hard as I could. I inhaled down to the depths of my gut and tried to feel my feet.

He pulled a chair up next to the counter and sat me down. I put my head between my legs and slowly sipped air, willing my pulse to slow down.

"Are you going to be okay?" J.W. asked. I nodded. "I shouldn't have pushed you. Do you want to lie down on the couch? I can put the fan on you."

"No, that's okay. I just need to chill for a minute."

"All right, sure. All right. I'm sorry. Guess I've caused enough trouble filling your head with my so-called wisdom. I'll conclude the lesson." He filled the pitcher with ice and poured the boiled tea over the cubes and stirred. "Once the tea's in here, you drop the lemon slices in a glass with some ice. You take the slices one at a time and twist 'em a little bit to let the juice out. Then you stir." He handed me a full glass. "There you go. Pretty as you please."

I didn't want any dinner and I was too wrung out to make the trip to Laramie with J.W. for Jubilee Days, so he put me to bed and I fell into a deep, dreamless sleep before the sun even set. I woke up after midnight, hot and parched, sweat soaking through my T-shirt and fusing my skin in the sheets. J.W., back from Laramie, slept motionless at my side, left arm folded over his eyes. I slid out to the kitchen for a drink. I took a jelly jar from the drainboard and the tea pitcher from the fridge. The night heat was so stifling I sank to the floor and rested with my legs stretched out against the cool linoleum tiles. I held the cold glass pitcher between my thighs. The tea was sweet and rich and went down like liquid sin, refreshing but not at all wholesome. I drank a full glass and poured another, savoring the gentle bite of lemon on my tongue.

I saw the outline of J.W.'s gear piled in the darkened living room. I set down my tea and walked quietly from the kitchen. I crouched down behind the arm of the sofa. My ears pricked up as I began sleuthing through his things. I unfolded his chaps and combed through the fringe with my fingers, feeling the nubby/smooth contrast on either side of the finely cut strips of leather. I stood and held the chaps along my legs; they trailed to the floor, six inches too long. I lowered onto my knees and slowly pulled the long zipper on his war bag, opening it wide. I dug through the contents—files, powder, a hole puncher, various wraps and tape, a small leather sack holding a sock full of rosin. I picked up his spurs, turn-down shanks angled 5 percent off-center, and touched the dull points of his rowels, spinning them on a loving fingertip. I rooted into every corner, as if somewhere in the rigging bag I could find the basis for his obsession, something, a single clue.

Maybe, I thought, it's a matter of biological destiny and for him, an adrenalized pursuit is its own reward. Maybe it's a hard reality of the heart, and passionate is just another word for stubborn. Stubborn with a higher purpose.

A can of rubber cement rolled from the rug onto the wood floor, startling me. I whispered *shit*. My eyes flicked to the loft. I scanned for sounds of motion from above. Nothing.

When I came upon J.W.'s glove, I pulled it from the bag. It was stiff and heavy, the fingers curled like they were beckoning me. Rosin stained the benzoin-girded palm and knuckles a sulphurous yellow-white. I slid in my hand, curving with the contours of the leather.

The rigging resembled a butterfly pinned in flight, the handle rising up like a twisting body from the folded wings. As with butterflies, each rigging is subtly different, customized with care to suit a man's form and style. Though flexible, the whole structure felt sturdy, solid as bone. I couldn't possibly calculate the gross tonnage of body weight that J.W. had flailed against the thing since the first time it braced a bronc's muscled back.

I sat spraddle-legged on the rug, the wool prickling the back of my knees. I placed the rigging over my thigh and rocked it down snug against the skin. My fingers were so small in the glove it slid easily through the narrow space in the handhold. When I closed my fist around the handhold, a wash of euphoric heat rippled from the root of my core right up the centerline of my back.

With my gloved hand in his rigging, I felt the way I feel when I run my kolinsky sable paintbrush across my lower lip. An almost libidinous hum, a quiet current swimming with minute, affirming sparks. These are more than mere tools of a trade. These are tools to fully inhabit life. I yearned to squeeze the rigging handle, turn my hand until I heard the owlscreech of rawhide on rosin on leather. Restraining the motion was like suppressing a shout.

I set to loving up the glove just like J.W. would. With my free hand, I opened the rosin pouch. I took out the sock, unwinding it, and when I did, a little glassine envelope fell into my lap. Inside were my lucky clover charm and the finishing nail that had started everything.

So I wasn't a speedbump on the rodeo road. I rosined the glove, glowing with the brightest happiness.

Lovers, I know, speak the same language in their embrace, but too often when they separate and face the world, they're alienated from each other by the gulf of years, background, gender, quirks of nature. Not us. I clenched the rigging handle tight and pantomimed pulling my arm down, as if cracking back in slow motion. I shut my eyes and envisioned that sacred place called "crazy" where art and rodeo intersect. I saw the old Indian behind the chutes in Cody, gnarled fingers gripping his cane top, the memory of a thousand rides boiling behind his eyes. *Once it gets in your blood, it stays there.* And I saw J.W. standing at the kitchen counter when I cut myself, the split-second greedy look when he licked his lip and swallowed. Shock sparkled along my legs. *Like me,* I thought. *My lover is just like me.*

19

J.W. AND I SPED DOWN HAPPY JACK toward Route 80 en route to Laramie for the final go at Jubilee Days, the sun a fuzzy white spot behind strips of gray cloud. J.W. wadded up a blue bandana and wiped the fog from the windshield, his spirits high. Having won first the night before, he was on quite a roll.

It had started to sprinkle after breakfast, rain misting the brown grass. We hadn't had rain in weeks. I stuck my head out the truck window. "This is awesome, isn't it?" The droplets felt cool on my face. I rolled the window all the way down and slid out. I sat on the door, the wind rushing around my body, and pounded the roof with my fists.

I felt J.W. yank me by the ankle. "Cowgirl, are you insane? Get back in here!"

I shouted at the sky. "Rain! This is amazing!" I dropped back into the passenger seat, my tank top soaked and my hair snarled from the wind.

J.W. had to yell over the sound of the engine roaring through the open window. "What would you say if I told you I was going to win that rodeo for you today?"

"What?"

He fixed his eyes on the road. "You heard me."

"No offense, cowboy, but I'd say you were more full of crap than a Christmas turkey." What he was proposing was outrageous. So much could go wrong. His horse could crush him against the rails before he even called for the gate. He could buck off halfway to the whistle. He could be on top until the very end of the round only to have someone knock him from the leaderboard with a killer ride. I shook my head.

"Well, I'm going to do it. I'm going to prove myself to you."

"You don't have prove anything to me, J.W."

"Sure I do, Daryl." He leaned over to catch a protein bar that was sliding across the dashboard as he took the curve. "After Casper, I couldn't figure it, you know, why you were uncomfortable. Then I finally figured it out. I was driving home and I said to myself, 'It's not her. It's you.' There's something that you're not doing, something she's not getting."

I rolled up the window and buckled myself into my seat. "What do you think that is?"

"Respect. You don't know me real well and I understand that. I'm going to win that Jubilee Days buckle for you as a tribute, to show you my respect."

I looked at him.

"The only people who ever got a buckle from me were family. You can ask anyone about that. What I'm saying is, I'm willing to do whatever it takes." An off-duty ambulance sped past us, sending sheets of water against the windshield. The cab went dark and gray, the engine hum muffling as in a cave.

I knew J.W. wanted me, and in a way that no man had, he understood me. And he was right—I really hadn't known where I stood with him. But I'd figured it out last night, when I was in his rigging bag. He didn't have to win me. I was already his.

When we pulled onto Route 80 at the Summit, the sky opened up and it began pouring. We could barely see the highway as we came down the steep grade into Laramie. In the parking lot at the rodeo grounds, everyone was ecstatic. The men working the rodeo ducked around in yellow slickers and clear plastic hat covers. The storm lowered the temperature a good fifteen degrees and kept down the dust. We needed this.

We rushed through the downpour amidst the glowing red lights of horse trailers. A siren mewled in the distance. J.W. found his buddies huddling under an RV awning. "Ready, boys?" They buttoned their collars to keep the rain off their necks and slopped over toward the pudding bowl arena.

Everyone packed in under the covered seating, sudsing away the chill. The beer guys were going nuts, skidding up and down the muddy stairs. I wanted to be as close to the bucking chutes as I could, so I sat alone in the open seating of the family section, shivering under my umbrella, J.W.'s Carhartt jacket over my shoulders and the black-and-white checkered blanket on my lap.

When J.W. nodded his head, the gate cracked wide and the horse stalled. I mean, just stood there like she was waiting for a bus. Someone swatted at her neck and she bolted from the chute and started a straight run along the fence. The crowd began yelling, the chant buffered by the rain. "Re-ride! Re-ride!"

I wanted to get out of the rain, but I knew J.W. would take the re-ride option, which meant I'd have to stay put until the end of the round.

They rolled in a new bronc named Satchmo. While J.W. set his rigging, the clutch of men helping him in the chute stopped what they were doing and looked over in my direction. He must have said something. Concentration in the chutes is sacrosanct, and seeing all those cowboys turn my way was as jarring as a group of surgeons pausing to give nod while elbow-deep in entrails.

I couldn't hear the gate crack for the sound of the rain hammering down. The horse had a couple ducks and lots of drop. J.W. flew up and away from the rigging, then bounced back down and flopped about like a rag doll. He kept his feet square and spurring throughout, toes cranked out to either side.

At the whistle, he jumped off Satchmo and churned through the mud. There was a dip near the fence and he skidded in it and slipped, landing flat on his ass, his legs straight out in front of him. He put his head in his hands, shoulders shaking as he roared with laughter. He pushed himself up and emerged from the mud, half-man, half-Fudgesickle. The audience cheered when the announcer boomed out that he'd won the round with his re-ride at seventy-nine points.

They brought out a saddled Appaloosa so J.W. could make his victory lap. It was still pouring thunderously. J.W. vaulted into the saddle and squinted against the raindrops as he kicked the horse into a gallop. The mudman cometh. He tipped his hat to the grandstand and when he galloped past me, he held his hat out from his chest and, safe from the eyes of the Sunday crowd, gave me a world-class raspberry.

When we got back to Red Hill we shucked our clothes in the laundry room and ran for the shower naked, dropping J.W.'s laundry bag next to the washer. The house was freezing so J.W., towel wrapped around his waist, knelt at the hearth and built a fire. With his wet hair slicked back, he looked sleek and vulnerable.

I combed out my hair and tightened the belt on my terrycloth bathrobe. J.W. sat on the couch and pulled me into his lap. "We did good today, didn't we, baby?"

"Considering everything we were up against, I'd say it turned out great. I wasn't sure we were going to get this one off the ground."

He shook the black velvet box at me. "I promised you this."

I opened the box. The Jubilee Days buckle was beautiful: a black enamel oval with a gold-and-red horseshoe inlay. I held it in my hand. It was cold and heavy. "So does this mean I'm officially a buckle bunny?"

He folded his arms behind his head. "Nope. A buckle honey, maybe."

"I could tell people I won it from you in a poker game."

"Sure."

"Or I could tell them I shot it off of you in a gunfight."

"Or you could just tell people I gave it to you. Would that be so bad?"

I put the box on the table and stood up. "I'm proud of you."

J.W. spread his legs so I could step between his knees. "Proud of me?" He reached forward and ran his hands up the outside of my calves. "It was you that did it."

"You're delirious." The fire warmed my back. I started to sweat but not from the heat. J.W. smiled slowly, a look both desirous and accusing. He sat up, his hands cupping the back of my calves, and pulled me closer. He untied the belt and my robe slid to the floor.

I drew back, stepping into shadow. I wanted to cover up the parts of me I didn't like but I was short about half a dozen hands.

"You're so pretty."

"You're crazy."

J.W. lay down on the quilt in front of the fire. "Come here."

I curled alongside him and he kissed me. He lowered his head, lips warm on my breasts and neck. I pulled the towel from around his waist and held his cock in my hand, stroking. His mouth went slack. He took one of my nipples between his lips and tenderly sucked. I closed my eyes as my hands found the back of his neck. After weeks of restraint, I was finally ready. His lips fluttered over my throat when he whispered, "You're my girl now, ain't you?"

My fingers rested in his wet hair. I opened my eyes to look directly at him. I nodded as he slid his hand up the soft flesh of my inner thigh. With a glint of his teeth, he had the condom wrapper shucked. He kneed my legs apart and with gentle force, he pushed inside of me. "That's right, you're Daddy's girl."

When we weren't playing our game, we never talked about it. I don't think either of us would know what to say, how to explain that connection. We slipped into role like sliding through a partition to a secret room. I was transfixed by the way he would open his arms to me or hold me down. How he whispered not into my ear but right behind it, and what he said.

Daddy. The word mystified as much as attracted. It wasn't an innocent endearment like sweetie or darling or babe. It implied a more dangerous relationship, more risk. To play this way meant hazarding a fragile trust that bridged deep wellsprings of shame and stopping seemed impossible.

He never hurt me; he just pushed me a little further than I thought I wanted to go. I was out of my depth and I think it was the same for him, too, for throughout every second of this he had a look of blatant need, as if caring for me this way, fucking me, nourished him. And behind that need was trepidation, like the game might get called at any time and that would kill him.

He called me so many things. Good girl, bad girl, best girl, favorite. The only thing I knew for sure was that I was *his* girl, and the simple thought of it made me feel as if fire were spiraling down my limbs.

Afterward, he bundled us up in the quilt. I felt worthy and surrendered, while he looked redeemed, respected. Proud. I closed my eyes and put my head on his chest. We lay wrapped in quiet, warm from the hearth glow, the body heat, and the searing lick of shame.

Hours later, I awoke. The fire had tamped down to embers and the dark room was freezing. Rain pounded the roof, mixed with the tinny ping of hail. J.W. clung to me, his erection pressing the small of my back. I writhed in his arms, trying to turn onto my stomach. I was tangled up in the quilt. He shuddered against me and woke up. His voice was a sleepy rasp. "I need you."

He entered me from behind and I bit my lips from the pain. Still shocky from before, I was tender and really tight. But I didn't stop him. There was no condom this time. I knew it was wrong but I was desperate to feel the naked heat of him inside me.

J.W. stretched out long and pulled me on top. I hated it. Hated the way it felt and hated being so exposed. I hefted forward onto my knees to slide him out. "I want to get off."

J.W. pressed his hips up. "I know you do, precious. Just take your time."

"No, I mean I want to get *off*." I squirmed onto my back.

He positioned himself over me. "Can we try it like this?"

"Daddy, don't."

"Shhh, just give it a minute and it'll stop hurting. I promise."

He slid his hands underneath me. I felt a cartilaginous creak from his shoulder, then a pop, as he pulled me close. He was barely moving inside of me when the ache shifted key. I felt like I was being swallowed up in warmth, my insides turning to simmering liquid. He took my hands and held them over my head as he leaned his full body weight against me. I wrapped my legs around his waist, trying to pull him further in, to grind against the hard slat of bone that floated just beneath his skin. The strength in his legs made it happen. I bucked once, hard, and arched off of the quilt. J.W. knew I never came this way and the surprise got to him. "Baby girl," he whispered, his pace quickening to meet mine. "Oh honey, oh God."

He tucked his sweaty forehead in the crook of my shoulder as he heaved against my breastbone. When I felt his humid breath on my skin, I started shaking. I couldn't control it. J.W. caught me right away and curved his body around mine, holding me to him while he rocked us back and forth. He kissed my eyelids and smoothed my hair. When the shaking finally stopped, I felt a radiant, otherworldly glow, almost a stillness inside. I had no words to describe how I felt, only the sense that being categorically, overwhelmingly wanted had transforming power.

J.W. whispered into my hair. "You happy, baby?"

"So happy. I love the way you make me feel."

He kissed the back of my neck. "How do I make you feel?"

I scanned for the perfect word. "Protected." He sighed and pulled me closer. I whispered over my shoulder, "How do I make you feel?"

J.W. tipped his head down. I felt his eyelashes against the skin on my back. "Hopeful."

J.W.'s cell phone rang. I held my breath and crossed my fingers. He took the call, said four words into the phone. "Yeah?" "Cool" and "See you."

I was almost afraid to look at him. "Well?"

"That was Brandon." Though quiet, the spark in his voice was unmistakable. "I made the short go in Calgary. I drew Ruby Jack."

Ruby Jack was the one everyone wanted—the crown jewel in the Calgary string. Clete had set an arena record on Ruby Jack in San Antonio two years back. Legends were made on a horse like that. J.W. lay down and I nestled into his embrace. Cradled where I lay, I felt like we could crush the world and remake it to our liking.

The sun rose in a cowl of ocher haze. The raindrops on the sage made it look shaggy. J.W. brought me coffee and rubbed my temples.

We drove to town in his truck and I dropped him at the airport. A circuit guy doing well enough to qualify for the short go at the Calgary Stampede—maybe there was some luck in our alliance. But it meant three days without him. How would I stand it? He turned to look at me, entreating me to reconsider. I shook my head. As I watched him board the chartered plane, I offered my prayer to God: *Keep him healthy, Lord. And thank you.*

20

I COULDN'T BLOW OFF JACE to go to Calgary. I'd been planning to see him for weeks. The only thing I put before meeting Jace was visiting my dad on the way down to Denver. South of Mead, the traffic was clotted, down one lane due to construction on the margins. I hadn't seen him in ages. My spontaneous call to him on the way out of Cheyenne was our first contact in four months. At Johnson's Corner, I stopped and bought some cinnamon rolls.

Dad was on the side porch rolling a cigarette. His house looked like it had been condemned, one green shutter hanging askew, an anemic-looking forsythia bush trailing yellow blossoms in the clots of grass, window shades lowered like drowsy lids. He reached his shaking hand out to Homer and scratched the fur under his red bandana.

"What are you doing out here, Dad?" I set the bakery bag down on the step and swatted Homer's nose away from it. My father was thinner than I'd ever seen him, with gray-brown and yellow whiskers like corn stubble on his neck.

"Got chased out of my own house for smoking."

Female humming came through the screen. The door squealed open and a woman backed out in leggings and a long T-shirt with kittens wearing cowboy boots on it. She carried a tray with a fussy flowered porcelain teapot and matching cups.

"JoAnn! This is my daughter!"

JoAnn put the tea tray on an upended clay flowerpot. She took my hands in hers and squeezed. They were ranchwoman hands, thick-skinned and lotioned to a shine. I could smell Jergens. "So nice to meet you after Pete's talked about you all this time," she said, nerves and sunshine. Funny, my dad had never talked about her. Her fingers were cold. She sat next to my dad on the step and smoothed her candy-striped leggings. A fine lace of red veins ranged across each ankle above her Keds. When Dad lit his cigarette, she raked through her thinning blond hair and wadded it up in a scrunchie she had around her wrist.

I hadn't come up Daddy's little princess. My father only paid me enough attention to figure out that I wasn't male, then turned me over to my mother. I always admired him through the long lens of the second-favorite: his sloped workman's shoulders, his gently mocking, back-slapping humor, the look of concentration on his face as he labored over a set of blueprints or charged across our property ahorseback with a rope between his teeth.

Dad picked a piece of tobacco from his lip. "How's your mother?"

JoAnn leapt up. "Why don't we have a nice cup of tea here on the porch?"

"Mom's doing fine. I saw her over Fourth of July."

Dad and I each took a full cup on a saucer from JoAnn. She shook two pink packets of artificial sweetener into the brown surface of her tea.

"How's your brother?" My dad held out his hand and I passed him a spoon.

"I think he's frustrated because Red Hill hasn't sold."

"He selling Red Hill?" The teacup rattled against the saucer as his fingers shook. My stomach crept up toward my heart. I thought my father knew. He slammed down the cup and JoAnn jumped to whisk it away. When he disappeared into the house, she gathered up her tea things, mumbled apologetically, and followed him in.

Most people regress when they visit their parents. Whatever their biological age, they slip back to fifteen, eleven, six. But whenever I see my dad, I instantly feel a hundred years old, the harried, constantly soothing and smoothing mommydaughter. When my dad refused to come out of the house, I tucked the bag of cinnamon rolls between the screen and the side door and called a good-bye. An invitation to the art show was folded in the bag. I was too tired of the routine to go in after him, and I couldn't explain this away, make like it was going to be fine.

The day heated up to a hundred degrees by the time I got to the Jefferson County fairgrounds. Small white rocks spelled out RODEO in the hillside dirt. The grounds were crowded already, everybody strolling around looking rodeo-fab. An old Dixie Chicks song pumped from the fairground speakers.

I saw my brother from behind in the beer tent, his hulking back sunburned under his ribbed undershirt. He had a phone clipped to his belt and a carpenter's pencil behind his ear, his sandy hair so long it was almost a mullet. I was so angry with him for not telling Dad about the house, I wanted to walk right up and shake him by the shoulders. But I didn't. I stuffed down my anger and dialed his cell phone number. When he answered I said, "Do you know what this is?"

Jace turned around, focused his squinty eyes on me, and we shouted at the same time, "This is the worst gay rodeo ever!" He smiled broadly, put his phone down, and held his big arms open. The first year I joined him here, a goat from the goat-tying contest had gotten hold of the hem of a Mexican drag queen's Tina Tuner mini-dress and eaten off four rows of silver fringe. The poor animal got sick, and the queen ran through the fairgrounds, trailing sequins and spackled foundation, wailing what became our *cri de coeur*. Somebody had to Heimlich the goat.

Homer sat down on Jace's feet, salivating at the grilled hotdog on his plate. "Here you go, Blimp Dawg." Jace tossed a piece in the air and Homer caught it and swallowed gratefully. Jace and I held hands and walked toward the arena, stopping now and then to say hello to folks we knew. Guys would check out Jace from the corner of their eyes as we passed; with his fireplug build and rural man's self-containment, there was no denying people found him attractive. I remember neighbor women coming by with covered dishes and single daughters, hoping to spark a connection with "that handsome Heatherly boy." Now, after years of struggle, he had to-hell-and-back radiating from every line, pore, and divot, and that aura of road-tested capability only increased his appeal.

Jace never formally came out. There was no pained letter home, no "very special episode" that ended with one parent storming out and the other at the kitchen table crying over a pecan ring with the understanding neighbor, played to the Emmy-nominated hilt by a former leading lady-turned-maternal type. The obvious was confirmed four years ago when Jace flew me down to meet him in New Orleans. He sneaked me a daiquiri in a paper cup down at Bourbon and St. Ann and introduced me to Ian, a towering forty-five-year-old former Marine he'd met online who had ham-sized biceps and a slight stutter. I knew I was hanging outside of a gay bar and Jace let me figure out the rest. I went up to the room he'd reserved for me at the Hotel Monteleone and tossed and turned the whole night, concerns about Jace playing against the do-wop soundtrack of the *a cappella* group on the sidewalk eight stories below. I never said anything to my parents, and I don't think Jace did, either. I do know he doesn't hector them and they never broach the subject. I'm not sure if the silence on all sides indicates acceptance or mutual deterrence, but it's a constant, everyone maneuvering around the lavender elephant in the middle of the room.

Jace and I watched a bit of the goat-dressing competition, six teams of two people in a mad hustle to wrestle a pair of tightywhities onto a goat's hindquarters. I heard PETA's animal humiliation platform made the treatment of goats at these rodeos a key issue. Unlike conventional rodeo, with its by-the-numbers conservatism and tradition, the gay rodeo always feels a little like a put-on, an amalgam of homey sincerity and country camp—beehive wigs mixed with Stetsons, farm kids in black leather biker chaps, and glamour dyke cowgirls in twenty pounds of rhinestones. Jace, who leaned toward the salty side, chafed at the outrageous bits, but he made do because these rodeos were the only place he could be everything he was all at once.

Kenny unloaded the horses from the Featherlite trailer, his stiff, dark purple shirt like fruit leather in the hot sun. He tipped his hat to me and tied Delaney to the fence. He checked Preston's boots and bridle.

Jace guzzled his Coke and belched neatly. "Where's Grits and Gravy? He didn't feel like coming down to hang with the boys?" He made a mocking limp-wrist gesture. Rude about J.W. once again, but I didn't rise to the bait.

"He's in Calgary for the short go. He flew up this morning."

"Impressive. He know where you are?"

"No."

Kenny ran a tube of ChapStick around his cracked lips. "Daryl, you might want to get out there and grab a seat. Team roping's starting soon."

I waited until Kenny rode away to warm up. "Jace, why didn't you tell Dad about the house?"

His face took on a pained look. "I thought maybe I'd wait until it sold. Let the old guy get a check in the mail instead of a bill for a change." He stood and quickly doffed his shirt. "You better grab a seat if you wanna watch us rope."

When I walked away, I turned around to wish him good luck just in time to see him tip a flask into his Coke can and take a deep belt. The wrecking ball swung into my chest. My hand went to my throat and I turned away. Why now, God? He'd been doing so well.

I lowered myself onto a concrete step behind a skeletally thin man hooked by plastic tubing to an oxygen tank on rollers. His friend ran after his straw hat when a wind gust carried it away. The wild drag race was concluding, the drag having jumped on the steer's back as his two teammates tried to coax it over the finish line.

This was Jace and Kenny's third rodeo of the summer—the gay circuit was tiny compared to the pros. They filled the calendar spaces in between visiting friends, fishing, and camping. Unlike me, Jace seized every leisure opportunity, though we each paid a price for our lifestyle, I supposed.

"Now in the box, we've got header Jace H. and Kenny M. on the heeling." At the shot, they came across the breakaway barrier on their matching bays and bolted after the stout red steer. Jace threw his rope, caught the horns, pulled him left, and Kenny skidded in behind to catch the back legs. Preston stepped backward to take the slack out of the rope, regal in his white leg wraps. They clinched it in under five seconds—a PRCA-worthy time. The excellence of their run made me think of J.W. I hoped he was doing okay up in Calgary. I missed him feverishly and couldn't wait for him to call.

Jace and Kenny bought me some cheese fries in the beer tent. A bad Reba McIntyre impersonator caterwauled "The Night the Lights Went out in Georgia" onstage. Kenny left to load the horses back into the trailer and the two men exchanged a look I didn't understand. When I came back from getting a couple of salt packets, Jace had popped the top on his fourth Coke.

I tilted the can and sniffed it. "So, we're drinking now?"

"A little."

" 'A little' meaning one drink or 'a little' meaning I have to take your truck keys?"

Love is letting go. How's that for a guiding principle? I'm always tapping around for that equivocal line—when do you get involved if an addict slips, and when do you let go, step back, and let them face the consequences? Recreational spirits were part of cowboy life, and for some, just a starting point. I heard rumors—so-and-so caught in the parking lot of the rodeo grounds snorting lines off the bumper of his horse trailer, guys sneaking into their veterinarian's medicine bag for whatever wouldn't lay them flat or make them sprout hooves and a tail, others who can't give an interview without gagging the reporter with a cloud of Jim Beam breath. But I did have one limit in place. If Jace was drinking too much and he was driving, there would be no detachment, no way, no how.

"You don't need to worry your cute little head about it, DeeDee. I've got it under control. See?" He pitched the Coke into a trash barrel crawling with bees. "How'd Mom look at her party?"

"Rich. Seems her midlife crisis is concluding nicely."

He clucked his tongue. "Why you always have to rag on Mom like that?" His tone was surprisingly nasty. I wondered how much he'd really pulled from that flask.

"I'm not ragging on Mom. She saw what she wanted, went after it, and now she's got it. How is that ragging on her?"

"Midlife wasn't the kind of crisis she had, Daryl." He ran his tongue over his teeth and spit a starchy white fleck onto the ground. "Think you know everything, don't you?"

"What are you talking about?" I pushed away my soggy fries. I was starting to understand why Jace was so ornery when he talked to me lately. I wasn't shrinking into little sister mode at the first sign of conflict. "If you've got something you want to say, then just come out with it. Stop treating me like I'm still a kid."

"Okay, since you're so grown up now and all, I guess it's time you found out the truth . . ."

When Jace told me, I felt a grinding crunch inside, like a dislocated joint being forced back into the socket. From the stage, the emcee called out, "Get your lasso, Mary. This is a live one!"

Jace's phone rang. His flipped up his belt and glared at the caller ID. "Oh shit, not this again." He opened the phone. "Don't call me anymore." He jammed the phone back into its canvas holster.

"Who was that?"

"Never mind, Daryl. Jesus."

I cradled my forehead in my hands, shivering in the stagnant heat of the beer tent. I wanted to take back the whole day and start over. I wished I'd gotten on that plane to Calgary. I wished I'd never visited my dad. I wished I hadn't gotten into it with my brother. Jace and I had never clashed like this before, and it felt like something was breaking inside of me. This really was the worst gay rodeo ever.

That night, I sat at the desk in my old bedroom, pulling down every prize ribbon that was tacked around the mirror, 4-H, the elementary school ag club, FFA. One by one, I fed them through the paper shredder. The shredder took them like whale's teeth sifting in krill until acetate strings and fluff clogged the blades. The shock inside of me had hardened into cold rage. I turned off the shredder and hacked through the blockage with my canvas knife, wondering if I'd ever felt this numb before.

When Jace told me about Mom, I had to know everything—how he found out, how much time had transpired between when it happened and when she left Red Hill. Jace wanted to drop the subject, but he couldn't make such a devastating strike and leave me in the wreckage. He crossed his ankle over his knee and worked at a rock stuck in the waffle sole of his boot. "You remember that weekend when they sent you to Goody's so they could go to a marriage counseling retreat with the church? That was just after Dad took Mrs. Evans down to Colorado. They were supposed to do the abortion then."

I remembered when my parents returned from that retreat. I was fourteen. That was when my fiery, feisty mother went away and never came back. She cried for weeks afterward. I had never seen her cry before. How long had the affair between my dad and Mrs. Evans gone on? And was her husband finding out what made him wrest the company from Dad's grip?

A queen in a tiger-striped unitard and curly ash-blond wig stopped in front of us and put her hands on her hips. She had a moustache, Buddy Holly glasses, and fifty or so strings of plastic pearls around her neck. She held out a strand to Jace and me. "Celebrate!" she sang along with Madonna.

Jace wound the beads around his fist. "From what I gather, the thing between them had gone on for years. Years. But I never did figure out if Mom knew all along, or only when Mrs. Evans turned up pregnant. Mr. Evans was cut years before, so he knew it wasn't his, and he put two and two together and came up with Dad as the guilty party.

"Before Mrs. Evans could even get in for the procedure, she miscarried. Say that's pretty common at that age. She went to the doctor for a D&C, and Mom and Dad did a week or two of counseling at the church and never talked about it after that."

Out of necessity, I'd learned to keep quiet about family matters, and I'd made understanding my strong suit. But I couldn't understand this. An affair, and plans for an abortion on top of it. It flew in the face of everything I believed, and I never hated my dad more in my life. I wanted to go back to his house and scream until I strangled and my tongue turned black. No. What I wanted was to never speak to him again as long as I lived.

★ ★ ★

Larry was surprised to hear my voice when I called later that night. In the past few years, had I dialed their number even a dozen times? "Your mother's in the stable, Daryl. Seems Circe might have a problem with her fetlock so she had someone out to take a look. Why don't you call over there? You have the number, right? No, wait, I'll transfer you out . . ."

My mother's voice was concerned. "Darling, it's late. Is something the matter?"

"No. I just wanted to make sure you knew what time the Opening Gala started for the art show." Years of contempt were crumbling around me and it took every ounce of strength I had to keep my tone casual.

"Seven o'clock. It's locked into memory, since I told every single person I know."

What I said was: "So you're definitely going to come then?" What I meant was: *I'm sorry, Mom.* Eight years of resentment she didn't deserve. Eight years of love withheld. I wanted to crawl through the phone wires all the way to Jackson and lay my head in her lap. *I'm so, so sorry. I didn't know.*

"What a question! Of course! I'm looking forward to being proud of you in public for a change."

I went down to the barn and brought an apple to Tad's stall, talking to her and smoothing her mane with my fingers as I had when I was a child and wanted to escape my parents' fighting, then later, their toxic silence. Then I went inside the house and walked around the studio, my flesh taut and edgy, jaws feeling stuck as a rusted gate. I cleaned every brush I had twice, separating the bristles at the ferrule to get out every last bit of dried acrylic. I needed order, needed assurance. I didn't hear from J.W., even after the rodeo was over. I assumed he was out having a good time and tried not to resent him for it. Maybe Jordan's hearsay rub-and-tug field report was accurate, and J.W. was whoring his way around Calgary. How well did I know the guy, anyway? How well could anybody know anyone? I paced the house that was and was not my home, vacillating between rage and regret, wondering how people who loved each other could destroy one another so effectively.

I was in my studio at around 2 A.M. mixing brown paint, mahogany and black cohosh. I began making dirt, jabbing at the canvas with my pouncing brush. Neanderthal art. I looked out the window when I heard a vehicle pull up. Doors slammed and a shadowy figure came down the driveway, slow as if dragging something. The dark outline of the truck slanted off but the figure kept advancing. My heart raced.

When the shadow came close enough, I could make out from the hat-shape that it was J.W. I heard the thud of his boots coming up the front steps. The screen door creaked open and slapped shut on loose hinges.

I put my head out the studio door and yelled toward the living room. "I thought you weren't coming home until Tuesday." I glared into the dark. "Thanks for calling to let me know."

"What's the matter?"

I yelled louder. My anger surprised me. "J.W., I'm working!"

"I'm sorry. I'll call next time." I heard him turn and walk toward the door.

I called after him. "I can spend some time with you if you come back later."

His footsteps halted. "I can't." He sounded strained and fragile.

"Why not?"

"I had to have someone drive me out here." His voice broke. "Ruby Jack bucked me off."

I rushed down the hall. When I saw him in the periphery of the yellow circle of light from the table lamp, I was stunned. He was half the man I kissed good-bye yesterday, bilious green shadows circling his eyes, right arm in a sling, his face a study in pain and misery.

I sat him down and he showed me everything. His knuckles were ground to red hocks, skin rolled away in thick waxy ridges. "He jerked my arm away from me and when I came off, I landed on my side and bruised a bunch of ribs. Knocked my shoulder around. I might have to turn out of everything for the next six weeks."

In the fantastical context of the road, the shock of seeing him injured fled quickly. But here at home, it cut deeper. It wasn't just that he was hurt, but that I felt ownership of his pain. Rodeo was populated with members of the he-man woman haters club, young bucks on the prowl, and self-proclaimed family men who were away from home two hundred days a year. In their own way, they kept a measured distance from women and their fate to themselves, but J.W. coming to me meant our luck was no longer separate.

I leaned over him on the couch, my arm carefully around his shoulders. "I'm sorry I snapped at you. I had no idea. Why didn't somebody call me?"

"I wouldn't let anyone call you." He wouldn't meet my eyes. "I didn't want you to worry."

"But I worry whether you call or not."

His nose began to run and he rolled his lower lip over his upper to stave off the tears. He choked out his words. "You're all I got anymore, Daryl. My kid barely knows I'm alive." He slumped, resting his head against my side. "I spent fifteen hundred dollars on that damn plane to Alberta." He sobbed once and inhaled in a hiccuping gulp. "I'm so tired."

I smoothed his feathery hair, rested my hand on his hot neck. "I know."

I knelt at his feet, and with gauze and tape and antibacterial ointment, I dressed his knuckles. I wrapped a bag of frozen peas in a towel and pressed it on the back of his neck to cool him down. No baby talk, no silly comfort food like cocoa with marshmallows. His dignity was a tenuous thread—clip it with a cutesy-poo gesture and the sword would come down. I dosed him with Tylenol, then helped him gently lower into the guest room bed.

He fussed and shook, shivering with fury. Tears bunched his lashes into starry spikes. I touched the back of my hand to his forehead. "The sheets are fresh, so they should be nice and cool. You let me know if you need anything."

When I switched out the light, I heard J.W.'s voice in the darkness. "I promise I won't bother you, Daryl. Just don't leave."

In the end, I couldn't do it, couldn't leave him on his own in the guest room. I set him up in my studio, building a nest of blankets so I could keep an eye on him while I worked.

At three-thirty, he was dozing evenly but with a crimped brow. I staggered into the kitchen and opened the hammered-copper flour tin with embossed roosters on the lid, sifting out enough flour for a dozen biscuits. I've always resorted to cooking or cleaning when I'm stuck, not only to procrastinate but also to remind myself that I can actually see something through, start to finish. My surroundings are never so spotless as when I'm on deadline.

Ground sausage for gravy browned in the cast iron skillet. I was getting a pot of coffee going when I heard the floor creak behind me. J.W. stood at the kitchen island with a blanket wrapped around his shoulders. I shook beans into the grinder. "What are you doing up?"

"Smelled the cooking. Couldn't sleep anyway."

"I can only guess why. When was the last time you ate something?" I measured flour and milk and stirred them into the skillet, then turned down the heat. The gravy would come up nicely.

He struggled to remember. "I got a pack of turkey breast at the mini-mart when we stopped for fuel in town."

"Turkey breast." I took two blue stoneware plates from the highboy. "I think you need to mind your diet a little better. If I laid you

sideways, I could play your rib cage like a marimba." He winced re-
flexively and put a hand on his bandaged side. "Sorry," I said.
"Graceless analogy. Have a seat, the biscuits will be done in less than
a minute."

He groped his way down into the chair. "Oh, none for me,
thanks. Maybe some of that coffee, though."

I took the biscuits from the oven, brushed the tops with butter,
and gave the bubbling peppery gravy a final stir. "I'm not giving you
coffee at this hour." What I knew for sure about the male of the
species could fit on a matchbook cover, but I was certain that a man
who staved off nurturing when he was well was only too happy to
be fussed-over and bossed when he was down. A lesson I learned in
this very kitchen watching my mom marshal homemade chicken
broth down my dad's flu-sore throat. "Listen, you've given me a
couple valuable lectures in the past few days, so here's one for you:
privation does not signify commitment."

"I don't follow."

I ladled the hot gravy over four biscuits and slid the plate in front
of him. "Translated from fancy college talk, I'm saying that fifty or
sixty fat grams between friends is nothing. Eat."

J.W. slept late. At ten, I brought in a tray with Tylenol, a couple biscuits wrapped in a napkin, marmalade, raspberry jam, and coffee.
"Well, you're a sight for sore everything," he said, sitting up to take
the mug. He blew on the surface. When he took a sip, a wisp of
steam floated into the air like a tiny ghost. In the rumple of blankets, he was subdued and docile, rubbing the sleep from his eyes
with the heel of his palm. He pulled a pillow onto his lap and toyed
with the faded tag. "How'd you sleep?"

I opened the bottle of Tylenol and shook out a couple for myself.
"I didn't."

21

ON TUESDAY, I WOKE UP with my chest constricted and something dragging a sharpened claw inside my throat. I recognized the symptoms—a genuine artist's panic. I'd spent Monday, my one day off, watching over J.W. He lay on the living room couch, dwelling on what he'd done wrong in Calgary: not enough drag on his spurs; wasn't set up right over the rigging, on and on. The depth of his obsessive self-review showed me how far I'd have to extend to match him in dedication, how much I'd have to give to support him emotionally. It got to the point where I wished I'd never heard the name Ruby Jack.

He did what he could to tend a cool flame, staying detached in that rodeo Zen space, but inside him, there was still that hungry kid, wanting and wanting. I knew that in his heart, he believed he only competed against himself, that whatever happened—or didn't—rested on his shoulders. But I couldn't help wondering, would it have been different if I'd gone with him like he'd asked?

I felt pretty bad and on top of it, I wasn't getting much work done. I'd even called in sick at the Twin Pines; I was that far behind. I'd made some progress on the Shane portrait, but it was due in twenty-four hours and "some" wouldn't cut it.

J.W. slouched on the sofa, positioned around a bunch of cushions against his strained ribs. He was peeling an overripe banana and the pungent smell of it was inexplicably nauseating. When I was in the kitchen pouring myself a fourth cup of coffee, he called over the back of the couch. "Hey, Daryl. Since you're up, could you get me a cold one?"

My silence could've frosted the windows. I left the kitchen and walked toward my studio.

His voice followed me, funneling down the length of the hall. "Precious, something wrong?"

He was probably seeking the kind word, but I had only a day's worth of Florence Nightingale in me and the clock had run out. He limped carefully into the room, half-eaten banana in his hand, and found me dragging on a Camel Light I'd taken from my emergency pack in the freezer. "You shouldn't be smoking."

I exhaled pointedly. "Yeah, well, you shouldn't be offering unsolicited opinions."

He laughed, thinking I was joking. He came over and pinched the cigarette from between my fingers, preparing to drop it into a jelly jar of clear fluid.

"That's acetone. It's flammable." I snatched the glass from him and set it down hard on the tarp-covered dresser.

He took a bite from the banana and folded down the peel. "Is something going on here that I don't know about?"

"I'm busy is all. I spent the better part of this month running around with you and now I've got to make up the lost time." My anger was so close to the surface, it was hard to form the words. I tossed the cigarette into the dregs of my coffee. The butt bobbed on the cream-streaked surface.

He chewed once and swallowed hard. "I wasn't meaning to create more work for you. I asked you to come along Fourth of July because I thought you'd enjoy it."

"And I did enjoy it. But I can't keep taking off with you when you travel, then hang out with you when you're home, and drop everything to take care of you on top of it."

"I didn't plan on getting hurt in Calgary, that's for dang sure. Sorry if that's an inconvenience to you."

I scraped paint from the palette and wiped my hands with a rag. "I'm not in a position to make my work second place to a relationship right now."

"Who asked you to?"

I couldn't even look at him. This was the conflict I had with Alex—my time versus his interest. That I was having the identical fight confirmed what I'd feared, that Alex was just a stand-in for every man who might come into my life. Knock down Alex and there would be another man just alike behind him, and another behind him. Same shit, different guy.

I took a deep breath and hardened my stance. "I know rodeoing is your priority, J.W., and that means sacrifice and a fair share of setbacks. I get that. But what about my priorities?"

"What are you saying here, Daryl?"

"I'm just saying that I'm on deadline and you're kind of getting underfoot."

He flinched like he'd been slapped. *But you said you liked taking care of me.*

But you said . . .

The shock and injury fled when his pride clicked in. He held up his hand, fingers and thumb touching, making a circle. "Do you know what this is?"

"No."

"It's a zero. That's how many more times you get to talk to me that way." He threw the banana peel in the trash, turned on his heel, went to the living room, and picked up his truck keys, trying valiantly to storm out, but it was slow going with the ribs and sling.

I slammed the door to the studio and sat on the bed. I didn't bother going after him because anything I might have said at that moment would have only made it worse. I swore that if I ever got into this bind again, I'd compose myself with dignity and press my point with the necessary feminine guile. I failed in spades. I was going for Scarlett O'Hara and ended up as Yosemite Sam.

I got up to call to him from the window and caught my foot on the tarp. My easel bumped up and fell forward, hitting the edge of the dresser. The painting slid off the easel and landed facedown with a sickening wet slap, the jar of naptha tumbling after. I leapt from the bed and grabbed the edge of the canvas and turned it over. My heart sank and angry tears exploded from my eyes. The solvent had soaked clear through the canvas. The painting was ruined.

I lay on my side on the daybed, sobbing, the white matelasse quilt balled up in my fist. It was stupid of me to think there could be room for two seekers in one relationship. In reality, one gets to wander the desert while the other keeps the tent from blowing away, and it's usually the female in the role of camp tender. What did I see over and over during Cowboy Christmas—beautiful, intelligent women stowed securely in second place. And why not? For a woman, second place pays better. The "supportive" spouse gets financial support in exchange for her sacrifice, and a shower of approving applause to boot. Were they content in their arrangement? I didn't know but I bet they weren't embroiled in screaming matches over priorities.

I cried so hard I got the hiccups. I looked around the room, my eyelids puffy and sore. The soft afternoon made the studio look serene and blameless, the bronze light burnishing the jars and metallic bands on the brushes. When I was quite sure I was done crying, I mopped my face with a fistful of tissues and left the studio with the door open. I swung down the deck steps, fed the dog, the cat, and the horses, then came inside and made myself a quick dinner of macaroni and cheese from a box. When I went back into the studio, it was dark. I changed into my crusty painting pants, snapped on the brightest lamp. I had an obligation to meet. Whether I'd gotten in a fight with J.W. or not didn't matter. I had to calm down and concentrate, and if he wasn't there when I came up for air, so be it.

There wasn't enough time to come up with a new sketch for a watercolor or an acrylic, so I blew the dust off of the Donna Dewberry one-stroke paint kit my brother gave me for my birthday last year. He'd ordered it off of a home shopping channel when he was up late drinking, and wrapped it with great pride, not knowing that giving it to me was like presenting a music major with the collected works of Barry Manilow. But I needed easy and I needed fast, and the kit might come to the rescue. I loaded up the scruffy brush with raw umber and nutmeg and started pouncing arena dust around the periphery of the canvas.

As I worked, I thought about how hard it is for me to muster up enough entitlement to just get the job done. I put up a great front of self-determination, but underneath it, I wonder if the professional advancement is going to cost me personal happiness. I worry that I'm assuming more than my due, but then I think, why should I feel less than entitled? Then I feel guilty about the guilt.

I have a room of my own, hell, I've got an entire house to myself. But it's not physical space I've got to defend, it's the psychic real estate, that place within, free from distractions and phobias, all the criticism and self-doubt and self-sabotage. A woman doesn't just need a room of her own. She needs an eight-hundred-pound gorilla guarding the door.

I squeezed blending gel into the center well on the green plastic palette and circled the easel to psych myself into mad composer mode, visualizing sitting down at the piano with my fingers over the keys, ready to crash down in genius arpeggios. In his videos, Shane charged around like he believed that if a guy gassed it and gave everything he's got, he'd excel, that the transformation from pretender to real thing was merely a matter of applying himself. It was up to me to capture that yearling zest.

Which, by midnight, I hadn't done. The half-empty canvas might as well have stuck out its tongue at me. No photo, video, or conjecture on my part would provide that critical missing element. I paced the room, finding every creak in the pine floorboards. At quarter past one, I picked up the phone.

J.W. answered on the second ring. I could tell he had been asleep. "Daryl, you all right?"

I forced out the three words I hate saying most. "I need help."

"You have to understand that when you rodeo, the dream of winning the World is the fire under you. When you're sleeping on the airport floor with your rigging bag for a pillow or paying your entry fees with quarters you were saving to do laundry, you've got that goal in mind." In between giant yawns that recalled a hippopotamus at the zoo, J.W. lay on the daybed and described his winning round at the Finals. The Las Vegas lights, the dismount of the last ride when he knew he'd clinched it, and him practically levitating to the ceiling of the Thomas and Mack arena when he heard the thousands of rodeo fans roaring as he was named the World Champion bareback rider.

I sat on the edge of the bed and sighed into my hands, exhausted and wired at the same time. "This is a million times harder than I thought it would be."

"Bear down and T-R-Y, Daryl. You can do it." He closed his eyes. "I've got to get some sleep or I'll never make it to work. But here's one last thing I'll tell you: when I realized I won the World, I felt like Clark Kent the first time he busted out of the phone booth as Superman."

Bear down. Well, all right then. I tripled loaded a one-inch brush and made a stroke on the canvas as if making an educated guess. Degas said, "Only when he no longer knows what he is doing does the painter do good things." A bull rider was no pretty ballerina, but I'd have to take old Edgar at his word because I couldn't tell if what

I was doing was good or not. Painting with no sketch was like working without a net. It was coming up on four-thirty and I was flying on faith.

I dragged into the kitchen, feeling like a massive greaseball, slugged back two glasses of J.W.'s sweet tea, then went back in and started working on Shane's dance partner. Kryptonite was a Charolais, fat and rounded like a beluga whale, with a high kick and lots of twist. I rendered Shane just as twisty and aggressive, lifted up off his rope, almost airborne. I pounced a final explosion of umber dust around him, like the big cloud that swirls out after a cartoon punch, then warmed it up with lots of pale yellow until it took on an almost sepia tone.

The sun was rising, thin, champagne-colored light peeking over the window ledge and onto the painting. I stepped away from the easel and looked at the canvas drying. It was fast, it was sloppy, and it was the best thing I'd ever done.

J.W. woke up when the sun warmed his face. He rubbed the length of his fingers along his eyelid and felt around for his glasses. "How's it going?"

"Almost finished. Just one more thing." I'd left an empty space next to my signature. I held out the #2 script liner brush to him. "You've got to sign it."

Mrs. McGurk knelt on the brick path in front of the tan ranch house, laying in a half-dozen Apache plume with a blue-handled spade and bare hands. The garage door was dented like someone had backed into it. I rode down with the truck windows open and the acrylic finished drying during the forty-minute trip to Longmont. The brown lawn hissed under my feet as I walked up to the house and the smoke from the wildfires had grown thick enough to make my throat itch. Mrs. McGurk wiped her hands on her flowered wrap skirt and came to me with a cool hug. "Daryl Heatherly!

Hello!" She ushered me into the house where her husband sat watching *SportsCenter* in his worn corduroy recliner, a crucifix on the wall behind him. On the polished oak coffee table a cut-crystal candy dish held pastel mints. Mr. McGurk pushed himself up from the chair. "Glass of pop?" When I said thank you, no, he held up the candy dish. "Care for a mint?"

"Luther . . ." His wife's voice was a caution over the sound of the kitchen faucet. She handed him a glass of lemonade as she crossed the living room, her red Easy Spirit sandals leaving imprints on the uniform nap of the carpet. "Let's go see the birthday boy."

Shane's small bedroom had the forced cheerfulness of a hospital gift shop, spilling over with flowers and potted plants, stuffed animals, and balloons, Happy Birthday and Get Well screaming from every corner. A black plush bull holding a puffy red satin heart in its hooves sat on the bedside table. The room was so full, it was hard to locate Shane in the bed, but there he was, flame-red hair shorn almost to the skull, his leg in traction. He lay on his back watching a Rockies game from a ceiling-mounted television. He only turned his head when his mother called, "You've got a visitor."

He couldn't place me as one of his friends or the millionth well-wisher who'd angled for a visit so she could extend the sentiment in person. "You look familiar."

"We danced together at a Ricky and the Redstreaks show at the Hitch last year."

He looked abashed, like that night had been whiskeyed from his brain pan before it was even over.

"Anyway, I brought you something."

"What is it?"

"Take a look and you tell me."

Shane shifted in the bed. I held up the canvas so his mother could unveil it. When the muslin sheet came off, the look on his face. God, it was priceless.

"You remember your old buddy Kryptonite, right?"

His eyes traveled from mine to his mother's, who had started to waver a little in the face. "That really what I looked like on that ride?"

His mother blinked rapidly and busied herself with the plastic laundry basket in the corner.

"Pretty much," I said, perching on the side of his bed. "I figured since you were battling Kryptonite, I'd make you into Superman, but I only had to pump you up a little. The rest is all you."

His mother turned away, busily putting faded T-shirts into a drawer. I leaned my elbow on his pillow and whispered in his ear. "By the way, I call this painting *Wild Thing.*"

Shane barked out a laugh. He remembered our dance now. His mother ducked out of the room with a pile of folded towels. I found her singing quietly to herself as she reorganized a shelf in the linen cabinet.

"If you frame it in barnwood, Mrs. McGurk, that might look really nice."

She tucked a fitted light green sheet under her chin as she folded it. "You know, even as far back as kindergarten, when someone would ask Shane what he was going to be when he grew up, he said a bull rider."

The portrait wasn't really for Shane, I knew. His mom wanted something to hang on to, and before getting involved with J.W., I never would have grasped the intensity of that need. While the cowboy you love is out chasing his dream, you're the white-knuckle support system, praying for dear life off to the side. When he's on the back of that animal, he's as alive as he'll ever be, but as vulnerable, too. When he's at the top of his game, you want that moment of invincibility to last. Your sweet boy at his strongest and best, forever.

Mrs. McGurk walked me out into the driveway. A cluster of pine-cones from a skinny ponderosa by the side of the garage had blown onto the truck hood. "Listen, I was wondering if it would be okay for us to take a while to give you the rest of what we owe you."

I pitched the pinecones into a yellow-blooming rabbitbrush and waved my hand to indicate that I'd already gotten payment enough.

I drove to the Frontier Mall to scope out a cheap dress to wear to the opening. I found something flattering that I thought J.W. would like—a deep red halter-top sundress with a flippy hem, fifty percent off markdown. He called me while I was in the dressing room trying it on.

"How'd it go down there?"

"Better than I could have hoped. How's your shoulder?"

"Oh, much improved. I ditched the sling. Even my ribs feel pretty good." Our cell connection cut out for a second, then I could hear him again. "I thought that after work, I might take an artistic genius to dinner, if that's all right."

"You're on. Listen, J.W., I didn't mean to run you off yesterday—"

"Don't worry about it. I appreciate what you were saying, Daryl. I just didn't appreciate how you said it. You practically snapped my head clean off before I could get a word in. I want to do right by you, but you have to give me a chance."

I supposed it was unreasonable to expect that a relationship could be both passionate and convenient. An alliance like ours could only work with careful adjustment, but it *could* work, even if it meant loving by the calendar page and teaching some manners to my eight-hundred-pound gorilla.

I beat J.W. back to Red Hill. He'd left his rigging bag behind so, exhilarated from having broken through the clouds, I dug in and did something I'd been fantasizing about. When he came into the house, I called him up to the loft and he found me, hip cocked on the dresser, wearing nothing but chaps and a heavy perfume. My hair was twined into buck rein braids, and I was baby-smooth and oil-soft from the neck down.

I swung my foot back and forth slowly. J.W.'s eyes traveled the length of my body. "Goddamn, you look amazing."

I stretched my neck and tipped back a little. "We missed you around here."

He leaned against the wall. I could see I was having the desired effect. "Goddamn," he said again, untucking his shirt as he approached. By the time he was halfway across the room, he had his glasses off. Three paces later, he reached me. I never did make it off the top of that dresser.

Afterward, he lay next to me on the bed. "Notice anything different?" He turned his head from side to side.

"I don't think so."

He rolled onto his stomach. "I got my stitches out! From Fourth of July."

I sat up and touched his cheeks. "You did! Well, if I'd known I'd have baked you a cake."

He laughed. "You're all the sugar I need, baby girl."

"God, you are greasy sometimes. Go on." I got up from the bed and put on my robe, walking toward the closet. "And don't tell me you got those stitches taken out when we both know you picked them out yourself." I took out my new dress and held it along my body. "Hey, what do you think of this?" I shook it on the hanger. "If you don't like it, I can take it back."

J.W. shinnied into his jeans and zipped them. "Important, is it?"

"Well, the gala is important, yeah. And I want to look good for you, of course."

He stood at the mirror and fixed his hair with his fingers. "Why? I'm not even going to be there."

I folded the dress over my arm and stared at him. "What do you mean you're not?"

He turned around and leaned back against the dresser. "I thought I told you—I drew good in Gunnison so I'm going."

"You didn't tell me." I couldn't believe I was learning this *now*. He was dripping out of me and edging down the inside of my thigh, for God's sake. I tightened the belt on the robe and sat on the edge of the armchair looking at my feet. "What about your shoulder? It's hurt again and you only just had it fixed."

"I got my shoulder fixed so I could keep going, not so I could quit." He crossed his ankles and steepled his fingers. "You're not mad, are you?"

I shrugged, silent. The hope I'd been nursing was nudging up against sour skepticism. I thought about the night after J.W. bucked off in Calgary and crumpled onto my couch in tears. I expected him to be as scared as I was, to tell me he couldn't keep going, but he was ready to crack back out like nothing had ever happened. The fear that I felt wasn't transmutable and the space it made between us was solid as an object.

This dedication of his, what did that mean for us, I wondered. Fast-forward a year or two and what would I do? Move to a trailer somewhere with this man to wait at home alone while he burned rubber following his bliss from Alberta to New Mexico? Conduct a marriage by cell phone? Call him to tell him our baby's cut his first tooth?

J.W. sat on the edge of the bed. "I'm sorry, precious. I should have told you I was going. Things got hectic and I plum forgot. I know you gave me that invitation, but I didn't write it down."

I fixed my chin and looked away, smarting from the boomerang slap of not coming first. Up until now, it had been fine. I didn't mind him coming and going; I liked it, in fact. But now, him leaving was the worst thing I could imagine. The anger scoured down and exposed a deep well of sadness.

J.W. raised his hands, then dropped them to his lap. His brow furrowed and his mouth tugged down. "Seems like every time I turn around I'm either disappointing you or annoying you."

"No," I said, an ache tightening my throat. I picked up the dress from the bed and went to the closet. "It's not that."

"Yeah? What is it, then?"

I hid behind the closet door as tears spilled from my eyes, streaking hotly from my cheeks to my chin. Why couldn't I say it? *I don't want you to go.*

"Daryl, will you please come out here so we can talk about this?"

I didn't answer him.

"You're giving me the silent treatment? Great. Let me tell you something . . ." He came around the door and when he saw that I was crying, his expression changed completely. "Oh." J.W. shifted forward. "Baby. I'm sorry. What did I do?"

Try as I might, I couldn't even look at him.

"Daryl . . . can you talk to me?"

I shook my head.

He turned me to him, enfolding me in his arms. "Girl needs her daddy, huh?"

I covered my face with my hands and nodded, sobbing.

He walked me over to the chair and sat down with me in his lap. I squeezed my eyes shut as he hugged me tight to his chest. In my heart, I didn't want J.W. to change. He was everything I could have hoped for. What I wanted was for me to change—to not feel so shaky, to not be so afraid. But the closer we got, the harder it was for me to watch him leave. As he held me, I thought for the first time, *I don't think I can do this.*

He swept back the hair that tears had matted to my skin. He looked in my eyes and stroked my damp cheeks with his thumbs. "Hi." He smiled.

"Hi." I tried to smile back but my lips were trembling. The dense muscle of his inner thigh relaxed when I put my hand there.

"No, baby," he said, taking my hand in his. "You just stay right here."

We sat like that for several minutes.

"J.W . . ."

"Mmm?"

"Do you have other girls? I mean, have you ever been somebody else's daddy?" I envisioned a nursery full of mewling, needy women, him standing over us, grinning—a smug patriarch. The thought of it almost made me sick.

He breathed deeply. "No."

"Why me, then?"

"I don't know. I guess because you're the girl I know I can take care of. And I feel like you need me to."

"What makes you think that?"

"There's no science to it, Daryl. It's just one of those deals. I don't question it. I don't even think I should."

The role was receding. I started to feel more like my grown-up self, like I was emerging from a trance. I sat up and scanned his face with my eyes, searching. "I want to take care of you, too." My voice scratched out raw, throat still hurting. "I don't want you to feel like you have to do all the heavy lifting."

He shook his head like I'd volunteered to take on a needless task. "I know you do. But here's the thing—you're not that heavy."

We sat there together, and J.W. rocked me like a cherished child. The sun transited the carpet, then the room went dark. I wanted to tell him everything—how Jace, who I had always counted on, had turned on me by telling me my mother's secret in the most punishing way, how I was so angry at my father I thought I might hate him and that scared me, and how I'd tried for so long to keep everything together and how it had come apart regardless. But I said nothing, J.W. listening silently as I cried out years and years of loss. I finally had a safe place to pour out everything I'd held in. I realized that for so much of my life, I thought that capable was the antithesis of fearful, and that busy was the remedy for lonely, but here in his arms I could finally face the fear and loneliness that had been straining under the surface the whole time.

I closed my eyes and felt a kiss on the top of my head. "I love you, Daryl. You're a good girl."

At the start of the gala, Charlie King walked up and handed me a small silver box. Charlie was a nice enough guy but with questionable grooming and a mold of premature gray hugging the knobby contours of his narrow skull, he looked like something you'd scrape off a shower curtain. "Hey, Daryl. J.W. wanted me to give this to you." A blue card was tucked under the ribbon, with a drawing of a sleeping star nestled in the curve of a smiling crescent moon, "To the star of the show" scripted above in glittered cursive.

I opened the card. Written in J.W.'s lucid southpaw:

Not together
But not apart
It's still our moon
Be still my heart.

—J.W.J., distinguished cowboy poet.

P.S.:Suitable rhymes for "dutch oven" include "turtle dovin' " and "monkey lovin'."

I lifted the lid on the box. Wrapped in light blue tissue paper was a braided copper bracelet. Engraved inside was a single word. PRECIOUS.

22

I BLINKED AND SWERVED in the syncopated pop of flashbulbs, plastic cup of jug Chardonnay in my hand, trying to find Shawna. The white partitions broke the room into a maze, and I finally spotted my friend, cornered by glittery-eyed critics. Her luxuriant hair was braided Kahlo style and she wore an emerald empire-waisted mini-dress with black spiderweb tights and jump boots buffed to a licorice sheen. As the youngest artist in the show, she generated a lot of curiosity. She periodically shook a limp hand or took a kiss on her cheek, frowning throughout. The frown's inspiration was not hard to figure. Her father stood right behind her, looking like a one-man trading post in a beaded yellow buckskin monstrosity, a feather headdress, and a chief's ransom in silver and turquoise. Next to him, a teenage girl examined the female figure in the largest of Shawna's paintings. "Is that Shania Twain?"

"I don't care how knocked-up I am." Shawna grabbed my arm. "Cigarette. Now."

We stole around the side of the building and leaned against the bricks, huddled together in a pool of pale green streetlight. She took the pack from her velvet clutch. I smelled the tobacco. "I'll take one."

"Chief Black Book is in fine form this evening," she said, blowing a jet of smoke from the corner of her mouth. She ground out the cigarette after one puff and gave an apologetic pat to her lower belly. "Some reporter from the Casper paper was interviewing me and he felt free to interrupt so he could introduce himself. Then he gave her a brochure about some bullshit Sacred Yoga and Sweat-lodge retreat he's doing. I didn't even invite him. I mean, my mom's coming."

"You sold a lot of work, though. I saw all those red dots by your stuff." The combined value of everything she showed was twelve thousand dollars, a sum I could only dream of. "And hey, at least your dad showed up!" I'd received my father's regrets this morning in the form of a good-luck card signed in JoAnn's handwriting.

We went back inside and looped arm in arm through the crowd of art lovers and cheese nibblers. When we got to my spot, Shawna squinted at the title card for *Passion Is a Lonely Road.* "Lookie here." She pointed to the red dot. "Congratulations!" A strange look came over her face. She took my hand and stood straight. I turned around to see what she was looking at.

Alex. It took me a second to recognize him. He'd shaved off most of his goatee, leaving just a soul patch like a blot of black shoe pol-ish. His eyes were wide and nervous, the gallery pot lights reflected as white wedges in the solid brown of each iris. He avoided Shawna's accusing stare "Hey, Daryl. *Westword* sent me to cover the show. Feel like doing an interview?"

I had the crazy idea that he had bought the watercolor, but I knew he wouldn't have eight hundred dollars. "Sure," I said. Shawna sloped off and left us alone. "I thought you were covering music for them."

"They've got me on arts now, too. I got promoted to associate editor."

"Oh. That's cool."

He took out a reporter's notebook. "So what can you tell me about these paintings?"

My first thought, which I didn't share, was that I found it highly amusing that he'd taken such a keen interest in my work. "I've never been interested in the static West," I told Alex while he scribbled. "There are many brilliant artists and photographers whose love of the land touch me—Ansel Adams and Charlie Russell being the most familiar. They say that being a Westerner is a state of mind, but I think it's more a physical spirit, an intimate engagement with your natural surroundings. That engagement is what excites me. I'm not interested in doing still lifes of a spurred boot in a stirrup, or a row of cowboy butts in Wranglers and chaps."

"Yeah. The genre's got enough cliché as it is." A quick jab in the guise of reportorial character sketching, or a backhanded compliment? He turned the page in his reporter's notebook. Of course, I'd shared my methods and philosophies a million times during our relationship, to increasingly impatient reception. But I guess there was something in it for him now. I was surprised that this realization had no significant emotional charge, and that in addition, I was enjoying being the center of his professional attention.

"Hey, Alex, I should've asked. Where's . . ."

"Jen? She's gone for the summer on a dig. Dinosaurs, somewhere up near Hell's Half Acre. She wanted to spend the summer on her own." I didn't point out the irony in that.

Alex read a question from his notepad. "Many Western artists feel compelled to document what they see as a vanishing way of life. Is that why you paint?"

I laughed. It was such an Alex question. "Weeping at the graveside of the American West is a tradition as old as the West itself. I think it's like the way some people go to sad movies because they enjoy a good cry, or a kid who wiggles a loose tooth just to feel that zingy pain. The anguish has some payoff, but not for me."

"So why do you do it?"

"I guess I paint to tell the world, 'Hey, we're still here.' "

"And finally, three words that describe your work."

"Simple . . . traditional." I bored into him with my eyes for word three. "Sentimental."

He flipped his notepad shut. "That's should just about do it, Daryl. Your work looks awesome. I'm happy for you." He scratched his chin. "Say, do they still have that wacky lounge over at the airport, where you can see the runway?"

"Sure. The Cloud 9. Why?"

"I thought maybe after this you and I could go get a drink. Watch the planes take off and land." He looked sheepish.

I couldn't believe it. The guy who for months had acted as if I were art's corny anti-Christ was asking me out again. Six weeks ago I was sure I would come apart if I ever saw him again, but now here I was, feeling stronger than I ever had in my life. "I don't think so, Alex. I'm, um, otherwise committed." I didn't bother telling him I was seeing J.W., but I was aware of the copper bracelet around my wrist. *Let him see it,* I thought. Let him see that someone thinks I'm just right the way I am.

I started across the floor to find Shawna. She wouldn't believe this. I wove through the crowd and heard a voice rise about the chatter. "There's the girl of the hour!"

I spun on my heel. "Mom!"

"Sorry I'm late. It was so windy, Larry insisted on pilot duties in the Cub. My God, I thought I was going to lose my cookies before we even left the airstrip."

I hugged her and I could feel her surprise at the embrace, but she grasped me tightly. She held my hand. As if trained by mother's intuition, her eyes went straight to my bracelet. "That's pretty. Is it new?"

I held out my arm. "Brand new. J.W. gave it to me."

"He's sure crazy about you, isn't he?" She rolled the show catalog in her hands.

"I guess."

"Don't try to fool me, Daryl. I saw the way he watched you over the rim of his coffee cup."

I felt my hackles rise. "If you're preparing to give me a lecture, Jace beat you to it."

"I'm not going to lecture. You're a grown woman, strange as that is to me. And I can remember a time when your own father used to look at me that way." She hesitated. "What I'm saying is, well, honey, be careful."

The mother I used to know would have confronted me, told me full-force how she really felt. But this was post-divorce Mom. She was cautious, resigned to salvage mode. There was a deepening in the cold spot I felt toward my father. It wasn't just that he'd betrayed my mother, but that he did something almost as bad—he took the fight out of her.

I stepped back so she could see the red dot. "Somebody bought the watercolor with the horse trailer."

"I know." She covered her mouth with her hand.

I had never let her give me money for school or be my parent-patron in any way. I turned down everything because I felt like she was trying to buy her way back from bailing on me. But now I knew there had been different forces at work.

She spoke from behind her fingers. "Don't be mad."

"I'm not."

The truck made a desperate wheeze when I tried to start it and I had a pretty good idea of where that eight hundred dollars would be going. I murmured endearments at it and kept tapping the gas until it turned over. I started toward home, envisioning a hot bath, a bourbon on the rocks, and a good twelve hours sleep. Well, maybe a quick call to J.W. first.

I ran my hand over the bracelet as that warm oily feeling in my hips started up. The relentless itch was new to me—being so aware of my own body's signals, wanting someone ten times a day. How many of us were there, I wondered, women with everything under control except for the wild longing to call up what was pure and innocent and offer it to someone who recognized submission as a gift? What would Alex think of me having gone from heartbreak kid to daddy's girl inside of six weeks? He'd sniff, probably, and make noises about archaic notions of masculinity and gender inequality. But I'd done equality with Alex—Young artistic type seeks same— and found myself quite belittled in the bargain. Thanks, but no thanks.

It was also quite possible that if he knew, he'd just laugh. Instead, it was I who laughed. A crazy, sleep-deprived cackle at something belched up from the recesses of memory. Alex's favorite novel was *Lolita*.

I pulled up to the house and patted the dashboard in thanks for an uneventful trip home. A light wind shifted the grass like hula fronds and moonlight colored the landscape a stark, chalky blue. The second I stepped in the driveway, the hair on the back of my neck pricked up. There was a feeling of foul weather but I couldn't tell exactly what was wrong. No sound beyond the sigh of grass and the truck engine ticking. As I drew toward the house, I saw the curtains fluttering in the breeze, the first sign that something was amiss. I hadn't left any windows open. Something else: no windows. Every single pane had been smashed out. I folded back into the truck and drove down to the barn. I could see the roof had been so shot up it looked like Swiss cheese. The horses, calling out in whinnying concert—*what happened, where were you*—were agitated but unharmed. In the tack room, I grabbed Jace's shotgun from its clip under the bench, then locked myself in the truck and dialed 911.

Blue-and-white police lights came up behind me. The police told me to wait outside while they swept the house to make sure no one was inside. They waved me out of the truck and together, we surveyed the damage. Even the panes at the very top of the living room were gone—blasted to bits by a shotgun, the detective said—leaving the whole west side of the house exposed. There were long, blade-shaped shards in the kitchen sink, crystalline chunks in the bathtubs.

The living room floor looked like an explosion of ice. What little glass remained in the window frames stuck out in jagged spikes like the teeth of Japanese cartoon monsters. Whoever had done it used a shotgun for the job—there were splintery buckshot holes everywhere, the walls a giant game of connect-the-dots.

The pretzel-thin junior cop looked like he might tip over from the weight of the accoutrements on his belt. The tic in his right eye was off-putting. He put his hands on his hips. "You staying out here alone?" Under the newly forged professional reserve was some genuine concern.

"For now. I called my brother."

Jace, who'd muttered, "Christ. Oh, Christ," when he heard the news, was on his way home as fast as Kenny, two horses, two dogs, and fifteen hundred miles of interstate would allow.

"Got a friend you can call? You really shouldn't be out here by yourself. Not until we can figure out who did this. Most vandals don't make personal appearances after the fact, but just in case." I could stay at Goody's. She had taken a group of Japanese tourists on an overnight trip to Devil's Tower. The cop made notes on a pad with a slender mechanical pencil. "You checked on your pets and animals, you said?"

Oh, God. Homer. I was headed toward the remains of the sliding glass doors before the cop could even close his notepad. The kennel door was open, the fenced-off area empty. The policemen came out when they heard me hollering my dog's name. They gave me a flashlight and we walked over the hills, searching. The older policeman drew up to my side. "You want to ride around with us in the cruiser? We can check the roads."

As we drove, I recited his description—yellow Lab, black nose, gray muzzle, about ninety-five pounds. My eyes started to water as I considered the worst. Whoever shot up the house might have gotten him, too. He could've run into the road and gotten hit by a car. The young cop handed me a tissue from the glove box. "Don't cry, ma'am. I bet you'll find your dog. Let's get you to your aunt's place."

The police officers headed back to town on another call. I didn't know what to do. I knew I shouldn't be at Red Hill on my own, but if I didn't go back and keep looking, how would Homer know where to find me? I sat on Goody's porch steps with the shotgun across my lap. Over the murmuring cluck of the chickens in the coop, I heard an unmistakably canine whine. I walked around the edge of the porch. Homer was sitting alongside the chicken-wire fence, crying. When he saw me, he barked once and dragged over. When I got a look at his face, I felt sick to my stomach. Blood and dirt were stuck to his muzzle, and from what I could see before I had to turn away, there was a deep gash near his right eye.

I called Twila, our family vet down the road, afraid I'd wake her family from sleep, but she was sitting up with her colicky four-month-old daughter. I begged her to come over.

"I can't, Daryl. I've got a sick baby here and my husband's gone for the week. Drive down and I'll see you right away."

I took down a set of Goody's truck keys and tried to herd Homer into the old blue F-350 without looking at him, which wasn't easy. He didn't want to move and kept whining whenever I tugged at his collar. I jostled him with my foot. "Don't let me down, old boy. Get in." When I shut the cab door, I could smell the blood on him and I felt my knees get weak. If I couldn't redirect my focus I would never make it.

When I finally had the vehicle pointed down the hill, I was so dizzy from the scent of blood I could hardly see. I grasped desperately for something to steady my nerves. Anything. And that's when it came to me. Try. What J.W. said he focused on before getting on a horse that seemed impossible. T. R. Y. I shaped the letters in my head: Behold the letter T. Unassuming, geometric, a pair of right angles, justly joined by a straight line, straight up the middle. R. I said this letter out loud. "R you serious about getting the job done here? You'd better be, Daryl. Y? Because you have to."

I squealed at top speed down Happy Jack, silently intoning T.R.Y. as the white stripes on the road flew at me, high beams boring phosphorescent tunnels in the dark. Two whitetail does sprung out of the gully and single-bounded over a wire fence. It's 90 percent mental, I said to the windshield. Mind over matter. Focus, focus. Then back to the word. I spelled it out like I was reading the letters off a page. T.R.Y.

Before I knew it, I was at the end of the long drive that led to the ranch house on the rise, lights in the windows glowing yellow. Twila was at the door of her converted garage waiting, her little daughter strapped to her chest in a sling, asleep. When J.W. told me about this T.R.Y. business, I had been skeptical. What, after all, could an athlete teach an artist about the higher mind? But damn if it didn't work. When I hopped down from the truck, my knees buckled and I stumbled. But I didn't fall.

"You're in luck, Daryl." Twila took off her examination gloves and closed her drawer of instruments. "He just got a sliver of glass near his eye. It looks worse than it is. We'll keep him in that bell collar for a few days so he doesn't scratch, and I'll give you ointment to put on him three times a day for the next week. No permanent damage, he's just going to be uncomfortable for a while." She'd cleaned and stitched the wound, and we were free to go.

I couldn't go back to the house by myself and I didn't want to be alone at Goody's, so I drove into town to wait for J.W. While Twila was stitching up Homer, I'd tracked down J.W. on his way back from the night show in Gunnison. I let myself into his apartment with the spare key hidden in the hallway planter. Homer wandered the strange apartment, sniffing and bumping into things because of the big plastic collar. I gave him some water and lunchmeat from J.W.'s fridge, switched on the radio to keep me company, sat on the couch under a blanket, and waited.

I felt my eyelids lower. After being up for two days straight, I had no choice. Sleep sucked me down, but the minute I drifted off, I'd be jolted awake by an alarming image. The thoughts and fears and music from the radio swirled in my brain and melded into the beginnings of a too-familiar dream.

I'm sitting by myself on a bench in a sunny, open field with a date book on my lap. The tips of the prairie grass are dried autumnal sere. A cold, wet wind comes up out of nowhere and the calendar pages begin blowing down the hill. I stand up and run after them, though I can't feel my legs move. I know I have to catch every page within a certain amount of time, or something terrible will happen. Always the deadline dreams—a test I slept through, an appointment I can't get to on time because the brakes give out in the car I'm driving.

After I gather up as many pages as I can, I come back to the date book and look down with a tight, heavy feeling of failure in my upper chest. My throat constricts as if I might cry, but no tears come. Though I want it to be different, the page that the book is opened to is the same as always. Life has its black-letter days. Mine was October 7, 1998.

I was sitting in the student center when I heard about Matthew Shepard. The TV in the lounge was tuned to the local news. The top story was that a gay University of Wyoming student had been found, bound and beaten and left to die, on a fence outside of Laramie. Everybody around me stopped what they were doing and turned toward the television. The kid at the coffee cart walked over and turned up the volume. Someone across the room started laughing. I recognized him, big, melon-headed, a hotshot on the wrestling team with red cystic acne and a tattoo of a screaming eagle on his calf. For whatever reason, he always wore shorts, unless there was more than two feet of snow.

I stared at the screen. I was frozen by incredulity melded to a grim feeling of fatedness—*how could this have happened? . . . I knew this would happen.* The anchorman said four kids had lured nineteen-year-old Matthew out of The Fireside on Custer, taken him to a remote area, tortured, and nearly killed him.

I'd asked years before if Jace told people, if they knew about that part of him. "Oh, they know and they don't know, if that makes any sense," he said. He didn't want to discuss it.

Jace didn't answer the phone when I called that day. I left the student center and got in my car, jamming the gas pedal to the floor as I sped up I-25. I drove a decrepit Honda Civic, wind rattling in through the taped-up passenger side window. I got to the house and tried the front door. It was locked. My heart dropped. Doors aren't locked around here. I ran to the barn and banged on the door, the steel vibrating against the side of my fist. I pounded so hard, green paint flaked off on my skin. "Jace? Jace, it's me. You've got to let me in!"

He peered through a crack in the door. He knew. I knew. Yet we stared at each other saying nothing.

I held my arms open and started sobbing.

"Now what're you crying for, DeeDee?" The radio played in the background. His shotgun was on the workbench.

I had that same feeling then, of something ominous howling in from the darkness. He wanted me to go back to Fort Collins but I wouldn't leave. Couldn't.

When I was a little girl, the winter wind would wake me up at night. Wind like torrents of water, a dark, howling wave that never breaks, the fearsome sound more haunting than anything I've ever known. If you don't live here, you can't imagine the bone-rattling racket. At ninety miles an hour, the character of the wind torques, sounding like a poltergeist moan. I'd cry in my bed, afraid. My father never came to me, and wouldn't let my mother, either. He thought it best for me to cry it out. But I couldn't stop. Jace would get into bed with me and lie by my side until I fell back asleep.

That night, picturing this young man I didn't know bound to a fence and left for dead not twenty-five miles from Red Hill, I curled in the corner of the bed in my old room. Somewhere in me was a scream, huge and strangled, welling up from an unfathomable depth. An unknown world spread out black before me, big and impossibly cold.

After midnight, Jace came in and curled up around me, just like when I was younger. Neither of us could sleep. I heard the calluses on his hands catching on the sheets.

I whispered into the dark. "Jace . . . are you scared?"

He took his chin from the top of my head for a moment. I could feel his breath in my hair. "No."

But what could he have said, really?

I used to pray for God to change Jace because I thought it was embarrassing. Plus, I wanted a sister-in-law someday, and nieces and nephews. But the night of the attack on Matthew Shepard I stopped petitioning and started bargaining. If you change him, God, I'll change. Be better, work harder. But I only prayed for such a thing because I couldn't change the rest of the world, make it safe for Jace, make it sane. God gave me my answer the next morning. I was in the kitchen fixing a bowl of oatmeal. On a flyer for Jace's company advertising a barn sale, he'd scribbled a note about an ordering error he offered to fix by cutting the customer's price. He'd written in red: DEAL. A practical response mooring life in the face of world-tilting events.

On October 12, Matthew Shepard died. That wasn't a black-letter day for me. Everything had gone gray by then.

I woke up, my mouth foul and gritty, the gala dress bunched up around my waist and stained over the ribcage with sweat. J.W. was on his way back to town, and so was Jace. No way around it—unless I invested all my energy into keeping them apart, they were bound to meet. Our vandalized house, the sight of shattered glass scorched into my memory. I had no idea who would do something so horrible. Was it someone I knew, or was it a random act? And what if they came back? What would I do then?

23

"WHY IS IT WHENEVER SOMEONE'S DRIVING halfway up my tailpipe, they've got Texas plates?" Jace thumped into the living room at eight the next morning, face haggard and sunburned the color of crackling pork. He hacked and threw his bag into the corner near the birch coat stand. "All the way up I-25 since Mead, stupid longhorn shitass grinding on my bumper." His eyes went round when Homer lurched over for a friendly scrub. "Jesus Fucking H. Christ, what happened to your dog?"

Homer looked bedraggled, as if smote by some dog-hating deity. He was still moping along, bumping into things because of the collar. Periodically, he'd haunch in a corner and scratch fruitlessly at the plastic funnel with his back leg.

Kenny fed the two hungry heelers wet food from a pull-top can. Their toenails clicked against the kitchen tile as their muzzles jostled for primacy in the red plastic bowl. He scraped chunks of meat from the bottom of the can with a dirty fork from the sink. "Where'd the plastic on the windows come from?"

After he'd come home from Gunnison, J.W. took me over to Dominion to pick up rolls of plastic sheeting. He worked until sunrise patiently measuring the windows, cutting plastic to fit, and stapling

it tightly in place. He'd left a half-hour before to catch a shower before starting his shift.

Jace, Kenny, and I spent the day sweeping. I picked glass out of
the yard so no shards would get stuck in paws and hooves. The afternoon discharged massive heat, the sun so bright on the hillside
shale it hurt to look at it. Salt and sunscreen stung my eyes.

Two police investigators came out to talk to us. The peach-fuzz
detective treated Jace with respect, as if the hostility of the crime
conferred tremendous worth. "There's no indication that this person wanted to harm you," Detective Diaz said. "If they did, they'd
have hurt your animals. The only thing we can tell you for sure is
that whoever did this really wanted to get your attention."

At sundown, Jace thawed out a container of venison chili and ladled it into yellow bowls. He took a deep sip of raspberry iced tea. I
yawned at the counter bar stool and refilled my coffee cup for the
fourth time. I was still in my dress from the gala. Jace spread butter
on a heel of pumpernickel. "Ken and I can wrap it up if you want to
go to Goody's and get some sleep."

My jaw muscle snapped from yawning so wide. "I want to stay
and help."

The piece of bread on his plate had big teethmarks in the butter.
"We don't know who did this or if they'll come back. I'd feel better
if I knew you were someplace safe. You can sack out for a while. I
can tell by looking you've been up for days."

Jace came into the loft as I finished changing into my jeans. I
started packing clothes in a bag. Jace reached out and snagged my
belt. He rolled his eyes at the Jubilee Days buckle. "Oh, I don't believe this."

"What?" I took the belt from him and threaded it through my
belt loops.

"Did he give that to you?"

"No. I mugged Ty Murray." The overnight bag was light in my

hand as I started down the stairs. "Who do you think gave it to me?"

"Where you going?"

"To town." I stopped on the landing, headed back upstairs to fetch my toothbrush. "J.W. said I could stay at his place until you got home but I wanted to wait for you out here. Now that you're back, I'm going."

When I came back downstairs, Jace followed me through the living room. "Well, ain't Grits and Gravy the giving kind? I told you to go to Goody's."

I turned at the front door. "What's the difference where I stay? I've got my cell phone. You can call me wherever."

"Because I don't like the sound of the guy, I never have, and right now I want you someplace where I don't have to worry about you." He was right on my heels. He caught the screen door when I pushed through it and came after me.

I kept going. "You don't even know him."

"I know enough to know I don't trust him."

I stopped. "Remember when I came to New Orleans and found out about you and Ian? I said I didn't care who you were with, as long as you were happy. Why can't you do the same for me?"

"This is different."

The porch ceiling was covered in miller moths, weaving and rotating around the tin lantern. "Ian was at least ten years older than you. How is this different?"

"It just is. You don't understand. Some guys just reel you in, get you crazy hung up, then turn around and hurt you when you least expect it."

I felt the cold anger percolating in my gut. "I sincerely doubt J.W. is like that."

"Yeah? Well, how do you know he didn't do this? Just so happens he wasn't around when it happened, then all of a sudden, he materializes to fix things up. Don't you think that's a little convenient?"

I turned away from him and started down the steps. "You're just saying that to upset me."

"I'm saying it because I'm your brother and it's my job to protect you."

"I don't recall asking for your help in the matter, Jace, and I'd appreciate it if you'd back the hell off." The gravel walk crunched under my feet.

I looked back and saw Jace on the porch. He crossed his arms. This talking back represented a change he didn't like. "What," he called from the railing. "You got some schoolgirl fantasy going with this guy? You think the big bad cowboy loves you?"

I stood at the edge of the apron of hard yellow light from the porch and faced him head-on. "No. I *know* he loves me. And whether you like it or not, I love him, too." I started up the hill toward my truck.

He yelled after me. "When are you going to grow up, Daryl?"

The words struck me like a brass-knuckled fist. I spun in the dirt and held my arms out. "I did grow up. You just don't like who I grew into."

24

RED HILL WAS A HIVE OF ACTIVITY when I returned from work the next afternoon. Goody's ranch hands were busy in every corner of the house, patching the roof and fitting in whatever panes of standard-size glass they could.

Jace put down the hammer and squinted at the pearl-green truck coming down the drive with a bed full of lumber. Brandon and Clete jumped out of the cab, and stomped by me holding a bundle of plywood sheeting. Clete crunched down on his toothpick. "Miss Daryl, next time you have yourself a little situation, make sure it's not during our busiest time of year, would you?"

Brandon, struggling with the other end of the bundle, passed me with a big smile. "Yeah, seriously. Anytime after Finals is good."

J.W. got out of the cab. "Thought we'd do what we could to help with what we had on hand at Dominion." Jace eventually sauntered over. He and J.W. shook hands, swapping suspicions. A clairvoyant would have fried every brain cell reading the fierce energy that coursed between them. Jace held himself stretched up to full height, chest out, and J.W. was the polite Southern boy, but that how-do smile was awfully tight.

I know Jace better than anyone and sorry isn't his strong suit. So I knew what it meant when he came up to me while I was in the kitchen making coffee. He set up a half-dozen mugs. "He's all right," he said, throwing the soggy filter in the trash before he went back out into the racket of drills and pounding hammers.

Everyone put their tools down when Harold Gwatney's Range Rover pulled up next to the house. Jace met him on the porch. He wiped the sweat off his forehead with the tail of his sleeveless flannel shirt. "Sorry, Mr. G. Looks like we've got some work to do before the next open house."

Gwatney waved his hand. "I don't imagine we'll need another open house. I've got marvelous news." He held up a sheaf of papers. "Darcey and Jordan Rivers made an offer on the property. I think you'll be very pleased."

My stomach turned and my eyes immediately went to Jace. He looked the way I felt—not pleased at all.

Surely the sale of a home was occasion to hoist a few and Ricky and the Redstreaks were playing at the Hitching Post so why the heck not? At eight o' clock, the red sun slunk behind Table Mountain and Jace called hammers down, and Clete, Brandon, J.W., and I headed to town for the show.

The Hitch was abuzz when we arrived. Never mind the burly singer onstage in the blond cocktail waitress wig, tossing a blow-up doll into the crowd. Forget the song he was singing that would make your grandma blush. Everyone was craning their necks and whispering about someone in the audience. Duff "The Dragon" Linsey! They may as well have spelled his name out in multicolored neon and slapped up a billboard in front. He stood at the bar with a crowd of rodeo guys around him. Duff showing up at Frontier Days was a matter of course; all roads led to Cheyenne this time of year. Over a hundred years running, million-plus purse, and more than a thousand contestants over the ten-day run, The Daddy of 'Em All was the country's biggest outdoor rodeo and, grumblings of sub-standard stock aside, a win was a huge coup, worth however many miles and dollars it took to get here.

Duff noticed us the moment we came in and cruised over immediately, slapping the boys on the back. Brandon, holding to some Hollywood dreams of his own, seemed a little star-struck but kept cool for J.W.'s sake. Clete met Duff's greeting with a grunt. Duff introduced himself to me and held onto my hand for an extra beat like J.W. had the night we met. "You know my brother, huh? He's one of the greatest bareback riders who ever lived! I worship this guy!"

Duff was smaller than I would have thought, as tall as J.W. but with much less bulk in the upper body. He had the same chiseled cheekbones and the smile of a vice-presidential candidate. Though it was hard to notice anything beyond the teeth so white they glowed under black light, his eyes had an anxious twitch when he looked at his brother. I recognized a false front of composure when I saw one, and behind the facade, this guy had *train wreck* screaming from every cell. He didn't reach out to shake his brother's hand. "J-dub! You up soon?"

"Yes." J.W. touched my arm, trying to maintain some hold on civility. "What can I get you, Daryl?"

"Hold off there, bro. I'm buying." Duff nodded my way. "What's your pleasure, Daryl?"

J.W.'s mouth set in a straight line. I felt uneasy. "Bud Light and a shot of apple Pucker, I guess."

Duff's laugh was oddly confrontational. "Pucker? That's a girl's drink!"

"I am a girl."

"I noticed."

J.W. cleared his throat, a gravelly scrape like a hoof pawing at pavement. "We'll be at our table."

I hissed into J.W.'s shoulder as he swerved us through the crowd. "Why the hell didn't you tell me he was in town?"

"Later, Daryl. Just let me get through this night."

Having made Duff as the type of guy who has no issue with dining off the dessert cart, I was surprised he wasn't courting any female attention. With *hey, cowboy* eyes beaming out from under the brims of pink and leopard print hats, every skirt hiked up short, and skimpy tops that would turn the joint into boobapalooza with one drunk ripcord pull, I expected Duff to be streaking about in a stud bunch—the superstar stallion surrounded by a clutch of adoring, willing women. But he moved from group to group of men, always returning to try to talk to us, but wherever Duff was in the room, J.W. managed to find his way to the other side.

The Redstreaks ground "Mustang Sally" into a fine dust, the room now so full it felt like the walls might bust out at any second. Beeber squeezed through the crowd, a Coors in either hand, and sat at our table. Duff came by and whacked him cheerfully between the shoulder blades. "Hey, Beeb!"

Beeber smiled like a guy taking a bite out of a shit sandwich. "Hey, Dad."

I looked at J.W., totally speechless. He raised his eyebrows sourly and looked away.

The Redstreaks launched into their encore number, and the crowd went ballistic, roomful of Wild Things hollering along, drinks held overhead. Women belly-to-belly dancing, some yuckster trying to swing from the chandelier. Beeber handed Duff one of his beers, straining over the song as the band worked toward its manic climax. "Dad, this colt I started yesterday, you should've seen 'im. I . . ."

Duff was distracted. There was no mistaking the focus of his attention. Kimber. The rock star of the rodeo had spotted Cheyenne's one and only buckle barracuda. She was near the stage swaying to the music, her hair swinging around. When she saw Duff, she stopped dancing. Their eyes met with all the subtlety of a thunderclap and the corner of Kimber's mouth curved up in her patented who-needs-you-anyway smile.

Wild thing, I think I love you!

Duff ambled up to Kimber and whispered something in her ear. She laughed at whatever he said and turned away. She started walking toward the exit with her languid panther step. The luring glance she cast over her shoulder worked like the devil's own magic. Duff left the beer on the table and followed her like she could lead him into boiling oil and he wouldn't even blink.

J.W. had six rodeo buddies crashing at his place, and we wanted to be alone. J.W. finally spilled it all when we were in the back of his truck off the Terry Ranch Road—his parents divorcing when J.W. was ten and Duff eight. His mom marrying Lucky Linsey, a schemer who did a good job of crowbarring the boys apart. J.W. went to go live with his dad and Uncle Royal who got him started on broncs out at their farm, while Duff stayed home, currying maternal favor and allowing Lucky to adopt him. Lucky viewed Duff as an investment, sinking some of his gambling money into rodeo school. The two boys managed to find peace when they were competing, while traveling together they could leave the family drama behind and steady themselves through sport. But when J.W. grew up—got married and got serious—and Duff refused to, the fissure widened into a yawning gap, and when there wasn't an eight-second agenda bringing them together, there wasn't much for the brothers to go on.

"Duff and Teresa were pretty much two of a kind," he said, sipping from the pop we were sharing. "They met in high school. Teresa was full Cajun, real dark like Beeb, the prettiest girl around for a dozen counties. Neither of them could parent worth a flip, that's for sure. My mother took up the slack when Duff was on the road but with Teresa partying all the time, it didn't do much to keep Beeber in line. I found a joint on him when he was twelve. When I got settled here with Melissa, I told Mama to ship him to me, see if I could straighten him out. Once he started working with horses, he fell in line."

Duff and J.W. had hardly spoken in ten years, and striking their relationship from the record wasn't hard. Friends and fellow cowboys were considerate enough to not bring it up, and there simply wasn't enough media interest in a lowly circuit cowboy for the press to look too closely at J.W.'s personal life. Duff's notoriety didn't draw the issue from the underbrush, either. The rodeo reporters could be counted on to omit tricky information with a little PR flak glad-handing, and the few mainstream publications that paid Duff any attention were more interested in his substance consumption than his family tree. A bastard son might make juicy copy, but only if there were enough ticket buyers to care.

"Duff offered to bring Beeber out to California and get him work as a wrangler on a movie set, but Beeber didn't want anything to do with that stuff. He just wants to be a cowboy." J.W. crinkled up the empty aluminum can. "This is old news, Daryl, and boring." His hand was hot as it traveled up the back of my shirt. "Now you come here and give me one of those sweet kisses, would you?"

We crept into the basement bedroom at Red Hill and overslept. J.W. had the day off but I didn't. I had to scramble to get to work on time. J.W. leaned on his elbow, watching me shuck his T-shirt and yank my tank top down over my head. "You sure seem in a hurry this morning. Someplace you've got to be?"

"Just errands."

"Anything you're wanting to tell me?"

I tightened my belt down another notch. With no time for decent meals lately, my pants were almost falling off. I checked my watch. I could already picture Grandma Dam's big hairdo shifting uniformly as she shook her head at me. "Not really."

He gave me an accusing look that burned like an eyeful of black pepper. Then he turned away.

Kimber, all hopped up on her latest conquest, talked me into meeting her out at Frontier Park after work to keep her company while Duff did a photo shoot for a big newspaper story. He'd scored eighty-nine points on his bull that afternoon, and wouldn't that make a nice lead for a comeback story? A reporter from New York stood near the photo set with a tiny notebook in hand. Her hair was polished mahogany, parted severely to the side, and fastened by a leather barrette at the base of her neck. Stern lines ran along either side of her mouth, as if she were strained from listening for applause that never came. She closed her notebook. "Okay, that covers it."

Duff sat in a canvas director's chair getting contour foundation sponged onto his jawline. "Catch up with you later, Rachel." He winked. Rachel nodded, charmed, marginally.

The Frontier Days committee makes media personnel dress in Western wear to keep the image consistent. Rachel wore her Wranglers like a dignitary forced to promenade the town square in clown pants. She buttoned her Western shirt over her camisole top, put on her new cowboy hat, and disappeared up the stairs to the media deck.

Kimber nudged me in the ribs. "Isn't this cool?"

"Well, it's different, that's for sure." I hadn't any idea if she knew of Duff's connection to Beeber, and I wasn't sure how to even approach the subject.

The photographer worked quickly, greasing Duff's ego as he shot. "The bull riding legend, yessir." Snap. Whir. "Look this way, Duff. Awesome." After changing lenses, he looked around for the stylist. "Can you make sure Natasha's ready? We need her in this shot."

While Duff waited, people closed in for autographs. To the older couple who thanked him for his charity work with underprivileged kids, he was the keeper of The Code. To the little boys who asked him to sign their hats, he was an idol. To the teenage girls who lined up for an autograph and a kiss on the cheek, he was a vintage heart-throb. With every different approach, Duff went through subtle changes in body language and vocal inflection, from four-square guy to whispering flirt. Through every personality shift, I wondered: would the real Duff Linsey please stand up?

Kimber watched his interaction with the crowd avidly. His slip-sliding personality didn't seem to bother her a bit. Role model, idol, sex god, whatever. To Kimber, he was the hottest thing in town and he was blowing kisses her way, and that was all that mattered.

Because of his concussion over Fourth of July, Duff had cut back his schedule and was now only entering at rodeos that, as it happened, received big media coverage. He stepped down from the platform and wandered off to get a bottled water. A chute hand in a dirty straw hat walked past and chucked his chin at him in greeting. "Hey, Tinseltown." It was barely affectionate.

The stylist returned from the sports-medicine trailer with a tall, Slavic model. She'd probably sought shelter in there because it was air conditioned. The model smiled for a nanosecond and adjusted her shiny pink top, flipped her designer red hair, and then climbed on the platform that Duff was standing on and wrapped herself around his ankles like a supplicant. He had a red metallic Fender Stratocaster strapped on.

Two steer ropers wandered by, ropes over their shoulders. One muttered under his breath, "You know how to play that?" Cowboys leaned against the chain-link fence of the ready area, watching the model. A couple of young bull riders snickered and pointed. The wind flipped up their back numbers.

"Hey, you!"

I turned and faced Tara Dunny, holding her little girls' hands. Both as angel-faced as their mama, they were ear-to-ear in blue cotton candy sugar. "Thought we might cross paths out here! How's J.W. doing? He up today?"

"Nope. Couple days yet. Saw Cord got some day money earlier.

You guys have to run off to another rodeo or can you stick around for some fun? Catch a night show or something?"

"We're here until tomorrow. Got tickets for Trace Adkins, and I can't wait. Last chance before I'm back to the grind. School starts in a couple weeks."

Her older girl squirmed when Tara wiped her face with a Wet-Nap. So cute. "Do you like school?" I asked her. "Are you excited to go back?"

Tara laughed. "I didn't mean their school. Mine." So she was a student as well as a wife and mother. Studying something practical, I'd bet. Cosmetology. Bartending. "A couple more semesters and you can call me Dr. Dunny."

"Doctor of what? Philosophy?"

"Bo-ring! No way. Forensics." She rubbed her hands together. "The good stuff. Lacey, Julia, come on, time to scoot if we want to see the trick riders in their pretty costumes." The three of them walked away, waving, leaving me standing ankle-deep in a steaming heap of my own fool assumptions.

Duff and the serpentine model were nearing the end of their poses for the camera when Beeber came clomping across the walkway that bridged the parking lot and the east stands. Beeber stopped dead in his tracks when he saw his father, Kimber waiting loyally for him, wearing his Oakley sunglasses. You could almost hear the poor kid's heart break. Beeber made an abrupt turnaround but Duff caught sight of him. "Beeb!" He yelled. "Come down here and snap a few with your dad!" He smiled at the photographer, who checked his light meter, looking bored. "Boy got his good looks from his mama, you can tell."

Beeber didn't have one thing to say about his dad's offer. Just a middle finger held aloft.

It was the Frontier Days edition of the Wigwam Wild Women Revue and the Wild Women were on the bar, outfitted in tiny crocheted bikini tops, cut-off denim shorts, and John Deere caps, grinding away to "She Thinks My Tractor's Sexy."

Duff was there, as well as half the town, everyone clustered in their little cliques—the tourists, the town people on the slum, the Air Force guys, the regulars, the cowboys, and the hangers-on. In the middle of her solo routine, Kimber slipped in a spilled drink and tumbled from the bar. Flyboy Jeff appeared out of nowhere, rushed forward, and caught her in his arms. Duff, who was autographing a girl's chest, was too busy to notice.

At midnight, Kimber got on the bar to introduce Duff and he climbed up next to her and manned the mic like a game show host. "I sure appreciate the hard work you Wild Women put into entertaining us, and I'm sure all the fellas do, too. But why don't the ladies get a show?"

The bar was packed to the rafters with tourist girls eager to get their chicken-fried freak on, and their approving squeals were deafening. Next thing I knew, Duff, Elvis Munce, and Cody Danko were on the bar shaking their butts to every rowdy cowboy song that came on, the women clapping and singing along.

Exhibitionism proved to be quite contagious. The Wild Women made space as more rodeo guys crowded onto the bar. The Wigwam was turning into a Who's Who of cowboy tail, and any guy who'd ever paid an entry fee at The Daddy of 'Em All was angling for space in the lineup. Shirts started coming off, showing scars, bruises, a bandage. A bullfighter dropped trou and spun around with his polka-dot clown boxers on. Someone started a basic pattern of steps, and soon the guys were synchronized in a turn-stomp-shimmy routine. Calf ropers, steer wrestlers, bull and bronc riders, the full range was spread across the fifteen-foot bar, the gaggle of girls waving dollar bills and smacking their chops at the masculine spectacle spread out before them.

Competitive showing-off made an interesting spectator sport, but I had a headache and wanted to go home. I found Kimber changing in the stockroom. I held my breath against the smell of turned beer and cheap hairspray.

Kimber grinned. "Duff's got 'em eating from the palm of his hand out there." She swept her hair up under her black Stetson. "I still can't believe he's really here."

"Guess it figures he'd come to town, given that he's got family here and all."

That was good enough bait. Kimber wiped her mascara wand on a bar napkin and swept two quick coats onto her lashes. "Yeah . . . Beeber's a doll. Now I know why. Duff's taking me out to eat after closing." She inserted the wand back into the Maybelline tube. "It's really something, isn't it?"

I didn't answer her.

"I said it's something, right, Daryl?"

"I never would have seen it coming, that's for sure. Makes me feel a little bad for Beeber, though. I mean, I think he kind of had his hopes up about you."

"He knew we were just hanging out. It wasn't anything serious." Where was basic consideration in her comprehensive index of human behavior?

"Not to you, maybe. But I think you really got him going there."

"So you're saying I led him on?" Kimber tied a black bandana around her neck. "What's that supposed to be, Daryl? A judgment?"

"No." Wow, it even sounded like a lie.

Kimber tore her Frontier Days T-shirt a little lower to show off her white satin bra and stomped her feet so the fringe on her starred chaps straightened out. "That takes some nerve. You don't think people are talking about you running around town with a guy who's old enough to be your father?"

"No, he's not."

"Let's see here. J.W.'s forty-one; you're twenty-three. That's a span of eighteen years. Do you meant to suggest that people don't have kids when they're eighteen, because if so, that sure sounds like another judgment to me."

"I am not judging you. And I don't care what anyone says about me and J.W., if you want to know."

"Well, it's real good you feel that way, because let me tell you, people are talking plenty. Like you're a five-foot-tall fix for some old cowboy's midlife crisis. And I always stick up for you. As far as choices go, you've got no right to come down on me." She pulled on a pair of fingerless black leather gloves. "Now if you'll excuse me, I've got a show to do."

25

FRONTIER DAYS MEANT EVERY ROOM in town was booked. Even the Twin Pines, the last on any recommended lodging list, had total occupancy. I worked my way down to Room Sixteen, at the very end of the east wing. I rapped on the door with my keys. "Housekeeping." When there was no answer, I unlocked the door.

I saw the straw Bailey first, brim-up on the dresser. J.W. sat on the bed, head in his hands. My feet were quiet on the carpet as I stepped into the room and closed the door behind me. He looked up, eyes heavy with contrition. "Why didn't you tell me?"

I wanted to back out of the room, to run away. "I wanted you to think I was a real artist." When I said it out loud, it sounded so stupid. Shouldn't I have been more proud to be a blue-collar trooper, the arty moppet with a mop?

"I have a day job, too. Do you think I'm not a real cowboy?"

"You've already proven yourself. I'm still a wannabe."

"You really think I'd care that you work here? Or that you had to keep it a secret, after everything you know about me?"

"I'm sorry, but I'm not exactly bursting with pride over cleaning motel rooms for a living."

"Well, shoot, Daryl, you don't always have to be a hero. Don't you know you could've asked me for money?"

"How did you find out?"

"My buddies from Ponca City are staying in Room Twelve. They recognized you from Big Sue's."

I sat on the floor and leaned my head against the bed. "Now that you know the truth, do you want to leave?"

He checked his watch. "I don't have to check out until eleven." He sat down on the carpet next to me. "Got something I want to show you." He put a Papa John's Pizza baseball cap in my hands. "Here."

"What's this?"

"I used to have to wear it. About seven years ago, I shattered my ankle so bad I couldn't rodeo for six months and I ran short of cash. So I worked construction during the day and worked for Papa John's at night. My hair smelled like cheese all the time. A thirty-five-year-old guy with a wife and kid, delivering pizzas. I'd already won the World then, too. And I was just like you—I never told anybody I was doing it. I keep this on the top shelf in my closet, right next to my good hats, to remind me that I could go from money to mud in a heartbeat." He pressed a roll of bills into my hand. "I want you to take this."

It had to be at least two hundred dollars. "No, J.W. No."

"Come on now, Daryl. It's not so bad having someone look out for you. I know you're independent but I'm a good old boy at heart and I can't change that. If you need help, I want to help you. I'm not saying you can't do for yourself. But you don't have to. Not all the time."

He took the money from my hand and tucked it into the pocket of my ugly yellow smock. "Jesus, Daryl, I wish you'd have told me. When I thought of you with somebody else, it about drove me out of my mind. You probably thought I was some crazy hillbilly hollering at you on the phone like I did in Calgary. I guess I'm not the most trusting person sometimes, and I'm sure sorry I got the wrong idea."

I sat looking at my paint-stained hands folded in my lap. "I don't even know why you'd want to be with a mess like me." My nails were filthy and the rubber gloves I wore while cleaning didn't keep the skin on my knuckles from toughening like rhinoceros hide. "My hands look like hell."

"Daryl, look at mine. I'm forty-one, I have the hands of a guy who's sixty."

"But I love your hands. I noticed them the very first time we went out."

"Why can't it be the same for you? I know what pampered looks like. I don't want it. You've got dedicated hands. Dedication isn't perfect."

He put his arms around me and cupped his hand around mine so my fist rested in his palm. "See that fit? It's just right." He kissed my knuckles and held our hands out together. "I want to take care of you but you've got to let me first."

I curled up in his lap. He kissed my hair and pulled me close. "You want to move to the bed?"

I sighed. "It's okay. I just vacuumed yesterday."

J.W. cruised off to work and I went back to sponging down tubs and making beds. I'd flipped the flowered coverlet off the California King in Room Six and folded it over the back of the chair to air it out, however possible that was in a room that hadn't had good ventilation since the Nixon administration, when Giselle came charging in. She clicked the television remote and tuned in channel five. "Isn't that your friend?"

Sure enough, it was Shawna, hands cuffed behind her back, policemen loading her into a squad car, right there on the twelve o'-clock news.

I didn't get the story until we were stowed away in a nonsmoking back booth at Shari's. Lan had no cell phone access in Sturgis, so I went to the jail downtown myself to pick her up. Shawna ordered hash browns and drowned them in ketchup. "Guess I picked the wrong week to give up cigarettes."

She was on her way into the gallery at the Old West Museum when she got cornered into a conversation with a group of steer wrestlers, Darcey Rivers among them. The talk turned to Brock Gasperson, son of a stock contracting dynasty and a rock 'n' roller who favored flame tattoos and earrings and the nickname "Kid Brock," and how he'd shown up that day to bulldog with his shoulder-length hair in cornrows. They'd asked Shawna why someone like him, like her, would want to walk around looking like "such a freak."

"If he wants to wear his hair like a goddamn nigger, he should do it on his own time," Darcey said. When Shawna told him that was fucked up, he said, "Oh, I do apologize. Wanna smoke my peace pipe?"

That set her off, as I could imagine. "Hey, squaw," he called to her as she stormed away. "Hey, Pocahontas!" Then he sealed his fate by jumping around, popping one hand over his mouth in a most offensive imitation of a war whoop. Shawna turned back, started at a run, and jumped him, bringing him to the ground with a punch to the temple.

She kept wailing on him until the other guys pulled her off. By then Jordan had shown up, screaming, and called the cops. Did they want to press charges, the policemen asked? Hell, yes, they did—Jordan because she was wired to do everything in the most dramatic possible fashion, and Darcey because not only had he gotten beaten up, he got beaten up by a girl. When the squad car pulled up, it attracted the attention of the channel five film crew, and her humiliating exit was captured for the lunchtime broadcast.

Shawna bent and unbent her drinking straw. She wanted a cigarette more than anything, I could tell. "I hate my life."

I took a cold bite of Denver omelet. "What's to hate? You've got a baby coming soon, a great guy who not only gets you but wants to marry you, and you make amazing money doing what you love."

"I'm *not* doing what I love. I'm a sellout of the highest order. I'm the same bullshit stereotype Darcey Rivers thinks I am."

"So stop painting the maids then. Paint something else."

"I can't, Daryl. If I don't paint what I paint, I don't eat." She pointed to her stomach for emphasis: baby on the way. Like I didn't know.

"How can you be so sure you wouldn't succeed? Have you ever tried to sell anything else?"

"Yeah. Once. And do you know what it got me? Nothing."

"Oh, I see. One unsold painting and you're a washout."

"Sometimes I fantasize about throwing myself off a bridge."

"Shawna, come on." I thought surely someone who pulls in five grand a month could find some reason to go on. Maybe I was just jealous. Maybe I was pissed that she hadn't bothered to say thank you for paying her bail with my credit card, but I was sick of it. It seemed like my relationships had mutated into a game of psychic whack-a-mole—hammer down one confrontation and another pops right up. "Take up tattooing, like you've always talked about doing. Or go work at an auto-body shop painting cars. Do something! Anything!"

Now that I'd cornered her, she went from angry to trapped animal. It was a total pity-play and I wasn't having it. "No. Oh, no. I'm not finished yet, Shawna . . ."

Honestly, I didn't know which was worse: to be a runaway success on an easy road that makes any other route seem scary, like Shawna, or to scrape by doing this and that, like me. I live pretty close to the edge but at least I know I've got the inner resources to not go over. Plus I like what I do. I started to think that maybe I got the better deal. I pulled my worried friend close to my side. "Listen, Shawnzy, Vincent van Gogh created incredible art and died broke.

Do you think that he stopped painting for lack of funds?"

"Yeah, but he ended up going batshit crazy and cut his ear off over some girl."

"Right. I know that. But my point is he kept painting. He had to keep painting, just like you, and just like me. But you seem to think that in order to live off of your art you have to paint something you don't like. The world doesn't owe you anything, but you've got to keep trying to get by on your own terms anyway." I motioned to the waitress to bring Shawna some water. She started sobbing quietly. I passed her my napkin. "You're so angry all the time you can't see your way out of it. And look where it got you. In jail, Shawna. In fucking jail." Her face went stone-flat. "If you keep going like this, you're going to do something really stupid. You can do so much better. I know you can. Everyone knows you can. Landy. Your mom. You just have to get out of your own way."

"Maybe." She honked into the napkin, then took another and started tearing off little pieces, pilling them between her thumb and forefinger. She looked down into her lap and spoke in a small voice. "Do you think I'll be a bad mother?"

"*What?* Shawna, no . . ."

"I mean, I was smoking and drinking before I knew." Her chin puckered and she started crying again.

"But once you found out, you stopped, right?"

She nodded and sniffed. "And the way I lose my temper . . ."

"Shawnzy, you have the biggest heart of anyone I know." This girl. She just had no idea of her effect, what it meant that she'd create flash art for Lan's shop, that she made vegetarian meatloaf dinners magically appear when I was in school and hardly had enough money to eat. I rubbed her neck. "A temper is something you can manage. A stingy little Grinch heart, not so much. You're the last person I worry about being able to care for someone." I stuffed a twenty into the black plastic billfold that held our check. I thought of Darcey and Jordan, off somewhere laughing over the fact that they'd sent Shawna to jail. "Goddamn, I can't believe Mr. and Mrs. Righteous Snot of God are moving into my house. I wish I could give them both a straight sock in the mouth."

"Don't bother," Shawna said. "They'll get theirs somehow. Karma wears boots."

Shawna's hippie-dippy retribution voodoo was forged between her mother's East Coast "Jewsoisie" high-mindedness and a Boulder private school, but I'm from the gritty root of this place, the gunslinger's sangfroid deep in my DNA. All I could think about was finding Darcey Rivers and pounding him into a puddle of teeth and blood. No matter how many housing developments, strip malls, chain stores, and tourist attractions you pile into this town, it was built on a bedrock of frontier justice. Maybe Shawna was right—maybe karma does wear boots. *But please,* I begged of whatever universal force would listen, *let me tie the laces.*

The party started right after the rodeo and by dinnertime, the house was full, people spilling out onto the deck and into the yard. Presumably we were celebrating the sale of Red Hill, but Jace draped the house with a FREE SHAWNA TWO TRIBES banner fashioned from of an old sheet. Someone rolled in a keg, and every person who came through the door brought a dish or a bottle. Guests climbed up on the ladder and spray-painted their brand on the plywood that covered the windows. Shawna, obviously touched and enjoying her guest-of-honor position from the living room's most comfortable armchair, made Jace promise he'd take the window covering down later so she could incorporate it into an art project. The music was loud and relentless.

I'd had a fair amount of tequila punch, so I only vaguely remember J.W. leaving early for a meeting with his boss at Dominion, and that Kimber and Duff never showed. Which was fine. I was still sore at Kimber and wasn't in the mood to see them draped all over each other anyway, and Beeber was in his stocking feet, executing a perfect moonwalk across the living room floor to Shawna and Lan's delight. Poor kid deserved the break.

I walked into my old bedroom. Crystal stood at the mirror with a cosmetic bag. She'd heard me on my cell phone at work inviting people, and I felt bad so I invited her, too. "Hey, Daryl." She smiled, dusting her nose with powder. "Great party." She swizzled on some pink lip gloss and clicked her compact shut.

"Thank you," I said, joining her at the mirror. "I credit the tequila. Though I suppose I could have had less." My mouth had that nice numb tequila feel. I put my glass on the nightstand, searching for a hair elastic. I found one and held it between my teeth while I swept my sweaty hair up into a ponytail.

"Nah, it's a party! So party!" She locked the bedroom door. "Keep the creeps out, you know? We don't need them barging in here." She had a bottle of Cuervo Gold with her, and a saltshaker by her lime-filled glass. "Had your body shot yet?"

"No. And I really shouldn't do any more."

"Bullshit. Don't you think we deserve it after scrubbing and vaccuuming all day?" She picked up the saltshaker and put the lime wedge in her mouth. "Come on, you go first, then me."

"Okay." The salt stuck to the light sweat on her neck. When I leaned into her, she smelled like Gummi Bear body spray. I licked as quickly as I could and pecked at the lime. The shot went down like liquid fire.

"Cheap ass," she said, spitting the lime into her palm. She was joking but there was menace to it.

I hadn't believed what happened until afterward, when I was pressing my fingers to my stinging lips. While it was going on, I couldn't process that Crystal had leaned in, pinned me to the bed, and started kissing me, that this small, wet mouth was connected to a girl who was connected to me. Even in my drunken state, I was aware of the force involved, that this was a sort of amazing, supersexualized kiss. Her tongue was eager, almost determined, and her lip gloss had a vile cherry taste. She bit my lower lip and tugged gently at it with her teeth, then ran her long nail along the hot seam of my jeans. She sat back on the bed and looked at me with a satisfied expression, like she'd put me in my place somehow. She crossed her legs and smiled. I couldn't think of a single thing to say. But after a shocked moment, the rabbit punch of Jose Cuervo hit me in the solar plexus. "That was something else, Crystal."

"Oh, if you want *something else,* check this out." She slid her skirt up her hips. Crystal Commando, her pubic hair a bleached platinum strip, lay back on the bed, spread her legs, and showed me the gold ring run vertically through the hood of her clitoris. A ruby-colored heart dangled from the ring. Even the vulgar presentation of a very drunk girl didn't stop me from thinking it was perversely exquisite.

There was rapping on the door. "Crystal, you in there?"

She didn't take her eyes from me. "Yes, baby," she called. "Be right out."

Without a word, she rose from the bed and opened the door. It was some guy I didn't know. She pressed up against him and slid her hand into his back pocket. "Sorry I was gone so long," she said. Her voice was high and girlish but underneath was a sultry hum like the purr of a cat with a goldfish sliding down its throat. "Girl talk."

A racket started up outside. We ran outside to find three trucks circling in the dirt. It was Doug Cathcart and his posse, attempting to crash. They'd not weighed the wisdom of pulling up to a hunter's house uninvited, especially a hunter with the foresight to extend a host's welcome to the cops who had come to his house when it was vandalized. Soon there were more men with weapons on the porch than you'd find at the local meeting of the NRA.

The Cathcart crew squealed off into the night and the party continued until six.

Morning was next to crash the party. At 8 A.M., a cell phone rang and a half-dozen cowboys reached for their belts, like a posse drawing their guns from their holsters in an old-movie standoff. It was the first of the good morning calls from all the girls left at home. Word came in that Wick Scuno was out with a broken leg, thanks to a rank one from Tiny Migden's practice pen in Pretty Prairie. But, someone else chimed in, Tiny had two teenage daughters, and the look that went with that bit of news suggested that the rank one who did the damage might have been Tiny himself.

Shawna stood on the back deck, explaining yoga to a couple guys from Medicine Hat. . . . *It's so good for your muscles, it's unreal* . . . and next thing I knew, she was leading a half a dozen hungover cowboys through the sun salute, two-time World champion bull rider Biscuit Taymor in downward-facing dog. Dannell Squires in cobra pose. I groped over the previous night's events. I wasn't worried that the interlude with Crystal had some huge meaning. If four years of college teaches a girl anything, it's the difference between lesbianism and tequila.

"Hey." Kimber stood at the screen door holding a bag of blood oranges and a bottle of champagne. I put the teakettle on the front burner and felt around the top of the refrigerator for a bunch of bananas.

Jace, unaware of any tension between Kimber and me got up to let her in. "Hey there, Miss Kimber. You missed a good party."

"I'll bet." She came into the kitchen and held out the blood oranges in apology. The Albertson's bag meant she had to drive way out of the way to get them. "I suck."

"How's Duff?" I could have said I was sorry, too, but I was still pretty mad. I wanted her to twist, just a little.

"I wouldn't know. I sent him packing. After dinner we went back to my place, and he took an OxyContin because he said his head hurt. Then he had a couple drinks. Then we went into the bedroom, and he couldn't get it up. He said he'd been having mood swings since his concussion so they put him on Zoloft and because of Zoloft he has trouble 'functioning.' By the time he was getting ready to pop a Viagra, I was like, Jesus, I'm fucking a Walgreen's!"

Jace came into the kitchen and started mixing batter for buckwheat pancakes. Kimber helped, and while they sifted flour, she dished the dirt on Duff Linsey. "He said he just signed on to play the lead in a remake of *Midnight Cowboy*."

Jace snickered. The batter slapped against the sides of the mixing bowl with a wet, sucking sound. "Oh, the boys'll love that."

"What do you mean?" I greased the griddle with some butter on a napkin and uncorked the champagne.

"Oh, come on, Daryl. Who do you think put the big bad Dragon on the map in Hollywood? 'Tweren't the Family Values folk." Kenny grinned like a maniac, showing his little badger teeth. He was enjoying this.

I opened the bag of blood oranges, sliced them in two, and fed them into the juicer. "What are you talking about?"

Jace gave me a bear hug that ended in a loving squeeze. "Daryl, DeeDee, my little sister, my love. Underneath it all, you are still country as corn. Pure and innocent as the day is long." He patted my head. "You stay that way now, 'kay?"

"Anybody home?" Jordan Rivers was at the door with a stout older woman carrying a book of fabric swatches. "I brought my decorator over for a quick peek. Is this a bad time?" Lan put his arm around Shawna's shoulder, hostility darkening his face.

While they wandered around inside, we sat on the deck, drinking blood-orange mimosas and eating pancakes. I had a thought that Jordan might have set someone up to blow out the windows so she could argue down the asking price for the property. Was she really that evil?

Goody pulled up in the blue F-350 with fresh poppy seed muffins, just as Jordan and her designer were leaving. Goody's Irish wolfhound paced the truck bed, panting. Jordan made a pissed-off, letter-to-the-editor face. "You know, you shouldn't let your dog ride in the back of the truck. It's dangerous."

The air fairly bulged with repressed laughter, everyone holding tongue. As she looked at the dwindling shape of Jordan's SUV up the driveway, Kimber drained her mimosa, licking a fat piece of pulp from her lower lip. "Probably thinks she deserves an Olympic medal because she still gives her husband head."

Jace put down his virgin mimosa and slapped his knee. "Girl, you are trash."

Kimber blew him a kiss. "That's right, teddy bear. I'm bona fide, certified one-hundred percent white trash."

Shawna lifted her head from Lan's lap. "By Jordan's saintly estimation, I'm trash. Is there such a thing as red trash?"

Lan looked at his tattoos. "I'm Technicolor trash, I suppose."

"And what about Homer?" I said. "He's yellow trash!" I looked over. "How about you, Kenny?"

"Aw, yeah," he said, flashing the pointy teeth. "I'm twenty different kinds of trash. I'm a compost heap."

We all laughed together on this fine day. Hot and clear and calm, smell of sage and meadowlark song on the breeze. Kimber lifted her glass and called out. "To trash!"

Jace joined the toast. "Trash. No value to speak of, but you always get taken out."

I raised my glass. "Brilliantly put, brother dear."

Lan chimed in. "Oh, hey, and to the trash heap! May your next home be twice as nice!"

Jace and I looked at each other, then each cast our eyes elsewhere. It hit us at the same time: this wasn't our home anymore.

J.W. showed up in the early afternoon and headed right for the barn, not a dozen words between us. "Let me get to those holes in the roof before it rains."

Jace and Kenny were shopping in town and wouldn't be back for hours. I showered and changed into my schoolgirl skirt, then climbed up the ladder to the hayloft with a Mason jar of fresh sweet tea with a lot of ice and lemon, a cold washcloth for J.W.'s neck, and a six-pack yanked from the freezer. J.W. worked on, half-ignoring me. He came down off the ladder for a drink. He stretched and yawned, resplendent in the stifling heat. He stripped off his shirt, the scar on his shoulder a ruddy pink stripe.

I sat on a hay bale and watched him work, hoping he'd notice me. As he sorted out the patching materials, he chewed gum. He was trying, he said, to kick his "dang expensive" can-a-day habit. At the bottom of his third beer, he looked at me. "Interesting."

"What?"

He pointed. I had sweat so much the undershirt went totally see-through. I recognized this distance in him when it was a byproduct of rodeo. Sometimes it wasn't just soreness that made him shut down. It was as if he were hobbled by moving too long in the world of men. We'd come together to shake the road off of him. If he won, he was snuggles and smiles the minute he came through the door. If he came up short, it took longer to get him back. But apart from rodeo, he had a lot on his mind—his brother being around, the tension between him and Jace. In his estimation, the best response to chaos was retreat. He popped the plastic lid off a jar of Vaseline and rubbed some over the torn knuckles.

My itch remained, unabated. I walked over and sat in his lap facing him, my legs wrapped around his waist.

J.W. was still sulking, looking at that torn knuckle. I was used to being pursued, and wanting sex when he didn't felt creepy, like I was out on a ledge by myself with a clammy wind around me. Was this how men felt all the time, that little signal flashing with no response to the call?

He held onto my hips, figuring out the agenda when he felt there was nothing underneath the little skirt. There was a downward tug to his mouth, a tired look in his eyes. "You still need your daddy, don't you, baby?"

"I've needed you my whole life and didn't even know it." I kissed his neck until I felt his shoulders loosen. "I wish you had been the one to teach me about sex," I said into the side of his hot neck. He had the confidence to lay any filthy old speech on me with a straight face, but I couldn't look him in the eye when I talked to him this way.

He exhaled. This was a game that would hold his attention for a while. "Really."

"Really. What would you do?"

"Well, I would . . ."

"Don't." I didn't want to talk. I wanted to writhe in silence. The hayloft pulsed with a wild throb of secrecy. As it turned out, we were perfectly compatible. Whatever reverse exhibitionism was, we shared it. I've known girls who put it on parade, especially at college, the news of whatever strange business they were up to exploding out of them in a starburst of sexual hubris. But I kept this part of me and J.W. a closely guarded secret; our bond a fragile thing that thrived in darkness. The concealment excited me, sure, but it was a cautionary measure, too. What people would think of me if they knew would be awful, but what they'd think of J.W. would be even worse.

There was none of the usual sweet stuff from J.W. this afternoon. As his fingers worked, deftly and to great effect, his face was sad, a little mean. He wasn't kissing me either, just chewing his gum, watching my face as I squirmed, a callous turn that was crude and a little shocking.

"Come on," he said, standing up, leaving me kneeling. He ankled a hay bale in front of me and I took the cue and put my elbows on it, spreading my knees a foot apart and rocking forward. I heard his fly unzip behind me, felt him moving around back there, then pushing in.

Afterward, we broke apart and folded around each other, my skirt tented between my legs, and napped in a sweaty heap.

I woke in the dark, woozy from the stultifying heat. My thighs were sticky, boots still on. I took the washcloth and shinnied down the ladder. I stripped off my skirt and undershirt and hung them on the hooks near the washing stall. I took the hose from the reel and stepped between the stall's metal rails. The water was ice cold. Our barn cat watched from under a bench. He yawned, pink tongue unwinding against his whiskers, and slunk away, back hunched against the dark shadows. I undid my pigtails and combed out the waves with my fingers, then bent at the waist, flipped my sweaty hair over my head, and wet my neck, shivering gratefully under the frigid spray.

I heard the ladder tick. From the corner of my eye, I saw J.W. leaning in the doorway, watching as I rinsed myself. I put the hose to my neck. The cold stream coursed down my chest, splitting around each nipple and rejoining, like water moving around stones in a brook path. I pretended not to see him, certain he was touching himself while he watched me in just my boots, washing off. I liked it.

I turned the hose over my shoulder and let the water run down my back. Still not letting on that I was aware of his presence, I leaned on the metal rails of the washing stall, my rear end thrust out suggesting a mare in season. I heard the hose turn off and felt J.W. come up behind me. Water dripped from the metal nozzle.

"Don't fight me on this." J.W.'s Vaseline-slick fingers were inside me, then he eased in an inch at a time. He didn't want to hurt me, risk me spurning his advance. I twisted around. I wanted to see what he was seeing. He was looking straight down, seeing everything. *Everything.* Who knew better than I the sublime of the visual? It wasn't his fixed gaze that caught me by surprise, but that it was me who excited him. My body. Mine. His breathing was perfectly rhythmic, shallow and smooth through his mouth, his nostrils flared. Now and then he'd squeeze his eyes shut and tip his head down, trying to hold on. He churned into me, doing everything to prove his strength, while showing me at the same time that I was his great weakness. His body was marbleized by moonlight, clay-white muscle and blue shadow, sweat streaming down his chest. How was it possible that he could feel so good and so far away at the same time?

The slap surprised me as much as it did him. He'd swung back and his hand landed on the side of my wet ass with an open palm. When I didn't protest, he did it again and heightened his effort. At full gallop, it felt good enough to hurt. When he got too close, he'd stop and pull back as slowly as possible. It was startling to be taken this way. I wanted him to do it over and over. He did until I was rubbed raw and his thighs were too tired to strain up toward me anymore.

He put me on my back, slapped more Vaseline on me and plowed forward, my ankles over his shoulders so he could bring me to a finish, my boot toes bobbing lewdly behind his neck. I could hear myself, not whimpering into his shoulder like I usually did, but open-throated and raw, not caring that I was in mucky water, that the concrete was taking layers of skin off my back.

He collapsed atop me with an exhausted wheeze. I stared at the ceiling, dazed. Somewhere in our coupling I had gotten so consumed I had just stopped thinking. I didn't worry what my stomach looked like, if my breasts were too small, or whether he'd come too fast, or if I'd come at all. We'd tapped off. As I held J.W.'s sweaty body against mine, I understood why a person would kill for love. I'm fairly certain that if someone had tried to intercede in what just happened, I'd have stabbed the fool in the neck.

We sneaked out in the moonlight and dunked in the stock tank. The stars winked in accordance. Far off in the night, the morbid throating of a coyote. The Big Dipper tilted over the horizon. J.W. dried in the air off the porch and stood looking up at Table Mountain. I came behind him, my hands joined, one fisted inside the other at his solar plexus. "Are you okay?" He patted my hands— once, twice—then walked away.

He joined me in the hayloft a few minutes later. I was staring out the window at the green belly of the moon. He stepped behind me quietly and touched my shoulder blade with the tips of his fingers. "Baby, look at you. Your back." He fetched the washcloth and sat behind me, dabbing at the broken skin. "I lost my job yesterday."

In the air around us was a sudden release of tension, like the breaking of a fragile glass bell. I didn't look at him. "What are you going to do?"

"Get another one, I guess." But it wasn't that easy. Everything he depended on was tied up in that job—the flexibility, the insurance, Troy's insurance. Where would he find something as good? Hadn't he just found out that his son needed braces?

"Did something happen?"

"No. My boss sat me down last night and said it wasn't anything I did. It's just that with the big chain stores coming in, business ain't what it used to be and they had to let a few guys go. And me being gone so much with the rodeoing, I was the logical choice."

I lay with my head resting on his hip. A barn owl flew in through the door and settled on the beam above us, its white heart-shaped face fringed in brown spots.

I kept my voice at the slightest whisper. "Look at him."

"Isn't he beautiful?"

I turned my head. In the bright moonlight, I could see the fine veins running just under the surface of J.W.'s neck. "You seem happy when you're here."

"Tell you what, if we had a coffee machine, I'd stay up here forever."

A beam of light coursed through the window, the tools dark shapes in shadow. He turned on his side and fell asleep. The thought I had, as I held him after he'd fucked me, was wrong. *This* is when you'd kill for love—when his Superman cape is slipping and you'd stab through anything or anyone to make it right again. I knew why he was reluctant to tell me—he was afraid I wouldn't want him anymore.

I watched the gentle rise and fall of his ribs as he breathed, then addressed his sleeping back. "I love you money or mud, Daddy Rabbit. I don't give a shit about your stupid job."

No answer. Just the moon above, seeing all and saying nothing.

"Absolutely not."

I put down my towel and crossed my arms. "But I want to."

Jace and Kenny left for town after breakfast, leaving J.W. and me alone on the property. We dipped in the stock tank, taking in the bright morning, the promise of intense heat already evident under the blue dome of sky. For the first time since I was a little kid, I was naked in the great outdoors. I felt newly uninhibited. *Yes, world, I'm pear-shaped. Deal with it.*

Bringing up such a crazy idea was testing J.W.'s mood but I wanted to share it. I had planned to tell him in the hayloft, but when I found out about his job, the agenda was rearranged. J.W. sat behind me now, brushing my hair, making me drowsy. I sat with my legs drawn up under my chin. J.W.'s hip bones were so prominent I had lilac bruises on the backs of my thighs from making love. I didn't mind. I wanted him to know that I'd go that far for him, that I'd take his mark.

I rested my cheek on my knees and took the brush from him, brushing my hair down over my face so I could make a center part. "I want to be marked for real. To show you how I feel about you. Something that I'll have on me every day. Like your scars." I couldn't see him from under the crackling curtain of hair. I needed a deep conditioning. "I can only wear that buckle so many hours of the day. I'd have this all the time."

"Why not just get another tattoo then?" Said with a hint of distaste.

"You can't get a tattoo where I want this."

That got his attention. But he shook his head when I told him I wanted a piercing just like Crystal's. "I can't stand the idea of you being in pain. Over me, especially."

I loved him for that, Mr. Safety Matches. "It doesn't hurt for more than a second."

"How do you know?" I thought he'd appreciate my wanting to prove that I was as brave as he was, as willing to go to extremes, but he just thought it was weird.

I changed tactics. "No matter what happens, it would always be there."

He wrapped my hair around his hand, kissing my neck. I was gambling that my suggestion would tap into who he used to be, before marriage, before fatherhood, before mellowing into Studly Do-Right. On the last kiss, he pulled my hair back a little hard, exposing my throat. "Okay. Let's do it."

After dinner, we drove to the Body Art Workshop in Laramie, J.W.'s knuckles rising up hard under the torn, chapped skin as he gripped the wheel. We wanted to keep this out of sight from anyone we knew. When I got the belly-button ring, I felt way better about my stomach. I wondered what this would do.

The girl behind the counter had long black-and-purple striped pigtails atop her head. Her eyes were ringed in deep plum liner, the whites of her eyes startlingly bright. I pored over the glass cases filled with barbells, studs, and rings in every size and color, and settled on a fifty-dollar stainless twelve-gauge ring with a pale blue bezel-set captive bead that suggested J.W.'s eye color.

J.W. busied himself by inspecting the art on the wall, a set of daggers with a primitive design airbrushed around the edge. His hands were balled up in his pockets. The tips of his ears glowed red. "That's different."

The other body piercers looked at him witheringly. In his cowboy preppy clothes—plaid golf shirt, jeans, and Ropers—he looked straight-laced, yet he knew pain and risk and bodies in ways they didn't. For all their edge-dweller trappings, they'd only tasted the blunt side of the blade.

The girl piercer, Nikka, filled me in on the aftercare ritual of salt-water soaking and keeping the jewelry clean. "Just so you know, there won't be any hanky-panky for a while. They say six weeks to heal, but off the record, I felt good enough after five days. Just make sure you follow the cleaning instructions very closely. Infection in that area is not fun."

J.W. focused on the wall. I could tell what he thought about wild-haired girls who informed strangers about having pierced privates.

She slid the consent form across the counter for me to sign. "First body piercing?"

I lifted my shirt to show her my belly-button ring.

"Hey, you're an old hand. This is nothing compared to that, I promise. Ear cartilage and navels are the worst, I think. This one's a piece of cake."

She led J.W. and me into the piercing area, then disappeared behind the curtain so I could disrobe. I took off my jeans and wrapped a paper gown around my waist. I looked over the tray of implements: needle, cork, blob of antibacterial ointment on a scrap of paper, the jewelry soaking in solution. I sat down on the edge of the vinyl-covered piercing table and concentrated on taking slow, deep breaths. J.W. sat on a chair up near my head, and held my hand.

When Nikka came back in, she snapped on a bright swing-arm lamp and sat down on a stool. She rolled over and positioned herself between my legs. "All righty. Feet in the stirrups, cowgirl." She pulled on a pair of purple examination gloves. Her hands were steady as she separated my outer labia. The clinical feeling of being analyzed down there had shades of a gynecological exam. We discussed the location. She started poking around with a cotton swab and decided that based on the way I was constructed, the piercing had to be horizontal. She examined me with a flashlight to avoid any blood vessels, then made two dots with a black Sharpie pen to mark where the piercing would go. My nostrils dilated at the scent of disinfectant cleanser. I felt a pinchy metallic jiggling down there when she clamped on the forceps.

I didn't want to watch. I turned my head to the side, keeping my breathing slow and deep as I silently chanted my manta. *T.R.Y.*

T.R.Y. A Georgia O'Keefe flower print hung on the wall next to a power towel rack. That had to be intentional.

J.W. squeezed my hand and licked his lips. I felt okay but he looked like he was about to faint.

Nikka picked up the needle and leaned forward. "When I say 'go,' give me a nice deep exhale through your mouth. Okay, first, Daryl, big inhale . . ."

I drew in a huge breath that made my lungs ache.

J.W. stood up. "Wait."

Ten minutes later, J.W. and I were heading up Route 80, me holding a paper bag containing a pair of gloves, forceps, a sterile twelve-gage needle still in its sleeve, surgical wipes, a couple corks, and the jewelry. J.W. had his hand on my thigh. "No, I ain't mad," he said when I asked. He glared in the oncoming headlights. "But if this is going to happen, I want to be the one to do it."

I was surprised that he felt so strongly but I trusted him. I was so invested in the depth and extremity of the gesture, I was willing to let him do this even though he lacked any relevant experience. As I lay back on his bed so he could locate Nikka's marks, I told myself that this was so much more meaningful than a clichéd, knee-jerk "I love you" that only scratched the surface. What I was offering to him was a bodily pledge to stand with him against any odds and against any judgment, that I'd never quit. Three words were nothing compared to a symbol installed under the auspices of the letters T. R. Y.

As he lined up the tools on a plate, he seemed distant but by now

I knew what nerves looked like on this man. He managed his emotions by concentrating on the task before him. I was half-terrified,
half-eager to show off my new stunt, this solidity that he'd helped
bring about. He fixed the forceps and turned the lamp to shine right
on me. I sipped air through my lips slowly, T-R-Y. From under the
rising panic, I heard the clean note of his voice. "Okay, deep breath
out." Then, a brilliant flash of pain, and a second later, it was done.
I was pierced.

He fixed the cork on the point of the needle. "You didn't faint."

I lay back, focusing on the faded brown spot on the ceiling. "I'm
wiggly, through. So I'd better be careful." There was a tight, sliding
pinch as he fit the open ring in the hollow end of the needle and
threaded it through, and another tugging pinch as he closed it. "In
my entire life, I never thought I'd do something like that."

"I want to see." I got up and opened the closet door, a row of hats
brim-up on the top shelf, neat line of shirts on wire hangers on the
rod below. I moved the chair in front of the mirrored door, sat
down, and spread my legs. In the midst of the smooth pinkness was
a brilliant pale blue glimmer.

J.W. stood behind me. "No, not in my whole life. . . ." Task complete, the hardhat attitude was softening. He ran his hands up and
down my arms and kissed a line up the side of my neck. "Guess
you're really mine now, huh?"

I nodded and closed my legs, feeling the swelling center of heat.
We swapped places, and with sure hands, I pulled him to the edge of
the chair and, after helping him wiggle from his jeans, spread his
thighs so I could kneel between them.

He never asked, but I knew he was thrilled that I was taking the
initiative. I loved the look he got, like a shy kid waved in from the
edge of the playground, like he couldn't believe I wanted it, and the
way he slid toward me, giving himself totally over. I opened my
mouth to him and he released his head all the way back with an ecstatic exhale. I knew the "girl, get yours" empowerment spiel by

now, but the truth of it was I'd trade a thousand hours of my own pleasure for those fleeting seconds of surrender.

After cradling his balls, I secreted my hand farther back. My finger entered him with a subtle, spit-lubed twist. He sucked in his breath. "Damn, baby." I moved carefully with the initiator's anxiety thought to be male province—Was I doing it right? The angle, the pace . . . did he like it? In and out I went, until that deep tremble came on. When I felt his orgasm start from the inside, I pulled back and held still as he spent himself, warm and sensuous, in milky ribbons over my lips and chest.

He pulled me up and kissed me, our chins skidding together in the mess. I was his, yes, but he was mine, too. I savored the symmetry of it. As J.W. slept with his hand wedged protectively between my thighs, I lay with my eyes closed, gliding on the rush of endorphins and lust, a surfer tucked inside the curl. I thought, *I did it*. I'd stopped inviting the chorus to judge. *We* had done it, everyone and everything else shut out, the totality of our world contained in that small circle of steel.

26

JACE AND KENNY, SIX OR SEVEN twenty-four-hour sobriety chips apiece in the nightstand, rarely made an appearance in a bar. But their friend Whitley was down from Gillette fronting the Graybull Band and she begged them to come see her, so we piled three across on the bench seat in Jace's truck to make it to the Outlaw in time for her ten o'clock set. I wore my new party-girl pants, a pair of baby blue Wranglers just like Kimber's. I was determined to break down the seams a bit, though in fact, it was I who was likely to end up breaking down, the stiff stitching on the inseams already burning my skin.

Beeber, soured on the Wigwam, was liquefying his meager paycheck at the Outlaw's outside bar. He was a small man, and after six or seven shots, he stumbled around, asking girls to dance and when they said no, he cussed them. "What are you all high-toned for, bitch?" He backed away from one girl who had laughed in his face, and plowed right into Doug Cathcart.

Cathcart poked Beeber in the chest. "I saw you out at that faggot's party the other night. You a faggot, too?"

Jace and Kenny came over, Jace stepping between Cathcart and tiny Beeber. "Is there a problem?"

"Problem?" Cathcart grinned coldly. "Yeah. There's a problem with you. You are a sick motherfucker." This from a guy who, in his lifetime, had ingested more crank than Elvis did ribs. Cathcart tried to take a swing, but Kenny whirled around back and kicked him in the kidneys. Cathcart fell forward. The move was dirty pool. Who knew that Kenny wasn't one to fight fair? Cathcart spun onto his back, trying to see who had kicked him.

Kenny had spittle in the corners of his mouth, his head raised on alert like a mongoose. "You know who done it."

Beeber's upper body swung forward, headed for the concrete. Envisioning picking tooth chips off the ground, Kenny swooped in and turfed him. Jace then scooped up Beeber and carried him off, throwing him over his shoulder like a sack of grain and then dumped him in the bed of the pickup. "Fresh air'll sober you up some," he said to Beeber's skinny butt. "And I don't want you puking your guts out in my nice clean cab."

Jace leaned over Beeber, tucked next to the toolbox under a green horse blanket. "Where we takin' you, Junior?"

Beeber rubbed his forehead. "Can't go home when I'm drinking. Linda's rules. J-dub's got seven people lyin' in sleeping bags at his place. Let me sleep it off in my truck." The three of us pictured the rattletrap Nissan nose-down against a highway median.

"We'll haul you home for a nap. Someone'll get you into town tomorrow."

By the time we got out to Red Hill, Beeber had already puked three times. Kenny fetched the hose off of the back deck. "Reckon I'll rinse down the truck bed for you."

Beeber thrashed in the basement pullout. "Women in this town . . . fucking bitches!"

Jace pulled the lamp cord and switched on a nightlight. "Son, you better shut the hell up and go to sleep." I had called J.W., roused him from sleep, and he was on his way out to fetch his pickled nephew so he could get back to Linda's in time for six o'clock chores.

Kenny and I were drinking leftover blood-orange juice at the kitchen island. Jace opened the refrigerator, cold yellow light a wedge over his rummaging form, and popped open a Coke. "I swear, one of these days that boy's jaw is going to meet the business end of a bar stool."

Kenny nodded and tightened his lip. "True story."

I picked up a sketchpad and charcoals, and walked down to the barn to pass the time until J.W. arrived. The night was cool and quiet. I sat on a wooden stool in Tad's stall, making quick sketches, grateful for her company. I put my arms around her neck and inhaled, smelling her coat. She had a scent unlike any other horse, sweet like cedar and healthy sweat. Before I sat down again, I grabbed my new jeans at the knees and pulled; they had bunched at the juncture between my hip and thigh, and hurt me terribly. I put down my pad and pen, went around the outside of the barn and climbed into the stock tank. I emerged soaking wet, leaving a dripping trail behind me leading to the horse stalls. If that wouldn't stretch them out, nothing would.

I felt the footsteps before I heard them and thought to myself, *Nice*. J.W. was squeezing in another barn ambush before gathering up Beeber to take him home. The tack room door creaked on its hinges. Feet shuffled through the dusting of straw, then something that sounded like a hand sliding along the wall, brushing the implements hanging on their hooks.

I spoke over my shoulder. "I was wondering when you were going to return the favor. I've been wanting you pretty bad, you know."

I felt a cold bar press under my chin and an arm close around my throat. "Is that what you want, little darlin'? You as much a get-around whore as your brother?" I smelled the tobacco-and-gin stench in the dirty khaki sleeve and recognized the voice. Doug Cathcart. His breath was rank and clouded. "Stand up."

I rose to my feet, slowly, his arm pulling me up, the blade pressing against my thyroid. Shocks came up from my hollow toes; my legs had fallen asleep. Ice water fanned through my veins, slow rivers of cold panic. The tinny taste of fear soured my mouth.

"What do you want?" I whispered hoarsely, his grip making it hard to breathe.

"You'll do." Cathcart's fingers were shaking. "Now don't you scream." With his free hand, he wrestled with the button on my jeans. I had a horrible image of him locating the piercing and yanking the ring right through the skin.

He pressed his knee into my lower back as he struggled with my wet pants. They were so tight he couldn't get them off. My thoughts were surprisingly clear: he's a fucking psycho. No. High. He's high. I had a surreal notion that I was going to die out here, a hundred yards from my house, but there was something ridiculous about it, this grotesque man playing movie bandit. Strange as it was, I felt a reeling urge to laugh.

He pressed the knife into my throat, a hot stripe of pain, the skin about to break. "Take off the pants."

I put my hands on my hips and made like I was going to wriggle out of the jeans, then I bent at the waist and bit into his arm. "Get the hell away from me," I yelled, as loud as I could. I stomped his foot hard and dove under the tool bench. When he stood up, I had the shotgun pointed at his chest.

The tack room door gaped behind him. We stood looking at each other, neither sure what to do.

"You wouldn't kill me, little flower. I know you wouldn't." The words scratched out of Cathcart's throat.

"She wouldn't kill you. But I sure as hell would." J.W.'s voice was cold as hell.

Cathcart stood straight up when he felt the steel barrel against his temple. His crazy eyes went wide at the click of the hammer pulling back. "I-I-I . . ." His mouth sagged open, chin quivering.

"Cathcart, I've got a witness here who could tell the exact same story about how you broke into this barn in the middle of the night wielding a weapon, and when you snuck up on me, I had to shoot you in self-defense." There was no mistaking the heat and rancor in J.W.'s voice, still it held steady. "Even if the police took me in, I bet they'd only hold me overnight. Odds are good they'd take my story and turn me loose in time to go to your funeral and shit on your grave. What do you say to that, Cathcart? Do you like those odds?"

Cathcart stammered unintelligibly. He was bookended by J.W. and his pistol, and me with the shotgun. He knew damn well if he moved he'd be plugged in the temple or peppered head to toe. Cathcart didn't move, just twitched.

Jace and Kenny came running in, each carrying a shotgun. My brother stopped in his tracks. "What in sam hell are you doing? I've had enough trouble out here lately without you showing up again."

Cathcart's smile was slow and malevolent.

Jace took a step forward, lowering the gun. "It was you, wasn't it? I knew it. All of it. The windows . . ." His mouth leveled. "Why would you do that to me?"

"Oh, you all but admitted it. I do believe you're in a mess of trouble." J.W. got right in Cathcart's face, shoving the barrel of the .44 under Cathcart's nostril, then tapped it down his neck, abdomen, groin. "Windpipe. Bladder. Entrails. You make a sorry hand, Cathcart, but you'd make an awesome gutpile." I really did believe J.W. would be more than willing to kill him.

"Now you listen good," he said. "If you ever come near her again, I will hunt you down, split you from balls to brisket, and pack you out of here in bloody chunks."

A dark spot bloomed at Cathcart's crotch and spread rapidly downward.

J.W. nodded. "In case you didn't notice, Cathcart, you're pissing yourself."

The last time any of us saw Doug Cathcart, he was running as fast as his boots would carry him and wet from his crotch to his knees.

★ ★ ★

Beeber was angry to have missed the excitement, sulking through breakfast, hungover and tearing his toast into pieces, mumbling, *"Aw, man."* The rest of us moved quietly about the kitchen, each treading in our own private emotional wake.

Whatever fear the night had wrought, it leveled the barrier between Jace and J.W. I was Jace's baby sister and J.W.'s baby girl, and while either man had his own interests to protect, they overlapped, too, and that served to unite them, if only in this instance.

Jace wandered off and drank ginger ale by himself on the deck. At first, I couldn't believe it, but when I examined the idea closely, it made sense. Jace always had a nose for the troubled ones. The drives by the house, the photo missing from the wall. It wasn't me Cathcart was after. And last night, I wasn't the one his advance was meant to hurt. Cathcart was yet another piece in Jace's puzzle of bad choices—the one just mad enough to hook you in and hurt you later.

I sat down beside him on a deck chair. "Did he mean anything to you?"

"Nah." He stood at the railing and sipped his ginger ale.

I supposed the best I could do for my brother was believe him. I put my arms around his shoulders and hugged him from behind. "You'll always be my family. You know that?"

He put his hand over mine. "Me, too."

When we went back into the kitchen, we let the story stand. J.W. was all over me, kissing me, saying he'd never let anyone hurt me, never. *If I hadn't had the window down and heard you scream. If I didn't keep a pistol in the glove box* . . . But I only half heard him. I kept hearing Jace out there in the barn, the rage in his voice. It wasn't the anger of violation; it was the anger of betrayal. I understood why he'd been on my case about J.W. He wasn't judging me. He was calling me in from the ledge.

27

THE FENCED-OFF READY AREA on the Frontier Days rodeo grounds looked like a cowboy chicken coop, full of anxious men strutting to shake loose muscles, shaking out chaps, and running stiff wire brushes up and down rosin-clogged lengths of bull rope. J.W. sat on a table outside the gate, slapping his face to wake up. I put down my day sheet. "Want some help with that?"

He laughed. "Sure." He was almost even keel, looking forward to two more weeks of rodeoing before he'd begin the hunt for a new job. Placing today would build a nice bridge over the misery of unemployment.

I slapped his cheeks with vigor. First one, then the other. *Wham! Wham!* I didn't worry about hurting him. I was hitting his game face, after all.

The chute boss walked by, surveying the scene with an earthy chuckle. "Looks like you got yourself a handful there, J-dub."

"Believe it, brother."

J.W. took off his shirt, two rolls of sports tape and some bandages at his side. He waved down a passing cowboy. "Hey, Kerry. Help, bud?"

Kerry taped up J.W., bringing the roll around and around, diagonally, like a ceremonial sash across his chest and shoulder. Suitably mummified, J.W. buttoned up, stood still while I pinned on his back number, and disappeared behind the chutes to prep his rigging.

I took a seat in the east stands next to Jace and Kenny. J.W.'s ride started out fine—textbook mark-out, a hard circle back to the right, and a few solid bucks. But J.W. fishtailed over the rigging, the shoulder not holding under all that tape. At the very last second, he reached up and double-grabbed. When he worked his hand out of the rigging, the horse bucked, and J.W. flew off, landing squarely on the hurt shoulder. The God of second chances had left the building.

I found J.W. lying in the red sports medicine trailer. The doctor, a film of perspiration on his high-domed forehead, was examining him. "How bad is the pain on a scale of one to ten, ten being the worst?"

"I don't know a number, doc, but I can feel my goddamn pulse up and down the whole arm every time my heart beats."

The doctor filled up a syringe. "Cortisone. Mixed with lidocaine," he said, answering my curious stare. He swabbed a spot on J.W.'s shoulder and, I assumed after turning away, sunk the needle in deep. He tossed the sharp in a red medical waste jug and started scooping ice into a plastic bag.

J.W. lay on his side, whispering, *Fuck, Fuck, Fuck.* I'd never heard him say the word before, such vicious rage rolling under the quiet words like a temblor. I turned my back as he leaned over the side of the exam table. The doctor vaulted over with a lined wastebasket and caught the dark spew of vomit just in time.

I sat at his side holding the ice to his shoulder. I was catching some definite attitude from the doctors and other cowboys wandering in and out. *What are you doing in here? It's not like he's really hurt.* The doctor heaved a freighted sigh. "Maybe you'd like to wait outside." He was well into his third decade of setting bones and shunting off girls who got underfoot. I left the trailer and sat on the green steel steps, worrying about J.W., and hating that I couldn't help. Sex aside, passion is a solitary pursuit. Whatever's going on in a person's little bliss-seeking bubble, you've got to gut it out on the other side. After weeks of following and listening and supporting, here I was, passion's helpmeet, banished. Lonely road, girl. Lonely road.

J.W. tramped out of the medical trailer an hour later. We were headed to my truck; I'd convinced him to come out to Red Hill for some TLC, but he insisted on carrying his own rigging bag. The rodeo grounds were emptying. "Daryl and Jamie, sittin' in a tree. K-I-S-S-I-N-G." Duff was sitting at a picnic table by the ready area, four beers into the decompression ritual, toasting himself for having won another round and nailing a spot in the short go. "Well, there's the reason you bucked off, J.W." He stood and cast a leering glance my way. "Don't you know it's bad luck to eat chicken the day of the rodeo?"

Someone off to the side said, *"Oh shit."*

What do you know—J.W. rode with his right hand but struck with his left. Duff dropped to his knees. J.W. picked up his pace. I started after him. "J.W.?"

"Leave me be, Daryl."

I stopped, watching him walk away. I turned to Duff. "Are you okay?"

Duff dusted off the knees of his jeans. "That punch hurt my head, I'll say that much." He felt along his jaw. "Did you see that story, Daryl? The one the New York lady did? Rachel." He laughed ruefully, like she was the one who had dumped him.

I had seen it online this morning. It was far from flattering, a two-column piece with the headline "Video Killed the Rodeo Star." On the first read, it seemed innocent enough, but when I read it the second time, words kept popping out at me: "spur-ious comeback," "road-weary," "affected," and "redneck chic." It wasn't the buckle-polish that Duff had been banking on, the writer even venturing that Duff signed on to revive the role of Joe Buck in *Midnight Cowboy* as a calculated career move, chasing publicity and the gay dollar both. "Sure I saw it, Duff. It was okay, I guess."

"You know, I used to ride bucking horses like J.W. When we were kids. But I quit. If I kept it up, I'd have one arm longer than the other. Besides, everyone wants to see the bull ridin'. But riding bareback, Daryl, there ain't nothing like it. So pure. Set to spurring, then you just lean back and look at the sky.

"But I got my own thing going now, something different. You don't want to get old in rodeo, all crippled up so no one cares about you anymore. They only love you when you win. But in movies, you can live forever."

"I hadn't thought about it that way, Duff. Guess you're right. Anyway, I better go. I should see how J.W.'s faring."

"J.W.'s always been a better athlete than me. Better person, too, I suppose, and everybody knows it. Studly Do-Right. I could win every rodeo on earth and I'd still come in second after that."

The admission took me by surprise. I didn't imagine there was much by way of substance hiding under Duff's hits-and-kisses demeanor. "Seems you do all right. You got that article about you. There's no such thing as bad publicity, right?"

He laughed. "That article? It was terrible. But you know what, Daryl? It doesn't matter what any media snob says. They can't stop me. I've got a plan." He tapped his temple with his index finger, then shook it at me. "I've always got a plan."

J.W., after a cup of coffee and a hot bath, had calmed down enough to sit still. He'd changed out of his riding clothes and was lounging in sweatpants on the bed in my old room, reading a copy of *Bowhunter* magazine.

I heard the truck pull up. Jace and Kenny came in looking proud and sly, like hounds that had flushed out a grouse. "Look who we found wandering around the rodeo grounds." Duff Linsey stepped in cautiously behind them. "Sorry. Can't find a room in town. Hope you don't mind the intrusion."

I shook my head violently. "J.W's in the bedroom . . ." I whispered.

"Oh, Jesus shit." Jace slapped his hand over his mouth. "Sorry, I just assumed you'd be at his place."

J.W. came out to see what was going on. When he saw Duff standing in the living room, he said nothing, but I could tell he was red-assed about it. He turned around and went back into my old room and shut the door behind him. J.W. managed to ignore Duff successfully until Duff came strutting into the living room when J.W. was eating a bowl of chili at the kitchen island. "Hey, maybe I ought to wear this when I'm up tomorrow." We looked up to see him standing there with J.W.'s World Champion buckle on.

J.W. put down his bowl. "What are you doing with that?"

Duff put his fists on his hips and grinned. "Figured I'd see how it looked, since I should've won it anyway. This is the one you should've given to me. Missed mark-out my ass."

"Bullshit. That is pure bullshit and you know it. Take it off, now."

Duff's eyes sparked with taunting glee. He rocked up on his toes and crossed his arms. "What are you gonna do about it, bro?"

"Take it off for you, maybe. Give you the chill out."

"I'd like to see that." Duff grinned.

In a split second, J.W. leapt from the stool and sent a sliding fist up Duff's right cheek. Duff rubbed his jaw and laughed. "Oh, that was something." He opened the sliding glass door and stepped out onto the deck. "Come on out here and continue this discussion. If you've got the sack to do it."

J.W. charged him. "You're an asshole. You're a fucking liar and a fake piece of shit asshole and you always will be."

They slugged at each other, J.W. favoring his good arm. Screw lidocaine—adrenaline is the world's greatest painkiller. J.W. dropped Duff with a punch to the gut. I was screaming for them to stop, but they paid no attention. Homer heard the ruckus from the dog run below the deck and started barking. It was chaos and my blood boiled.

I hollered for Jace and Kenny, hoping for their intervention, but I saw them high up the ridge, running their horses. I looked around frantically for something to use to intercept. The hose was coiled in the corner. J.W. had Duff on his back and was just about to smash him in the face with an open hand when I set the nozzle to a stinging needle spray. I pointed it right at his face, then at Duff's. J.W. coughed and gagged, and Duff rolled out from under him. They both sat back, soaked to the skin. I kept on spraying them in the chest, one then the other.

J.W. glared at me, his cheek swollen. "Quit, Daryl." Duff touched his lip, checking for blood. They were both panting, their hair sticking up in crazy angles.

I yelled at them with a fury that raged up from the soles of my feet. "You two can either calm the fuck down or get the hell out of my house and never come back!" I threw down the hose, forcing it to unkink and swivel around. The nozzle wound out and clipped J.W. on the neck.

I went to bed early. J.W. came in and tried to justify what he had done.

"I had to live with fighting in this house every day of my life. I don't want to hear it." I could've stopped there, but I was ready to pounce. "I don't care if you get mad but at least be a man about it." His expression snapped. I could tell he was offended and I was glad.

He stripped off his sweats and T-shirt and tried to get into bed next to me.

I flipped over to face him. "What do you think you're doing?"

"I'm going to sleep."

"Not in here you're not. You want to act like an animal you can sleep like one, too." I threw a pillow on the floor.

"Why you gotta be so stubborn, Daryl? Jesus."

I turned my back to him and stared at the wall. I felt the pillow land on the bed behind me. "Well, I ain't sleeping on a floor so I guess I'll be seeing you."

I rested my head on my arm. A fly landed near my elbow and I nabbed with a quick swat. "He's jealous of you, you know."

"Jealous? What's he got to be jealous of?"

"You don't think living right counts?"

"I'm no saint, Daryl, I . . ."

I held up my hand. "I know. And what I didn't figure out on my own, people were kind enough to tell me. But what you're talking about is of a different magnitude. You didn't run out on anybody. You aren't propped up on twenty different so-called medications. You don't ask for more than you deserve."

"It's a dead issue."

"The hell it is."

J.W. sat next to me on the bed. "What could he possibly want from me?"

"Forgiveness, looks like."

"Yeah, right."

"If that's not what he wants, then why is he still here?"

"He's waiting around for Kimber, wouldn't you say?"

"Bullshit." I lifted my head so we were eye-to-eye. "Kimber told him she didn't want to see him anymore. I assure you he's not hanging around on account of her."

J.W. looked surprised.

"He's got Hollywood on the brain and he's half-stoned all the time. Someone in his shape doesn't know any better. You do." There was so much in my family that I couldn't fix. That J.W. would squander the opportunity to make things right galled me. I recognized the envy and anger tightening his mouth. I said, "If Duff's got anything worthwhile left in this world, I'd like you to point it out to me." J.W. said nothing. I took his hand and pointed his finger at his chest.

"This is your moment to be the bigger man." I balled up the pillow and lay my head down. I'd said my piece.

When J.W. came back to bed, the red digital numbers on the clock said two-twenty. "He said he was sorry."

"For what?"

"For everything."

28

PERFECT DAY FOR A SHORT GO.

At 9 A.M., J.W. and I sat on the living room couch, looking out the newly restored picture window, mugs of steaming coffee clasped in our hands. The sun shone across the valley, and we blinked sleepily in the bright orange morning light. I'd turned the horses out when I woke up, and they stood in a tight cluster near the wash. Dish and Tad nuzzled sweetly like teenage lovers.

We tried to wake Duff, but whenever one of us stuck our head into the bedroom and called his name, an arm emerged from beneath the tangled sheets waving us away, and a muffled voice groaned from underneath a pillow, "Ten more minutes!" We'd try again and he'd be asleep on his stomach, deep in dreaming, the tops of his feet whistling along the sheets as he drove his legs up and down. "Looks like he's spurring a bad one," J.W. whispered over my shoulder, then shut the door.

Duff wandered into the living room at about ten, shirtless and wild-haired. He looked like hell, even for a hard-partying cowboy first thing in the morning. The top button on his dirty jeans was unbuttoned, and he was bruised from armpit to hip on the right side. Blackened bits of tape adhesive stuck to his ribs. His eyes, skirted with thready red blood vessels, were sunken in the hollows over the sharp ridge of his cheekbones.

He poured himself a glass of orange juice and washed down a couple pills he'd unearthed from his jeans pocket. "Feel like I'm a hunnert years old today. You know what they say, 'Ain't the years, boys, it's the miles.'" He scratched his tender, tape-gummed ribs and yawned widely. He seemed eerily serene.

Duff sneezed loudly. "I'm allergic to your damn dog." He took the box of Benadryl from the lazy Susan and popped two out of the blister pack, swallowing them dry.

"I wouldn't do that if I were you," I said. "That stuff makes you tired."

"Well, what do you know," he cawed. "I took my keep-awakes and something that'll make me sleepy. Then after I eat, I gotta take my glucosamine and OxyContin up. I am a goldang science experiment!"

The clang and hustle of the final go-round pealed across Frontier Park, competitive energy rolling out in radiant waves in every direction.

The caged-off ready area behind the chutes was a sacristy. Cowboys, buckled into favorite chaps, squatted in meditation with hats in hand. Prayers for protection and form were offered. Competitors measured lengths of rein, kissed amulets and fingered crosses, danced crazily to loosen a tight quadriceps or calf muscle. Duff sat near where he'd dropped his gear bag on the concrete pad, checking over his arm brace. He was the last guy scheduled to get on in the first round of bull riding. His motions were slow and methodical as he checked his rowels and slipped on his spurs. Bud Meeks, the funny guy—and today, the first rider up—was walking around, drinking honey out of a plastic bear-shaped bottle to get his energy up, and slapping everyone on the back. The fellows nodded back solemnly. "Get 'im rode, Buddy." The vibe was sepulchral, but everyone was pumped.

J.W. hung around behind the chutes, helping Duff get ready. Though Duff left a companion pass for him at the rodeo office, Beeber never showed. A thumb in his daddy's eye.

At 1:05 P.M. the show began. The best of the best cowboys were taking on the elite bucking bulls. Competition was fierce. Bud Meeks, just behind Duff in the average, took off on the back of Rum Runner, and all he got for his effort was an immediate buck-off and a mouthful of dirt. Curt Zane cracked heads with his bull and got knocked out, but he came to right away and walked out of the arena on his own—with matching goose eggs on his head and the scoreboard. But some of the guys were riding well. Joe Don Amichi scored an 83 on Sweet Potato, a nasty brahma, and Kenton Whitley turned in an 84-point ride on an up-and-coming Charbray named Zip Drive.

Duff had drawn the notorious Seventh Heaven, a Watusi with huge stabbers and a jiggling dewlap that gave him the profile of an aged magistrate. In seventy trips out of the chute, he'd been ridden once. Duff nodded his face, and man and beast spun out of the chute backward and proceeded to give the capacity crowd its money's worth, from the press box up to the cheap seats. Through every spin, Duff kept his balance and spurred. With every jump, he held tight. In this oppositional dance, both partners were showing maximum grit. After one last fearsome buck, Seventh Heaven turned to the left showing the loose skin on his belly to the people in the East stands, and Duff made the buzzer. The announcer came in, "Look out, leader board, that's a show-stopping great ride for Duff Linsey! What you expect when two legends meet!"

The crowd was up off its denim, clapping and hollering. All we had to wait for was Duff to come off Seventh Heaven, fling his hat in the air, and do his trademark spin around, which he would surely do when he saw what was bound to be a jaw-dropping score.

Duff pulled his rope, landing a-stumble on his feet, but before he could run for the fence, Seventh Heaven whipped around and hooked him right under his flak jacket, flinging Duff up and over his back. Duff landed, looking up at the clouds as the bullfighters darted in, trying to lure Seventh Heaven away. Duff rolled onto his belly and paused, as if frozen in fright. Seventh Heaven horned his way through the pair of bullfighters and stood stock-still. Bull and rider looked at each other for a fraction of a second. Then Seventh Heaven charged.

Seventh Heaven ran right over Duff, each hoof eager to sample his hide, then circled fast and hooked him right under the chin. The stock contractor himself raced in and snapped a quirt at the bull's behind, and Seventh Heaven headed at last for the out gate. Duff pushed up to his elbows and knees in the arena dirt, spitting out ropy strands of bloody saliva. Then he rose to his feet swaying a bit, and raised his arms to signal, "I'm okay."

The crowd exploded in applause and a mighty roar rose throughout the arena. Then Duff's head dropped to his chest and his knees buckled. He spiraled down and to the right, falling to the dirt in a crumple-legged heap.

In the stands, a collective breath drew in, followed by the eerie decrescendo of ten thousand people going dead silent at once. All you could hear was the banging of the bulls in the chutes and, just barely, the sickly sweet carnival music whirling in on the breeze from the midway.

This eternity lasted about fifteen seconds. The chute boss and the cowboys who were watching on the sides of the chutes vaulted over the gates and ran toward Duff. The sports medicine team was across the arena like a shot, carrying a backboard between them. The announcer cut in, "We got a wreck, folks, but let's let the doctors from the Justin sports medicine team do their job. Stay where you are, folks. A cowboy can't get better care than what he's got here. All right, folks, thank you."

Next to me Tara Dunny murmured, "Oh my God, oh my God, oh my God." Her older daughter, Lacey, drew a lank piece of her strawberry-roan hair across her lip and rocked back and forth. Julia, the young one, tugged at her mother's arm and looked up at her with a curious twist to her head like a baby bird.

J.W. and I got to the hospital before the ambulance. The waiting room was cool and dark. The red numbers on the digital clock said 1:58. Less than an hour ago, everything had been completely normal. The ambulance screamed up, the automatic doors slammed open, and paramedics wheeled Duff in on a gurney. He was unconscious, strapped under an oxygen mask. An IV bag dripping clear fluid swung from a pole. J.W. pulled me out of the way as they raced past us toward the operating room. We heard the EMTs reciting a list of injuries to the doctors. Broken ribs. Possible punctured lung. Sustained trauma to the head. Broken hand, wrist, forearm. We watched the doors to the trauma center swing shut with a rubber-buffered wheeze.

An OR nurse wearing scrubs patterned with multicolored fish came out while Duff was in surgery and told us that neither his neck nor back were injured, thank God, and his legs and feet were fine. But, she said, there was a lot of internal bleeding and they were working as quickly as they could to get things under control. A damp gray curl hung in her eyes and she brushed it back with a veiny hand. She wore blue stretchy booties over her shoes, stained with dark red blotches crusted to dark brown along the elastic gathers. She caught me staring and smiled kindly. "It's Betadine. We use it to create a clean surgical field."

We drank cup after cup of vending machine coffee. It tasted overstewed, rank, and bitter. A beefy guy in a palm leaf hat, brand-new

Wranglers, and one of those dreadful Brooks and Dunn shirts came into the waiting room. He checked us out, marking the dirty boots and rodeo wear with his eye. "Hello? Hi," he extended his hand, to whom I wasn't sure. "Micky Schenk, sports reporter for the *Wyoming Tribune-Eagle*. What's the status of Duff's condition?" He zeroed in on me. "Are you his girlfriend?"

"No." I motioned robotically in J.W.'s direction. "I'm here with him."

He glanced over at J.W., and registered the resemblance but wanted to be careful. He'd already figured out that this was a tough room to work. Rookie sweat gathered at the edge of his sideburns. "Are you his friend? His traveling partner?"

J.W.'s face clouded over. "No," J.W. said, his voice measured, "I'm his brother."

He said it. I kept my eyes on the floor and touched the toe of my boot to his.

Schenk kept his cool, but I could tell he felt like a fox with a hen in its mouth. "Do you mind if we talk a while? We could walk around a few minutes, if you like."

"Sorry, man. Not free to talk just now."

I watched Schenk leave the building, his shirt plastered to the middle of his back by a wide stripe of perspiration.

Judging by the weakening sunlight it must have been about dinner-time when a summer shower began and just as quickly ended. "Good. We need the rain," J.W. mumbled. The wet asphalt in the parking lot shone like an oil slick. Small wrens hopped through a puddle in the grassy median. What was going on inside J.W.? Was he eating himself up with worry? Breaking down the agglomeration of regrets? I was staring at the floor, counting out how many tiles there were between me and the opposite wall when the rubber-soled shoes stopped in front of me. "We can take you back now if you'd like to see him," the OR nurse told us. I wouldn't be able to stand the sight, tubes running in and out of Duff like a lab animal. J.W. followed her to the ICU.

Another nurse's voice floated in from someplace far, far away. "We're doing everything we can. There's still a risk of more internal bleeding."

As the night wore on, we'd seen one labor, a bull rider with a broken foot, and two asthma attacks from the dust the wind had blown up. Just past nine-thirty, the doctors came into the waiting room. Their eyes were pouchy with fatigue, scrubs rumpled. One of the surgeons asked us to follow her to Dr. Morley's office. It was so small we barely fit inside. J.W. and I stood side by side in front of the doctor's desk, forming a somber, flat-featured wall.

Don't say it, doctor. Please.

He didn't. He simply looked at us, eyes sweeping across our faces, and clasped his hands in front of him. "I'm sorry."

When we came out, we found Beeber in the waiting room. He had just come from working out at Linda's. The expression on his face was searching, desperate. He took a step toward us, and opened his mouth to speak, but J.W. just shook his head.

The funeral was held that following Sunday at St. Mark's Church downtown. The street was so swarmed it seemed as if the entire town had turned out. It had fallen to J.W. to make the funeral arrangements, which he did quickly, efficiently, and without complaint.

Duff's coffin was glossy black and trimmed in brushed silver. I had no doubt as to who paid for it. As a special favor, Schrader Funeral Home arranged for a horse-drawn Victorian hearse with glass sides to take Duff from the funeral home to the church. The coffin lay inside, covered in a blanket of ivory-hued roses and dark blue ribbons sent by Duff's agent. The stock contractor whose bull had killed Duff lent his own mount for the funeral procession. The beautiful white-starred black quarter horse was tethered to the hearse behind the two blinkered draft horses and mounted with a saddle, riderless, on his back. His boots were stuffed, cavalry-style, backward in the stirrups.

As it advanced along Central Avenue the cortege had a morbid
dignity. The hearse came to a stop in front of Saint Mark's and the
driver dismounted and opened the back door. The pallbearers, Beeber among them, hoisted the coffin up on their shoulders. The
crowd parted as the men carried the coffin up the church steps. I followed behind.

The inside of the church glowed with the light of hundreds of
candles, and the organ played low. Huge arrangements of flowers
crowded the altar, filling every spare inch around the casket. The
oily perfume scent of lilies and gladiolas gathered in the back of my
throat, making me nauseous. At the head of the casket an easel
propped up a board covered in deep blue velvet. Tacked to the fabric
were all of Duff's buckles, arranged in a large horseshoe shape. In
the middle of the horseshoe was Duff's photo, and underneath, his
Frontier Days back number.

Jace and Kenny sat in the row right behind me and J.W. Jace kept
his hand on my shoulder. The church overflowed with mourners
from every corner. Those who hadn't driven in had flown. J.W. held
my hand, but he looked a million miles away. Beeber sat next to J.W.
and cried like someone who'd been robbed. The buckles in the
arrangement had come from him—Duff had been sending them to
him all these years, and Beeb kept them in a tackle box under his
bed. Beeb insisted on putting together the arrangement himself, sitting up half the night at the workbench in King's Metal Shop, at-
taching them to the board just so.

The candles guttered and wept. Hank Vollmar, his face and neck
sunburned red, sat in the pew across from us. He was doleful as a
man could be, for it was his bull that did the damage. He kept dabbing at his downcast eyes with a bandana and tugging on his bolo tie
as if it were strangling him.

The eulogy flickered before me like an old silent movie. Moments clicked past frame by frame, several people spoke, but all I

could recall was that a baby was crying, and I'd never seen so many people in suits in my entire life. The air felt static, and the whole proceeding seemed surreal, like I was in the choir loft watching from above.

At the end of the eulogy, the minister led us through Badger Clark's Cowboy's Prayer.

"Oh, Lord, I've never lived where churches grow.
I love creation better as it stood
That day you finished it so long ago.
And looked upon your work and called it good.

Just let me live my life as I've begun
And give me work that's open to the sky;
Make me a partner to the wind and sun
And I won't ask a life that's soft and high.

Make me as big and open as the plains
As honest as the horse between my knees
Clean as the wind that blows behind the rains
Free as the hawk that circles down the breeze.

Just keep an eye on all that's done and said
Just right me sometime when I turn aside
And guide me on the long, dim trail ahead
That stretches upward towards the Great Divide."

After *Amen*, the strains of "Go Rest High on That Mountain" swelled, enveloping us in mournful melody. Vince Gill's voice was once described as being shaped like a teardrop. Bluegrass, high and true, it sounds as sad as its shape. *I know your life on earth was troubled* . . . When that first line sang out of the buzzy old church speakers, it seemed to hover in the air above the pews. Through the deep sadness of song, some restraining cord was cut and the immense grief that people had been holding back finally overtook them. Brows furrowed. Tears flowed freely. Shoulders shook. Duff made a dilapidated dignitary—he was no spotless primetime hero like Gene or Roy—but he was a loyal athlete who helped keep the beloved sport of rodeo in sight, and he would be missed.

The viewing line wound around the church and spilled out the door onto the sidewalk. Rodeo athletes from around the country, stuntmen, actors and actresses from L.A., townsfolk, old hands with their wives, kids, and grandchildren approached the altar, but the bronc and bull riders hung back, moving into the church vestibule to let everyone else queue up to pay their respects.

When the last person left the coffin's side, the cowboys formed a single, silent line. Duff's travel partners led the way as they walked down the aisle, a slow procession of long faces and black hats, from aged, retired veterans to pink-cheeked rookies. Digby Ryan, who was crippled five weeks ago when a bronc fell on him and crushed his leg in Sisters, swung along on crutches. Brandon, Clete, so many guys I'd met on the road. One at a time they filed past Duff, each placing one of their buckles into his casket. I sat in the front pew and watched them go in: Denver. Guthrie. Dodge City. Houston—twenty-five in all. I knew the depth of their gesture and what it meant. It said, eloquently, wordlessly, *If you go down, brother, we go with you.* You will not make that last ride alone.

Beeber remained glued to his seat, his head down. Shuffling at the tail of the line, listing like an old timber about to give way in a hard wind, was J.W. When he got up to the casket, he unpinned Duff's Frontier Days buckle from the blue velvet and put it in with the other cowboys' buckles. Then he reached toward his waist and unhitched his belt. He drew it from the loops, the leather making a soft, snaky hiss. Not taking his eyes from Duff's face, he popped the snaps. He paused for a moment and looked down at the engraved gold medallion in his hand—it was his World Championship buckle, which he'd won over Duff all those years ago. He placed the buckle with great care on Duff's abdomen, just above his interlaced fingers. J.W. blinked rapidly and heaved a great, conflicted sigh. Then he squared his shoulders and stepped quickly away from the casket.

Duff, the son of a gun, had gotten that Finals buckle after all.

29

AFTER DUFF'S FUNERAL, THE MEDIA CIRCUS roared into Cheyenne. Reporters from all the local newspapers and TV stations, the rodeo magazines, *Sports Illustrated,* even *Entertainment Tonight* combed the city for stories about what had happened. Everybody in town had their tale to tell, their own version of events, from the chute boss to the vendors in the stands to the doctors who treated Duff when he came into the hospital.

Duff had passed on only three days before when J.W. next hoisted his rigging bag into the cab of his truck. I wasn't shy about voicing my opinion. "Maybe this isn't such a good idea, you rodeoing so soon. I think you need more time. You've been through an awful shock."

"I'll be back soon, same as always, Daryl. What are you worried about?"

"I'm not just worried, I'm scared. Scared for you. About what might happen if you keep going the way you do. Why don't you just sit out a month or two and get totally sound? You've got plenty of time; you can get the proper medical attention."

He grunted.

"That's right, I forgot I'm talking to a man whose idea of medical attention is ibuprofen and sports tape." I threw up my hands. "Fine. Go ahead, go. I understand."

A vein pulsed in his forehead. "No, child, you do not understand. You don't know the first thing about it. What you do, you will do until the day you die. Me, I'm almost finished."

I walked back to the porch and spoke through the screen door. "Oh, please. It doesn't matter how long I paint for. An artist is worth more dead than alive."

He took measure of the words, shaking his head back and forth. "That is not the point. I'm not talking about worth—yours, mine, or anybody's. I'm on the fine line here. It's not much longer before I'm too far gone to go anymore."

For the first time, I felt our age difference acutely. I flashed back to the first day he came out to Red Hill. A smile in barn shadow. *I'm a fossil.*

He came back toward the porch, anger bolstering each step. "Do you know what they call guys like me? Weekend warriors. Like I'm not committed enough to get after it full-time. But I did that already, away from home two-hundred-fifty nights a year, so sored up all the time you can't hardly drive. So much a stranger to your wife that she . . ." He shook his head. "I been doing the right thing, working and taking care of my son. But I've sacrificed as much as I'm willing. I want what all I've kept for myself and I won't be made to suffer for it, Daryl. I won't."

His boot heels echoed loudly as he came up the porch steps. I reared back, unsure. I was waiting for lightning to strike. A cuss and a slap. Something.

J.W. rolled his eyes, aggravated, and extended his hand. "Oh, I ain't gonna hit you. You know that. Come on now."

I didn't go to him. I opened the door a little further and balanced on my right leg, leaning warily against the door sill. I dusted off the bottom of my left foot against the side of my calf.

J.W. leaned back on the porch railing, not meeting my eyes. He took off his hat and raked his fingers through his sweat-matted hair. Several times, he started to say something, then stopped. He pulled his hat back on, put his hands on his knees, and pushed himself up to standing. "Daryl, I'm gonna go. But before I do, I want to tell you something."

I crossed my arms, suddenly cold. "Okay." My voice was small and wavered on the wind.

"Last year I rodeoed down in Durango and I brought my boy with me. On the way back he got tired, so we stopped in a ghost town. You know, one of those little old corny places that used to be something, they dress it up to look old-timey with saloons and people acting out horse stealing and hangings and stuff? You know what I mean?"

I nodded.

"Well, they had this high-noon shootout where two guys with them big mustaches come into the street and pretend to have a gunfight. Troy wanted to see it, so we lined up on the hitching rail with our Cokes. One of the gunfighters was a skinny Mexican, maybe twenty, twenty-two years old. Just some kid, probably making extra money over the summer. Do you know who the other gunfighter was?"

I said nothing, just shook my head, trying to rub down the hair on my arms that now stood on end.

"It was the guy who won the World three years before me." J.W. laughed. "When I started out rodeoing, I used to idolize him, thinking, 'I'm gonna be like him. I'm gonna be a hot shit cowboy and win it all just like he did.' Now here he is playing shoot 'em up in the middle of nowhere. For what, maybe minimum wage? He's about as cowboy as a sideshow geek, Daryl."

"But . . ."

"No, don't." He held up his hand. "Don't say anything. It doesn't matter a flip what anyone tells me, 'Don't worry, buddy, that won't be you,' or, 'He just didn't plan right. You won't end up like him.' I know that for every so-called legend with a gold buckle, there's ten other World Champions no one remembers at all. Some of 'em are working mucking out stalls! From hero to horse shit, how do you like that?"

I'd never before seen the expression that was on his face, resigned yet almost mocking. It was the first time I'd seen him look cynical.

"I ain't educated like you, Daryl; I don't have a lot of options. Way I see it, this is my last shot at something good. So when you think about how much *time* I have," he smiled an ugly smile, "I want you to remember that."

He turned and trod heavily down the steps. Pebbles spun from under his heels. He opened the door to his truck.

I started after him, stepping gingerly on the rocky path. "J.W., wait!"

He climbed in the cab. "Nah, I ain't got time for you now, either." He looked purely disgusted. "Just go back to your work, Daryl. And get on inside. You shouldn't be out here barefoot." A slam, then a spin-around in the driveway, and I was seeing taillights.

I stood there stunned. A cold wind blew down from the side of the hill, lifting my hair in tangles. My nose began to run. I felt shamefully stupid. How could I not have figured it out? A cowboy's most unforgiving opponent isn't a bronc or a bull or a calf or a steer. It's time.

A guy might fancy himself a wild one storming life's stage, but the curtain sweeps down to tame him eventually. His luck may change, his skill might improve, he can condition his body to its very limit, but no matter what, time keeps bearing down, constant and indifferent.

I sped past Jace, at the end of the driveway yanking the FOR SALE sign back and forth, working it out of the ground. He kicked dirt off of the steel pegs. The truck tires squealed as I made the hard left,

Homer's paws gripping the truck bed. The more I drove, the angrier I got. To hell with Wyoming. To hell with obsessed cowboys, and drunk racists, and love-struck tweakers, and men who hold the Bible in one hand and their dick in the other. To hell with the whole lot of it. So the Wild West was becoming extinct. Maybe it was dying because it didn't deserve to live. Maybe the wildfires would rage up and finish off the whole mess with a holy purge of flame.

Yeah, burn it, I thought as I crossed the Colorado state line. *Burn it all.*

The closed-in feel of my tiny Denver apartment was just what I needed, the sound of the traffic outside the living room window as soothing as the rush of river water. Homer relaxed with his paws in my lap. It wasn't Giverny, but it would do. If I crashed soon, I could get up early for ham and eggs with a short stack at Pete's Kitchen, then scrounge around for some quarters and head to Smiley's to wash the dust out of my jeans.

My phone rang. When I said hello, Jace was indignant. "I had to call six different numbers to find you, Daryl. Shawna didn't know where you were at. J.W. didn't know. Goody didn't know. Why didn't you answer your phone and where in the devil are you?"

"I'm back in Denver. I needed some time to myself."

"You left Cheyenne without telling me? Listen, I let you run off twice already, Fourth of July and that time you went to Casper. Gwatney just called and the deal fell through on the house . . ."

"What?"

"You heard me. Darcey Rivers pulled out. Just like that. *Bam.* The deal fell through and I need to hustle. You've got to stay on and help me out a little longer."

"He and Jordan didn't give a reason why?"

"No, Goddamn it, they did not. I need you to get back up here because I've got to scare up some work or I'll get behind on the mortgage."

"I don't want to. I'm sick of Cheyenne."

"Oh. Oh, I see. It's all poor Daryl, innit? Let me tell you, you've got a mulish way about you that hurts more than it helps. You've got responsibilities now. To me. Now you get in that shittin' truck . . . Excuse me, you get in *my* shittin' truck, and hightail it back to Red Hill. I mean it."

I didn't. I went to the Grizzly Rose instead, leaving Homer tied to the toolbox, vowing to dance with twenty different men and leave alone. But as I stood on the perimeter of the dance floor, I surveyed the men with disapproval—this one's boots were new, that one's hat creased wrong. I sniffed at the slack in a shirt collar, the unsatisfactory cant of a heel. I left the bar inside of an hour, longing to go back where I belonged. The truck idled at the entrance to I-25. South would take me to downtown Denver, north to Cheyenne. Two directions to carry me, but which way was home?

I had a cup of coffee at the Village Inn on Lincolnway. It was almost 1 A.M. Too late to call on someone, really, but I couldn't wait.

I climbed the stairs next to King's Metal Shop and knocked on the door. J.W. answered, his arm back in the sling, cheeks smogged with days' worth of facial hair. He looked tired. The television was playing low in the living room, the lights turned off.

My mouth felt dry. "I just want you to know something."

He leaned on the door sill. "What's that?"

"Remember that Wild West town you went to? Where you saw that guy you used to worship?" J.W. nodded. If I'd had my hat in my hands, I'd have been wringing it. "Well, just down the street from him is a gal drawing ten-dollar caricatures, and she's got a Master of Fine Arts diploma on her wall at home."

J.W. shifted off the door sill and opened the door further with his foot. "You want to come in?"

"Can I go get my dog?"

"Sure."

I watched his stiff gingerbread-man gait as he went to the kitchen and put down a bowl of water for Homer. "Pulled my groin pretty bad in Eagle."

"You really need a shave."

"I'm dying for one but it's too hard with my arm hurt."

"I'll do it."

"Naah. I should be good enough to do it tomorrow."

"Oh, come on." I led him into the bathroom and began pulling shaving items from the medicine cabinet. Spice-scented shaving cream, his good silver razor, a box of fresh blades. "Here, sit on the floor." Homer came in and lay on the bathmat with his head in J.W.'s lap.

J.W. held up his hand. "Light's hurting my eyes." I lit a couple candles. He sat up. "Forget it, Daryl. You can't see what you're doing."

"Sure I can. I just have to be careful is all."

"I can't ask you to do that."

"You need it." I pointed to the floor. "Sit."

He sat on the bathroom tile and rested a basin I'd filled with hot water on his knees. I perched on the side of the tub, his head leaned back and resting between my thighs. The blade made a satisfying rasp as it sloughed through whisker and foam. He closed his eyes. "When I had my first shoulder surgery, I was in a sling for a long time. Melissa and I weren't doing so good around then, you know, but she had to cook for me and cut my meat and everything. It took a lot longer than I thought to get my coordination worked out with just the one arm working. I wasn't flat on my back helpless like when I broke my pelvis, but pretty damn close."

He kept his eyes shut. "One time, I was standing at the kitchen counter trying to make something to eat. I got a can of soup out but I couldn't work the can opener. Then I thought I'd make a sandwich but I couldn't open the mayonnaise jar or spread mustard on the bread. I stood there with my arm flapping, trying to hold the bread still and I kept pushing it across the counter and into the stove. Either that or I'd knock it off the counter. I called for Melissa and she pretended not to hear." His Adam's apple bobbed as he swallowed hard. "I knew she could hear me. She wouldn't help."

I put down the razor. A tear rolled to the tip of my nose and dropped onto his face. It was followed by another, then a steady stream down my cheeks. "A woman who loved you would do whatever she could to help. Even if it's just a shave."

He reached up and pinched the bridge of his nose like he had an itch. When his eyes opened, they were glistening. "Money or mud, huh?"

Damn. He'd heard me when I said I loved him that night up in the hayloft. I nodded, even though I couldn't say it here to his face. *I love you. Money or mud. Absolutely.*

Later, when I was in his bed, J.W. came to me in the dark. He pulled me to the edge of the bed and knelt on the floor beside it. He spread my legs wide and made love to me with his mouth until I came and then came again, the pressure of the steel ring against the tender flesh the perfect erotic shock.

When he got into bed beside me, I straddled him. He tried to stop me. "But you don't like it."

I put my fingers over his mouth. "I want to." Rocking my hips, I angled forward so I could lower fully down. I moved slowly, shifting in silence. The mood was quiet and reverential because we knew, as much as we were showing we loved each other, we were apologizing, too. *I'm sorry. I'm sorry. I'm sorry.* I clenched every muscle I had tight like I might trap him inside me. I closed my eyes and rocked until he clutched my hip with his free hand and stabbed up into me once, fiercely, then dropped back down against the mattress. I felt his release as if it were my own, though there was no pleasure for me, only undulations of regret. When I opened my eyes, he was watching my face as if to memorize it.

* * *

The freight trains rattling along the tracks across the street woke me the next morning, the metal-on-metal screeching forcing me from a dream. J.W. shifted to the edge of the bed and hurriedly wrapped a sheet around his waist.

When he stood, I grabbed the corner of the sheet and ripped it away. "J.W.? What are you trying to hide from me?"

Before he could answer, the air sucked from my lungs at what I saw—both his thighs savagely bruised from knee to pelvis. On the inside of one thigh, a huge, spreading stain of port wine under the skin, on the other, territories of brown, purple, and red—the map of a murderous continent. I curled my fingers under the comforter. "What the hell happened to you?"

J.W. covered himself with the sheet. "Just the groin pull. It's nothing, Daryl. It'll fix itself."

I swooned, like a heavy crimson cape was swinging toward me, blotting out the light. I struggled to focus: *He said it's nothing. You can get over this. T.R.Y. Try, Daryl. T.R.Y.* A jet-engine whine started in my head. It was just three little letters, why couldn't I do it? But then, "I love you" was just three little words—why couldn't I do *that?*

T.R.Y. I couldn't visualize it. All I could see when I closed my eyes were J.W.'s thighs looking like a slaughterhouse floor. He took a cautious step toward me. "Baby, don't. Come on. It's not that bad."

What rodeo did to his mind, I could handle. And his job. And his relationship with his family. The deterioration of his quality of life I could take, but the piecemeal destruction of his body, I couldn't. The effect of seeing yet another man I loved led to the brink of ruin by a dangerous impulse dropped on me like a ton of bricks. "Is there some part of you that wants to die? Is that why you do it?"

"No. Exactly the opposite. You know that about me. It's what I live for. It's my heart."

I leapt from the bed and starting pulling on my clothes. "That's what you don't get. It's my heart, too!" My stupid, stupid heart. Are we really supposed to take our lead from that ridiculous, blood-pumping machinery? Because following my heart had led me here, to a sad, run-down apartment by the railroad tracks, terrified at the sight of a man who looked like he'd been beaten from the waist down with a lead pipe. "They say that love is letting go, J.W., but that's bullshit. Love is attachment. Love is me giving a damn whether you're hurt or you're healthy, or whether you live or die. I can't watch you get hammered like this anymore." My breath burst from my chest, shallow and fast. I sat down on the ladder-back chair, my head in my hands, on the verge of hyperventilating.

J.W spoke calmly. "I told you way back in the beginning what would have to happen to me before I'd quit this, Daryl."

"Yeah," I snapped. "I remember that. As long as you're not shitting blood, it's okay, right?"

J.W. came to me with an ice pack. I sat with the ice pack on my neck, silent. He stood looking down at me, as if awaiting a verdict. I was coming to believe that for J.W. and the men like him, rodeo was not about dedication, but addiction—once it gets in your blood, brother, the hell with everything else. Heartsick and angry, I felt like the last eight weeks I'd been floating around in some pink-cloud dream state and I'd just now woken up to the ugly truth. The images were unavoidable: Jace kneeling on the living room floor in front of a buck's head, so high he'd plucked the black glass eyes from the sockets; Dad pulling Uncle Dee, frostbitten and blue, from the truck where he'd spun to his drunken death in a snowstorm. I met J.W.'s eyes. "You are all alike. I knew it."

I stood on the sidewalk of Fifteenth Street, watching him secure his rigging bag in the truck. We'd spent the last few hours in the kitchen, sitting in stony silence, neither wanting to be the first to tip their hand. The sky had darkened, a shower rolling in. I didn't move from my spot on the pavement as the clouds gave way to a classic afternoon soaker, fat raindrops flattening my hair and drenching my clothes. "You've got to understand what this is like for me, J.W."

J.W. turned his collar up and buttoned his Carhartt. "If you really don't want me to go, I won't. And I ain't ever said that to anyone before. Ever."

I couldn't do it. I could not be the girl who issued the ultimatum, who made him choose between something and someone he loved. There was a different choice to be made, and it was mine. "I want you to go because I know you have to." I was numb as I forced out the words, dreading every one. "But I also know that if you really want to keep living this way, if what's in your heart is to ignore what the rest of your body is trying to tell you, then I can't be here when you get back. I'm sorry, but I can't."

He tipped his head down and the rain that had pooled on the brim of his hat funneled down into the crease, a curtain of water pouring across his face. This was a variation on a conversation he'd had before, in another context, another life.

I reached for his hand. "Please don't be angry with me."

He brought his head up and looked at me. "I'm not angry, Daryl. I just didn't think I'd hear the words 'I can't' coming from you is all." His eyes were squinted almost shut from pain. "But if you don't have the want-to for this, there's nothing for me to do." He took his hand from mine. "I'm ready to go. Maybe I'll give you a holler in a while." He walked around to the driver's side of the truck.

"Really?" I followed him. "Will you? Because I'm worried about you, J.W."

"I will. I'll call you." Of course he'd say that. Rejection never did hurt his manners.

The truck pulled away from the curb, dirty sprays of rainwater splashing up from the tires. Homer started after it. I called out, "Get back here, boy. He's gone. You'll never catch him."

30

AFTER J.W. LEFT, WE HAD BLOOD MOONS for a week. The fires in Weld County had started up again and the ash turned the sky moody and the air thick. The red moon glowered as it waxed its way toward full. Everything around me—grass, the dry earth—crackled.

I tracked J.W.'s path on the Web—I could at least partly tell where he'd been by finding rodeos where he'd placed. He was making just enough—a thousand, maybe a couple hundred here and there—to keep going until he had his points racked up. Or until whatever he was trying to avoid went away. Relief would come in long highway silences, the blotting effect of getting on, and in the meditative concentration before and after.

In my mind's eye, I saw him preparing to get on, tightening up his glove, the thong clenched between his teeth as he pulled, another junkie tying off. Could I have argued with him, begged him not to leave? Yes. But by now I'd figured out that people go whether you want them to or not. Leaving's what they feel they need, and there's no talking back to need. You can either waste your breath or yield to their exit remedy with some dignity.

I pulled into the Twin Pines to pick up my last paycheck on the morning of August first. I had quit, effective immediately, the day

J.W. left, the same day the check from my mother cleared. When I came out of the office, Jordan Rivers came screeching into the parking lot in Darcey's Bronco. She stopped at the desk and asked for a room number.

I saw her standing on the sidewalk in front of Crystal's room. When the insistent rap of her knuckles yielded no response, she pounded on the door with her fist. Keely answered the door. The lamplight from the parking lot made dark wells under Jordan's eyes. She did not look well.

Crystal swept Keely aside and stood looking at Jordan, tired and clearly confused.

Jordan poked her finger at Crystal's chest. She took a deep breath. "I just want to know. Do you love him?"

Crystal tugged and smoothed the straps of her black mesh tank top. "Who? I . . . no."

"Then why? Why are you doing this? Is it because you need the money? Gotta couple mouths to feed?" The tendons in Jordan's neck stood out, steel cables under the reddening flesh. "Don't just stand there with your cheap little miniskirt and high heels. I want you to answer me."

Crystal started sputtering.

Jordan hit the door frame. "ANSWER ME!" Tears started pouring down her face. "I kept asking him, what's wrong with your back? The scratches. Is it a rash? Something in your shirts, the way I do laundry?" Snot dripped from her nose. She sniffled deeply. "He said it was nothing, to quit asking. Then last week I followed him. I followed him here and I saw you.

"You think you're giving him something that I can't? That I won't? I want you to know I never denied him." She sobbed and wiped her nose with the back of her hand. She stood on her toes to peer around Crystal, her voice a hateful whisper. "You got a little girl in there, don't you, huh? Well, how do you think she feels, knowing that her mommy's doing those awful things with somebody else's daddy? Maybe you think she's too young to know. She isn't.

"You think what you do is okay? That it's between consenting adults? Nobody gets hurt, right? Well, it's a sin. It is wrong in the eyes of God and it's not just you who you're hurting. When you think about that, think about how you ruined everything I ever worked for, everything I ever wanted." She dug into her designer purse. "If you need the money, then I've got it. What does he pay you? Fifty dollars a go? A hundred? Two?" She pulled a handful of bills from her purse and held it out to Crystal, who just stood there staring with her mouth half open. "Here it is," Jordan hissed. "Take it. But know that when you take it you've gotten more from me than some stinking money. You've taken everything that I had in this world and destroyed it." Jordan pulled herself up straight and tried to suck in her pregnant belly. She was crying harder now. "If you like what you do with him, go ahead and keep him. I don't want him anymore."

Jordan threw the money and the bills fluttered to the cracked concrete sidewalk. A crisp twenty took the current and landed in an empty clay flowerpot. Walking in heavy, eighth-month steps, she headed to the Bronco and sped down the back alley so fast her tires screeched.

Giselle and Mrs. Dam had come out of the office, drawn by the commotion. They looked at each other, and then looked at me. Mrs. Dam held her hair as she shook her head disapprovingly. Giselle had her hand over her mouth. "I had no idea."

I looked back and forth between their shocked faces. "Me, either." And judging by Crystal's stunned expression as she shut the door to her room, her hand on Keely's skinny shoulder, I don't think she even remembered whose wife she was dealing with.

A tow truck behind me honked at me to get moving. How long had I been sitting at the stoplight on Lincolnway? I turned right and joined the traffic heading up Capitol Avenue. I'd thought that when

Jordan got hers, the revenge would be so sweet I'd relish every drop. I'd pictured her comeuppance so many ways, but this was a million times worse than anything I could have imagined and it wasn't sweet at all. It was horrible.

I stopped into the Wigwam to see Kimber. The wood bar gleamed under a fresh polish of lemon oil. Her mood was low. "Guess what? Teal sold out. The whole hotel's getting made over and the bar got bought by a gourmet coffee franchise."

"Wow, that's the shits, Kimber."

She buffed the curved corner of the bar with a soft white cloth. "Yeah. I have seen the future, and there's a pound of fresh-ground beans in it. We're goin' mocha, baby." She turned her back. Top-shelf liquors beckoned her and she started mixing a potion in a highball.

The latest *Sports News* sat on the bar. The Rivers family was on the cover with the headline, "A Family Affair." I opened the magazine and looked down at the layout in front of me, Darcey with his arms around Jordan's shoulders, their two kids in her lap. I read the quote from Jordan about how tough a woman has to be to love a cowboy. "Everyone knows that when it comes to this sport, it's not a matter of if you get hurt, but when and how bad." I closed the magazine and pushed it away. When she said those words, had she any idea she was predicting her future so eloquently?

Kimber caught me staring into space. "Missing somebody?"

"Nah, I'm fine. Just dealing with the clean up from a summer fling that got flung."

"Sure, honey." She put a Bloody Mary in front of me, squeezed my hand, and walked away.

Day three after J.W. left, I decided I'd brooded long enough. I knew that if I got back to work, everything would settle down. That evening, after the showers stopped, I ate a box of animal crackers for dinner and sat on the deck, arms wrapped around my knees on a rain-soaked cushion, watching the sun set behind Table Mountain. Redtail hawks glided against a backdrop of threadlike purple clouds. Jace whistled out the basement door and the horses swung back toward the barn from the wash, their hooves and fetlocks muddy socks. I stayed still and quiet until the last light vanished and darkness closed around me like a sheltering hand.

The noon heat woke me up. I was alone in the house. I didn't bother dressing, scuffing around in my leopard-print slippers and a long Copenhagen T-shirt, hair a wild tangle. I fed Homer and loafed on the couch. I read an old issue of *Western Horseman* and drank an entire pot of coffee sweetened with condensed milk. At about two, I tried to paint but ended up standing there gawping at the canvas like a dumb cart horse that wasn't sure where to go or what to do. Art used to be my great comfort, my safety zone, the one place where my troubles couldn't get me. But nothing was safe anymore.

I gave up, headed upstairs, and ran the hottest bath I could stand. With a beer resting on the tub ledge, I lay in the steaming water and played every rodeo hurting song I could think of on the CD player: "I Can Still Make Cheyenne," by George Strait. Susie Boggus singing "Someday Soon." Chris LeDoux's "Riding for a Fall." *Last night you told her you could never hold her, 'cause cowboys just got to be free . . .*

When the water started to cool, I opened the spigot and ran more. I kept the bath so hot that beads of sweat blistered along my upper lip and my skin flushed as if fevered. With my fingernail, I etched a line up my stomach, watching the skin in its wake turn white, then fill in again with color. Where sadness should be was just a dull, empty ache.

I set my jaw and leaned back in the bathtub until I was completely submerged. Bad as I felt, I was tempted to stay underwater, to give up and fade away. I held my breath until I thought my lungs would explode, then at the last second, I sat up. The water sluiced from my scalp, my hair a cascading sheet down my back. I spun to face myself in the mirror. My eyes were glassy, my skin red as rage. *A sucker for love,* I thought grimly, *is still a sucker.*

By the weekend, I'd put away my easel, my paints and canvases and brushes, tossed J.W.'s Jubilee Days buckle and the copper bracelet into the bottom of my steamer trunk under my clothes. Jace was home for good now. My services were no longer needed.

I was doing okay until the morning I prepared to leave for home. I brought my dirty clothes to the basement in a plastic basket. As I was sorting lights and darks, I noticed something red stuffed in the small space next to the washer. There it was, J.W.'s laundry bag with his shirt, his jeans, his clothes—and mine—from Jubilee Days balled up together and caked with mud at the bottom of the bag.

I soaked his shirt and washed it in cold water with a lot of detergent. After two turns in the gentle cycle, the dirt came out. I took it out of the dryer, tumbled warm and wrinkled, and lay it flat on the ironing board. As I ironed, I sank lower, getting flashes of J.W.: a rigid collar on a rigid neck with the razored line of sorrel hair just above, the way the shoulder fit the sleeve, his arm tunneling through to the cuff. At the first blast of spray starch, he came rushing fully back to me. This was his scent, Daddy scent, clean and crisp and uptight. I ran the iron along the monogrammed placket, hitting the steam button as I smoothed around the buttonholes and realized I was weeping. I kept ironing, creasing the sleeves like I knew he'd want, and soon I was bawling. I flattened his jeans on the ironing board and creased each leg with fanatical precision. The clothes were steam-damp and hot in my arms as I bundled them to my face. I sank to my knees and rocked, unable to contain myself. "I miss you so much," I whispered, then howled out my pain and loss into the bunched fabric.

I fell asleep around ten and dreamed of J.W. curled up in his wife's lap. In the dream, I knew she was pregnant, but that she was also nursing. Her face a smooth ivory mask, like the Sacred Virgin. She offered her milky nipple to him, and he latched on to her, milk spilling down his cheeks. His eyes were closed but he clung to her like she was offering him her very life through her sustenance. I couldn't tell if he was her child or her lover. I felt a queasy mix of revulsion and arousal.

I woke clammy with sweat. *What if I'm pregnant?*

Every time J.W. and I made love was a gamble, a primitive flirting with *having* each other. I hate condoms, always have, the plastic screechy texture, or the greasy lettuce feel of the lubricated ones. The first few times he hesitated, as if expecting me to say, "wait" but I never did. *What if* fled the instant I felt the throbbing heat of him press inside of me.

My period started when I was in the shower the next morning. I twisted the nozzle to the hardest spray, then sat down in the tub and rinsed away the evidence, the water a thousand liquid needles on my skin. Blood of this kind never bothered me. The sight of it didn't make me feel sick, just sad.

I remembered the night during Frontier Days, when J.W.'s apartment was full of guests and I feared the disapproving eye of my brother. We fled, parking on a dark country road where there was no one to scandalize but the fence posts. Me on my back, J.W. on his knees atop his piled clothes, the rhythmic ticking of the rivets on his Wranglers as they hit the truck bed, he was in me as far as he could go, not driving toward a finish, but relaxed and languorous. As he fucked me slow and deep, he leaned into my neck. I barely heard the words before the hot wind carried them away. "I want to make you a mama." It was the most profoundly erotic thing he'd ever said to me, and my response was immediate and convulsive.

I sat on the shower floor with my chin on my knees as red swirled around the drain and disappeared, and found myself immersed in a strange sadness, as if our last possible physical connection had been cut. From the very first time I had touched J.W., my senses ventured in where my head and heart could not. My head had urged caution and my heart was riddled with doubt, but my body was different; my body believed.

I had a go at the piercing with a set of needle-nose pliers, but hunched over and fiddling with the implement between my legs, I couldn't get the right angle to open the ring, and trying to remove it was more than I could bear, so I stopped. I got the piercing as a stand in for I Love You, to play it safe, to beat back the cliché, and now here I was with just my startling originality for company.

Raw with exhaustion and self-pity, I went over to Goody's and moped in her kitchen. She was busy spreading lingonberry jelly on fat-free toaster crumpets for the High West tea. I watched how dutifully she worked. When Dee died, she'd sunk every bit of energy into the Little Wyo to distract her from the pain. She offered me the copies of the *Sports News* with J.W.'s picture in them, but that only made me cry. I let her hug me, feeling the wet wool of her sweater against my forehead. "I wish I knew how long it would take to get over him."

She glanced out the window at the cross high up on the hill. "You don't always get over somebody. Sometimes you just go on."

On the way down South Greeley Highway, I stopped in to see Shawna. I opened the rusted gate and walked up the front path to the trailer house. The lawn was overrun with tough bunches of crabgrass. From the porch, I could see through the screen door into the living room. Lan was stretched out on the plaid couch watching a cooking show. A raffish man in a white chef's hat flipped veal chops in a copper-bottomed pan, the flames leaping in wild arcs from the stove. When I knocked, Lan got up to let me in.

"Daryl. Come here, you." He opened his arms and folded me into a big, tight hug. He knew. He had to know. His T-shirt smelled sharp, of cigarettes, pot smoke, musk incense, and sweat.

"Hey."

I turned. Shawna stood in the kitchen, her hair cut to shoulder length and clipped up in silver barrettes. Her bangs were streaked hot pink. She wore a black A-line minidress and combat boots.

"When did you cut your hair?"

"Oh, this?" She ran her hands up the back of her head. "Last night. I decided I needed something different. I didn't have the right scissors so I used kitchen shears."

"Well, it looks great."

Shawna drew a breath and stepped toward me. "Daryl, I just want you to know I'm so sorry about everything. Not just about J.W., but how horrible I was when you came to bail me out."

Every ounce of energy drained from me. I sagged at the knees. "Oh, Shawnzy, I know you're sorry. It's okay." I loved her for wanting to apologize, but my grief was so huge it blacked out everything around it; I probably couldn't even sketch the jail from memory at this point.

She came over and put her arms around me. "Thank you. I hope you'll be okay. I mean, I know you will." She paused. "Has he called?"

"No. And I doubt he will. I guess it's better this way, you know?"

Shawna nodded. "Listen, I want to tell you something. We're moving. My aunt has a house in Santa Cruz she'll rent to us. Lan wants more work than he can get out here." She rolled her hands over and over her stomach. Her fingernails were bitten to the quick. "It's time for a change."

31

THE SECOND SATURDAY NIGHT in September was Kimber's last stand. The Wigwam was closing for good that weekend, and in the spirit of making a dramatic exit, Kimber called off all the rules. The Wild Women were dressed like nineteenth-century saloon girls. Kimber didn't care if there were butt cheeks showing or boobs flashing or tips being tucked straight into bras and thongs. "Let 'em arrest me," she yelled over the music. "I'll go down like Mother Featherlegs and they'll build a monument to me later," she said as Alizé leapt off the bar and bodysurfed the crowd all the way back to the pool table. She started dancing in the middle of someone's game of Eight Ball, tearing up the felt with her spike-heeled boots. Brandy wore a six-petticoat skirt with a leopard-print lingerie set underneath, a pearl-and-ruby choker, and feathers in her hair. Bubbles was collecting twenties every time she hiked up her heavy black velvet skirt to adjust her satin garters. Kimber looked just like Miss Kitty—brocade corset, bustle, and all. She walked the bar with her hands on her hips and shook her head as two men swung at each other over Tequila Rose, Sherry running by screaming as a girl chucked maraschino cherries into her top and chased her through the bar with a bottle of Cuervo Gold. Kimber swatted the girl with her lace parasol, then just stood there laughing like a woman face up on the guillotine.

The Wigwam was slated to become a Java Jane's Coffee Corral. Wild women and whiskey giving way to barristas and biscotti—if that didn't mean the West was tamed, then it was gelded, at the very least. The Wigwam Wild Woman Revue was a short, rowdy party powder-kegging out in a final-night flash of stocking-top and two-dollar drafts, and after a few weeks of swift renovation, a man would be able to take his pleasure in fussy caffeinated blends, three sizes to choose from: Lil' Bit, A Skoch, and Whoa, Nellie—foam and cinnamon dash optional. Teal had already put his house on the market and trailered his Harley for the move to Daytona.

For their finale, the Wild Women did a cowgirl can-can that ended with all six women on the bar, skirts flipped up, ruffle-thonged bottoms wriggling, with "SCREW YOU, TEAL" written one letter per cheek across their buttocks, then they turned and blew him a farewell kiss. Teal, stowed as ever in his watchdog spot in the corner, dabbed at the sides of each eye with a bar rag, then returned the love by flipping the girls the bird.

When the house lights came up and the crowd cleared out, Kimber sat down at one of the round tables and put her feet up on a chair. She surveyed the empty room, chairs knocked over, pool cues snapped in half like toothpicks, her eyes clear behind a pair of pink-tinted granny glasses. "You know what, kid? A good time is a lot of hard work."

"I know, Kimber. You worked harder than anyone this summer. But after tonight, you're gonna be a legend in this town."

"Yeah. But I've got my kid back, and now I guess I'll try to pull together a personal life, or something like it." She toyed with a silver Wigwam matchbook. "I don't know, Daryl," she said, "I'm thinking of giving Flyboy Jeff a shot. I mean, there's something to a man who works for something larger than himself. I know the cowboys think they're keeping certain traditions alive, but Jeff keeps actual people alive. I cracked the code on the whole cowboy thing anyway. You want a gentleman? Get a cowboy. You want a bad boy? Get a cowboy. It's all something you cook up in your head, and nothing can stomp your little dream because there's not enough of them around to check facts against the real thing. Lord knows I had the fever myself, but not anymore. If you want to know the truth, I think the only reason the so-called cowboy mystique stuck around so long is because it's like Silly Putty. You can pretty much pull it any direction you want."

"You got that right. I know I'll be keeping my distance from cowboys in the future." I balled up a couple of used cocktail napkins and tossed them behind the bar. "You thought about where you might work next?"

"Oh, I don't know. They offered me a job as manager of Java Jane's but I'd have to wear a polka-dot blouse buttoned up to the neck and a bolo tie with a coffee cup slider and I was like, 'No, thank you.'"

Tazer Mendez rolled through the lobby. His biceps flexed as he grabbed the stainless rims of the wheels to push forward. He leaned his head in the door. *"Hola*, Kimber."

Kimber fluffed her hair. *"Hola*, Tazer. *Que pasa?"*

"Nada." He spun around in his wheelchair, a neat 360. "What's goin' on with you?"

"Just getting ready to shoot out the lights here at the Wigwam."

"It was a real good party. We'll miss having you around." He spun around again and pushed forward toward the glass door. "See ya."

Kimber and I looked at each other. Tazer was awfully cute. I flicked her arm with my fingernail. "You sure *no mas* on the cowboy thing?"

"I'll be right back." Her heels clicked on the hotel lobby tile.

When she came back into the bar, Tazer's number tucked into

her bra, Kimber unhooked her corset and sat down on the bar cross-legged, her big Miss Kitty skirt puffed up around her. At heart, every good-time girl knows that the gig wasn't meant to last, but Kimber was savvy enough to go out with both barrels firing. She watched a hot pink brassiere spin around and around on one of the blades of the ceiling fan. "Well, it's official," she said, her unruly blond curls springing back as she downed one last shot of top-shelf whiskey. "This place has seen more ass than a toilet seat."

I passed out on Kimber's couch at three A.M. and woke to the first frost of the season. I drove north of town, the brown grass on the prairie stiff under a lace of ice. The washboard road that led to Linda Kenney's place was empty but for a Yukon towing a green gooseneck trailer just ahead of me. My poor old truck ate a lot of dust on that five-mile stretch, and my shocks were so bad, I think I might have shaken loose a few fillings.

I found Beeber in a stall with a gorgeous little Morgan. "Hey, Daryl."

"Hey. Got time for a visit? Just wanted to see how you're doing."

"Sure. If you don't mind hangin' out while I work. This little girl's ready to go and I don't want to wait."

I sat on the fence while Beeber led the filly into the round pen. He'd haltered her with no lead, and closed the gate so it was just the two of them in the circular enclosure. Beeber took a long plastic strip from his pocket and the horse stood shyly near the fence while he unfurled the ribbon. Beeber walked to the exact center of the pen, cedar shavings piling up at his ankles and snapped the ribbon at her, not making contact. She took off running around the perimeter of the pen.

Beeber kept flailing the ribbon, over and over, and the Morgan ran and ran. She began to lather, but Beeber worked silently on, his posture easy and straight. A breeze came up and the horse's coat rippled. She ran for almost half an hour, and by then, she began dipping her head down and chewing. She was submitting.

Beeber stood stock-still, eyes cast on the ground. The filly stopped running and pressed her side to the fence, watching him, her eyes wide and careful, hind legs straight in that characteristic Morgan stance. Beeber didn't move a muscle. The horse took a tentative step toward him and Beeber flexed his right hand, curling his fingers into a fist to keep the horse used to him moving.

A few minutes later, the Morgan edged to Beeber's left side. Beeber began talking softly into the horse's shoulder, then reached down and tested the horse's front leg. His face was serious but gentle. "Are you going to let me have your hoof? It's okay." Beeber seemed settled in his skin now, more like a man. I guess few things will grow you up faster than hoisting your own father's coffin. He said he was going to go home to Louisiana to find his mother.

Duff was a shoo-in for induction into the ProRodeo Hall of Fame, and if they couldn't get him in this year, then surely next—hang the chaps and buckles in a Lucite box, cut a ribbon, watch the flashbulbs pop. The press was divided on the matter of his death. To some, he was an old guy who should have known better than to sign up for one last shot at glory. To others, he was a tragic rodeo god, and what coincidence that he met his fate on July 30 at Frontier Days, the same day and same place that rodeo's favored son, Lane Frost, was killed in 1989 by a bull named, ironically, Taking Care of Business. Either way, by dying at Cheyenne, Duff would not be forgotten. I knew I'd never forget the look in his eyes when he saw that bull coming toward him for the last time, that split second when it looked like he could roll away, hump into an all-fours cowboy crawl, and run for his life, but he didn't.

The filly let Beeber lift her front hoof about six inches off the ground. "That's good. See I didn't hurt you, did I, girl?" Beeber went around behind the horse and she started. "It's okay, girl. You take your time." Beeber patted and rubbed her flank. When the little Morgan finally let Beeber lift up her hind hoof, I felt a lump rise in my throat. I was witnessing the birth of trust. This simple animal could trust somebody. Why couldn't I?

A crowing voice cut through the autumn afternoon. "Well, look who it is."

I turned around. "Hey, Clete."

"What's new, Daryl?" He tossed a couple dusty horse blankets over the railing. "Talk to J.W. lately?"

"No. You ought to know that."

Clete hopped up and sat on the top rail of the fence. "Ah, you disappoint me, girlie."

"Pardon?"

"Tell you why I wasn't so nice to you at first. I was sick of hearing about you before we even met. 'She's so talented.' 'She's so nice to me, I can't hardly believe it.' I was jealous, I guess, that he could find someone that'd have that effect. I told him a young one was going to be trouble but when I saw how you were with him after that kick-in-the-eye business up in Cody I gave you my endorsement." He tucked a fresh toothpick in his cheek.

"I thought I had you figured right. You know, I was the one who told him to go to you, after he bucked off in Calgary and his ribs hurt him so bad the lone shot that could make it better was the stuff that only a woman can do. That was when you did it to him, girlie, when you really sunk the hook in deep. I heard about those sausage biscuits for days." He shook his head and looked up into the low-scudding clouds. Another cold front was blowing in. "I know you got some fire in you and I respect a strong will, but I told you how that old boy works and I don't appreciate what you did."

"What did I do?"

"You held out when ya should've hung in."

Margie came out of the tack room with a bridle around her neck.

I gave her a little wave, my hand balled up in my jacket sleeve to keep warm. "Hi, Margie."

"Hi, honey." A tendril of kindness in her voice reached toward me but she kept her distance because of Clete.

I drew my hands farther up into my sleeves. "So, how's he been doing? Is he okay?"

Clete twisted his lower lip. "He's out there doing what he can."

"Well, if you talk to him, maybe you could tell him I asked after him."

He flicked his toothpick to the ground. "I might say something to that effect. But then again, I might not, 'cause the way I see it, girlie, what you got broke here ain't for me to fix."

I zipped my fleece up to my neck and got back into the truck. Winter would come on quick and I was glad. I wanted the snow to blanket the dull agony, the winds to blow in and sweep my heart clear. At a stoplight in town, I heard the distinct chug and ping of a diesel in the next lane and turned my head. Pavlovian heartache.

Shawna and Lan shipped off to northern California. Jace slashed the price of Red Hill, but because he'd refused to subdivide the land, interest was slight. Jordan had a healthy, seven-pound baby girl. Darcey, I heard, was living out of his horse trailer on the road.

I turned my truck into the Bluffs Ranch drive, my pens and pencils jangling in their wooden case as I bounced over the cattle guard. Hawley and his dog Deuce were sitting on the porch, Hawley rubbing the grease off a set of wrenches with a blue chamois. The stock truck was idling, the engine sputtering and belching as Richie Meadows worked the pedals. They were getting ready to haul the ranch's twenty-four head of bucking stock down to New Mexico for the winter.

Hawley eyed the truck warily, then flopped the greasy rag over his shoulder when he saw me jump from the cab and land ankle-deep in a glazed-over mud puddle. "Have to pack around a change of britches if you're going to make that kind of dismount," he said, with his cloudy-lung laugh.

"Just want to sit a while and do some drawing, if you don't mind, Mr. Bolinger. I won't be any bother." The wind picked up, blowing gum wrappers and cigarette butts at my feet. I shivered inside my fleece layers and winter coat.

"Go right ahead," he said, fitting the wrenches into foam-padded slots in a red plastic case. Deuce, tied to the porch rail with a frayed nylon rope, gnawed a steak bone. "You can have the run of the place, far as I'm concerned."

I sat on the riser where I first laid eyes on J.W., calling up every memory of him that I could. My fingers were freezing in my thin wool gloves as I tried a simple outline of him lowered down in the chute, chin tucked, lips snarled, ready to nod. The focus, the hot flexion before release, when he was nothing but faith and strength and instinct, braced for that life-and-death grip around his heart. His dedication, his style, his athleticism—I wanted to capture everything that had made me love him, so I could finally let him go. But something in me had coarsened, and through the calcified pain and anger, I could no longer grasp what was good. What swam before my eyes was the look on his face as his friends helped him limp, dazed and bleeding, from the arena in Cody. Him crying and exhausted after he bucked off in Calgary. The gruesome, blood-dark bruises on his thighs that brought me to the limit of what I could take. I didn't see a hero or a legend or a lover. I saw a man following his bliss right into a brick wall.

I had my theories—addiction, obsession—but I really didn't understand what would make a man like J.W. put so much on the line. What made rodeo worth risking everything? If I wanted to lay down this burden of pain, I needed to know. I tucked my sketchpad under my arm and walked up to Hawley. "Got a favor to ask of you, Mr. Bolinger." Half a dozen horses were milling around the stock pen, grass and leaves stuck in their thickening coats giving them the look of mothy woolens. I swung my foot in a semicircle in the frozen grass. "How about you let me get on one?"

Hawley howled and adjusted his blaze-orange cap. "You gotta be shittin' me, Daryl." He saw by my expression that I was serious. "You ever been on a bucking horse before?"

"No. But that doesn't mean I can't."

"I known you since you was a kid. You're good at chasing the cans, I'll vouch for you on that, but this is dangerous. I'm not supposed to say this with the women's lib and all, but it's not a girl's sport. Besides, we're breaking down the bucking chutes today so you pretty much missed your chance."

"Hawley . . ." A stone-solid feeling was fast hardening along my bones. I didn't recognize it but I knew it wasn't fear. I held out the two hundred dollars J.W. had given me at the Twin Pines.

The roll of bills disappeared into Hawley's plaid jacket pocket. He spit and cursed. "All right. But goddammit, if you get hurt—" He whistled for Richie. "Go get Royce and William out of the engine guts they're messing with."

"No." I didn't want anyone else to see me. I didn't want anybody to know.

"Darlin', somebody's got to pull the gate. Can't be the guy who helps you set your mount."

They fished out a kid's flak jacket and chaps for me. I paced the riser behind the chutes, looking at the ungroomed arena soil, while William and Royce pulled a gray mare from the herd and rolled her in. Royce had an orange-and-blue-striped Broncos muffler stuffed under the collar of his army coat. The wind turned everyone's earlobes crimson. From the distance of anxiety, I observed my hand in the junior bareback glove with an almost scientific eye. I stretched forward to touch my toes. My muscles felt remarkably stiff. Then, when they said okay, I swung my leg up over the worn wooden slats of the chute. Hawley and William helped me lower, thighs shaking, onto the horse's back. I felt the mare sigh and shift beneath me. Her eyes rolled back, white showing at the rim. In that claustrophobic weathered wood chute, she seemed enormous. Rosin squawked as William showed me how to work my hand into a passable bind. My pulse was in my ears, blood red waves pounding the shore of my skull, every beat of my heart bringing me closer to what I was seeking. On the other side of the gate, Royce held a stopwatch in one hand and the gate rope in another. When I was ready for the snap of latch and shriek of hinge, I bit my lips hard and nodded.

At the very first jump, the frost-singed landscape shifted hard and spun. I forced myself to keep my eyes open. Fence. Sky. Shed, house, sky, all in a tilt-a-whirl blur. My head snapped back and my arm burned ferociously up to the shoulder as I pulled up on the rigging with all my might. The horse and I moved as two parts of a disjointed unit, vaulting and clacking like a runaway roller coaster car on a bumpy track. It felt like something had taken violent hold of me; I rattled like a pair of dice in King Kong's fist. No wonder J.W. didn't think when he rode. For what was happening to me, I couldn't have formed one shred of a thought.

After what felt like an hour, my hand got jerked from the rigging. I pitched over the horse's side and hit the ground with an impact so savage I saw a faceful of stars. I lay in the dirt feeling the calm of a shipwreck survivor at last washed ashore, then sat up slowly and started laughing, huge hyena yips of adrenaline and exploded fear. A white-hot bolt shot from my arm to my neck. Tears streamed down my cheeks. I felt like I'd been pitched up to heaven and slammed back down.

I heard a voice behind me, felt the reverberation of several sets of footsteps taking the rocky dirt. "Easy now, sweetheart. I think you might have broken your collarbone." Careful hands eased me to my feet. I couldn't turn my head without releasing another blinding bolt. Was I hurt? I couldn't tell, but the energy coursing through me was so great, I decided it couldn't be anything other than pain. A gust of cold wind tumbled in, blowing hard grit into my face and freezing the sweat on my scalp.

Royce's grinning face loomed over me, yellowed saliva crusting in the corners of his mouth. "Well, ya lasted two-point-eight seconds. That's a real good try, cowgirl."

I held onto Hawley's faded sleeve and hobbled out of the dirt, shaking. Satisfied. When we reached the fence, I stood straight, dust caking my lips and coating the inside of my mouth. I'd closed the gap between what I'd guessed at and what I knew as truth. I finally understood. The minute I'd hit the ground, I wanted to get right back on again. I vibrated from the virago shriek in every muscle of my body, but I wasn't angry anymore.

32

"HOLY MOLY, I'M HUGE." Shawna surveyed her behind in the mirror over her old oak dresser. The California sunlight tinted the lace on her tea-dyed sack dress the color of old parchment. There was no denying it—she was showing, and the baby weight was starting to come on. But the pounds gave her a beautiful roundness. With her ruddy, pillowy cheeks, her face had taken on the softly regal look of an *infanta de* Goya.

Kimber tugged down the fabric skimming Shawna's hips, then looked at her own reflection, running a foam make-up wedge around the border of her perfectly glossed lips. "Not huge, spooks. Pregnant."

"Hugely pregnant. And I'm only four months."

"Okay, Hormonal. I hear you!" Kimber shot a glance at me. "For God's sake, we're going to need a bottle of tequila to get through this wedding."

I wrestled with the buttons on my black flowered dress, which was no easy task given that I was still in a sling because of my collarbone. "She can't drink."

"I didn't mean for her."

Shawna and Lan picked the Autumnal Equinox for their wedding because of its pagan significance. Fertility. Harvest. Preparation for renewal and all that jazz. Kimber and I flew out three days ago to act as the "babes of honor" at the friends-only ceremony, a barefoot ritual on the beach.

For weeks, Lan and Shawna campaigned heavily for me to fly out to Santa Cruz for a visit. Then, once they set the date for the wedding, I no longer had an excuse. Shawna's aunt Judith, a realtor down the coast in Monterey, let them rent her five-room pink stucco bungalow a few blocks from the beach. The yard overflowed with red bougainvillea, and ridiculously cheerful orange and yellow poppies lined the driveway. Velvet-purple morning glories climbed the trellis near the front door. Since I arrived, I'd been assaulted by balm and color at every turn.

Lan secured work right away tattooing. "That's one good thing about California," he said. "No shortage of ink-hungry bodies." Shawna was still practicing on oranges, but she was rapidly approaching skin-readiness. I bet she'd be tattooing live human flesh within months. I claimed dibs as her second client. Lan was first in line. He wanted her to tattoo a band of Gashleycrumb Tinies around his calf as a wedding gesture.

Kimber kept herself busy by acting as Shawna's apprentice's assistant. She slathered petroleum jelly on oranges and grapefruits for Shawna to practice her hand with different needles and techniques—shading, outlining, filling in. The rind of the fruit was a time-honored tattooist's substitute for skin, and it made the house smell wonderfully of citrus. I sat around watching, drinking giant mugs of Tension Tamer tea to calm my nerves. Every so often, Shawna would press down too hard with the tattoo gun, sending a grapefruit shooting across the room, where it'd roll into a corner and come to rest in dust and crumbs. When he'd hear her swearing, Lan called in from the drawing table in the breakfast room, "Babe, tell Kimber she doesn't have to grease the whole grapefruit!"

Newbie frustration aside, Shawna showed a real gift with the needle and a surprising willingness to accept Lan's tutelage. They wanted to open their own shop once the baby was old enough for a sitter. If things went well, Shawna would never have to paint another moon-kissed Indian maid as long as she lived.

She hadn't stopped painting, but her work had changed drastically. The first night of our visit, Shawna poured Kimber and me huge tumblers of vodka and organic orange juice and showed us what she'd been up to. It was a series of three oils called, *It's an Indian Thing, You Wouldn't Understand (but I will trade it to you for twenty-four dollars and some beads)*. First in the series was a supersaturated comic panel she called *Squaws on the Stroll* that depicted the cartoon Pocahontas and the SueBee Honey girl dressed in fishnet stockings and tarty loincloths, leaning against the wall in an alley off a city street. You could just glimpse a pair of male legs in fringed buckskin trousers and the tip of a walking stick coming around the corner—an Indian pimp. Her Dad, I knew. The second painting she called *Native American Gothic*, an exact replica of Grant Wood's portrait, but with her and Lan looking aggro and bitter, Lan holding a devil's trident instead of a pitchfork, their Santa Cruz bungalow behind them, flames pouring from the windows. The last work she showed us was of the Land O' Lakes dairy mascot as a young girl, with an elderly woman kneeling down, clutching her tiny chin. The little maid's eyes were filled with tears, and the woman, who I recognized from photos as Shawna's estranged Nana from Rhode Island, gazed at her with adoration. "This one is called *Like Buttah*." Shawna choked up a little when she said it. Normally, self-portraits made me gag, but these had real bite, and Shawna making herself the center of these paintings was truly an act of redemption—she'd been absent from her work for too long. And should she find a gallery to launch her to the same level of success she had with the maidens, she'd no longer be a boutique minority, she'd be a boutique rebel, and that, I thought, would suit her just fine.

* * *

Throughout my visit, Kimber, Lan, and Shawna treated me with great care, coddling me like a fragile egg. We prowled through Stearn's Market, hiked into the Santa Ynez Mountains, and ate at Mexican restaurants and tapas places and sushi bars, with not one peep of veggie proselytizing. But my favorite thing was the beach. I couldn't get enough of the smacking salt breeze in my face, the *foom* of the surf, the way the white coastal light caught the sand. I spent hours walking the shoreline alone, pants rolled to the knee, wading calf-deep into the foam, the cold water distracting me from the tight pain in my heart.

Much as I missed having Shawna and Lan around back home, I had to admit that the California lifestyle agreed with them. They had good record stores, ten kinds of tofu in every supermarket, and numerous kindred spirits in their neighborhood. They had so many punky folks stopping in to chat, the house looked like a safe house for escaped Muppets. The guy with green dreads who lived next door was teaching them how to surf. I asked Lan if he missed Wyoming, but he just rolled his eyes.

Shawna swept her pink-streaked hair behind her ears with antique tortoiseshell combs and put on a pair of tinkly crystal strand earrings. She puffed out her cheeks and exhaled. "Okay, I think I'm ready."

She never looked more beautiful. The high-button shoes. The handmade dress, the stacks and stacks of silver bracelets. The soft glow of hope in her face. "You make an amazing bride, Shawnzy."

"Like a regular nightmare dream girl," Kimber agreed.

"Let me just check here. Something old—my dress. Something new." Shawna touched the black, filigree-style bracelet Lan tattooed on her left wrist. "Something borrowed—Kimber's crystal earrings. And something blue. Something blue . . . ?

"Oh!" I pawed through my satchel and held out my mother's

handkerchief embroidered with faded violets. She'd carried it at her First Communion.

She tucked the handkerchief into her brown velvet vintage cocktail purse. "Thanks." Her eyes started watering, which made mine well up.

Kimber picked up a crown of dried ivory, pink, and apricot roses and pinned it atop Shawna's head. She sniffled.

Shawna ducked her head from under the flowers and looked up. "Oh my God, Kimber. Not you, too?"

"I'm not crying, spooks. Your goddamn hippie incense is making my eyes water."

The beach was almost empty when we arrived. We promenaded down the boardwalk to the steps, Lan looking vampiristically handsome in his black suit with maroon pinstripes, his great-grandfather's silver watch fob draped from his vest pocket. He'd dyed his hair black and tinted his sideburns, too. His antique satin cape blew back in the wind, the red lining showing like the flesh of a plum. Surfers, wet suits unzipped and folded down at the waist, toted their boards up from the water. The smell of popcorn and the sight of the Ferris wheel lights on the midway made my throat constrict. I shook it off, trying to make some room around the stubborn sadness to be happy for Lan and Shawna.

The priestess, Morgaine, was a friend of Shawna's from her women's spirituality group. She met us on the boardwalk in long purple brocade robes, her curly gray hair swept off her neck by a pair of chopsticks and topped with a gemstone-studded moon-and-stars headdress. No one gave her a second look. California.

We walked down close to the water, and everyone joined hands and formed a circle with Lan and Shawna in the center. Morgaine took a three-foot golden cord from her green velvet pouch and began the hand-fasting ritual. "Blessed be this union with gifts from the east . . ." Then the south, west, and north. Shawna and Lan joined their left hands and Morgaine wrapped them loosely with the cord. "Here before witnesses of friend and family, Lan and Shawna will swear vows to each other. With this cord, I bind them to those vows. But know that this binding is not tied, so that neither is restricted by the other, and the binding is only enforced by both their wills."

Shawna and Lan faced each other and recited, in unison:

"Heart to thee,
Soul to thee,
Body to thee,
Forever and always,
So mote it be."

We all affirmed, *"So mote it be."* I tasted the salt-sting as the wind filled my mouth. Morgaine raised her voice over the crashing surf. "Let Lan and Shawna now exchange their rings." Kimber stepped forward, proffering the rings, slid up the stems of two stargazer lilies laid across a crimson pillow. "The symbolism of the ring was explained by the great Native American leader, Black Elk, who said: 'Everything the power of the world does is done in a circle. The sky is round and I have heard that the earth is round like a ball and so are all the stars. The wind, in its greatest power, whirls. Birds make their nests in circles, for theirs is the same religion as ours. The sun comes forth and goes down again in a circle. The moon does the same and both are round. Even the seasons form a great circle in their changing and always come back again to where they were. The life of a man is a circle from childhood to childhood, and so it is in everything where power moves.' "

Lan took Shawna's hand from where she'd rested it on her growing belly. "Shawna Shalom Two Tribes, you are an artist in everything you do, and you have redrawn my world and made it a bigger and more beautiful place." When he slid the white gold band on her finger, a tear ran down my cheek, turning cold in the ocean wind. They seemed so sure of each other, so utterly devoid of doubt.

Shawna trembled as she put the matching ring on Lan's finger. "Lander Marshall Abbott, I can't in good conscience stand here today and tell you that I will always be agreeable. But I promise with all my heart and soul that I will never be ungrateful. You have gone from my friend to my family, and you've made my heart into a home."

Kimber sniffed loudly and patted her powdered face with a tissue.

Their rings on, Lan and Shawna joined hands and said together, "I commit myself to the bond that exists between us, and pledge to nurture its life and the life that we've created. As the circle, symbolized by these rings, has no end, neither shall my devotion to you. You are my once-in-a-lifetime love."

At seeing their love consecrated in a way both old and new, bravely and unambiguously, a voice inside me asked, *Did I let fear cost me my best chance?*

The priestess smiled beatifically, though the wind had blown her headdress askew and made a mad snarl of her long gray curls. "You may now seal your pledge with a kiss."

Lan insisted on having the wedding at sunset so we could all be together to witness what he calls The Ultimate Flash Art—the atmospheric dispersion of light that happens when the sun sets, making a green explosion of light on the horizon. While the priestess poured plastic glasses of sparkling cider, we stood close to each other, talking and huddling under blankets, waiting for the sun to accelerate its descent. My cell phone rang inside my satchel. I scrambled to where I dropped it on the sand and fished around in the outside pocket. I checked the caller ID: J.W.

Curse these eyes. Were they playing tricks on me in the fading light? I flipped open the phone with shaking hands.

There was no mistaking that drawl. "Hey, what's a cowboy daddy gotta do to get a girl around here?"

With rubbery legs, I walked to the water's edge. "Where you calling from, sir?" I dug my toes into the wet sand. I hadn't smiled in so long the expression felt foreign to my face.

"I'm in a strange and unfamiliar place."

"Sorry, pard, I don't think I can help you. Word is all the quality girls are in California."

"You don't say."

Twenty different emotions and impulses were warring inside of me. *Where have you been?* I wanted to ask him. *Why did you wait so long to call? Don't you think I'd have given up by now?*

"Daryl, are you there? Hello?"

"Yeah, I'm here."

"So, California, huh. California." He drew the syllables out, feeling them one by one. "That sounds nice. Maybe I could visit."

Pause. "I don't know about that. I'm going back home soon."

He got real quiet. At the water's edge, two seagulls sliced through the gloppy sand with thick webbed feet. J.W. cleared his throat. "So, you didn't say. Would you mind a visit?"

"I suppose I could stand it." I held my breath for a beat. "But do you have the time?" My voice sounded challenging, maybe a little defiant.

"Yes. Now I do, ma'am. Yes." Wind made the phone crackle. "You must be freezing."

"I'm sorry?"

"I said you must be freezing. You should grab a blanket or something."

"What are you talking about?"

"Turn around."

I looked behind me. J.W. was standing twenty feet away at the surf line, leaning haphazardly with the phone jammed up to his ear and the black-and-white checkered blanket draped over one of the crutches that held him up. A long, narrow box wrapped in a baby-blue bow was at his feet. I turned back toward the wedding party.

Shawna and Lan snuggled together, looking our way, hands clasped under their chins.

J.W. shifted on his crutches. "I said I'd call you, didn't I?"

"You're insane." I walked toward him.

"What's with the sling, cowgirl?"

"Oh, this? Just a little horse problem."

He swung his crutch up as a pointer. "Did it hurt to get that?"

"Yeah, kinda." I pointed to his foot. "Did it hurt to get that?"

"Yeah, kinda." We both laughed. Back where we started. Life—a circle, indeed. He hopped forward a few steps.

"No, no. You stay put." I picked up my pace. "Pretty rude to crash a wedding, you know."

"I'll have you know I was invited by the bride *and* groom. Lan asked me to be a witness, as a matter of fact."

"Some witness. You missed the whole thing."

"I did not. I witnessed the entire ceremony, just from a considerable distance."

When I got to his side, we hung up our phones and stood looking at each other. So much to say and no clever opening line. I nodded at the box. "That a gift for the happy couple?"

"It's for you, actually. Open it."

We laughed because neither of us could pick up the box. I dropped down on my knees and pulled off the bow and tape with my good hand. I tore carefully through the white tissue and saw the glint of a blued steel barrel.

"You got me a shotgun?"

"What can I say? You made a heck of an impression that day on your deck. I go plum foolish for a girl who's a good shot." He reset his hat nervously. "There's something else. Look under the gun."

I lifted it to see an ivory business-size envelope. "What's this?"

"Something I got from a couple friends of mine. You can have a look if you'd like."

I braced the envelope between my knees and slit the top of the envelope with my nail and unfolded the piece of paper inside. I recognized Jace's canted script. "PROMISSORY NOTE: I, Jace Henry Heatherly, in advance of contract and transfer of title, pledge to sell Red Hill to James Willis Jarrett . . ." A gray notary seal marked the lower left corner.

If my heart was pounding before, it was positively racing now. "But how did you . . . ? How?"

"My brother. Son of a gun didn't have much when he died, but he left a bunch to Teresa and the rest to me. And his fancy Hollywood agent sold the rights to his life story, so any money from the movie deal will go straight to Beeb, and it looks to be quite a bit. What I got is still in probate and it's barely enough to cover the down payment and closing costs but I figure what the heck."

"Jace didn't tell me."

"I asked him not to. I wanted to tell you myself. In person."

I dusted the sand off my palms. "Aren't you going to be lonely out there all by yourself?"

"Nah, I told Jace he could stay as long as he wanted, and Beeb might come back up if he gets run out of Louisiana. And maybe a little gal down in Denver will come up and visit with us now and then, powder a few clays off the back deck."

We stood looking out at the foamy surf. The tide was rising, curling in jade green and crashing into the hard sand, one wave after another. The moon and Venus were in their slow float toward mid-heaven. A cold wavelet rippled over my feet and swirled around my ankles.

"So, you still think we're all alike, us cowboys?"

"I'm willing to reconsider." I curled my toes in the wet sand. The breeze off the ocean blew down the beach. Cool sand stirred at my feet. I shivered, gooseflesh pimpling up my arms.

In silence, we watched the California sun sink lower, and lower still. Lan yelled out, "Look out, everybody. Here she comes!" The sun dipped below the sight line and an eerie green light flared over the water—a split-second burst of otherworldly color limning the horizon, then nothing. With that little cosmic pop, the day was extinguished.

I tipped my chin up and smiled into the wind. There were no words to describe what I was feeling. Hopefulness and happiness and enormous, heart-settling relief.

J.W. bracketed my legs with his crutches and rested his chin on my shoulder. His body felt warm but brittle, like he might fold in two any second. "You know, I was serious back there in Cheyenne. I'd have laid off it if you really wanted me to."

"Yeah, well, it's good that you didn't because I had a change of heart in that department. How about this instead: If you don't quit, then I won't."

The jackknife tension left him. He had come back to me completely now, I could sense it. "So, that money or mud deal still stand?"

I leaned back against him and took hold of each crutch so he could get his arms around me. "That's right, cowboy. Money or mud. Or neither. Or both."

Funny, I thought, how the acid edge of hope cuts through skepticism. But then, if try teaches you anything, it's how to turn fear into faith. As we stood in the settling dark, I saw us, two slightly broken people who might heal each other in time. There was a feeling of bones knitting back to whole, of things falling into place. No hurt between us that a little courage couldn't fix.